SPIRAL
Koji Suzuki

Translation
Glynne Wolley

‖VERTICAL.

Published by Vertical, Inc., New York.

Originally published in Japan as *Rasen* by Kadokawa Shoten, Tokyo, 1995.

ISBN 1-932234-06-3

Manufactured in the United States of America

First American Edition

Vertical, Inc.
257 Park Avenue South, 8th Floor
New York, NY 10010
www.vertical-inc.com

Prologue

Mitsuo Ando awoke from a dream in which he was sinking into the sea. The trilling of the telephone insinuated itself into the sound of the surf, and the next minute he was jerked into wakefulness, as though the waves had taken him.

He stretched his arm out over the side of the bed and picked up the receiver.

"Hello."

He waited, but no sound came through the line.

"Hello," he said again, sternly this time, urging the caller to reply. There came a woman's voice, so morose it made him shudder.

"Did you get it?"

The voice filled Ando with fatigue. He felt as if he were being dragged into a dark ditch. The dream from which he'd just awakened flashed before his eyes. A huge wave had suddenly sucked him up off a beach: as he sank to the bottom of the sea he lost all sense of up or down, right or left, until he was helpless against the current... As always, he'd felt a tiny hand grasping at his shin. Every time he had the dream, he felt on his feet the touch of that little hand, those anemone-like fingers slipping away to vanish into the depths of the ocean. There was absolutely nothing he could do to prevent it, and it tortured him. He stretched out his arms, sure that he should be able to reach the body, but he just couldn't get a grip on it. It eluded his grasp every time, leaving behind only a few soft, fine strands of hair.

The woman's voice reminded him with unpleasant vividness of the soft feel of that hair.

"Yes, it arrived," Ando answered, annoyed.

The form for their divorce. It had arrived two or three days ago, with his wife's signature and seal already affixed. All Ando had to do was sign it and stamp his own seal on it, and the paper would have fulfilled the purpose of its existence. But he hadn't done it yet.

"And?" There was weariness in his wife's voice as she prodded him. How could she be so blasé about putting an end to seven years of married life?

"And what?"

"I want you to sign it, stamp it, and return it to me."

Ando shook his head. How many times had he tried to make it clear to her? He wanted to start over. But every time he told her so, she would set terms he couldn't meet, as if to prove to him the strength of her determination. He'd been perfectly willing to give up all self-respect and grovel, but lately, he was getting a bit tired of even that.

"Alright. I'll do what you want." Ando surprised himself, giving in so easily.

His wife was silent for a moment, and then rasped, "I think you owe me an explanation."

"About what?" It was a stupid response.

"About what you did to me."

Still clutching the receiver, Ando squeezed his eyes shut. *Is she going to harangue me every morning even after she gets her divorce?* It was a crushing thought.

"It was my fault." But he said it too easily, without putting feeling into the words, and that set her off.

"You never cared for him."

"You're talking nonsense. Listen to yourself!"

"Well, then, why..."

"Don't ask. You already know the answer."

"How could you do such a thing?" Her voice trembled, a harbinger of the frenzy she was warming up to. He wanted to tell her never to call again and then slam down the receiver, but he restrained himself. This was the least he could do. The only reparation he could offer was to silently bear his wife's recriminations, to allow her to vent her grief.

"Say something." She was in tears now.

"Like what? For a year and three months now, we've talked about nothing else. There's nothing left to say."

"Give him back to me!"

It was a cry of pain totally devoid of reason. He didn't need to ask whom she wanted back. Ando wanted him back, too. It was what he'd been praying for every day knowing full well how useless it was. *Bring him back, I beg You! Give him back!*

"I can't," he said simply, trying to calm her down.

"I want him back!"

He couldn't bear to hear his wife like this, wrapped up in past misery, unwilling to start a new life. Ando was trying, at least, to live a little more constructively. There was no recovering what was lost, and he'd done his utmost to repair their marriage—to convince her to think about the new life they'd have, if they could. He didn't want to get divorced over this. He was prepared to do anything. It would be worth it, if only they could again be the happy couple they'd once been. But his wife didn't want to look to the future, and she blamed him for everything.

"Give him back!"

"What more do you want me to do?"

"You don't know what you've done!"

Ando sighed, loudly enough to be heard on the other end of the line. She was repeating the same barren phrases; her nerves were clearly fraying. He wanted to introduce her to a psychiatrist friend of his. But his wife's father was a doctor, the head of a hospital; she'd just take it as meddling.

"I'm hanging up now."

"That's it, run away like you always do."

"I want you to forget this. To get over it." He knew it was useless, but he couldn't think of anything else to say.

Ando started to put down the receiver. As he did so, a cry of desperation came from the earpiece. "I want you to bring Takanori back..."

Even after he'd hung up, the name kept spilling from the receiver until its echo filled the room. Without knowing it, Ando was now muttering it himself.

Takanori, Takanori, Takanori.

Ando lay unmoving on the bed for a while, curled up in the fetal position, head in his hands. Then he glanced at the clock and knew he couldn't stay that way forever. It was time to leave for work.

Ando unplugged the phone from the wall jack so she couldn't call back, then went to stand by the window. When he opened it to get rid of some of the gloom, he heard the cry of a crow. They always flew over from Yoyogi Park to perch on the power lines, but this one sounded closer than usual—it gave him a start. But the avian cry, airy and expansive, also lightened his mood. It was such a contrast to the black depths of the ocean of his dream, and to the desperate cries of his wife for their son. It was Saturday morning, a clear autumn day.

Maybe it was the wonderful weather rubbing him the wrong way, but tears welled up in his eyes. He blew his nose. He was alone in his studio apartment. He collapsed back onto bed. He thought he'd managed to fight back the tears, but now they came streaming out of the corners of his eyes.

Soon he was sobbing, hugging his pillow and calling his son's name. He hated himself for falling apart like that. Grief's visits weren't regular; it waited until something set it off, and then it kept on coming. He hadn't wept for his son for a couple of weeks. Although the hiatus between his crying spells was getting longer, when the sadness did come, it was just as deep as ever. How long was this going to continue? He could hardly bear to wonder.

Ando took an envelope out from between two books on a shelf and withdrew from it several tangled strands of hair. They were all that was left, physically, of his son. His hand had brushed the child's head, and when he'd tried to pull the boy toward him, these strands had come off. It was some kind of miracle that they'd stayed stuck to his hand all the while he'd been thrashing about in the ocean. They'd gotten twisted around his wedding ring. The body never surfaced. They had been unable to have a proper cremation. The lock of hair was Ando's only relic of his boy.

Ando held the strands to his cheek and recalled the touch of his son's skin. When he closed his eyes, Takanori came back to life in his mind. Ando could almost believe the boy was right there...

When he finished brushing his teeth he just stood in front of the mirror, naked from the waist up. He put his hand to his jaw and rubbed it lightly. He felt the back of his teeth with his tongue: there was still a little plaque clinging to them. He saw a spot on his neck, just below his chin, that the razor had missed. He brought the straight razor to his neck and shaved off the little stumps of beard, and then froze, arrested by his own reflection. He raised his jaw and looked at his pale neck outstretched in the mirror. He shifted his grip on the razor and brought the back of it to the base of his throat, then slowly lowered it from his neck to his chest and then down to his midriff, finally resting it near his navel. A white line ran along the surface of his flesh, between his nipples and down his belly. Imagining his razor was a scalpel, he pictured dissecting his own body. Ando spent his days cutting corpses open, so he knew perfectly well what he'd find inside his chest. His fist-size heart sat cradled between his two pink lungs and was beating firmly. If he con-

centrated, he could almost hear it. But that persistent pain in his chest—
where in his innards did sorrow lodge? Was it the heart? He wanted,
with his bare hands, to scoop out the clump of remorse.

The razor felt as if it were going to slip on his sweaty skin, so he put
it down on the shelf over the sink. He turned his head to see a thin line
of blood on the right side of his throat. He'd nicked himself. He should
have felt a little stab of pain where the edge of the blade bit into his skin,
but as he stared at the blood he felt nothing. He was lately growing
numb to physical pain. Several times already he'd only learned he'd been
hurt after seeing the wound. Maybe he was losing his passion for life.

He pressed a towel to his neck and picked up his watch. Eight-thir-
ty. He'd better leave for work. His job was his only salvation these days.
Only by immersing himself in work could he elude the clutch of his
memories. Ando, a Lecturer in Forensic Medicine at Fukuzawa
University Medical School, was also a coroner for the Tokyo Medical
Examiner's office. Only when he was conducting an autopsy could he
forget the death of his beloved son. Ironically, playing with dead bodies
released him from the death that had touched him.

He left his apartment. As he walked through the lobby of his building he looked at his watch. A habit. He was five minutes behind schedule: the five minutes he'd taken to sign and stamp the writ of divorce.
In a mere five minutes, the bond that had connected him to his wife had
been severed. He was aware of three mailboxes between his apartment
and the university. Ando made up his mind to drop the envelope into the
first one along the way. He hurried off to the train station.

PART ONE *Dissecting*

1

Today was Ando's turn on autopsy duty. In the M.E.'s office, he ran his gaze over the file for his next corpse. As he compared the Polaroids of the scene, his palms started to sweat, and he had to walk over to the sink several times to wash his hands. It was mid-October and it wasn't warm, but Ando had always been a heavy sweater. He was in the habit of washing his hands several times a day.

He spread the photos out on the table once more. One in particular held his attention. In it, a stocky man sat with his head resting on the edge of a bed, the position he'd been in when he stopped breathing. There were no evident external wounds. The next photo was a close-up of his face. No evidence of blood congestion, no signs of strangulation. In none of the photos could Ando find anything to establish a cause of death. Which was why, even though there was nothing to indicate a crime, the body had been sent to the M.E.'s office for a post-mortem. It looked to be a sudden death, an unnatural one at that, and under the circumstances the body couldn't legally be cremated until the cause of death was discovered.

The corpse was found with both arms and both legs spread wide. Ando knew the man, knew him well—an old friend from college, whom Ando had never dreamed of having to dissect. Ryuji Takayama, who'd been alive up until a mere twelve hours ago, had been a classmate of Ando's through six years of medical school.

Most graduates of their program were aspiring clinicians, and when Ando decided to go into forensic medicine, people called him an oddball behind his back. But Takayama had gone even further off track. He'd led his class at med school, but after graduation he'd started over as an undergraduate in the Department of Philosophy. At the time of his death, he'd been a Lecturer in Philosophy, specializing in logic. Lecturer was the position Ando held in his own department. In other words, even granting that the school had let Takayama re-enroll as a junior, his rise in the department had been meteoric. Thirty-two at the time of his death, he'd been two years younger than Ando, who'd spent a couple of years after high school cramming to get into the university of his choice.

Ando's eyes came to rest on the line where the time of death had been noted: 9:49 the previous evening.

"This time of death is awfully precise," Ando said, glancing up at the tall police lieutenant who had come to observe the autopsy. As far as Ando knew, Takayama had lived alone in his apartment in East Nakano. A bachelor, living alone, dying suddenly at home—it shouldn't have been possible to get such a precise fix on the time of death.

"I guess you could say we were lucky," the lieutenant said nonchalantly, seating himself in a nearby chair.

"Lucky? How?"

The lieutenant glanced at his companion, a young sergeant. "Mai Takano's here, isn't she?"

"Yes, sir. I saw her outside in the waiting room."

"You wanna go get her?"

"Yes, sir."

"She's not a relative, but she's the one who discovered the body. One of Professor Takayama's pet students—his lover, in fact. If you find anything suspicious about her report, feel free to ask her some questions yourself. Any question, Doc."

It was policy to turn the body over to the next of kin directly following the autopsy. In Takayama's case, that would be his mother, or his brother and sister-in-law. They were out in the waiting room, where they'd been joined by Mai Takano.

The woman in question stepped into the office, then stopped and shook her head. Upon noticing her, Ando immediately stood up, bowed, and offered her a chair. "I apologize for putting you through this," he said.

Mai, dressed in a plain navy dress, had a white handkerchief clutched in her hands. Ando wondered if proximity to death brought out a woman's beauty. Her body was slender, her arms and legs delicate, and the subdued simplicity of her dress emphasized the paleness of her skin. Her face was a perfect oval in shape, with smooth, balanced features. Ando could see the beautiful curves of her skull without dissecting her. No doubt, beneath her skin, her organs had a healthy hue and her skeletal frame was perfectly regular. He had a sudden urge to touch them.

The lieutenant introduced them, and they exchanged names. Mai went to sit down in the chair Ando had indicated, but she faltered. She had to steady herself on the desk.

"Are you alright?" Ando peered at her, examining her complexion. She suddenly looked ashen under the surface whiteness of her skin. He wondered if she was anemic.

"I'm quite fine, thank you." She stared at a point on the floor for a while, her handkerchief pressed to her forehead, until the lieutenant brought her a glass of water. She drank it, and it seemed to calm her somewhat. She raised her head and spoke in a voice so soft Ando could hardly make it out.

"Sorry, it's just that I'm..."

Ando understood immediately. She was having her period; that, plus the emotional stress, was responsible for her anemic state. If that was all, it was nothing to worry about.

"It so happens that the late Mr. Takayama and I were buddies back in college." He told her this partly to set her at ease.

Mai raised her eyes, downcast until now. "You said your name was Dr. Ando?"

"Yes."

She gazed intently at him. Then, with evident pleasure, she narrowed her eyes and bowed slightly as though she were meeting an old friend. "Pleased to make your acquaintance."

Ando thought he knew how to interpret her expression: she probably felt she could trust his friendship with Takayama to keep him from treating the body callously. But, in truth, his friendship or lack of it with the deceased had no effect on how he wielded his scalpel.

"Excuse me, Ms. Takano," the lieutenant broke in. "Would you mind telling the doctor exactly what you told us about how you discovered the body?" He seemed determined not to let down his guard on this case just because there were no signs of foul play. There was no time to waste in exchanging fond memories of the dear departed. He'd brought Mai here for the express purpose of having her present her story to Ando. She'd been the first person to see the body, and Ando was the medical examiner in charge of the autopsy. Hopefully between them they could establish the cause of death. That was why they were gathered here today.

In a hushed tone, Mai began to tell Ando more or less the same story she'd told the police the night before.

"I had just gotten out of the bath and was blow-drying my hair when the phone rang. I looked at my watch immediately. I suppose it's a habit of mine. If I know what time it is when the phone rings, I can usually guess who it is. Professor Takayama rarely called me; usually, *I* called *him*. And he hardly ever called after nine o'clock. So, at first, I didn't think it was him. I picked up the receiver, said 'Hello,' and a moment later I heard a scream from the other end of the line. At first I thought it was a prank. I held the phone away from my ear, in surprise, but then the scream faded into a moan, and then it gave out altogether. I felt like I was wrapped in…in a stillness not of this world… I brought the receiver back to my ear and listened for signs of anything, all the while dreading what I might find out. And then, suddenly, like a switch flicking on, Professor Takayama's face was in my mind. I recognized the scream. It sounded like him. I hung up the phone and then dialed his number, but the line was busy. And so I concluded that it was he who had called, and that something bad had happened to him."

"So you and Ryuji didn't have any sort of conversation?" Ando asked.

She shook her head. "No. I just heard that scream."

Ando scribbled something on a memo pad and urged her to continue. "What happened next?"

"I went to his apartment to see what had happened. It took me about an hour to get there, by train. And when I went in…he was there, by the bed in the room past the kitchen…"

"The front door was unlocked?"

"He'd…given me a key." She said this with a certain artless bashfulness.

"No, what I mean is—it was locked from the inside, then?"

"Yes, it was."

"So then, you went in," Ando prompted her.

"Professor Takayama had his head on the bed, facing up, his arms and legs spread out." Her voice caught. She shook her head vigorously as if to repel the scene replaying itself before her eyes.

Ando hardly needed her to elaborate. He had the photos before him. They spoke of Ryuji's lifeless body more eloquently than words could.

Ando used the pictures as a fan to send a breeze over his sweaty brow. "Was there anything different about the room?"

"Nothing that I noticed… Except, the phone was off the hook. I could hear a whining sound coming from it."

Ando tried to collate the information he'd gleaned from the incident report and Mai's story to reconstruct the situation. Ryuji had sensed something was wrong with him and had called his lover, Mai Takano. He must have hoped she could help him. But then why hadn't he called 911? You have a sudden pain in your chest—if you have the time and strength to use the phone, normally your first call would be for an ambulance.

"Who dialed 911?"

"I did."

"From where?"

"Professor Takayama's apartment."

"And he hadn't done so, correct?" Ando shot a glance at the lieutenant, who nodded. He'd already confirmed that there had been no request for an ambulance from the deceased.

Ando briefly considered the possibility of a suicide. Distraught at his lover's cruel treatment of him, a man decides to take his own life and swallows poison. He decides to call the woman who's driven him to it, to accuse and torment her. Instead, all he can manage is a dying scream.

But, according to the report, suicide didn't seem to be a possibility. There were no signs on the scene of anything that might have contained poison, nor any proof that Mai had taken such an object away from the premises. Besides, one look at the shape she was in dispelled any such suspicions. One had to be quite obtuse to the subtleties of relations between the sexes not to see at a glance how deeply Mai Takano had respected her professor. The moistness that welled up in her eyes now and then was not due to guilt about having driven her lover to take his own life; it came from profound sorrow at the thought of never being able to touch his body again. For Ando, it was like looking in a mirror; he confronted his own grief-stricken face every morning. That kind of devastation couldn't be faked. Then there was the fact that she'd come down to the M.E.'s office to claim the body after the autopsy. But most important of all, Ando couldn't imagine a guy as dauntless as Ryuji Takayama killing himself over something like a break-up.

Which left the heart or the head.

Ando had to look for signs of sudden heart failure or cerebral hemorrhaging. Of course, he couldn't rule out the possibility that an examination of the stomach contents would turn up potassium cyanide. Or signs of food poisoning, or carbon monoxide poisoning, or one of the other unexpected causes that he occasionally came across. But his suspicions had never been far off the mark before. Takayama had sensed something wrong with him all of a sudden, and he'd wanted to hear his girlfriend's voice one last time. But there hadn't been enough time to do more than scream before his heart stopped beating. That had to be it more or less.

The technician who was assisting Ando that day poked his head into the office and said, "Doctor, everything's ready."

Ando stood and said, to no one in particular, "Well, time to get started."

One way or another, he'd have the facts once he'd dissected the body. He'd never failed to establish a cause of death before. In no time, he'd figure out what had killed Takayama. The thought that he might not didn't even cross his mind.

2

The autumn morning sunlight slanted into the hallway leading to the autopsy room. There was something dark and dank about the corridor, nonetheless, and as they walked, their rubber boots made a sickening sound. There were four of them: Ando, the technician, and the two policemen. The rest of the staff—another assistant, the recorder, and the photographer—were already in the autopsy room.

When they opened the door, they could hear the sound of running water. The assistant was standing at the sink next to the dissecting table, washing instruments. The faucet was abnormally large, and water cascaded from it in a thick, white column. The 350-square-foot floor was already covered with water, which was why all eight of them, including the two police witnesses, wore rubber boots. Usually, the water was left running for the duration of the autopsy.

On the dissecting table, Ryuji Takayama awaited them, stark naked, his white belly protruding. He was about five-three, and between the layer of fat around his middle and the muscles on his shoulders and chest, he was built like an oil drum. Ando lifted the body's right arm. No resistance, other than gravity. Proof that life had indeed left the body. This man had once prided himself on the strength of his arms, and now Ando could move them about as freely as he would a baby's. Ryuji had been the strongest of any of them in school; nobody was a match for him at arm-wrestling. Anybody who challenged him found his arm slapped flat on the table before he could even flex his biceps. Now, that same arm was powerless. If Ando let go, it'd flop helplessly onto the table.

He turned his gaze to the lower torso, to the exposed genitalia. The penis was shriveled amidst thick black pubic hair, and the glans was almost entirely hidden by the foreskin. The member was incredibly small, almost cute, given the robustness of the body. Ando found himself wondering if Ryuji and Mai had been able to have normal sexual relations at all.

He took up the scalpel and inserted it below the jaw, slicing the thick muscle in a straight line all the way down to the abdomen. The body had been dead for twelve hours and was completely cold. He broke the ribs with bone-cutters, removing them one by one, and then took out both lungs and handed them to his assistant. In med school Ryuji had been a diehard anti-smoker, and from the looks of his lungs, he'd remained one to the end. They were a handsome shade of pink. With practiced movements, the assistant weighed and measured the lungs, announcing his findings to the recorder, who wrote them down. All the while, the room was bathed in flashes of light as photos were taken of the lungs from every angle. Everybody knew his job well, and everything went forward without a hitch.

The heart was enveloped in a thin fatty membrane. Depending on the light it looked either whitish or yellowish, and it was a bit larger than average. Eleven ounces. The weight of Ryuji's heart. Point thirty-six percent of his total body weight. Just looking at the outer surface of the organ, which a mere twelve hours ago had still been pumping life-blood, Ando could tell it had suffered severe necrosis. The left part of the heart, below the fatty membrane, had turned a dark reddish-brown color, darker than the rest of the heart. Part of the coronary artery, branching off the surface of the organ to coil around it, was blocked, probably by a thrombosis. Blood had been unable to flow past that point, and the heart had stopped. Classic indicators of a heart attack.

Based on the extent of the necrosis, Ando had a pretty good idea where the blockage had occurred: in the left coronary artery, just before it branched off. With a blockage there the chance of death was extremely high. The cause of death, then, had pretty well been established, though he'd have to wait for test results, which wouldn't come in for a day at least, to know what had caused the blockage. Ando pronounced with confidence a case of "myocardial infarction due to blockage of the left coronary artery" and moved on to extracting the liver. After that, he checked for abnormalities in the kidneys, spleen, and intestines, and examined the stomach contents, but nothing caught his eye.

He was about to cut the skull open when his assistant craned his neck suspiciously.

"Doctor, take a look at that throat."

The assistant pointed to a spot inside the throat where it had been split open. Part of the mucus membrane on the surface of the pharynx had ulcerated. The ulcer wasn't large, and Ando might have overlooked it had it not been for his assistant's alertness. Ando had never seen any-

15

thing like it before. It was probably unrelated to the cause of death, but he cut out a piece of it anyway. He'd have to wait until they ran tests on the tissue sample before he could tell just what it was.

Now, he made incisions in the skin around Ryuji's head, and peeled back the scalp from the back to the forehead. The man's wiry hair now covered his face, his eyes, nose, and mouth, and the white inner surface of the scalp was exposed to the overhead light. Anyone who saw it could tell that the human face was constructed out of a single slab of flesh. Ando removed the top of the skull and lifted out the brain.

It was a whitish mass covered with innumerable wrinkles. Even among the elite students who were assembled at their medical school, Ryuji had stood out for his brains. He was good at English, German, and French, and he'd ask questions in class that you couldn't follow if you weren't reading the latest foreign bulletins. That managed to intimidate even the lecturers. But the deeper he'd gotten into medicine, the more Ryuji's interests had shifted toward the pure realm of mathematics. For a while, everyone in their class had been hooked on code games. They'd each take their turn devising a code, and the others competed to see who could break it first. Invariably, it was Ryuji. When it was Ando's turn and he came up with a code he was sure couldn't be cracked, Ryuji figured it out with ease. At the time, Ando had been less exasperated by Ryuji's mathematical genius than chilled by the feeling that his mind had been read. He simply couldn't believe that his code had been broken. Nobody else was able to solve it. But, in turn, Ando was the only one who ever broke one of Ryuji's codes. Although he could claim that one triumph, nobody knew better than Ando himself that it had come through sheer luck, not through any logical acumen. He'd gotten tired of wrestling with the code and gazed out the window, where his eyes happened to settle on a sign for a flower shop. The phone number on the sign gave him an idea, and he stumbled on the key to the sequence of characters. It was pure chance that his thoughts had traveled in the same direction as Ryuji's. Ando was convinced to this day that his moment of triumph had just been a fluke.

Back in those days, Ando had felt something akin to envy toward Ryuji. Several times he'd felt his self-confidence crumble under the burden of knowing that he'd never dominate Ryuji, that he'd always be under Ryuji's sway.

And now Ando was staring at that brain that had been so remarkable. It was only slightly heavier than average, and looked no different from any normal person's brain. What had Ryuji been using these cells to think about when he was alive? Ando could imagine the process that had led Ryuji deeper and deeper into pure mathematics until eventually he'd abandoned numbers altogether and arrived at logic. If he'd lived another ten years, he'd surely have contributed something major to the field. Ando admired, and hated, Ryuji's rare gifts. His brain's cerebral fissure looked deep, and the frontal lobe loomed like an unconquerable ridge.

But it was all over now. These cells had ceased functioning. The heart had stopped due to a myocardial infarction, and the brain had died, too. In effect, physically at least, Ryuji was now under Ando's dominion.

He checked to rule out cerebral hemorrhaging, and then replaced the brain in the skull.

Fifty minutes had elapsed since he had taken his scalpel. Autopsies usually took around an hour. Ando had basically finished the examination, when he paused, as if he'd remembered something. He reached a hand into Ryuji's now-hollow abdominal area and felt around with his fingertips until he pulled out two round objects the size of a quail's eggs. The pair of testicles, a grayish flesh-color, looked curiously adorable.

Ando asked himself who was more to be pitied, Ryuji, who'd died without issue, or himself, who'd accidentally let his son die at the age of three years and four months.

Me, of course.

He thought so without hesitation. Ryuji had died in ignorance. To the end, he'd never been tormented by the kind of sorrow that bored into your chest. There were no limits to the joy of having a child. But the sorrow of losing that child just never went away—would never go away, Ando felt, even if he lived another thousand years. His heart full, Ando dropped the testicles onto the dissecting table. They were dead now, without having created anything.

All that was left was to sew the body back up. Ando stuffed the empty chest and abdominal cavity full of rolled-up newsprint, to give it volume, and began stitching. He stitched up the head, too, then washed the body clean and wrapped it in a bathrobe. Stripped of its internal organs, the body looked skinnier.

17

You've lost weight, Ryuji.

Ando couldn't figure out why he'd addressed the corpse in his head like that. Usually he didn't. Was there something about Ryuji's cadaver that made him want to talk to it? Or was it simply because he'd known the guy? Of course, the conversation was one-way—Ryuji didn't answer. But when the two assistants picked up the body to put it in the casket, Ando thought he could hear Ryuji's voice from somewhere deep inside his own chest. He got a ticklish feeling around his navel. He scratched himself, but the feeling didn't go away. Before long it was as if the itch had left his body and was hovering in the air.

Disconcerted, Ando stood next to the coffin and stroked Ryuji's body from the chest to the belly. He felt something sticking out near the abdomen, and he opened the bathrobe. Looking closely, he saw that the edge of a piece of newspaper was sticking out through the stitches just above the navel. Ando thought he'd sewn up the incision carefully, but somehow there it was, just a corner. The newspaper they'd packed the cavity with must have shifted when they moved the body, and the corner had found its way into an opening. It was lightly blood-stained and had bits of fat clinging to it. Ando wiped away the white membrane until he could see numbers printed on the paper. They were small, hard to read. His face drew closer to them. He read the numbers, six digits arranged in two rows of three:

178
136

He couldn't tell if this was part of the stock market report, or maybe two telephone numbers that had happened to be in alignment, or perhaps program codes on the television schedule. In any case, what were the chances of the corner of a randomly folded newspaper containing nothing but six digits? For no reason he could think of, Ando etched the numbers into his brain.

178, 136.

Then he poked the newspaper back into the belly and gave it a couple of taps with his latex-gloved fingers. After making sure the paper didn't pop out again, he closed Takayama's bathrobe and once again ran his hand down the body's chest. There was nothing anomalous to interrupt the roundness of the torso. Ando took a couple of steps back from the coffin.

Suddenly, inexplicably, he shuddered. He raised his hands to peel off his gloves and found that the hair on his arms stood on end. He leaned on a stepladder standing nearby and stared at Ryuji's face. The eyelashes trembled as if the eyes, now peacefully shut, would open any minute. The splashing of the water was suddenly very loud. Everybody else in the room was busy with his own tasks, and Ando seemed to be the only one aware of the intense aura rising from the body. *Is this guy really dead?... Bah! What an idiotic question.* The swatches of newspaper, which occupied the cavity where the guts used to be, shifted, causing the abdomen to rise and fall gently. Ando marveled at how the assistants and the cops could be so detached.

Ando felt the urge to urinate. He imagined the dead Ryuji walking around, complete with the rustle of crumpled sheets of newspaper, and the need to evacuate his bladder became almost unbearable.

3

Having finished the morning's autopsies, Ando headed toward Otsuka Station on the JR line to get some lunch. Walking along, he stopped over and over to look behind him. He didn't know what caused his anguish, or what it meant. It wasn't that his son was on his mind. And he'd probably performed over a thousand autopsies. So why did this one in particular bother him so? He always performed his work meticulously. He couldn't remember ever seeing newspaper sticking out from between his sutures. It was a mistake, though a minor one to be sure. But was that what was bothering him? No, that wasn't it.

He entered the first Chinese restaurant he passed and ordered the lunch special. The place was far emptier than it usually was at five minutes past noon. The only customer aside from Ando was an older man sitting near the register slurping noodles. He wore a leather alpine hat and shot Ando an occasional glance. It bothered Ando. *Why doesn't he take off his hat? Why does he keep looking at me?* Ando was looking for significance in the tiniest thing; his nerves, he realized, were on edge.

His mind was like a sheet of photosensitive paper, and on it were imprinted the digits from the newspaper. They flickered against his eyelids, and he couldn't brush them away. They were like a melody stuck in his head.

Something made him glance at the pay phone that sat behind the alpine-hat man. Maybe he should try dialing the numbers. But only small towns had six-digit phone numbers—there certainly weren't any in Tokyo. He knew full well that even if he dialed the number, there'd be no connection. But what if someone picked up anyway?

Hey, Ando, that was a hell of a thing to do to a guy. Pulling out my balls—oh, man!

If Ryuji's voice came on the line to cajole...

"Here you are, sir." A voice spoke in a monotone, and the lunch set was placed on the table before him: soup, a bowl of rice, and stir-fry. Among the vegetables in the stir-fry there lurked two hard-boiled quail eggs. They were the same size as Ryuji's testicles.

Ando gulped once, and then drained his glass of lukewarm water. He didn't categorically deny supernatural phenomena; still, he felt stupid

for being so obsessed with the numbers. But obsessed he was. *178, 136.*
Did they mean something? After all, Ryuji had been into codes.

A code.

In between sips of his soup, Ando spread a napkin out on the table,
took a ballpoint pen from his pocket, and wrote down the numbers.

178, 136

He tried assigning each letter of the alphabet a number from 0 to 25,
so that A equaled 0, B equaled 1, C equaled 2, and so on. This would
make it a simple substitution cipher, the most basic kind of code. He
decided first to treat each number as a one-digit numeral, substituting
the corresponding letter of the alphabet for each.

BHI, BDG

Put it all together: "bhibdg." Ando didn't have to go to a dictionary
to see that there was no such word in any language. The next step was
to break down the numerals into combinations of one- and two-digit
numbers. Since there were only twenty-six letters in the alphabet, in
terms of a simple substitution cipher this meant that he could, for the
time being, rule out numbers larger than twenty-six, such as 78 or 81.
He began writing down the possible combinations on the napkin.

17	R
8	I
1	B
3	D
6	G

Or:

1	B
7	H
8	I
13	N
6	G

Or:

17	R
8	I
13	N
6	G

Only one of the combinations produced an actual word: R-I-N-G. *Ring.*

Ando thought it over, recalling what he knew about the English word. He was most familiar with its use as a noun to mean "circle." But he also knew that it described the sound a bell or a telephone makes; it could be a verb meaning "to cause a bell or a telephone to sound," and by extension, could mean calling someone on the phone or summoning someone by means of a bell.

Was it nothing more than a coincidence? A piece of newspaper sticking out of Ryuji's stomach, six digits on that scrap of newspaper—and Ando had played with them until he came up with the word "ring." Was this all pure chance?

Somewhere in the distance he heard an alarm. He remembered the fire bell he'd heard once as a child in the small town he'd grown up in. Both his parents worked overtime and never came back until late, so he was home alone with his grandmother. They covered their ears when the clamor of the bell broke the night's silence. Ando could remember curling up on his grandmother's knees, trembling. Their town had an old fire-watch tower, and the bell meant that fire had broken out somewhere. But he didn't know that. All he knew was that the sound carried with it an air of terrible dread. It seemed like a harbinger of tragedy to come. And in fact, a year later on the exact same day, his father died unexpectedly.

Ando found that he'd lost his appetite. In fact, he felt nauseated. He pushed aside the food, which had only just arrived, and asked for another glass of water.

Hey, Ryuji, are you trying to tell me something?

When they'd signed over to the family the coffin containing his body, all hollowed out like a tin toy, Ryuji had seemed to relax his white, square-jawed visage a tiny bit, giving the impression, almost, of a smile. Only an hour ago, Mai had seen that face and bowed, to no one in particular. They'd probably hold the wake tonight, and then cremate the body tomorrow. This very moment, the hearse was probably well on its way to the family's house in Sagami Ohno. Ando wished he could watch Ryuji's body turn to ash. He had the strange feeling that his old classmate was still alive.

4

They were to meet at the benches near the library. Ando finished auditing a lecture at the law school on the main campus, checked his watch, and then headed for the appointed spot.

Only the day before, Mai Takano had placed a call to the M.E.'s office. Ando happened to be there—it was his turn on autopsy duty again—and when he heard her voice on the phone, he instantly recalled her face. It wasn't all that unusual to get calls from relatives or friends of people he'd worked on, but usually they were calling to ask about the cause of death. Mai had a different reason for calling. She said that on the evening of the day of the autopsy, she'd slipped out of the wake early and gone to Ryuji's apartment. She'd needed to set in order an unpublished manuscript he'd been working on. In the process, she'd discovered something that bothered her. She hinted, subtly, that it might have something to do with Ryuji's death.

Of course, Ando was interested in anything of value she might be able to tell him, but he was also eager to be in the presence of her pristine beauty again. He'd told her he had to attend a lecture on the main campus, but after that he could make time for her. She could tell him all about it then.

He'd told her when the lecture was scheduled to end, and then she'd suggested the place.

The benches in front of the library, under the cherry trees.

He'd spent two years on the main campus getting his general education requirements out of the way, but he and his friends had never used these benches as a rendezvous point. His future wife, who'd been a liberal arts major at this university, had preferred to meet under the gingko trees.

Before he even got close to the benches he recognized the woman sitting there as Mai. Her one-piece today was a primary color, making her look younger than she had at the M.E.'s office ten days ago. He circled around in front of her to get a look at her face, but she was immersed in a paperback and didn't look up.

He accosted her, with intentionally loud footsteps, and she raised her head.

"Ms. Takano?"

She started to stand up, saying, "Thank you for...the other day." She plainly couldn't figure out quite how to greet a man who had just dissected her lover.

Ando was holding a briefcase. His hands looked nimble and his fingers long and thin enough to proclaim what he did for a living.

"May I sit down?"

Without waiting for her reply, he sat down next to her and crossed his legs.

"Have the test results come back yet?" she asked in an inflectionless voice.

Ando glanced at his watch. "How are you for time? If it's okay with you, why don't we go have a cup of tea? There are a couple of things I'd like to ask you."

Without a word, Mai stood up and tugged at the hem of her dress.

They went to a café of her choosing. For a student hangout, it was surprisingly quiet—it felt more like a hotel lounge. They sat at a table next to the window, where they could look out onto the street, and the waitress brought them water and hot towels.

Mai didn't hesitate before ordering. "I'll have a fruit parfait."

Surprised, and unable to settle on anything, Ando could only say, "Coffee for me." Ten days ago, he'd gotten an impression of meekness from her. That was beginning to change.

"I love fruit," she shrugged after the waitress left. For a moment, Ando thought she'd said *I love you*, and then kicked himself for indulging in such a ridiculous fantasy. *A man of your age!*

It was truly a gorgeous fruit parfait, nestled on wafers and topped with a cherry. From the way she tore into it, it was clear that Mai was partial to this shop's confections. She had the same kind of intent look that Takanori used to wear when he was eating something he loved. It just about broke Ando's heart. He didn't even sip his coffee, but simply marveled at the utter concentration with which she wielded her spoon. Even if he could have convinced his wife to come to a place like this, she wouldn't have ordered a fruit parfait. She would have stuck to lemon tea, no sugar please, or something like that: she was always on a diet, and never let anything sweet pass her lips. But Mai, at least with her clothes on, looked thinner than his wife had been back in her better days. To be sure, his wife had gotten *so* thin by the time they'd separated that Ando had often had to avert his eyes; when he thought of her now, however, he always pictured her face as round and soft as it had been when they got married.

Mai took the cherry into her mouth, and then demurely spat the seed out onto an oval-shaped glass dish before wiping her lips with her napkin. He'd never met a woman so fun just to watch. She munched away on the wafers, spilling crumbs on the tabletop, and then gazed longingly at the cream that clung to the bottom of the dish. No doubt she was wondering if she could lick it up.

When she'd finally finished eating, she asked Ando what sort of tests had been performed on Ryuji's organs after the autopsy. It felt incredibly strange to be talking about the treatment of cut-out organs to a young woman whom he'd just watched eat a fruit parfait. *But here goes.*

Not long ago, he'd gotten burned trying to explain similar tests to a bereaved family member. There'd been a lapse in communication: the other person hadn't really understood what was meant by a tissue sample. The family member was imagining his loved one's organs in jars, pickled in formaldehyde, and Ando and he had wasted a lot of time in meaningless back-and-forth. Tissue samples were as mundane to Ando as ballpoint pens were to an office worker, but he had realized then that most people had no idea what they looked like, how big they were, how they were obtained, etc., unless it was spelled out to them. So he decided to start by telling her about tissue samples.

"It's almost all lab work, you see. First, we cut out a small piece of the heart in the area where the infarction took place and preserve it in formaldehyde. From it we slice a smaller portion in the shape of a sashimi and embed that in paraffin. You know, wax. Then we slice from that a microscope specimen, take the wax off, and stain it. Then we have a tissue sample, which we send off to the lab for analysis. After that, it's just a matter of waiting for the results."

"So I should imagine a thin slice of the organ squeezed between two glass plates?"

"That's about right."

"And that makes it easier to examine?"

"Of course. We stain it so its cellular structure can be examined with a microscope."

"Did you have a look?"

A look? At what? Ryuji's cells, of course. Regardless, Ando thought Mai's question had an odd nuance.

"I gave it a quick peek before sending it off to the lab, yes."

"How was it?" She was leaning forward now.

"There was a blockage in his left coronary artery, just prior to the left circumflex branch. The blood couldn't get past it, and Ryuji's heart stopped. As I think I explained, we took circular sections of the tissue in question and examined them under a microscope. I was surprised by what I found. You see, usually, when there's a heart attack, what's happened is that the arteries have hardened: cholesterol or other lipids have built up, narrowing the passageway, until one of these atheromas breaks off, clogging the artery. But in Ryuji's case, while there was blockage, it wasn't due to hardening of the arteries. That much was clear."

"So what was it?" Mai's question was short and to the point.

Ando's answer was just as concise. "A sarcoma."

"A sarcoma?"

"That's right. We haven't determined yet if the cells belong to a specific tissue or if it's an undifferentiated tumor, but at the very least, we've never seen it before in the *tunica intima* or *tunica media*. Simply put, he developed a strange lump that blocked his blood flow."

"So these were like cancer cells?"

"It's probably safe to think of it in those terms. But normally, sarcomas don't occur inside blood vessels. It's impossible."

"But when the test results come back, you'll know what caused the sarcoma, right?"

Ando shook his head, laughing. "Unless there are other symptoms, we probably won't. I'm sure I don't even have to mention AIDS as an example..."

Even in today's world, in which science, seemingly, is omnipotent, there are still a whole host of illnesses whose causes are unknown. There was no way to tell whether the symptom in question would prove to be part of a larger, identifiable syndrome or not.

Ando continued. "There is one more possibility. Ryuji might have had a congenital defect in his coronary artery."

A layperson could figure out what that meant. If Ryuji had been born with that lump in his artery, it would have seriously impaired his ability to live an active life.

"But Professor Takayama..."

"I know. He was a track star in high school. His event was the shot-put, I believe."

"Yes."

"So it's hard to imagine it had been there since birth. Which is why I want to ask you if Ryuji ever complained about pains in his chest, that sort of thing."

Ando's relationship with Ryuji had basically ended upon graduation. They said "hi" if they passed each other in the hall at the university, but that was about it. Ando certainly wouldn't have noticed any change in Ryuji's physical condition.

"We were together for less than two years."

"That's fine. Did he ever mention anything to you during that period?"

"He was tougher than other people. I can't even remember him catching a cold. He wasn't the type to whine, though, so even if he had a problem he might not have mentioned it. I certainly never noticed anything."

"Nothing? Nothing at all?"

"Well...that's just it, you see."

Ando remembered suddenly that he hadn't called Mai here to give her a report on the autopsy. She had summoned him, to tell him about something that had happened when she'd been going over Ryuji's papers the night of the wake.

"Right. Well, let's hear it."

"I'm not sure if it has any connection with the professor's death, though." Mai was maddeningly cute as she dithered. Ando fixed her with an intense gaze, trying to urge her onward.

"Please tell me."

"Well, ten nights ago, I slipped out of the wake early. I went to the professor's apartment to put in order an unpublished article of his. While I was doing that, the phone rang. I didn't know what to do, but in the end I picked up the receiver. It was 'Asakawa,' a friend of the professor's from high school."

"Do you know this person?"

"We'd met once. We ran into each other at the professor's apartment four or five days before he died."

"A man?"

"Of course."

"Right. And?"

"He didn't seem to know that the professor had died. So I told him, briefly, about what had happened the night before. Mr. Asakawa seemed really shocked. He said he'd be right over."

"Meaning..."

"To Professor Takayama's apartment."

"Did he show up?"

"Yes, much sooner than I'd expected. He came in and glanced all around the apartment as if he were searching for something. And he asked me over and over if I had noticed anything. He looked like a man driven into a corner. He kept asking me if I'd noticed anything strange about the place immediately after the professor's death. But what really struck me as odd was what he said next."

She paused and sipped some water.

"So...what did he say?"

"I remember it exactly. He said: 'He didn't tell you anything there at the end? No last words? Nothing, say, about a videotape?'"

"A videotape?"

"Yes. Strange, isn't it?"

What an unexpected, inappropriate thing to bring into a discussion about Ryuji's sudden death the night before. Why bring up such a matter?

"Well, had you heard anything about a videotape from Ryuji?"

"No. Nothing."

"A videotape, huh?" Ando muttered, leaning back in his chair. He sensed a shadow over the image of this Asakawa who'd visited Ryuji's apartment the night of the autopsy.

"In any case, I was wondering—I'm not an expert, but is it possible that whatever was recorded on this videotape was so shocking it gave him a heart attack?"

"Hmm."

Ando thought he understood what had been troubling Mai. She

would have been too embarrassed even to bring the matter up until she'd ascertained the cause of death. It reminded him of a thriller he'd seen on TV two or three days ago. A woman is having an affair with one of her husband's subordinates, but she's been ensnared. Somebody has videotaped the two of them going at it at a love hotel, catching everything, and the tape is mailed to her with an extortion letter. At home, she puts the tape into the VCR and glares at the screen. Snow, and then an image cut its way in. The naked body of a woman pressed up against a young man's. Panting. The instant she realizes that it's her on the screen, she faints. It was such a common and vulgar scene that Ando had felt like a fool watching the drama.

No doubt it was possible to use a videotape to provide simultaneous visual and aural stimulation and shock somebody's system. If the wrong kind of conditions were met, the possibility of it resulting in death couldn't be ruled out. But Ando had examined Ryuji's body in detail. He'd even taken slices of his coronary artery and made tissue samples.

"No, that's out of the question. He definitely had a blockage in his left coronary artery. Besides, you know Ryuji. Can you really imagine him dying from shock just from watching a videotape?" He laughed as he said that.

"No, of course not..." Mai allowed herself to be coaxed into a weak laugh. Their impressions of Ryuji jibed, then. He'd been a man of almost disgusting daring, real steel in his spine. It would have taken something extraordinary to get to him, body or soul.

"Do you happen to know how I might contact this Asakawa person?"

"I'm sorry..." Mai started to say she didn't, but then she brought a hand to her mouth. "No, wait, I think I remember the professor introducing him as Kazuyuki Asakawa from the *Daily News*."

"Kazuyuki Asakawa from the *Daily News*." Ando made a note in his planner. If he called the newspaper, he shouldn't have much trouble finding the man's contact info. He might need to talk to the man yet.

Mai seemed to have caught a glimpse of what he'd written in his planner. She brought her hand to her chin and said, "Huh."

"What?" Ando looked up at her.

"So that's how you'd write Kazuyuki."

Ando looked back down at the page.

It took him a minute to get what she meant. There were several different combinations of characters that could be used to spell the surname "Asakawa." The same was true for the given name "Kazuyuki." Normally, he would have had to ask which characters were used, or just written the name down phonetically. But instead, he'd written the ideograms without hesitation, as if the name were one he'd known all along.

Mai's eyes opened wide as she asked, "How did you know it's written that way?"

Ando couldn't answer. Was this some sort of premonition? He felt he'd be coming into close contact with the man fairly soon.

5

For the first time in nearly a year and a half, Ando had allowed himself some saké with his dinner. This was the first time since the death of his son that he'd even wanted alcohol. He had liked to drink. It wasn't that he'd given it up out of a sense of guilt for the boy's death. Alcohol tended to amplify whatever mood he was in to begin with. If he was in a good mood, it made him jubilant; if he felt sad, it just made him sadder. For the last year and a half he'd been shrouded in grief, and so naturally he'd been unable to drink. He had the feeling that if he took one swallow he wouldn't be able to stop until he was falling-down drunk. He was afraid he'd be unable to control an impulse to die should it arise. He didn't have the courage to go there.

It was raining, rare for late October. It was a misty rain, wafting underneath his umbrella like smoke, wetting his neck. He didn't feel cold. A faint glow from the saké warmed his body. As he walked back to his apartment, he kept sticking his hand out from beneath the umbrella to see if he could catch raindrops on his palm, but it didn't work. The rain seemed to be coming not down from the sky, but up from below.

On his way down the road from the station, he wavered in front of a convenience store, thinking to buy a bottle of whiskey. Brightly lit skyscrapers towered over him. The cityscape was more beautiful than any natural landscape. The government edifices, all lit up, glowed cannily in the rain. He stared at the flashing red light at the very top of a building until it began to seem like a message in Morse code. It flashed on and off, slowly, like some thickheaded, barely articulate monster.

Ever since he'd separated from his wife he'd been living in a dilapidated four-story apartment building facing Yoyogi Park. It was definitely a step down from the South Aoyama condo he'd lived in before. There was no parking, so he'd had to give up his brand-new BMW. In his miserable little studio apartment he felt like he was a student again. There was nothing in the place to suggest that he cared about how he lived. The only furniture was a bookcase and an aluminum bed.

He went inside and walked over to the window to open it. The phone rang.

"Hello?"

"It's me."

He recognized the speaker immediately. There was only one person who'd start a conversation with him like that, without bothering to identify himself: Miyashita, another classmate from his med school days. Miyashita was currently an Assistant Researcher in Pathology.

"Sorry not to call earlier." Ando knew why Miyashita had called, so he apologized before he could be reproached.

"I was at your lab today."

"I was at the M.E.'s office."

"Must be nice having two paying jobs."

"What are you talking about? Your job's tenure track."

"Never mind that. You haven't RSVP'd about Funakoshi's farewell party."

Funakoshi, over at Internal Medicine, was leaving to take over his father's clinic back home; the old man was retiring. Miyashita had taken it upon himself to organize a send-off for him. He'd already told Ando the time and place, and Ando was supposed to get back to him right away to tell him whether or not he'd be attending. He had gotten wrapped up in other things and forgotten. If his son hadn't died, Ando would probably have been the one getting the big send-off. His stint in forensics was only supposed to be temporary, a stepping-stone. He'd planned to get the basics down pat, then switch to clinical work in preparation for taking over his wife's father's clinic... One moment of carelessness, and the whole blueprint had been ruined.

"When is it again?" Ando wedged the receiver in between his ear and his shoulder as he flipped through the pages of his planner.

"Next Friday."

"Friday, huh?" He didn't need to check his schedule. Only three hours ago, as he and Mai had parted, they'd made a dinner date for that evening. *Six o'clock next Friday.* It was clear which commitment should take priority. For the first time in ten years, he'd asked a young woman out to dinner, and somehow, she hadn't bolted. There was no way he was going to send things back to square one. Ando felt the date could be the moment of truth as to whether or not he was ever going to wake up from his long nightmare.

"So how about it?" Miyashita nagged.

"Sorry, but I can't make it. Prior engagement."

"Really? You sure this isn't the same old thing?"

The same old thing? Ando didn't know what that meant. He couldn't remember if he used any excuse habitually to turn down his friend's invitations.

"What same old thing?"

"Your not being able to drink. When I know for a fact you used to drink like a fish."

"It's not that."

"Look, if you don't want to drink, you don't have to. Fake it with oolong tea or something. But you've got to be there."

"I said it's not that."

"So you *can* drink?"

"Sort of."

"Wait—is it some girl you're after?"

Miyashita's intuition was sharper than one would have guessed from his rotund physique. Ando always tried to play things as straight as he could with Miyashita, but he wasn't sure he could say he was "after" a woman he'd only met twice. He didn't know how to respond, so he said nothing.

"She must be something if she made you forget Funakoshi's send-off."

Ando still had nothing to say.

"Well, I'm happy for you. Don't worry—hey, why don't you bring her along? We'd welcome her, you know? With open arms."

"We're not at that stage yet."

"You're taking things slowly?"

"I guess you could say that."

"Hey, I won't twist your arm."

"Sorry."

"Do you know how many times you've apologized during this conversation? I get the picture. I'll put you down for a no-show. To make up for it, I'm going to spread the word that you've got a girl, so brace yourself."

Miyashita laughed, and Ando knew he wouldn't be able to get mad at the guy. The only comfort Ando had been afforded during the gut-wrenching days after his son died and his wife left him had come from a present Miyashita had given him. Miyashita hadn't told him to "cheer up" or anything meaningless of that sort; instead he'd given Ando a novel, saying, "Read this." It was the first Ando had heard of his friend's interest in literature; he also discovered for the first time that books could genuinely give strength. The novel was sort of a *Bildungsroman*, the story of an emotionally and physically scarred youth who learns to overcome his past. The book still occupied an honored place on Ando's bookshelf.

"By the way," said Ando, changing the subject, "did you learn anything from Ryuji's tissue sample?"

It was Miyashita's Pathology Department that usually handled any diseased samples that needed to be analyzed.

"Oh, that." Miyashita sighed.

"What's wrong?"

"I don't know quite what to tell you. I'm at my wits' end with that. What do you think of Professor Seki?"

Seki was the doctor in charge of the pathology lab. He was famous for his research on the initial formation of cancer cells.

"What do I think of him? Why?"

"The old man says some funny things sometimes."

"What did he say?"

"It's not the arterial blockage that he's focusing on. You remember the throat was ulcerated?"

"Of course."

It wasn't very noticeable, but he definitely remembered it. He'd overlooked it until his assistant had drawn his attention to it. After the autopsy, he'd cut the affected portion out complete.

"He took one look at it with his naked eye, and what do you think the old man said it looked like?"

"Knock it off and just tell me."

"Alright, alright, I'll tell you: he said it looked like what you see on smallpox victims."

"Smallpox?" Ando yelped in spite of himself.

Smallpox had been stamped out through a concerted global vaccination effort. Since a case in Somalia in 1977, not a single patient had been reported worldwide. In 1979, the WHO had declared the disease eradicated. Smallpox only infects humans. No new victims meant that the virus itself had effectively ceased to exist. The last specimens were being kept frozen in liquid nitrogen in Moscow and in a lab in Atlanta, Georgia. If a new case had appeared, it could only have come from one of the two research facilities, but, given the tight security the virus was under, it was unthinkable.

"Surprised?"

"It has to be a mistake."

"Probably is. Still, that's what the old guy said. Respect his opinion."

"When will you have the results?"

"In about a week. Listen, if we actually do turn up the smallpox virus, it'll be huge for you."

Miyashita sounded bemused; he didn't believe it himself. He was sure it was an error of some sort. It was only natural, since medical professionals their age had never even had the chance to see a real smallpox patient. The only way for them to learn about the illness was through specialist works on viruses. Ando had seen a picture once, in a book, of a child covered with smallpox eruptions. A cute kid, mercilessly defiled by the pea-sized pustules, turning a hollow gaze on the camera. Those sores were the primary visible characteristic of smallpox. Ando seemed to remember reading that they reached their peak seven days after infection...

"First of all, Ryuji didn't even have a rash on his skin."

That much had been clear at a glance. His skin had glistened smoothly under the glare of the lights.

"Listen. This is so stupid I don't even want to say it. Did you know there's a strain of smallpox that produces obstructions in blood vessels, with a near 100% mortality rate?"

Ando shook his head, ever so slightly. "No."

"Well, there is."

"Don't tell me that's what caused Ryuji's arterial blockage."

"Fine, then, I won't. But listen, that sarcoma he had on the interior wall of his artery—what was that? You looked at it under magnification."

Ando didn't answer.

"What caused it?"

Ando couldn't answer.

"I hope you're inoculated," Miyashita laughed. "It'd be pretty funny, though, wouldn't it? If that's what it turned out to be."

"Jokes aside, I just thought of something."

"What's?"

"Forget smallpox, but suppose the sarcoma in his artery was actually caused by some sort of virus. There should be other people who've died with the same symptoms."

Miyashita grunted. He was weighing the possibilities. "Maybe. Can't rule it out."

"If you have the time, could you ask people at the other university hospitals? You've got the connections. It shouldn't be too hard."

"Gotcha. I'll see if any other bodies presented the same symptoms. If this turns out to be part of a larger syndrome, we could be in trouble."

"Don't worry. We'll have a good laugh over this, I'll bet."

They said goodbye and hung up at the same time.

The damp night air had stolen in through the open window. Ando went to shut it, sticking his head out before he did. The rain seemed to have stopped. The street directly below was lit by streetlamps at regular intervals; tire tracks stretched into the distance, twin dry stripes. Headlights streamed past on the No. 4 Metropolitan Expressway. The seamless whole of the city's din had become waterlogged, turning into a listless eddy. He shut the window, abruptly cutting off the sound.

Ando took a medical dictionary down from the bookshelf and leafed through it. He knew next to nothing about smallpox. It was the kind of thing there was no point in researching unless you had a scholarly interest in viruses. Smallpox was the common name for the viruses *variola major* and *minor*, genus *orthopoxvirus*, in the poxvirus family. *Variola major* had a fatality rate of thirty to fifty percent, while *variola minor*'s was under five percent. There were also pox viruses that affected monkeys, rabbits, cows, and rats, but there had been hardly any cases of these in Japan; even if they did break out, they involved no serious danger, causing only localized rashes.

Ando closed the dictionary. The whole thing seemed ridiculous. Professor Seki had only glanced at the sore with his naked eye. And what he'd said was hardly a conclusive diagnosis. All he'd said was that the affected area looked like what happened with smallpox. Ando made denial after denial to himself. Why was he trying so hard to deny the possibility? Simple: if by some chance a virus was discovered in Ryuji's body, then he'd have to worry about whether Mai Takano had been infected. She and Ryuji had been intimate. In the case of smallpox, eruptions would occur in the mucous membrane inside the mouth; when they ulcerated, the virus would spread. As a result, saliva was a major medium for the spread of the disease. Visions of Mai's lips touching Ryuji's danced in his head. He hurriedly shook them off.

He poured whiskey into a glass and drank it down straight. The alcohol, after a year and a half of temperance, had a powerful effect on him. As it burned his throat and seeped into his stomach, he was engulfed in lethargy. He sat on the floor, leaned back against the bed, and spread his limbs carelessly. Only a part of his brain remained alert. He stared at the stains on the ceiling.

The day before his boy had drowned, Ando had dreamed of the ocean. Looking back now, he knew the dream had come true. He'd known his son's fate ahead of time, and he still hadn't been able to do anything about it. Regret had made him a more cautious man since.

And now, he was having a definite premonition. A piece of newspaper had poked its way out of Ryuji's belly after the autopsy, and he'd been able to take the numbers written on it and find the word "ring." He couldn't believe it was just a coincidence. Ryuji was trying to tell him something—in his own way, using a medium only he could manipulate. By now, most of Ryuji's body had been reduced to ash, all but a small part which remained in the form of a tissue sample. Ando got the feeling that even in his dismembered, tissue-sampled state, Ryuji was speaking to him. Which was why he felt his friend was still alive. His body had been cremated, but Ryuji was not without words and some means to communicate them.

Ando kept fiddling with this notion as he loitered just this side of incoherence. A certain delusion—it could be a joke or it could be for real—was producing a new storyline.

Utterly ridiculous.

Objective reason reared its head. In that instant, Ando felt as if he were gazing with the eyes of a disembodied spirit at his own body, spread-eagled on bed. His body posture looked familiar to him. He'd seen that pose somewhere recently. In the midst of an overpowering sleepiness, he recalled the Polaroids of Ryuji's dead body. It was the same pose: head back on the bed, arms and legs flung wide. He fought off sleep and got to his feet so that he could crawl into bed and pull up the covers. He couldn't stop trembling until he dropped off to sleep.

6

He finished his second autopsy at the M.E.'s office, then headed back to the university, leaving the clean-up to his colleagues. Miyashita had contacted him, hinting at a development in the pursuit of Ryuji's cause of death, and Ando had been on tenterhooks ever since. He darted up the steps out of the subway.

He entered the university hospital by the main entrance and then crossed over to the old wing. The new wing, which housed the main entrance, was only two years old. It was a totally modern seventeen-story building connected by a complex of halls and stairways to the old wings, which crowded around like high-rise apartments. The whole place was like a maze. First-time visitors invariably got lost. New and old intertwined, and the color, width, and smell of the hallways—even the squeak of his shoes on the floor—shifted as he pressed on. When he stopped at the iron door that marked the boundary and glanced back at the new wing's wide corridor, he lost his sense of perspective momentarily. He was overcome by an illusion that he was gazing at the future.

The door to the Pathology Department was open a crack, and he could see Miyashita's back where he sat on a stool. Rather than being ensconced in his lab equipment as Ando had expected, he was turned toward the central table, going through some literature. His face was down close to the book opened before him, and he was flipping its pages rapidly. Ando approached him from behind and tapped him on a burly shoulder.

Miyashita turned around and took off his glasses, then turned the book over and laid it on the table. The title on the spine read, *A Beginner's Guide to Astrology*. Ando was taken aback.

Miyashita twirled on his stool until he was facing Ando and then asked, with a straight face, "So, what's your date of birth?"

Ignoring him, Ando picked up the *Beginner's Guide* and leafed through it.

"Horoscopes? What are you, a high school girl?"

"You'd be surprised at how often this stuff hits the mark. Now tell me when you were born."

"Never mind that. Listen." Ando pulled another stool out from

40

under the table and sat down. He moved carelessly, though, and knocked the *Beginner's Guide* off the table. It fell to the floor with a thud.

"Calm down, will ya?" Miyashita bent over—it looked like it pained him—to retrieve the book. But Ando wasn't interested in any book.

"So did you find a virus?" he demanded.

Miyashita shook his head. "My first step was to check with other universities' forensic medicine departments to see if bodies had been brought in with the same symptoms as Ryuji. I've got the results of that inquiry."

"So, were there any?"

"Yup. Six altogether, as far as I could determine."

"Six deaths." But Ando had no idea yet whether or not that was a lot.

"Everybody I asked was astonished. They'd all figured they were the only ones who'd stumbled across this."

"What universities are we talking about?"

Letting the table edge wedge into his belly, Miyashita reached for the file folder that had been placed unceremoniously on top of it.

"Shuwa University had two, Taido University had one, and Yokodai University in Yokohama had three. Six total. And there's every chance we'll see more."

"Let me have a look," Ando said, taking the folder from Miyashita.

That morning, Miyashita and his counterparts at the other schools had faxed each other the relevant files. The folder contained faxes of copies of the original death certificates and autopsy reports. As such, they were somewhat blurry and not very easy to read. Ando took the printouts from the folder and skimmed them for relevant info.

First, the body dissected at Taido. Shuichi Iwata, age 19. He'd died on September 5th, at about eleven at night; he'd been on his 50cc motorbike in the intersection in front of Shinagawa Station when he'd fallen. The autopsy had determined that his coronary artery had been blocked by unexplained swelling and that a cardiac infarction had ensued.

Two of the three bodies autopsied at Yokodai belonged to a young couple, and they'd died together. Takehiko Nomi, age 19, and Haruko Tsuji, age 17. Sometime before dawn on September 6th, their bodies had been discovered in a rented car parked at the foot of Mt. Okusu, in

Yokosuka, Kanagawa Prefecture. When the bodies were discovered, Haruko Tsuji's panties were down around her ankles, and Takehiko Nomi's jeans and briefs were pulled down to his knees. They'd obviously pulled over into a wooded area intending to have car sex, when their hearts stopped simultaneously. The autopsies had discovered strange lumps in their coronary arteries, which were, again, blocked off.

Ando raised his eyes to the ceiling, muttering, "What the hell?"

"The couple in the car, right?"

"Yeah. They had heart attacks at the same time in the same place. And, counting this Shuichi Iwata autopsied at Taido, we have four people experiencing blockage of their coronary arteries at about the same time. What's going on here?"

"Those aren't the only symptoms, either. Have you looked at the mother and child?"

Ando looked down at the files again. "No, not yet."

"Take a look. They had ulcerations on their pharynxes, just like Ryuji."

Ando riffled through the pages until he found the notations for a mother and daughter autopsied at Shuwa. The mother was Shizu Asakawa, age 30, and the daughter was Yoko, only eighteen months old.

When Ando saw the names, he felt something tug at his mind. He rested his hands for a moment, thinking. Something didn't sit right.

"What's wrong?" Miyashita peered at him.

"Nothing."

Ando read on. On October 21st, at around noon, a car driven by Shizu's husband and carrying Shizu and Yoko had gotten into an accident near the Oi off-ramp of the Metropolitan Bayside Expressway. Heading from Urayasu toward Oi, it was not uncommon to encounter traffic near the entrance to the Tokyo Harbor Tunnel. The Asakawas' car had slammed into a light truck at the end of a column of vehicles waiting to exit at Oi. The car was badly wrecked, and mother and daughter, together in the back seat, had lost their lives, while Mr. Asakawa had sustained serious injuries.

"Why did they get sent in for autopsies?" Ando wondered aloud. There wasn't much call to autopsy people who had obviously died in a traffic accident. A full forensic autopsy such as they'd received, with a public prosecutor presiding, usually didn't happen unless a crime was suspected.

"Don't get ahead of yourself. Keep reading."

"Why don't you buy a new fax machine anyway? I can hardly read these. It's making my head hurt," Ando said, waving the curling page in Miyashita's face. He just wanted to know what had happened, and he was having trouble grasping the situation from the blurry printouts cranked out by the antiquated fax.

"You are one impatient bastard," Miyashita said by way of preface. Then he began to explain. "At first, the feeling was that they'd died, indeed, in the collision. But further examination showed no life-threatening injuries. The car was completely wrecked, but on the other hand, mother and daughter were in the back seat. This probably raised some doubts. They did a meticulous post-mortem on both of them. And sure enough, they found bruises and lacerations from the accident on their faces, their feet, et cetera, but the wounds showed no vital reaction. And I think that brings us to your territory."

It was easy to tell if a corpse's injuries had been sustained before or after death based on the presence or absence of a vital reaction. In this case, there was none. Which meant only one thing: at the time of the crash, mother and daughter were already dead.

"So, what, the husband was driving his dead wife and child around?"

Miyashita spread his hands. "So it would seem."

That would immediately justify the forensic autopsy. Perhaps the husband had decided to kill himself and taken his family with him; he'd strangled his wife and child and driven off with them looking for the best place to end his own life, but had gotten into an accident on the way. The autopsies, however, had cleared the husband, for Shizu and Yoko had both had arterial blockages identical to the other cases. They couldn't have been murdered. They'd both died of heart attacks on the expressway, shortly before the accident.

Once that was established, it was easy to guess how the husband lost control of the vehicle... He doesn't realize for a while that his wife and daughter are dead—maybe they just quietly stopped breathing—so he drives on, thinking they're asleep in the back seat. They've been curled up like that for an awfully long while. He tries to wake them up, keeping one hand on the steering wheel and reaching with the other into the rear of the car. He shakes his wife. She doesn't wake up. He glances back to the front again before putting his hand on his wife's knee. Then, suddenly, he realizes the change that's come over her. He panics and just stares at his wife and child, not realizing that the traffic's clogged ahead of him.

That had to be more or less what happened. Having lost his own son, Ando could well understand the panic the husband must have felt. It had been the same for him. If only he'd been able to overcome the panic, maybe he needn't have lost Takanori... In the driver's case, though, overcoming panic wouldn't have accomplished anything. His wife and daughter were already dead.

"So what happened to the husband?" He felt sympathy for the man, who'd lost his family only two weeks before.

"He's hospitalized, of course."

"How bad are his injuries?"

"Physically, he doesn't seem to be that bad off. Mostly it's his mind that was affected."

"Emotional damage?"

"Ever since they brought him in with the bodies of his wife and daughter, he's been catatonic."

"Poor guy." He could think of nothing else to say. The facts spoke volumes about the violence of the psychological shock Asakawa had received in losing both wife and child in a single moment. He must have loved them deeply.

Ando grabbed the faxes out of Miyashita's grip, licked his fingertips, and began paging through the flimsy sheets again. He wanted to know which hospital the man was in. He was curious about the symptoms, and he thought that if Asakawa was in a hospital where Ando knew somebody, specifics could be obtained.

The first thing that leapt into sight was the name.

Kazuyuki Asakawa.

"What's this?" Ando let out a stupid-sounding yell, so surprised he was. "Kazuyuki Asakawa" was the same name he'd inscribed in his planner the other day. The man who'd gone to Ryuji's apartment the night after his death and peppered Mai with questions about some videotape.

"You know him?" Miyashita yawned.

"No, but Ryuji did."

"Really?"

"The driver, this Asakawa guy, was a friend of Ryuji's."

"How do you know?"

Ando gave a brief explanation of what Mai had told him about Asakawa's visit. "This doesn't look good."

There was no need for Ando to specify what didn't look good. Including Ryuji, seven people had died of the same thing. Four on September 5th, one on October 19th, and two on October 21st. The pair at Mt. Okusu had died simultaneously, as had the mother and daughter whose car had been in the accident near the Oi exit. The surviving member of that family had been a friend of Ryuji's. All these people, who seemed to be connected in one way or another, had died from some newfound sarcoma that blocked off the coronary artery. Naturally, the first thought to occur to Ando was that he might be dealing with a contagious disease. Judging from how limited the circle of victims was so far, it probably wasn't airborne. Perhaps, like AIDS, this new epidemic was relatively difficult to contract despite its deadliness.

He considered Mai. He had to assume she'd had physical contact with Ryuji. How he was going to explain this development to her weighed heavily on his mind. All he could tell her, basically, was that she was in danger. Would it even do any good to warn her, if it turned out that was all he could do?

I'd better go to Shuwa U.

The files he held in his hand simply didn't contain enough information. He couldn't do any better than to speak directly with the doctor who'd conducted the autopsies on Asakawa's wife and daughter. He asked Miyashita if he could use the phone, and picked up the receiver to call Shuwa University.

7

On the Monday after the three-day weekend, Ando paid a visit to Shuwa University Medical School, located in Ota Ward. When he'd called from Miyashita's lab he'd pressed for an immediate appointment, but the party on the other end hadn't been impressed, calmly saying he could make time on Monday, if that would do. Ando had to acquiesce. This wasn't a murder investigation or anything of that sort. His curiosity had been piqued, that was all.

Ando knocked on the door of the Forensic Medicine Department and waited. He heard nothing from beyond the door. He looked at his watch and realized that there were still ten minutes to his one-o'clock appointment. Forensic medicine usually had a smaller staff than surgery or internal medicine. The three or four people in it here had probably all gone out to lunch.

While he stood wondering what to do, from behind him a voice called out, "May I help you?" Perfect timing.

He turned around to see a short young man who wore rimless glasses. Ando thought he looked too young to be a lecturer here, but on the other hand, he thought he recognized the slightly shrill voice. Ando offered the young man his card, introducing himself and stating his business. The young man said, "Pleased to make your acquaintance," and handed over his card. Just as Ando thought, it was the man he'd spoken to on the phone Friday. His name card said he was Kazuyoshi Kurahashi, Lecturer in Forensic Medicine at Shuwa University. Judging by the man's position, Ando figured they had to be about the same age, but Kurahashi looked young enough to be in his early twenties. Probably it was to avoid being taken for a student that he spoke in an overdone tone of authority and stolidity.

"Come right this way," Kurahashi said punctiliously, ushering Ando in.

Ando had learned just about everything he could by fax. His purpose today was to see with his own eyes things that couldn't be faxed, and to speak directly to the doctor who'd been in charge of the autopsies. He and Kurahashi exchanged small talk, and then began to share their observations of the bodies they'd dissected. Apparently, Kurahashi had been quite surprised by the unidentified sarcomas he'd found blocking the coronary arteries. As soon as the conversation turned to them, his cool demeanor cracked.

"Would you care to see?" So saying, he went to get one of the tissue samples from the blocked arteries.

Ando had a good look at it with his naked eye, then placed it under a microscope and examined it on a cellular level. One glance told him that these cells had undergone the same transformations as Ryuji's. When cells are treated with a hematoxylin-eosin stain, the cytoplasm turns red while the nucleus turns blue, allowing them to be differentiated with ease. Here, the diseased cells' shapes were distorted; their nuclei were larger than normal. Whereas normal cells had an overall reddish tint, these cells looked bluish. Ando stared at the red, amoeba-like speckles floating on the blue. He had to find out what had caused this change—the culprit, as it were. Obviously, it wasn't going to be easy. He had to deduce the murder weapon and the criminal entirely on the basis of the damage done to the victims' bodies.

Ando lifted his eyes from the microscope and took a deep breath. Somehow, the longer he looked, the harder it was to breathe. "Whose cells are these, by the way?"

"The wife's." Kurahashi turned his head only slightly to answer. He was standing by the shelves which covered one wall, removing and replacing files. He kept shaking his head, evidently unable to locate what he was looking for.

Ando bent over the instrument again, and again the microscopic world assailed him.

So these are Kazuyuki Asakawa's wife's. Knowing who they belonged to, he found himself trying to imagine, in detail, what had happened to their owner. Last month, a car her husband had been driving had collided with a truck near the Oi exit ramp on the Metropolitan Bayside Expressway. Sunday, October 21st, noon. Autopsies had confirmed that mother and child had expired an hour prior to the accident. In other words, they had died simultaneously, at around eleven in the morning. Of the same cause, no less. And that was what he just couldn't wrap his mind around.

So small these lumps of flesh were compared to the rest of the body, yet big enough to block off an artery and stop a heart. He had a hard time imagining that these sarcomas had been growing gradually over a long period of time, since they'd claimed two lives at virtually the same instant. Even if the victims had contracted a virus of some sort, if the virus required an incubation period of months before producing its symptoms, there was no way the two victims should have died nearly simultaneously. The physical differences between the victims should have assured some sort of lag. There was a thirty year age difference between Shizu and Yoko Asakawa, and that should have had some effect. Maybe it was just a coincidence? But no, that couldn't be. The young couple autopsied at Yokodai had died simultaneously, too. And if it wasn't just a coincidence, he had no choice but to conclude that the period between infection and death was extremely short.

The viral hypothesis didn't seem to make for an adequate explanation. Ando momentarily laid aside that scenario, wondering if it could have been food poisoning or the like. With food poisoning, when two people eat the same spoiled item, it's not uncommon for both to fall prey to the same symptoms at the same time. Of course, "food poisoning" could involve a wide range of things; there are natural, chemical, and bacterial toxins. But he'd never heard of any toxin that caused sarcomas in the coronary artery. Perhaps some lab somewhere had been performing ultra-secret bacteriological research, and something had mutated and escaped...

Ando looked up again. He was merely speculating, and he knew all too well that guessing would get him nowhere.

Kurahashi approached the table where Ando was sitting and pulled out a chair. He held a file folder, from which he drew out ten-odd photos.

"These are from the scene of the accident. I don't know if they'll be of any use to you."

Ando hardly expected that shots of the scene would give him anything to go on. He was convinced that the problem was rooted in irregularities at the cellular level, and not in a driver's carelessness. But since Kurahashi had gone to all the trouble of digging out the photos, Ando didn't feel right about returning them without at least taking a look at them. He glanced through them, one by one.

The first photo was of the wrecked automobile. The hood had been crumpled up until it was shaped like a mountain. Both headlights and the bumper were crushed. The windshield had been shattered, too, but the center pillars hadn't been bent. Although the car itself had been totaled, most of the shock evidently hadn't carried to the back seat.

Next was a shot of the surface of the road. It was dry, and there were no skidmarks, suggesting that Asakawa hadn't been watching where he was going. Where was he looking, then? Most likely at the back seat. Maybe he was even touching the cold bodies of his wife and daughter. Ando recalled the sequence of events he'd worked out in Miyashita's lab three days before.

He flipped through two or three more pictures, laying them on the table like playing cards. There was nothing in them to catch the eye, he thought, but then his hand stopped. He was holding a photo of the car's interior. The camera had been lodged against the passenger's side window and aimed so as to take in the front of the cabin. The seatbelt was draped over the driver's seat, and the passenger's seat was pushed forward. Ando stared, momentarily unsure of what in this picture had aroused his interest.

He'd had the same experience paging absently through books before. Sometimes a word would return to mind and keep him from turning the pages, but he'd be unable to remember where in the book he'd seen it, or, for that matter, what the word was. His palms started to perspire. He could feel his intuition at work. This photo was trying to tell him something. He brought the picture so close to his face that his nose was almost touching it. He examined every corner of it. Then he concentrated his vision on one point, and finally found the thing that had been hiding there.

On the passenger's seat sat the black thing, mostly hidden because the back of the seat had been pushed forward. A section of the front and one of the sides were the only visible portions. A similar flat, black thing rested on the floor of the car, also on the passenger's side, held down there by the headrest of the passenger's seat. Ando gave a little cry of excitement and called Kurahashi over.

"Hey, what do you think this is?" He held the photo out to Kurahashi and indicated where he should look. The short man took off his glasses and looked closely at the photo. Then he shook his head, not so much because he couldn't make out the thing, but because he couldn't figure out why Ando was interested in it.

"What is it?" Kurahashi muttered without taking his eyes from the photo.

"It looks to me like a video deck," said Ando, seeking confirmation.

"That *is* what it looks like." As soon as he recognized the object for what it was, Kurahashi thrust the photo back at Ando. The object on the passenger's seat could just as well have been a candy box, given its black, rectangular shape. But a close look at the front of the object revealed a round black button. It certainly looked like a video deck, but it could also have been a tuner or an amp. Regardless, Ando had decided that a video deck was what it was. The thing on the floor, under the headrest, looked like a portable word processor or a personal computer. Considering Asakawa's profession, it wasn't odd that he'd be carrying around a word processor. But a video deck?

"Why's it there?"

His conclusion that it was a video machine, of course, had to do with what Mai had told him. According to her, the day after Ryuji's death, Asakawa had visited Ryuji's apartment and asked her repeatedly about a videotape. The very next day, he'd put a video deck on the passenger seat of a car and gone somewhere, only to get in an accident on his way home to Shinagawa. Where had he been with that deck? If it was just to get it repaired, there was no need to get on the highway; surely there were electronics shops in his neighborhood. It bothered Ando. Asakawa couldn't have been driving around with a bare VCR for no reason.

Ando went through the photos again. When he found one that showed the wrecked car's license plate, he took out his planner and noted it. A Shinagawa plate, WA 5287. From the WA, Ando knew it was a rental. So not only was Asakawa driving a video deck around, he'd gone to the trouble of renting a car for the purpose. Why? Ando tried to put himself in Asakawa's position. If he were carrying around his own video deck, why'd he be doing so?

Dubbing...

He could think of no other reason. Suppose A calls B saying he has a fantastic videotape. B wants a copy, but A owns only one video deck, naturally. If B really wants a copy, he has no alternative but to take his own deck to A's house and ask him to let him make a copy of it.

Even so... Ando lowered his head. *What could a video possibly have to do with these deaths?*

Ando was possessed by an urge he couldn't reason with. He wanted to get his hands on the tape—if at all possible, he wanted to watch it. The accident had happened near Oi. What police precinct was that? The wrecked car had to be stored temporarily at the traffic division of the local precinct. If there had been a video deck in the car, the police would have taken possession of it, too. With Asakawa's wife and daughter dead and he barely conscious, perhaps no one had come to pick up the deck; perhaps it was still at the stationhouse. As an M.E., Ando had quite a few acquaintances on the police force. Getting his hands on that video deck wouldn't be too hard.

But first, Ando realized, he needed to meet Asakawa. It'd save Ando a lot of time if he could learn the facts of the case from Asakawa himself. According to the fax, Asakawa had been catatonic when he was taken to the hospital, but that was over ten days ago. Maybe there had been a change in his condition. If there was any chance of communicating with Asakawa, then the sooner the better.

"Do you know which hospital Kazuyuki Asakawa is in?"

"The Saisei Aid Society Hospital in Shinagawa, I think." Checking his file, Kurahashi said, "I was right. But it says here the patient's catatonic."

"I'm going to pay him a visit all the same," Ando remarked, nodding several times as if to persuade himself.

8

Ando had dozed off with his face pressed up against the window of the cab. Then his head slipped off the support of his right hand, and he collapsed forward so that his face banged into the back of the driver's seat; at the same time, he heard something that sounded like an alarm bell, off in the distance. Reflexively he looked at his watch. Ten past two. Immediately on leaving Shuwa he'd hopped in a cab, and he couldn't have been riding for more than about ten minutes. He'd probably only dropped off for a couple of those minutes, but somehow he had the feeling that a long time had elapsed. It felt like days had passed since Kurahashi had shown him the photos of the accident. Feeling as if he'd been spirited somewhere far away, Ando sat in the sealed cab and listened to the clanging alarm.

The cab wasn't moving. It was in the left lane of a four-lane road, and it must have been a turn lane, since all the other lanes were flowing. Only they were stopped. He leaned forward and peered out through the windshield. Ahead and to the left he could see a railroad crossing: the bar was down and the signal light was flashing. It could have been his imagination, but the rhythms of the light and the bell seemed to be slightly out of synch. The crossing for the Keihin Express line was about a hundred feet ahead on the No. 1 Tokyo-Yokohama Freeway, and Ando's taxi had been waiting for a train to go by. Shinagawa Saisei Hospital, his destination, was on the other side of the tracks. A train went by, bound for Tokyo, but the bar still didn't rise; the arrow indicating a Yokohama-bound train began to flash now. It didn't look like they'd be able to get across any time soon. The cab driver had resigned himself to waiting and was flipping through a sheaf of papers bound by a paper clip, writing something down now and then.

No need to hurry. Visiting hours last until five, so there's still plenty of time.

Ando suddenly raised his head from the headrest: he thought he'd felt somebody's gaze on him. Somewhere close, outside the car, a pair of eyes was staring at him. Maybe this was what it felt like to be placed between slides as a tissue sample and examined under a microscope. There was something of the observer in the gaze that had been turned on him. Ando looked all around. Maybe somebody in one of the other cars had recognized him and was trying to catch his attention. But he didn't see a familiar face in any of the cars, and there was nobody on the sidewalk. He tried to convince himself it was just his imagination, but the gaze showed no signs of relenting. Once again Ando turned his head right and left. To the left, just beyond the sidewalk, the ground rose in a grassy embankment that ran alongside the railroad tracks. Something in the shadow of the weeds was moving. It moved and froze, moved and froze. Without once taking its gaze off Ando, some creature was crawling along on the ground, alternating between stillness and motion. It was a snake. Ando was surprised to see one in such a place. Its tiny, intense eyes glowed in the autumn-afternoon sun. There was no doubt that this was the observer he'd sensed, and it dredged up memories of a scene from his grade school days.

He'd lived in the country, in a little town surrounded by farmers' fields. Once, on his way home from school—Ando remembered it as a peaceful spring afternoon—he'd seen a snake on a concrete wall that flanked a ditch filled with water. At first the threadlike gray snake had looked to him like just a crack in the wall, but as he got closer he could see the roundness of its body emerge from the surface. As soon as he saw it was a snake, he scooped up a rock the size of his fist. He tossed the rock in his palm a few times, gauging its size and weight, and then went into a pitcher's windup. It was several yards from where he stood to the wall on the other side of the ditch. He really didn't think he'd hit the bull's-eye. But the rock arced high in the air and came down from above directly onto the snake's head, crushing it. Ando recoiled with a cry. He was standing more than a dozen feet away, but it felt like he'd smashed the snake's head with his own clenched fist. He wiped his palm over and over on his trousers. The snake had fallen into the ditch like a suction cup peeling off a stainless steel surface. Ando took a couple of steps into the tangle of grass on the bank of the ditch and leaned forward, trying to catch the snake's last moments. He got there in time to see its corpse float away. At that moment, he'd felt the same gaze upon him that he did now. It hadn't been the dead snake's gaze, but rather that of a bigger snake that lay in the grass watching him. Its smooth face betrayed no expression as it entangled him in its insistent, unwavering stare. Ando had been shaken by the malevolence of that gaze. If the little snake he'd killed had been the big snake's child, some catastrophe would befall him for sure. The big snake was laying a curse on him: that was the purpose of the insistent stare. His grandmother had told him many times that if he killed snakes something terrible would happen to him. Repentant, Asakawa pleaded silently with the snake, hoping it'd understand that he hadn't meant to kill.

That was more than twenty years ago. But now, Ando recalled the incident with startling clarity. Snake curses were nothing but superstition, he knew. He doubted reptiles even had the ability to recognize their own offspring. Yet...the alarm kept on ringing. *Enough! Stop thinking!* Ando cried voicelessly. But still the image of a baby snake, white belly upturned, floating away in the ditch, parent snake swimming along behind, continued to pester him like threads that wouldn't come untangled.

I was cursed.

He was losing control of his thoughts. Against his will, he could see the chain of karmic cause and effect looming before him. He couldn't shake off a vision of the murdered baby snake getting caught in the tangled vegetation lining the sides of the ditch, of the parent snake catching up with it and entwining itself around it, the two of them floating there... The image reminded him of DNA. The DNA within a cell's nucleus, he realized, looked like two snakes coiling around each other and flying up into the sky. DNA, by which biological information is transmitted endlessly from generation to generation. Perhaps a pair of snakes perpetually ensnared humanity.

Takanori!

His silent call to his son was filled with misery. He was afraid he wouldn't be able to hold himself together for much longer. Ando lifted his head and looked out the window. He had to distract himself, to interrupt this chain of associations at once. Through the windshield he could see the bright red Keihin Express train go by, slowly. With Shinagawa Station right ahead, it was moving no faster than a slithering snake. *Snakes again.* There was no way out. He closed his eyes and tried again to think of something else. The tiny hand grabbed at Ando's calf as it slipped away into the sea. He could feel the touch again. It was the snake's curse, it had to be. He was about to let out a sob. The situations were too similar. The baby snake, its head crushed, carried away by the flow. Two decades later, its parent's curse had manifested itself. Takanori was close by, but Ando couldn't save him. The beach in June, before the season had officially opened. He and his son, paddling out to sea, holding onto a rectangular float. He could hear his wife, back on the shore, call:

Taka! That's far enough. Come back!

But the boy was too busy bobbing up and down and splashing about. Her voice didn't reach him.

Honey, come back, okay?

Hysteria was beginning to tinge her voice.

The waves were getting taller, and Ando, too, thought that it was time to turn back. He tried to turn the float around. Just at that moment, a whitecap rose in front of them, and in an instant overturned the float and thrown both him and the boy into the sea. His head went under, and it was then that he first realized they were so far out that even his own feet didn't touch bottom. He started to panic. When his head broke above the surface again, his son was nowhere to be seen. Treading water, he turned around until he could see his wife running into the sea toward him, still fully clothed. At the same time, a hand grasped at his leg. His son's hand. Ando tried hastily to turn around towards the boy to draw him up, but that had been the wrong move. Taka's hand slipped away from his calf, and all Ando's hand managed to do was graze his son's hair.

His wife's half-crazed cries shot over the early-summer sea as she rushed through the water. *I know he's close, but I can't reach him!* He dived under the surface and moved blindly about but couldn't manage to make contact with that small hand again. His son had disappeared—for good. His body never surfaced again. Where had it drifted to? All that remained were the few strands of hair that had tangled in Ando's wedding ring.

At the railroad crossing, the bar finally lifted. Ando was weeping, holding his hand over his mouth to stifle his sobs. The cab driver noticed anyway and kept glancing at him in the rear-view mirror.

Get a hold of yourself, before you totally fall apart!

It was one thing to break down alone in bed, quite another to do it in broad daylight. He wished there were something, anything, he could think about that could bring him back to the here and now. Suddenly he saw Mai Takano's face in his mind. She was working on a fruit parfait with such enthusiasm that he thought she might lick the dish when she was through. The collars of a white blouse peeked out from the neck of her dress; her left hand rested on her knee. Finished with the parfait, she wiped her lips with a napkin and stood up. He was beginning to see. Sexual fantasies about Mai were the only thing that could draw him out of the abyss of his grief. He realized that he hadn't fantasized about a woman once since his wife had left him—or rather, since the death of his son. He'd lost all of his former attachment to sex.

The cab jostled up and down until it was straddling the tracks. At the same time, Mai's body was bobbing up and down in Ando's mind.

9

Mai Takano got off the Odakyu Line at Sagami Ohno and went out to the main street, but she couldn't decide which way to turn. She'd walked this route in reverse two weeks ago, but now she'd lost all sense of direction. When she'd gone to Ryuji's parents' house for the wake, it was in a car from the M.E.'s office. This time, making her way there on foot from the station, she hadn't gone more than a hundred feet or so before she found herself in unfamiliar surroundings. It wasn't a new experience for her. She always got lost when she tried to get somewhere she'd only been to once.

She had his parents' phone number, so all she had to do was call. But she was embarrassed to ask his mother to come pick her up. She decided to trust her intuition a little more. She didn't have far to go, she knew. It was only a ten-minute walk from the station.

Suddenly she saw Ando's face in her mind. She'd made a dinner date with him for the coming Friday, but now, she wondered if it'd been careless of her to accept. She was starting to regret it. To her, Ando was a friend of Ryuji's, someone with whom she could share memories of him. If she could get Ando to tell her stories about Ryuji's college days, maybe she'd understand Ryuji's impenetrable ideas better. In other words, she had to admit that some calculation had gone into her decision to go out with Ando. But if Ando started entertaining the sort of thoughts a man can have about a woman, things could turn unpleasant. Since entering college, Mai had learned the hard way that men and women wanted vastly different things. What Mai wanted was to keep the relationship on a level where she and the man could provide each other with intellectual stimulation; her boyfriends' interests, however, always tended to gravitate toward her nether parts. She was forced to turn them down as gently as possible. The trauma her rejections caused them was always more than she could take. They'd send her long apologetic letters which only rubbed salt in her wounds, or they'd call and the first thing out of their mouths would be, "Listen, I'm really sorry about what happened last time." She didn't want them to apologize. She wanted them to learn and grow from the experience. She wanted to see a man turn embarrassment into energy and engage in a genuine struggle toward maturity.

If the man did that, she'd resume the friendship any time. But she could never be friends with a guy whose psyche remained forever, and unabashedly, that of a child who refused to grow up.

Ryuji was the only man she'd ever been serious about. He wasn't like the juveniles who surrounded her. The things she and Ryuji had given each other were invaluable. If she could be sure that a relationship with Ando would be like the one she'd had with Ryuji, she'd accept any number of dinner invitations from him. But she knew from experience that the chances weren't very good. The likelihood, in Japan, of her meeting an independent guy, a man worthy of the name, was close to zero. Still, she couldn't quite put Ando out of her mind.

Just once, Ryuji had mentioned him to her. The conversation had been about genetic engineering, when suddenly he'd digressed and dropped Ando's name.

Mai hadn't ever gotten the difference between genes and DNA. *Weren't they just the same thing?* Ryuji had set about explaining to her that DNA was the chemical material on which hereditary information was recorded, while a gene was one unit of that nearly infinite amount of hereditary information. In the course of the discussion, he'd mentioned that the technology existed to break DNA down into small segments using restriction enzymes, and to rearrange it. Mai had commented that the process sounded "like a puzzle." Ryuji had agreed: "Absolutely, it's like solving a puzzle, or deciphering a code." From there, the talk had gone afield, until Ryuji was telling her a story from his college days.

When Ryuji had learned that the nitty-gritty of DNA technology involved code-breaking, he'd started to play cipher games with his friends in med school, between classes. He told her an interesting anecdote about these games. Many of the students were fascinated by molecular biology, and so, before long, Ryuji had recruited about ten guys to play with. The rules were simple. One person would submit a coded message, and then everybody else would have a certain number of days in which to decipher it. The first one to get it right won. The game tested their math and logic skills, but also required flashes of inspiration. The guys loved it.

The codes varied in difficulty, depending on the skill of the person devising them, but Ryuji had been able to solve most of them.

Meanwhile, only one classmate had ever been able to crack any of Ryuji's codes. Mitsuo Ando. Ryuji told Mai how shocked he'd been when Ando had broken his code.

I got chills. It was like he'd read my mind.

And so the name Mitsuo Ando had made a deep impression on Mai.

Which was why she'd been so astonished when the detective had introduced her to Ando at the M.E.'s office. He had to be *the* Ando—he'd even introduced himself as an old friend of Ryuji's. Knowing Ando had been the only one to ever unlock one of Ryuji's codes, Mai had felt she could trust him. She just knew his skills with the scalpel had to be way up there, and that he'd easily figure out the cause of death.

Mai was still under the sway of the words of a man who'd been dead for two weeks. If Ryuji hadn't mentioned Ando to her, she probably never would have been able to call the M.E.'s office to ask about the cause of death; she never would have ended up seeing Ando again on campus. She certainly never would have made plans to have dinner with him. One chance word from Ryuji had subtly bound her.

Mai turned off the main road into a maze of residential streets. There she spotted a convenience store sign that she recognized. She knew where to go from there. Once she turned at the convenience store, Ryuji's parents' house would be straight ahead. As two-week-old memories started to come back to her, she quickened her step.

It was a nondescript house, built on a parcel of about four hundred square yards. From the wake, she remembered that the first floor contained a largish living room adjoined to a smaller Japanese-style room.

No sooner had Mai rung the doorbell than Ryuji's mother appeared at the door. She'd been waiting impatiently for Mai, and showed her up to the second floor, to the room Ryuji had studied in from grade school on through his sophomore year at college. After his junior year, Ryuji had moved out of the house, even though it was well within commuting distance, and taken a room near campus. The only times the room had been used as a study since were when Ryuji had come home to visit.

Ryuji's mother set down a plate of shortcake and a cup of coffee and left the room. As Mai watched her shuffle down the hall, head drooping, she was touched by the woman's grief at losing her son.

Left alone, Mai took her first good look around the room. It was a Japanese-style room with a matted floor. In one corner a carpet had been spread out under a desk. Bookshelves lined the walls, but she could only see their upper portions; the lower shelves were hidden by the confusion of cardboard boxes and appliances that littered the floor. She took a quick count of the boxes. Twenty-seven. These held everything that had been carted over from Ryuji's East Nakano apartment after his death. The larger furniture—the bed, the desk, etc.—they'd given away. The boxes seemed to contain mostly books.

Mai sighed, then seated herself on the floor and had a sip of coffee. She was already trying to resign herself to the possibility that she wouldn't be able to find it. Even if it were in there somewhere, it'd be quite a task to find a few manuscript pages among all those things. Perhaps the pages weren't even *in* those boxes.

The twenty-seven boxes were all sealed with tape. She took off her cardigan, rolled up her sleeves, and opened the nearest one. Paperbacks. She picked up a few. One turned out to be a book she'd given him as a present. Longing washed over her. The smell of Ryuji's old apartment clung to the cover.

This is no place to let yourself wallow in emotion.

She choked back her tears and went back to work taking things out of the box.

But when she got to the bottom, there was still no sign of the pages. Mai tried to deduce what they could have gotten mixed in with. Maybe one of the books he'd been using as a reference, or one of the files in which he'd kept his research materials. She kept breaking the seals on the boxes.

Her back started to break into a sweat. Taking books out of boxes and putting them back in was surprisingly strenuous work. After she'd finished her third box, she took a breather and entertained the idea of filling in the missing pages by herself. Ryuji's challenging theory of symbolic logic had already been made public, albeit in piecemeal form, in specialist journals. The project at hand, however, wasn't quite so esoteric. Ryuji had also been writing a book-length study aimed at the general reader that dealt with logic and science in the context of various social problems. What he was saying in it wasn't too difficult. In fact, the work was being serialized in a monthly put out by a major publisher. Mai had been involved from the start, when she'd volunteered to make clean manuscript copies of what Ryuji wrote; she'd even attended meetings with his editor. As a result, she felt she had a good handle on the flow of Ryuji's argument as well as on his writing style. If one or two pages were all that was missing, she felt confident she could come up with something to fill in the gap without creating any inconsistencies.

But that's only if I could be sure only one page is missing.

If that were the case, she'd probably give in to the temptation. Each installment had averaged forty manuscript pages, but that was only an average. They'd ranged from thirty-seven to forty-three. This was the twelfth and last installment, and she had no idea how many pages Ryuji had actually ended up with. That meant she had no way of knowing how many were missing. When she'd slipped out of the wake to put the manuscript in order, she'd found the installment, thirty-eight handwritten pages. The final page was numbered 38, and there were thirty-seven pages preceding it. So she had no inkling at first that anything was amiss. What with the funeral and all, she was late in sitting down to make a clean copy, and the deadline was upon her when she finally sat down and read through it. It was then that she realized that there was a lacuna between the last two pages. In terms of page numbers, they looked okay—37 was followed by 38—but something important was missing. In fact, the conclusion. And without it the argument made no sense. The last two lines of page 37 had been crossed out in ballpoint pen, with an arrow leading to the edge of the page. But the next page did not contain the head of that arrow. She could only surmise that he must have added something and that that something had disappeared.

Turning pale, she'd read the whole thing again from the beginning several times. But the more she read, the more obvious it was that there was a gap at the end. His line of reasoning, which had been reiterated and expanded upon in installment after installment, came to a sudden halt with the words, "However, for that very reason..." The phrase seemed to promise an antithesis, but the sentence was cut off there. The deeper she got into his train of thought, the more she was convinced that a very important passage, probably several pages long, had disappeared. And the whole thing—twelve installments, some five hundred pages—was already slated for publication in book form. This was the conclusion she was dealing with. This was serious.

So she had immediately called Ryuji's parents and explained the situation to them. Within two or three days of the funeral, they had emptied out Ryuji's apartment and had had all his books and personal effects brought to his old room. If the missing pages had gotten mixed in with something else, they had to be somewhere in the room, Mai had explained to Ryuji's parents. She needed their permission to look through Ryuji's things.

But now, confronted with the stacks of boxes, she felt like whining. *Oh, why did you have to go and die on me?*

What a feat, though, drawing his last breath immediately after finishing his manuscript. She found it hateful.

I want you to come here right this minute and tell me what happened to those pages!

She reached out for her coffee, now quite cold. If only she'd read through the manuscript sooner, she wouldn't have been in this mess. She couldn't regret that enough. If she couldn't find the missing pages, she'd have no other option but to try to supply them herself. She shrank in fear from the thought that what she wrote might diverge from Ryuji's intentions. It would really be quite presumptuous of her. True, she had already been accepted into graduate school, but for a girl barely twenty to doctor the conclusion of the very last work of a logician from whom everybody had expected such great things...

I can't do it.

Telling herself she'd just have to find the pages, she opened the next box.

Sometime after four, the room, which faced east, began to get dark, so she turned on a light. It was November, and the days were getting noticeably shorter. But it wasn't cold. Mai got up and drew the curtains. For a while now, she'd been bothered by the feeling that someone was watching her through the window.

She'd already gone through half the cardboard boxes, and she hadn't yet found the missing pages.

Suddenly, Mai could hear her heart beating. The inside of her chest was pounding. She stopped what she was doing and sat there, one knee up, back bent, waiting for the palpitations to subside. This had never happened to her before. She pressed a hand over the left side of her chest and tried to figure out what was causing it. Was it guilt over having lost her teacher's work? No, that wasn't it. Something was hiding in the room with her. A minute ago, she'd thought it was outside the room staring at her, but evidently she'd been wrong. She half expected a cat or something to dash out from behind a box.

She felt something cold on the back of her head and neck. A stabbing gaze. She turned around. She saw her pink cardigan draped over a box where she'd left it when she got to work. The spaces between its fibers glittered like eyes, reflecting the lamplight. Mai picked up the cardigan to reveal a video deck.

The jet-black deck sat on top of a box, its cords wrapped around it. It had to be the one that had been in Ryuji's apartment. There was no TV set to be seen, however, and the deck hadn't been hooked up.

Gingerly, Mai reached out and touched the edge of the deck. The cords were wrapped around its middle, top to bottom, leaving the deck resting on them as on a see-saw.

Did I put my cardigan on this?

She couldn't remember. Of course, there was no other explanation. Before starting on the boxes, she'd taken off her cardigan and carelessly laid it on the video deck. That had to be it.

She locked gazes with the deck for perhaps a minute, and all thoughts of the missing pages disappeared from her mind. In their place swirled questions about a video.

She couldn't forget what Kazuyuki Asakawa had asked her the day after Ryuji's death. "He didn't tell you anything there at the end? No last words? Nothing, say, about a videotape?"

Mai uncoiled the cords from around the body of the machine. She picked out the power cord and looked for an outlet. An extension cord lay unassumingly under the desk. She plugged the deck into it. Four zeros started flashing on the machine's timer display—its pulse, like that of a dead person brought back to life. Mai extended her right index finger and waved it around in front of the deck. She couldn't decide what to do. A voice told her not to touch it. Mai pushed EJECT anyway. The slot opened, a motor whirred, and a videotape emerged. There was a label on the spine, and a title written on the label.

Liza Minnelli, Frank Sinatra, Sammy Davis, Jr./1989

Sticking out of the deck like that, the tape looked like a huge tongue. The deck resembled an obnoxious child, winking and wiggling his tongue at her.

Mai took firm hold of the black tongue and pulled it out.

10

Just when it was about to pull up to the hospital, Ando's cab was overtaken by an ambulance whose siren was wailing. They were on a narrow, one-way street lined with shops, and in order to let the ambulance pass, they had to wedge the car between two delivery trucks parked on the side of the road. It looked like it might take a while to pull out again, so Ando decided to get out then and there. The eleven-story hospital towered over them, almost close enough to touch. It would be quicker to walk.

As he stepped off the street toward the main entranceway of the hospital, Ando could see the ambulance that had just passed them pull into the space between the old and new wings. It had taken the ambulance so long to negotiate the narrow streets that it had ended up arriving at the same time as Ando had on foot.

The siren fell silent, but the ambulance's rotating light remained on, throwing its red mottled pattern onto the hospital walls. Stillness descended from the clear blue sky and created a zone of silence around the ambulance like the circle of brightness from a spotlight. To go in, Ando had to walk past the ambulance. The red light finally stopped rotating, and the echoes of the siren were disappearing into the sky. The atmosphere was thick with the prospect that, any second now, the back doors of the ambulance might burst open and spew forth emergency medical personnel unloading a stretcher—but nothing happened. Ando stood and watched. Ten seconds, twenty seconds passed, but the doors didn't open. Silence prevailed. Thirty seconds. The air was frozen. Nobody came running out of the hospital, either.

Ando snapped out of his reverie and resumed walking. And suddenly, the ambulance doors opened with great force. A paramedic jumped out and helped his colleague inside the ambulance unload a stretcher. Ando didn't care what had prevented them from carrying out the patient immediately—these guys were too damn slow. Now they were holding the stretcher at a slant, and Ando's face came momentarily level with the oxygen-masked face of the patient. Their eyes met. The patient seemed to twist toward Ando, and stopped just as abruptly. His eyes were lifeless. He'd been picked up in critical condition, and now he'd met his end. In his line of work, Ando had witnessed any number of deaths. But never like this, by chance. Taking it as an ill omen, Ando averted his eyes from the dead man. He was no different from Miyashita with his astrology. First the snake on the embankment, and now this chance encounter with death. Lately, Ando had been looking for meaning in a lot of trivial events. He'd always scoffed at people who believed in jinxes and fortunes, but now, he realized, he was one of them.

Shinagawa Saisei Hospital was a general hospital connected to Shuwa University, and the man Ando was going to see, Dr. Wada, actually belonged to the university. Kurahashi, his superior, seemed to have contacted him already. No sooner had Ando stated his business than he was shown to a room on the seventh floor of the west wing.

Ando peered into Asakawa's eyes where he lay prostrate on his sickbed, and was immediately reminded of the eyes of the patient he'd just seen. Asakawa's eyes had the exact same quality to them: they were the eyes of a dead man.

Arms hooked up to a pair of I.V.s, face turned toward the ceiling, Asakawa moved not a muscle. Ando didn't know what the man used to look like, but he guessed the poor soul must have been at about half his normal weight. His cheeks were sunken and his beard was turning white.

Ando moved to the bedside and addressed him gently. "Mr. Asakawa."

No answer. Ando thought to touch him on the shoulder, but hesitated and turned to Dr. Wada for permission. Wada nodded, and Ando placed a hand on Asakawa's shoulder. The skin under his gown had no resilience. Ando could feel the shoulder blade, and drew back his hand involuntarily. There was no reaction.

Backing away from the bed, Ando turned to Wada and asked, "Has he been like this the whole time?"

"Yes," Wada answered flatly. Asakawa had been brought in from the accident site on October 21st, meaning that for fifteen days now he hadn't spoken, hadn't cried, hadn't laughed, hadn't gotten angry, hadn't eaten, hadn't evacuated his bladder or his bowels on his own.

"What do you think is causing it, doctor?" Ando asked in his politest voice.

"At first we thought he'd sustained a brain injury in the accident,

66

but tests showed no irregularities. We suspect a psychological cause."

"Shock?"

"Most likely."

Probably the shock of losing his wife and daughter at the same time had destroyed Asakawa's mind. But Ando wondered if that had been the only cause. Probably because he'd seen the photos of the accident scene, Ando had a surprisingly clear image of the moment of the collision. And every time he envisioned it, his gaze was drawn to the passenger seat and the video deck enshrined thereon. It loomed larger and larger in his imagination. Why had Asakawa been transporting a VCR? Where had he gone with it? If only the man could explain himself.

Ando pulled a stool up next to Asakawa's pillow and sat down. He stared at Asakawa's face in profile for a while, trying to imagine what dreamland the poor man was lost and floating in. Which was more pleasant to live in, he wondered, the world of reality or the world of delusion? Probably Asakawa's wife and daughter were alive in his dream world. He was probably holding his daughter to his breast and playing with her right now.

"Mr. Asakawa," said Ando, with all the sympathy of one who felt the same grief. Since Asakawa had been a high school classmate of Ryuji's, he must have been two years younger than Ando. But to look at him one would have thought he was past sixty. What had brought about such a change? Sadness accelerated the aging process. Ando was aware that he himself had aged rapidly over the past year, for instance. He used to be told he looked young for his age, but now, people often thought he was older than he really was.

"Mr. Asakawa," he called a second time.

Wada couldn't bear to watch. "I don't think he can hear you."

It was true. No matter how many times Ando called Asakawa's name, there was no reaction. He gave up and got to his feet.

"Will he recover?"

Wada threw up his hands. "God knows."

Patients like Asakawa could get better or worse without warning. Medical science was usually helpless to predict what lay ahead in cases like these.

"I'd like to ask you to notify me if there's any change in his condition."

"Understood."

There was no point in staying any longer. Ando and Wada left together. At the door Ando stopped and took one last look at Asakawa. He couldn't detect the slightest change. Asakawa kept his dead gaze fixed on the ceiling.

11

Mai reclined the adjustable backrest as far as it would go, and then lay back and stared at the ceiling. This was what she did when she was at an impasse. With her back arched like this she could read the titles on the bookshelves behind her, upside down. Not minding that her still-damp hair was touching the carpet, she closed her eyes and stayed in that awkward position for a while.

Her whole studio apartment, including the bathroom and kitchenette, measured less than two hundred square feet. One entire wall was taken up with bookshelves, leaving her without enough room for a bed or a desk. At night, she pushed the low table she used in lieu of a proper desk into the corner so she could unroll her futon. She'd had to sacrifice space in order to afford a place near campus on just her monthly allowance from home and the money she earned tutoring. Her three conditions for an apartment had been that it be close to school, that it have its own bath and toilet, and that it offer some privacy. Rent counted for nearly half of her monthly expenses, but even so, she was satisfied with the arrangement. She knew that if she relocated a little farther out toward the suburbs she'd be able to find a bigger place, but she had no intention of moving. She actually found it convenient to be able to sit at her table in the middle of the room and have everything she needed within arm's reach.

With her eyes still closed, she felt around until she found her CD boom box and turned it on. She liked the song. She tapped her thighs in time with the music. She'd been on the track team in junior high and high school; she'd been a sprinter, and her legs were still pretty firm. She regulated her breathing until her chest, under her flowered pajamas, swelled and fell along with the music. She opened and closed her nostrils in rhythm, praying for a flash of wisdom. The discomfort of knowing that she had to finish the manuscript this very night had totally zapped her concentration.

She had an appointment tomorrow afternoon with Kimura, Ryuji's editor. She was supposed to turn over the clean copy of the last installment then. And she still hadn't come up with a solution for what to do about the end. She hadn't found the missing pages at Ryuji's parents' house, and she had no more time to spend looking for them. She'd even started to wonder if there were any pages missing to begin with. Maybe Ryuji had meant to add something later but died before he had the chance. In which case, she'd be better off giving up the search and concentrating her energies on coming up with adjustments worthy of the final installment.

But she'd been stuck for words for ages now. She hadn't written a line. She'd taken a shower to clear her head, but still her pen would not produce. She'd write something only to cross it out, to tear up the paper and throw it away.

Suddenly it struck her. She opened her eyes. *You're not getting anywhere because you're trying to add something.*

All her suffering came from the fact that she was trying to fill in the blank towards the end of the book with her own words. But it was only to be expected that she'd find it impossible to guess where Ryuji's line of thought would have gone. It tended to skip and jump at the best of times. It followed, then, that the best she could hope to do was to delete passages before and after the blank and smooth things over.

Mai got up and fixed the backrest so that it was nearly vertical. She'd been a fool. Taking words out was a lot easier than putting any in. Ryuji himself would undoubtedly have preferred it that way, even if it meant leaving some of his thoughts unexpressed. That would be far better than seeing them twisted beyond recognition.

Mai felt herself relax, now that she'd hit upon a solution. And as though to seize upon her relaxation, the videotape leapt into sight. She'd brought it back from Ryuji's parents' house without telling them. Ever since she'd discovered it there in the study, she'd wanted to see what was on it. But there hadn't been a TV set in the room, and the deck hadn't been hooked up. The only way she could watch the tape was to bring it home with her. At first she'd fully intended to ask Ryuji's parents if she could borrow it. But when she'd finally decided to leave, having given up on finding the pages, all the phrases she'd prepared vanished, and she couldn't figure out how to broach the subject.

Excuse me, but this videotape has really got me intrigued. Would you mind if I borrowed it?

What a vague way to put it. What did "intrigued" mean, anyway? If they asked her, she wouldn't be able to answer. So at last she'd simply left with the tape hidden in her bag.

Liza Minnelli, Frank Sinatra, Sammy Davis, Jr./1989. Chances are he'd just recorded a music show; the cassette itself was totally ordinary. And yet it had taken hold of her. She couldn't even remember when she'd taken it out of her bag. There it was, sitting on top of her fourteen-inch combination TV/VCR, tempting her. Even in Ryuji's room, when it had been shut inside the deck, that mechanical box, the tape had been attracting her in some way. Now, out of its shell, exposed, it seemed almost to have the power to suck her in whole.

The title didn't seem to mesh with Ryuji's taste in music. As a matter of fact, as far as she knew, he didn't listen to music all that much. When he did, it was light classical. In any case, from the handwriting on the label it was clear enough that the tape hadn't belonged to Ryuji. Someone else had made it. In the course of events, it had been taken to Ryuji's apartment in East Nakano. And now, it was in Mai's own apartment.

Without getting up, Mai reached over and put the tape in the VCR. The machine switched on automatically. She turned to the video channel and pushed PLAY.

Mai heard a *thunk* as the tape started to roll, and she hurriedly pressed PAUSE. What if it was something she was not meant to see? She balked. Once certain images were burned into your brain, she knew, it was impossible to wipe them away—to ever return to a state of purity. Maybe she'd better stop now before she regretted it. But in the end her doubts couldn't overcome her curiosity, and she released the pause button.

There was the sound of static as the picture wobbled. A second later, the screen went black as if ink had been splashed over it. There was no going back now. Mai braced herself. What then unfolded before her eyes was a series of scenes whose meaning she could not understand and whose nature she could never have guessed from the title.

As soon as she'd finished watching it, Mai felt like throwing up, and she ran into the bathroom. She wished she'd turned it off halfway through, but she couldn't resist the power of the images. She'd watched until the very end. No, it was probably more accurate to say that she was *shown* it. She simply couldn't press the stop button.

She was drenched with sweat and was shivering. She felt something force its way up from her stomach into her throat. She felt more revulsion than fear—something had come inside her, deep inside her. She knew she had to get it out. She stuck her finger down her throat, but she only vomited a small amount. She choked on the taste of bile, and tears streamed from her eyes. Turning a hollow, helpless gaze around the room, she slumped to her knees. For a while she could feel herself being destroyed—and then her consciousness receded, to some place far, far away.

PART TWO   *Vanishing*

1

It was already fifteen minutes past the time they were supposed to meet. Ando started to fidget. He took out his planner and checked the schedule again.

There it was: Friday, November 9th, 6:00 pm, in front of the Moai statue at the west exit of Shibuya Station. *Meet Mai for dinner.* He hadn't misremembered.

Ando inserted himself into the flow of passersby and made a brief circuit of the area. Each time he saw a woman of roughly Mai's age he peered at her face, but none were hers. Half an hour had passed now. Thinking maybe she'd forgotten, Ando called Mai's apartment from a pay phone. He let it ring six or seven times, fancying he could hear from the echoes how small her apartment was.

It's really tiny, she'd said. *Less than five mats!*

Ten rings. Obviously, she wasn't home. He brought the receiver away from his ear. No doubt something had happened to make her late. She was probably on her way. At least he hoped so, as he hung up.

His gaze kept stealing back to his watch. It had been almost an hour now.

At seven I'll give up.

It had been so long since he'd dated that he didn't even know if it was proper to wait any longer. Come to think of it, he'd never been stood up before. His wife had been pretty punctual when they were dating. He'd kept her waiting occasionally, but never she him.

He spent a while thinking back over various times he'd waited for people in the past, and as he did so, seven o'clock came and went. But Ando couldn't make himself leave. He couldn't give up while there was still some slight ray of hope. As he kept telling himself, *Five more minutes!...* All week long he'd been looking forward to this. He couldn't give up now.

In the end, Ando waited in the Shibuya throng for an hour and thirty-three minutes, but Mai never appeared.

He entered the hotel lobby and headed straight for the front desk to ask where the farewell party was being held. Funakoshi's send-off. Now that Mai had stood him up, he had no reason not to come. Plus, after standing in the chilly evening air in a throng of countless young people, he just couldn't bear to go straight back to his empty apartment. Seeking some way to salvage the evening, he'd hit on the idea of showing up at the party after all. It wouldn't hurt to kick up his heels with his friends for the first time in a while, he reasoned.

The organized-gathering part of the evening was just ending, and people were getting together in groups of threes and fives to hit the bars. This was how it always worked. The professors would go home after the main party, allowing the younger faculty to speak freely in their informal post-party binge sessions. Ando's timing was perfect; he'd come just in time to join in on one of those sessions.

Miyashita was the first one to notice him. He came over and put a hand on Ando's shoulder. "I thought you were out on a date?"

"Oh, she stood me up," Ando forced himself to say cheerfully.

"Ah, sorry to hear that. Hey, come here a second." Miyashita grabbed him by the cuff and led him over to the space by a door. He didn't seem interested in pursuing Ando's strikeout.

"What is it?" Something seemed fishy.

But before Miyashita could tell him anything, Professor Yasukawa from the Second Internal Medicine Unit walked by. Miyashita whispered, "You'll come drinking with us, right?"

"That's why I'm here."

"Great. I'll tell you later."

And then Miyashita was off to make nice with Yasukawa. As organizer, he thanked the professor for attending. Miyashita smiled and joked, his jowly face glowing. Ando couldn't but admire the way his friend managed to get liked by all the profs. If anybody else acted in such a way it would have come across as smarmy, but Miyashita knew how to carry it off.

Ando stayed by the door, waiting for Miyashita and Yasukawa's conversation to end. In the interim, several familiar faces passed by, but none did more than offer a greeting. Nobody cared to stop and talk to Ando.

His circle of friends had narrowed considerably in the time since he'd lost his son to the sea. He bore not a smidgen of a grudge toward those who'd distanced themselves from him, though. He knew that the fault lay with him. Right after it had happened, everybody had crowded around him to offer help and comfort, but Ando hadn't been able to respond appropriately. Instead, he'd just dragged his misery around interminably, acting morose with his friends. "Cheer up," they'd say, but how could he? Gradually, one by one, they'd deserted him. Before he knew it, Miyashita was the only one left. Miyashita always had a joke ready, no matter how melancholy Ando's expression. Miyashita knew how to find something to laugh about in misfortune no matter whose. The only times Ando could forget his sadness was when he was with Miyashita. By now, Ando could put his finger on what it was that set Miyashita apart from his other friends: while everyone else came to him to *cheer him up*, Miyashita had come to *actually have fun*. There was no more meaningless phrase in all of language than "Cheer up!" The only way to get someone to cheer up was to help them forget, and saying "cheer up" had quite the opposite effect, only reminding the person why he or she was depressed in the first place.

Ando knew quite well that he hadn't worn a sunny expression once all year. He tried to imagine, objectively, how he must look from Mai's perspective. Terribly gloomy, no doubt. No wonder she didn't want to have dinner with him; he'd only depress her more.

The thought, in turn, depressed him. A year and a half ago he'd been full of confidence. The future had stretched out before him, wide open and full of promise. He had a loving wife and a darling son, a ritzy condo in South Aoyama, a BMW with a leather interior, and a position as chief administrator waiting for him down the road. But he realized now that everything had been in his wife's name, or her father's, and a simple twist of fate had made it all slip through his fingers.

Miyashita was still talking with Professor Yasukawa. At a loss for what to do, Ando let his gaze wander idly around the lobby until he noticed a row of three pay phones. He took out a phone card and went over to them, thinking to dial Mai's number one last time. Cradling the receiver on his shoulder, he looked back over at Miyashita. If he lost track of his friend and missed out on the drinking session, he'd have come all the way in vain. Miyashita was in charge, here. As long as Ando stuck close to his friend, he wouldn't be stranded.

He let it ring eight times, then hung up and looked casually at his watch. Almost nine o'clock. It was three hours past the time they'd agreed to meet, and Mai still wasn't home.

I wonder where she went. He was beginning to worry about her.

Miyashita was bowing deeply to Yasukawa. Their conversation seemed to be over. As Miyashita moved away from the professor, Ando went and stood by Miyashita.

"Hey, sorry to keep you waiting." His tone was informal, a 180 degree reversal from how he'd been speaking to Yasukawa.

"No problem."

Miyashita took a scrap of paper out of his pocket and handed it to Ando.

"This is where we're going. I think you know it—it's over in the Third District. Would you do me a favor and go on ahead? I have to wrap things up here." He waved and started away, but Ando touched his elbow.

"Hold on a second."

"What?"

"What is it you want to tell me?" Miyashita's tease had been bothering at him.

Miyashita licked his lips with his thick tongue. They'd served roast beef at the party, and he was enjoying the last drops of grease. His lips glistened red as he said, "I found something."

"What?"

"A virus."

"A virus?"

"I got a call this afternoon from Yokodai University. Remember the two kids they autopsied over there?"

"The ones who died in a car of simultaneous heart attacks?"

"Yeah. Well, the thing is, a virus was found in their damaged tissue—from both of them."

"What kind of virus?"

Miyashita frowned and exhaled. "You're not going to believe it, but it looks identical to the smallpox virus."

Ando was speechless.

"Seki's diagnosis was right on the money. All he had to do was look at the ulcerations on the pharynx, and he came up with smallpox."

"This is unbelievable," Ando muttered.

"You can say that now. But I have a feeling we're going to find the same virus in Ryuji's tissue sample. Then you'll have no choice but to believe it."

Miyashita's complexion was even ruddier than usual due to the alcohol he'd consumed. It made him look vaguely happy about the whole thing. Maybe the appearance of an unknown virus was more exciting than frightening for a student of medicine.

But not for Ando. His mind had already raced ahead to wonder about Mai. The fact that she was not answering her phone bothered him no end. Her absence and the discovery of a virus that resembled smallpox seemed somehow connected. He had a bad feeling about where all of this was going.

Maybe what happened to Ryuji is happening to Mai. Maybe it's already happened.

The hotel lobby was filled with the clamor of drunken knots of people. Somewhere in the hullabaloo he could hear an infant laughing. *A baby here at this hour?* Ando wondered, checking the couches. But he didn't see any baby.

2

Wednesday, November 14th.

Ando went to the main campus, to the philosophy department, to ask Mai's professors if she'd been attending classes recently. But everyone he asked said the same thing: they hadn't seen her for a week now. As one of the few female students in the department, she stood out like a flower. When she missed class she was conspicuous by her absence.

Ever since last Friday, Ando had been calling her place two or three times a day, but no one was ever there to pick up the phone. He couldn't imagine her camping out at a boyfriend's house that whole time, and now his inquiries at her department had only exacerbated his concern.

It occurred to him that she might have gone home, so he went to the registrar's office. He explained the situation to the person on duty there and managed to get a look at her file. He discovered that her hometown was a place called Toyoda, in Iwata County, Shizuoka Prefecture. It was two or three hours from Tokyo if you took the bullet train en route. Ando wrote down her phone number, and then her address, too, just in case.

As soon as he got home from work that night he dialed the number. Mai's mother answered. When Ando explained who and what he was, he heard a sharp intake of breath on the other end of the line. Mai's mother was panicking upon learning that she was talking to someone from the med school at Mai's university. Even a call from her department would have been alarming, but one from a residing doctor could only mean Mai had fallen seriously ill. Her mother was probably bracing herself for the bad news. Students at the university all got free medical examinations at the university hospital, so Mai wouldn't have had to ask her mother before going in.

But Mai's mother couldn't figure out exactly why Ando had called. She was in touch with her daughter at least two or three times a month. True, she hadn't spoken with Mai in three weeks now; when she'd called last week, Mai had happened to be out. But she couldn't understand why a doctor from her daughter's university would be calling her parents' house just because he hadn't seen her for a week. Ando could hear suspicion in the woman's voice as she carefully probed his every remark.

79

"So, you say your daughter wasn't at home when you called last week." Ando knitted his brow. He'd hoped to find out she'd just gone home for the week. He'd prepared himself for that minor embarrassment, but now, his bit of optimism was gone. Mai hadn't been around when her mother called the week before, either.

"I'm sure it's nothing, doctor. We had a stretch last year, too, when we kept missing each other's calls. We went almost two months without talking then!"

Ando felt antsy. He couldn't explain the situation even if he wanted to. Just the day before, they'd found in Ryuji's tissue sample the same virus that had shown up in the two Yokohama kids. They hadn't been able to establish how the contagion was passed on, or by what route it had traveled. Depending on what they turned up, perhaps the truth had to be withheld from the media. He couldn't let Mai's mother know what was going on, either.

"Excuse me for asking, but does your daughter spend the night away from her apartment often?"

"No, I don't think so," her mother said firmly.

"Do you happen to remember exactly what day it was you called her last week?"

The woman thought for a moment, then said, "Tuesday."

So she had already not been answering her phone on Tuesday. Today was Wednesday. Over a week...

"Is it possible that she's traveling?"

"No, I don't think so."

Ando wondered how she could be so sure. "Why not?"

"Well, she has a part-time job as a tutor just to pay her daily expenses. She doesn't want to be a burden on her parents, she says. I simply don't believe she has enough money to travel."

All of a sudden Ando was sure that Mai was in some terrible trouble. The Friday before, Mai had stood him up. It wasn't as if he was difficult to get hold of. If she couldn't make the date, all she had to do was give him a call the day before and tell him. But she hadn't done that. And now, he felt sure he knew why. She *couldn't* contact him. He recalled the Polaroids of Ryuji's corpse. No matter how hard he tried, he couldn't rid himself of the picture of Ryuji's limbs splayed out in death. It was still branded on his brain.

"Would it be possible for you to come up to Tokyo tomorrow?" As he made the request, Ando bowed even though he was talking to her over the phone.

"I'm not sure I can get away on such short notice," she sighed. Then she was silent. Ando supposed he couldn't expect her to feel a proper sense of urgency when he hadn't given her the facts of the situation. All the same, though, she seemed a little too unconcerned about the whole thing. Ando wanted to tell her just how easy it was to lose someone you loved. How you could hear her voice, turn around, and find her gone.

Mrs. Takano broke the awkward silence. "If I did go to Tokyo, what exactly would you have me do? File a missing person report?"

"I'd at least like you to take a look at her apartment. I'll accompany you. We can think about a missing person report after that." But Ando didn't really believe they'd have to do that. This was—unfortunately— not that kind of case.

"I just don't know... Does it have to be tomorrow?"

She couldn't make up her mind. What errand could she have that was important enough to keep her from possibly finding her daughter dead? Ando couldn't coddle her along any longer.

"Alright, then. I'll go over to her apartment alone tomorrow. I understand she lives in a small studio. Do you happen to know if the building has a superintendent?"

"Yes, it does. I met him when I helped her move in."

"Well then, I'm sorry to impose, but could I get you to call him and tell him that Mitsuo Ando will be coming by tomorrow afternoon, between two and three, and that I'd like to take a look at Mai's room, in his presence of course?"

"Well..."

"Please. I doubt he'll give me the key if I just show up unan- nounced."

"Alright. I'll make the call and set it up."

"*Thank* you. I'll call you if anything comes up."

Just as he was about to hang up, Mai's mother started to say some- thing. "Listen..." Ando waited for her to continue. "Say hello to Mai if you see her."

She doesn't understand. Ando didn't know what to feel as he hung up.

3

Mai's apartment was only a short train ride from the university, no transfer required. Ando passed through the gate, left the station, and started to search for her apartment, map in one hand and the planner where he'd written the address in the other.

He spotted a little girl in an orange kimono walking down the side-walk ahead of him with her parents. He was reminded today was the tra-ditional 7-5-3 festival, a celebration for boys of three and five and girls of three and seven. As he overtook and passed the trio he glanced at the child's face. She seemed a little big, her features too well-developed, for her to be just seven years old. But her festive attire was bright and cheery in the afternoon sunlight. Ando thought her incredibly cute as she wobbled down the street in her unfamiliar lacquer sandals, clutch-ing her mother's hand. Even after he'd passed them, Ando kept stealing glances back at the three, imagining that in fifteen years the girl would grow up to be as beautiful as Mai.

He eventually located a seven-story apartment building facing a shopping arcade, the address of which matched what he'd written down in his planner. The facade was nice, but even from the outside, he could tell that the units had to be pretty small. They'd kept the rent low by cramming as many tenants as possible onto the property.

He found the superintendent's office in the lobby and pushed the buzzer. Through the window, he could see him emerge from an inner room. An older gentleman. He opened a small door in the window, and Ando gave his name.

"Oh, yes. Miss Takano's mother told me you were coming." Jangling a thick bundle of keys, he came out of the office.

"I appreciate this," Ando said.

"No, *I* ought to thank *you*. I'm afraid things haven't been going well lately with that girl."

Ando didn't know exactly what Mai's mother had told the man, so he didn't know how to respond to this, except to say, "I guess not," and follow him.

On the way to the elevator, they passed a bank of mailboxes. From one of them protruded several newspapers. Guessing it was Mai's box,

Ando had a closer look. As he'd suspected, the nameplate read TAKANO. There were four rows of mailboxes, and hers was in the top row.

"That's Miss Takano's. It's hardly ever like that."

Ando took the newspapers from where they'd been wedged into the mail slot and checked the dates. The oldest one was the morning edition from Thursday, November 8th. This was the seventh day since. It had been a full week, then, since Mai had last come down to pick up her newspaper. She could be sleeping somewhere else, but he doubted it. She was in her room, alright. It's just that she couldn't come down for the paper. All signs pointed in that direction.

The super interrupted Ando's thoughts. "Okay, then, are you ready?" He sounded as if he thought Ando would back out.

"Yes, let's go." Plucking up all the courage he could muster, Ando followed the man into the elevator.

Mai's apartment was on the third floor, room #303. The super took out his bundle of keys, chose one, and inserted it into the keyhole.

Without realizing it, Ando took a step back. *I should have brought surgical gloves.* The virus that had brought about Ryuji's death was probably not airborne. He imagined it to be like AIDS, fairly difficult to catch. Still, it was an unknown quantity, and he should have taken precautions. Not that he was all that attached to life, but he didn't want to die just yet. At least not until he'd figured out this puzzle.

A click echoed in the hall as the lock sprang open. Ando took another step backwards, but focused his sense of smell on whatever lay beyond the door. He was well-acquainted with the stench of death. It was mid-November, a fairly dry season, but he could expect a decomposing corpse to give off a powerful odor. He steeled himself until he was confident that even if the door opened to reveal what he expected it to, he could defend against the shock.

The door opened a few centimeters, and a gust of air blew out of the room and into the hallway. The window was probably open. Catching the wind full in the face, Ando breathed in, carefully, through his nostrils. He couldn't detect the unmistakable scent of a dead body. He inhaled and exhaled several times. No smell of decay. His sense of relief was so strong that it threatened to knock him off his feet, and he put his hand against the wall to steady himself.

"After you," urged the super, waiting in the doorway. Just standing in the entrance, he could see the whole interior of the apartment. There wasn't really any "looking around" to be done. Mai's body was nowhere to be seen. So Ando's premonition had been an idle one; he relaxed and let out a deep sigh.

He took off his shoes and stepped past the super into the room.

"Where's she gone?" grumbled the super from behind him.

Ando felt a strange sort of gloom steal over him. He should have felt relieved that he hadn't found what he'd thought he'd find, but instead his heart continued to race. The room had a strange air about it, and he didn't know why.

So she hasn't been back here in a week. It was the only conclusion he could draw. *Where is she now?* He wondered if the answer to the new question he was left with awaited him somewhere in the room.

Directly next to the entrance there was a small bathroom. He opened the door a crack to make sure it was empty, then returned his gaze to the main room.

He could see how she'd tried to make efficient use of her limited space. A futon was neatly folded and stashed in a corner. There wasn't enough space for a bed, nor was there a proper closet for the futon. Instead of a real desk there was a low table that had an electric space heater attached to its underside. The table was covered with manuscript pages. A discarded page had been folded up to serve as a coaster for a coffee cup, which was a quarter full of milk. Bookshelves covered one wall, and a combination TV/VCR was nestled in among the books. All the other appliances were arranged around the room almost as if they'd been built in, suggesting the care she'd put into choosing what to buy for her tiny apartment.

In front of the table sat an adjustable backrest that rocked unstably. It was covered with a penguin-print cloth. Pajamas, neatly folded, lay on the seat, with a bra and panties wadded up next to them.

Maybe it's just because I'm in a young woman's apartment? Ando was trying to figure out why he felt so uncomfortable. His chest was tight and his pulse was pounding. Seeing her underwear made him wonder if he was just an overexcited voyeur.

"What do you think, Doctor?"

The super was still standing in the doorway. He made no move to enter; he hadn't even taken off his shoes. Since she clearly wasn't to be found in her room, he seemed to have concluded that their business was finished and that it was time to go.

Ando didn't reply, walking over to the kitchenette instead. The floor here was wooden, but for some reason it felt like a thick carpet. He looked up: a ten-watt fluorescent light had been left on. He hadn't noticed it before because of the afternoon sunlight streaming in. Two glasses were in the sink. He turned the tap on, and after a while the water heated up. He pulled the string dangling from the bulb, turning out the light, and walked away from the kitchenette. When the light went out, he felt gooseflesh rising all over his body.

Nothing he saw gave him any clue as to Mai's whereabouts.

"Shall we go?" Ando said, not looking at the super. He wore his shoes back on and left the apartment. He heard the key turn behind him. He finished tying his shoelaces, straightened up, and walked to the elevator ahead of the super.

As they stood there waiting for the elevator, an autopsy Ando had performed the previous summer came back to him all of a sudden. It was on a young female who'd been strangled at home in her apartment. They'd told him she'd been dead for eleven hours, but when he cut her open he found to his surprise that her organs were still at something close to normal body temperature. When a person dies, the body temperature drops at an average of one degree Celsius per hour. Of course, that's just an average, subject to all sorts of factors, such as the weather and location. All the same, it was extremely unusual to find a body still perfectly warm after eleven hours.

The elevator came up to the third floor and the doors started to open before Ando's eyes.

"Hold on a minute," he said. He didn't want to leave while any doubts lingered. The oppressive feeling he'd gotten as he'd stepped into Mai's room, the weird sensation of the wooden floor as he stepped on it, almost as if it were melting away.

There was only one way he could describe the odd atmosphere of that room. It was like cutting into a body that had been dead for eleven hours and finding its insides still warm.

The elevator doors were fully open, but Ando did not step in. He was blocking the way, so the super couldn't get in either.

"Aren't you going to get on?"

Ando answered with a question of his own. "Are you sure you haven't seen her at all this last week?"

The elevator shut its doors and began its descent to the ground floor.

"If I have, then we wouldn't be here, would we?"

The super hadn't seen her. She hadn't shown up for class for a week, despite a near-perfect attendance record until now. She didn't answer the phone no matter how many times he called. A week's worth of newspapers were stuffed in her mailbox. It was clear that she'd been away since last Thursday. And yet, there was something about that place... It didn't *feel* like an apartment whose occupant had been away for a week. There was warmth there, and it had nothing to do with the temperature of the room. It was just that something in the air said some-one had been there until just a moment ago.

"I want to have another look," Ando said, turning to the super, who looked first surprised, then troubled, and then, briefly, afraid. This last emotion did not escape Ando's notice.

The old man's afraid of something.

The super handed Ando the key ring, saying, "Just drop them off in the office when you're done." He gave Ando a look as if to say, *If you want to go back, be my guest, but count me out.*

Ando wanted to ask the super what his impressions of the place had been. But he'd probably be at a loss for words, even if Ando asked. That kind of thing wasn't easy to express. Ando wasn't sure if he himself could explain what he'd felt there.

"Thanks, I will," Ando said, accepting the keys and turning on his heel. He was afraid that he'd lose his nerve if he hesitated. In any case, he made up his mind to get out of there as soon as he figured out why the place felt so weird.

Once again, he opened the door. He wished he could leave it open while he was in the apartment, but it swung shut automatically when he let go. The moment it shut, air stopped flowing through the room.

Ando took off his shoes again and walked to the window. He closed it and opened the lace curtains as wide as they'd go. It was past three in the afternoon, and the window faced south; rays of sun slanted into the room. Bathed in light, Ando turned to have another look. The décor did-n't strike him as particularly feminine, though it certainly wasn't masculine. If it hadn't been for the penguin design on the backrest, he wouldn't have been able to guess the inhabitant's gender.

Ando seated himself next to the backrest and picked up Mai's underwear. He brought them close to his face and sniffed them, then held them away, then sniffed them again. They smelled like milk. Takanori's undershirts had smelled like that when he was a toddler.

Ando put the underwear back where he'd found it and twisted his body until his eyes came to rest on the television. The power light glowed red: the VCR had been left on. He pushed EJECT and a tape popped out. There was a white label on its spine, with a title on it.

Liza Minnelli, Frank Sinatra, Sammy Davis, Jr./1989.

This was written in large letters, none too neatly, with a felt-tip pen. It didn't look like a woman's writing. He took the tape out and examined it. It was fully rewound. After he'd scrutinized it for a while, he slid it back into the VCR. Ando hadn't forgotten how this whole series of incidents had something to do with a video. There was the story Mai had told him about Asakawa, then the fact that Asakawa had been carrying a video deck on the passenger seat at the time of the accident.

Ando pressed PLAY.

For two or three seconds the image on the screen looked like ink being mixed with some viscous fluid. Then a point of light appeared amidst the roiling blackness. Flashing, it moved around to the left and right, and then finally started to grow. Ando felt a momentary, but distinct, unpleasantness. Then, just when the point of light looked like it was about to turn into something else, a TV commercial came on. He recognized it as one he'd seen several times already. The contrast, as the darkness gave way to sunny ordinariness, was stunning. Ando felt his shoulder muscles unclench.

The ad was followed by another, and yet another. He fast-forwarded through more of them. Then came a weather report. A smiling woman was pointing to a weather map. He fast-forwarded some more, and got to what looked like a morning talk show. The scene changed again: a reporter was looking into the camera and speaking into a microphone, something about some celebrity getting divorced. Ando kept on fast-forwarding but couldn't find anything that corresponded to the title on the label. The tape must have been recorded over.

As he watched, Ando began to relax. Of course, he hadn't been

expecting to see American singers, but something altogether more horrifying. Aside from the first few seconds, however, his fears had been
misplaced: all the tape contained was mundane TV programming. The
talk show came to an end and was followed by a rerun of an old samurai adventure. Ando stopped the tape and rewound it. He wanted to
examine the weather report segment.

He found the beginning of the forecast and pressed PLAY. The
woman said, "And now here's a look at the weather for Tuesday,
November 13th."

He pressed PAUSE and the image froze.

November 13th?

Today was the fifteenth. Which meant that this had been recorded
the day before yesterday. But who'd been around to press RECORD?

Was Mai here just two mornings ago?

But then how to explain the newspapers in her mailbox? Had she
simply forgotten to pick them up?

Or maybe... He opened the front panel of the VCR and tried to see
if there was any evidence it had been programmed. It was possible that
when she'd left the room a week ago, Mai had set the VCR to record
something on the morning of the thirteenth.

At that moment, he heard something. It sounded like the faint
splash of a drop of water. Without getting up, he turned his torso until
he could see the sink in the kitchenette. But there didn't seem to be a
drip there. He got up and peered into the bathroom.

The door was open a crack, just as it had been the last time he
checked. He turned on the light and tried to push open the door. But it
would only open halfway; the toilet blocked it. Ando leaned in through
the narrow opening and saw a bathtub just large enough for someone to
sit in if she drew her knees up to her chin. A nylon curtain draped down
into it. He pulled the curtain out of the way and looked inside. Water
dripped from the ceiling, landing with a splat; there was water pooled in
the bottom of the tub. While Ando gawked, another drop fell, rippling
the surface of the water. It was about four inches deep, and in one end
of the tub it was swirling gently. Several strands of hair floated on the
surface, and a few of them had gotten tangled as they swirled.

Ando wedged his way into the bathroom, leaning down until his
head was inside the tub. The drain was a round black hole, that is to say,

the plug had been pulled. Ando didn't immediately realize what that meant. The drainpipes were clogged with soap, or hair, or something, and the water wasn't draining well. But as Ando stared, he could see that the level was falling, if only gradually.

It finally occurred to Ando to ask himself who had pulled the plug.

It clearly hadn't been the super. He hadn't taken one step into the room. He hadn't even taken off his shoes.

Then who?

Ando took another step into the bathroom and crouched down. He held out his hand and hesitantly touched the surface of the water. It was still slightly warm. A few strands of hair tangled themselves around his fingers. It felt just like…sticking his hands into an eleven-hour-old corpse and finding it had maintained body temperature. The apartment had supposedly been vacant for a week. But only an hour ago, someone had filled the tub with hot water and, even more recently, pulled the plug. It was for ventilation that the window had been left open.

Ando hurriedly pulled his hand back and wiped it on his trousers.

On the other side of the toilet, directly below the toilet paper, he noticed a brownish stain. It wasn't fecal matter, but rather, like something that had been vomited up. Covered in a thin film, it retained the outline of undigested food. A reddish, square object—perhaps a piece of carrot?

Did Mai vomit this?

Ando was squatting with one foot in the tiny bathroom, but in order to examine the vomit he had to lean over. When he did so, though, he lost his balance.

He came to rest with his face pressed up against the edge of the toilet. The cream-colored porcelain digged coolly into his cheek, and he could only imagine what kind of expression he was making.

At that moment, he thought he heard someone laugh behind him.

Ando fought back the urge to scream, and froze in that ungainly posture.

It wasn't his imagination. He'd heard a distinct giggle behind him, from a point rather low to the floor. As if it had welled up from the floor, like some plant shoot poking up from the ground, blossoming forth in laughter. Ando tensed his muscles and held his breath.

"Hee-hee." There! The same giggle. He wasn't hallucinating. He was absolutely certain someone was behind him. But he could hardly move, much less turn around and look. He couldn't figure out what to do. With his face still pressed up against the smooth porcelain, he managed to call out, rather stupidly, "Is that you, super?" He couldn't prevent his voice from trembling. One foot still sticking out of the bathroom door, he thought he felt a current of air on it. Something was moving out there. Now, that something touched him on the patch of exposed skin between the hem of his slacks and the top of his socks, where they'd scrunched down. It brushed against him as it moved past, leaving behind the memory of its slithery touch. The lower half of his body shrank from it, and he let out a cry. He tried to tell himself that it was nothing; maybe a cat that'd been trapped in the room had licked his Achilles tendon. Nothing more. But it didn't work. Every one of his five senses knew that it was something else. Some unknown thing was behind him.

His face was below the top of the bathtub, so he couldn't see inside, but he could hear the water inside trying to gurgle out. There was a faint slurping sound as the water swirled down the drain, hair and all. But above that sound, he heard the floorboards creak. The creaky noise receded slowly from him.

He couldn't stand it any longer. He raised his voice in an inchoate yell, banged the bathroom door with his knee repeatedly, and even flushed the toilet. All the racket he'd caused finally gave him the courage to creep to his feet. Using his hands to steady himself, he raised himself until he was almost fully upright, and then he stopped to listen behind him. He desperately tried to think of a way to step out of the room without turning around. The hair on the nape of his neck stood on end, as if countless tiny spiders were crawling up his back.

He inched backward towards the entrance, making sure that his heel wasn't touching anything, and then he whirled around, grabbed the doorknob, and stumbled out into the hallway. He banged his shoulder on the wall, but he ignored the pain as he watched the door swing shut.

Gasping for breath, Ando headed for the elevator. The super's keys jangled in his pocket. Thank God he hadn't left them in the apartment! He certainly didn't want to go back in there again. He was sure something was in there, even though he could recall every corner of that room and he couldn't think of a single place for anything to hide. The futon was folded up neatly. The built-in wardrobe was neither wide nor deep enough. There was no place for any living thing to hide—unless it was pretty small.

An out-of-season mosquito buzzed in his ear. He tried to swat it away, but it kept right on droning about him. Ando coughed weakly and jammed his hands into his pockets. Suddenly he felt cold. The elevator was taking forever to arrive. Finally, frustrated, he looked up, only to see that it was still on the first floor. He'd forgotten to push the button. He pressed it two or three times, just to be sure, and put his hand back in his pocket.

4

"Hey, what's up?"

Ando didn't realize he'd been drifting away until Miyashita spoke to him. The sensations of two hours ago had become a tidal wave, threatening to rip his consciousness out by the roots. He resisted frantically, and got gooseflesh for his efforts. Miyashita's fervent monologue reached his brain only intermittently.

"Are you even listening to me?" Miyashita sounded annoyed.

"Yeah, I'm listening," Ando replied, but his expression said his mind was elsewhere.

"If there's something eating at you, maybe you ought to tell me about it."

Miyashita pulled a stool out from under the table, plopped his feet onto it, and leaned back. He was a visitor in Ando's office, but he acted as if the place were his own.

Ando and Miyashita were the only ones in the forensic medicine lab at the moment. Despite how dark it was getting outside, it was still not quite six in the evening. After his harrowing experience at Mai's apartment, Ando had come directly back to the office to meet Miyashita. As a result, he hadn't had any time to regain his equilibrium. And Miyashita had been telling him about the virus the whole time.

"No, nothing's bothering me." He had no intention of telling Miyashita what he'd experienced in Mai's apartment. He had no words to express it, first of all. He couldn't think of an appropriate metaphor. Should he compare it to that feeling you sometimes get, standing at the toilet in the middle of the night, that there's someone behind you? The one where, once you've sensed them, the monsters in your imagination just keep growing and growing until you finally turn around and dispel the illusion? But what Ando had experienced was no such run-of-the-mill affair. He was sure there'd been something behind him when he lost his balance in Mai's bathroom and hit his cheek against the toilet. It wasn't a product of his imagination. Something had emitted that high-pitched laughter. Something that had made Ando, not normally a coward, too scared even to turn around.

"You look pale, though. Paler than normal, that is," said Miyashita, wiping his glasses on his lab coat.

"I haven't been sleeping well lately, that's all." It wasn't a lie. Recently, he'd been waking up in the middle of the night and having trouble getting back to sleep.

"Well, never mind. Just don't keep asking me the same questions over and over. No one likes to be interrupted."

"Sorry."

"Now. May I go on?"

"Please do."

"About that virus they discovered in those bodies in Yokohama..."

"The one that's just like smallpox," Ando volunteered.

"That's the one."

"So it resembles smallpox visually?"

Miyashita slapped the tabletop. He flashed Ando a look of exasperation. "So you really weren't listening. I just told you: they ran the new virus through a DNA sequencer in order to analyze its bases. Then they ran it through a computer. Turns out it corresponds closely to the library data on smallpox."

"But they're not identical?"

"No. We're talking maybe a seventy percent overlap."

"What about the other thirty percent?"

"Brace yourself. It's identical to the basal sequence of an enzyme-encoding gene."

"Enzymes? Of what species?"

"*Homo sapiens.*"

"You're kidding."

"I understand it's pretty unbelievable. But it's true. Another specimen of the same virus contained human protein genes. In other words, this new virus is made of smallpox genes and human genes."

Smallpox was supposedly a DNA virus. If it were a retrovirus, then it would be no surprise to find it had taken human genes into itself. Such a virus would have reverse transcription enzymes. But since DNA viruses didn't have them, how did this one pick up human genes and incorporate them into itself? Ando couldn't think of any process. And with one virus containing enzymes and another proteins, it meant that together they contained human genes, but in separate components. It was as if the human body had been broken down into hundreds of thousands of parts, and those parts apportioned out individual specimens of a virus for safekeeping.

"Is the virus from Ryuji's body the same?"

"Finally, we come to that. Just the other day, we found a nearly identical virus in a frozen sample of Ryuji's blood."

"Another smallpox-human combo?"

"I said 'nearly.'"

"Okay."

"It's almost identical. But in one segment, we found a repetition of the same basal sequence."

Ando waited for Miyashita to continue, and he did.

"No matter where we cut it, we kept coming up with a repetition of the same forty-odd bases."

Ando didn't know what to make of it.

"Are you following me? They didn't find this in the two bodies in Yokohama."

"So you're saying that the virus found in their bodies is subtly different from the one that killed Ryuji?"

"That's right. They look alike, but they're slightly different. Of course, we really can't say much until we get data from the other universities."

At that moment a phone rang two desks over. Miyashita cursed under his breath. "What now?"

"Excuse me a minute, okay?" Ando leaned over and picked up the receiver. "Hello?"

"I'm Yoshino from the *Daily News*. I'm calling for a Dr. Ando."

"That's me."

Yoshino wasn't quite satisfied. "Are you Dr. Ando the lecturer in forensic medicine?"

"Yes, yes."

"I understand you performed an autopsy on a Ryuji Takayama at the Tokyo Medical Examiner's Office on the twentieth last month. Is that correct?"

"That's right, I was in charge of that one."

"I see. Well, I'd like to ask you a few questions about that, if I may. Can we meet?"

"Hmm." While Ando deliberated, Miyashita leaned over and whis-

94

pered in his ear.

"Who is it?"

Ando covered the mouthpiece with his hand before answering. "A reporter from *Daily News*." Then he quickly brought the receiver back to his mouth and asked, "What is this about?"

"I'd like to ask your opinion regarding a certain series of incidents."

The man's phrasing took Ando by surprise. Had the media already caught a whiff, then? It seemed far too early for that. Even the various med schools in charge of the autopsies had only begun to discover a connection among the deaths of the last two weeks.

"What series of incidents do you mean?" Ando decided to play dumb to try to find out how much Yoshino knew.

"I mean the mysterious deaths of Ryuji Takayama, of Tomoko Oishi, Haruko Tsuji, Shuichi Iwata, and Takehiko Nomi—and of Shizu Asakawa and her daughter."

Ando felt as if he'd been hit upside the head with a board. Who'd leaked all that? He didn't know what to say.

"So how about it, doctor? Think you have time to meet with me?"

Ando wracked his brain. Information always flowed downhill, so to speak, from those who had more of it to those who had less. If this reporter had more information about the case than Ando, then perhaps Ando should try to get it from him. There was no need for Ando to show all his cards. The thing to do was to find out what he needed without giving up his own secrets.

"Alright, let's do it."

"When would be best for you?"

Ando took out his planner and looked at his schedule. "I assume you'd like it to be as soon as possible. How about tomorrow? I'm free for two hours after noon."

There was a pause as Yoshino checked his schedule.

"Okay, good. I'll come to your office at noon sharp."

They hung up nearly simultaneously.

"What was that all about?" Miyashita asked, tugging on Ando's sleeve.

"It was a newspaper reporter."

"What does he want?"

"He wants to meet me."

"Why?"

"He said he wants to ask me some questions."

"Hmmph," sighed Miyashita, thinking.

"It sounds like he knows everything."

"So what does that mean? A leak?"

"I guess I'll have to ask him that when I see him tomorrow."

"Well, don't tell him anything."

"I know."

"Especially that it involves a virus."

"If he doesn't know already, you mean."

Suddenly Ando remembered that Asakawa also worked for the company that published the *Daily News*. If he and Yoshino knew each other, maybe Yoshino was in pretty deep. Maybe tomorrow's meeting would turn up some interesting information. Ando's curiosity was piqued.

5

Yoshino kept reaching for his water glass. He'd pretend like he was going to pick it up, and then look at his wristwatch instead. He seemed to be worried about the time. Maybe he had another appointment right afterwards.

"Excuse me for a moment, will you?" Yoshino bowed and stood up from the table. Threading his way between the tables on the café terrace, he went over to the pay phone next to the cash register. As Yoshino flipped open his notepad and started punching buttons on the phone, Ando was finally able to stop for breath. He leaned back in his chair.

An hour ago, at exactly noon, Yoshino had shown up at his office at the university. Ando had taken him to a café in front of the station. Yoshino's business card still lay before him on the tabletop.

Kenzo Yoshino. Daily News, Yokosuka Bureau.

What Yoshino had told him, Ando couldn't believe. It had left his head spinning. Yoshino had come in, sat down, and launched into a monologue that did nothing but seed Ando's mind with doubts. Now he'd gone off to call God knew whom.

According to Yoshino, the whole thing had started on the night of August 29th, at a place called Villa Log Cabin, a property of the South Hakone Pacific Land resort, located where the Izu Peninsula met the mainland. A mixed-gender group of four young people who stayed a night in cabin B-4 had found a videotape recorded psychically by some woman. A videotape that killed anyone who watched it, exactly a week later. What the *hell*?

It sounded like nonsense no matter how many times Ando went over it in his head. "It's probably something akin to psychic photography," Yoshino had said, as if that explained it. Mentally projecting an image onto a videotape? That was out and out impossible. And yet... Suppose he told somebody about the numbers he'd found on the piece of newspaper that poked out of Ryuji's belly? Or the strange vibes he'd felt in Mai's apartment? Wouldn't people think he was talking nonsense? There was just no equating what you've experienced yourself with what you've heard from someone else; one could never feel as real as the other. But Yoshino had been directly involved, and what he said was substantiated by Ando's own experience, at least. He'd helped Asakawa and Takayama investigate the case. His words were not entirely lacking in persuasiveness.

"Sorry to keep you waiting," Yoshino said, returning to his seat. He quickly wrote something in his notebook, then poked his bearded cheek with the tip of his pen. His beard looked wiry, and it was long and full, as if to compensate for the thinning at the top of his head. "Now, where was I?" He leaned forward, bringing his hirsute visage closer to Ando. He had a certain charisma that came through when he spoke.

"You were starting to tell me how Ryuji got involved."

"Right. Now, if you don't mind, what was your relationship with the late professor?"

"We were classmates in med school."

"Okay, that's what I'd heard."

Ando interpreted the remark to mean that Yoshino had run a check on him before contacting him.

"By the way, Mr. Yoshino, have you watched the tape yourself?" The question had been weighing on Ando's mind for a while.

"You've got to be kidding," Yoshino said, wide-eyed. "You'd have met me in the autopsy room then. No, I don't have the guts." He chuckled.

Of course, Ando had had a sneaking suspicion for some time now that a videotape was involved in these deaths. But never in his wildest dreams did he suspect the existence of a video that killed anybody who watched it in exactly a week's time. He still couldn't quite believe it. How could he? He couldn't accept such a thing, short of watching the video himself. Even then, he'd probably only truly believe it a week later, at the moment death came for him.

Yoshino drank his now-cold coffee, taking his time. He must have gained a little leeway in his schedule, because his movements no longer signaled haste.

"So why is Asakawa still alive? He watched the tape, didn't he?" There was a note of scorn in Ando's voice. Asakawa might be catatonic, but he was still alive. That didn't seem to square with Yoshino's story.

"You've hit the nail on the head, there. That's exactly what's bothering me, too," Yoshino said, leaning forward. "I suppose the best thing to do is to ask the man himself, but I tried that and it got me nowhere."

Yoshino too had visited the hospital in Shinagawa, and he too had failed to communicate with Asakawa.

Then Yoshino seemed to have an idea. "Maybe..." he trailed off portentously.

"Maybe what?"

"I think you know what I'm talking about. If we could just get our hands on it."

"On what?!"

"Asakawa's a reporter for our weekly news magazine."

Ando had no idea what Yoshino was getting at. "I know."

"Well, he mentioned to me that he was putting together a comprehensive report on all this. I mean, the whole reason he got interested, to begin with, was that he thought he was onto a scoop. He teamed up with Takayama, and the two of them rushed off to Atami, and then to Oshima Island, hoping they'd find clues to unlock the riddle of the videotape. I think they found something. And I'll bet you anything that it's all written up and stored on a floppy disk." Yoshino turned his head, leaving Ando staring at his profile.

"Ah-ha."

Yoshino faced Ando again, this time with a bitter expression. "I just don't know where it is. I couldn't find it in his apartment." Having said this, he stared off into space.

Asakawa was hospitalized, and his wife and daughter were dead. The apartment was empty. Was Yoshino saying he'd broken in and searched it? "His apartment?"

"Yeah, well, the building manager's an old softie. All I had to do was come up with a good excuse, and he let me right in with the master key."

It was the same thing Ando himself had done just the other day, out of concern for Mai, so he knew he couldn't criticize Yoshino's behavior. The motives may have been different, but in the end, they had both done the same thing: they had ransacked apartments in their occupants' absence.

Yoshino didn't look ashamed in the least, only annoyed. "I searched every corner of that place. Didn't find anything. Not his word processor, not the floppy disk." Yoshino bounced his knee with nervous energy. Then he noticed and placed a hand on the knee, flashing Ando a rueful smile.

Ando was recalling the photos he'd been shown of the scene of Asakawa's accident. He remembered the one that showed the interior of the car from the vantage point of the driver's side window. The thing he understood to be a video deck sat on the passenger's seat, wedged under the back of the seat where it had been pushed forward; on the floor on the passenger's side lay what looked like a laptop. The pair of black objects had made a deep impression on Ando. And now they gave him an idea. He turned his head, desperately trying to think, pretending to watch the crowd flowing out of the station like a human tidal wave.

Ando realized he knew where to find the report that could explain everything. No doubt Yoshino had searched Asakawa's apartment with great diligence, but the word processor and disk weren't there at all. Yoshino didn't know that Asakawa had brought them with him wherever he'd last been to, that they were in the car at the time of his accident.

Ando was now fairly confident he could get his hands on that disk, and he had no intention of sharing the information with Yoshino. He'd decide whether or not to tell the media only after he'd read Asakawa's report. Right now, all he knew was that this smallpox-like virus had been found in all seven of the corpses in question. They weren't ready yet to announce their findings in professional circles. In fact, they were only beginning to put together a research team consisting mainly of Shuwa and Yokodai people. If he went and let the media in on it at this stage, there was no telling what kind of panic they'd whip up. He had to proceed with utmost caution to make sure things didn't get out of hand.

The rest of their meeting Yoshino spent lobbing predictable questions at Ando. What were the results of the autopsy? What did he determine was the cause of death? Was any part of Yoshino's story suggestive in terms of the results of the autopsy? The reporter kept his face buried in his notebook as he went through his list.

Ando tried to answer each question as politely and as unobjectionably as he could. But all the while, his thoughts were lunging in another direction. He had to get his hands on that floppy disk right away. What did he need to do to make that happen?

6

The next day was Saturday. After finishing two autopsies, Ando took aside the young cop who was there as a witness and asked him what happened to cars that had been in accidents. If a car had been wrecked in an accident near the Oi exit of the Metropolitan Bayside Expressway, for instance, what was done with it?

"Well, first we'd inspect it." He was a trusty-looking young man with glasses. Ando had seen him several times before, but this was the first time he'd spoken to him.

"Then what?"

"Then we'd return it to the owner."

"What if it's a rental?"

"We'd return it to the rentacar agency, of course."

"Okay. There were three people aboard this car, a young couple and their daughter. They, ah, lived in a condo in Shinagawa, just the three of them. The wife and child died in the accident, and the husband is in critical condition. Now, what happens to the items that were in the car?"

"They'd be kept in temporary storage in the traffic division of the local precinct."

"For an accident that happened at the Oi offramp of the Metropolitan Expressway, what's the local precinct?"

"The exit?"

"Yeah, that's right. Near the exit."

"No, I mean, was it on the expressway or off it? They're different jurisdictions."

Ando thought back to the photos of the accident scene. He was certain it had happened on the expressway itself. He seemed to remember seeing the phrase "Tokyo Harbor Tunnel entrance" written in a file somewhere.

"It was definitely on the expressway."

"Then it'd be the Metropolitan Expressway Traffic Patrol Unit."

Ando had never heard the name before. "Where's the headquarters?"

"Shintomi."

"Alright. So the items would be stored there temporarily. What next?"

"They'd contact the family and have someone come and get the items."

"Suppose, like I said, everybody in the family's dead."

"Even the siblings and parents of the man in the hospital?"

Ando knew nothing about Asakawa's parents and siblings. Judging from the man's age, there was a good chance that his parents were still alive. It raised the possibility that they were in possession of of whatever was in the car. Asakawa and Ryuji had been classmates in high school. Since Ryuji's parents lived in Sagami Ohno, Asakawa's probably lived somewhere in that area, too. In any case, the first thing Ando should do was to look them up and contact them.

"I see. Thank you very much."

Ando released the young cop and straightaway set about locating Asakawa's parents.

He determined that they were both alive and living in the Kurihara section of the city of Zama, not far from Sagami Ohno. He placed a call and asked what had happened to the items from their son's car. Asakawa's father told him, in a strained voice, to call his eldest son, who lived in Kanda, in Tokyo. Kazuyuki, it turned out, was the youngest of three brothers: the oldest worked in the art book division of Shotoku, a major publisher, while the middle son was a junior high school Japanese teacher. Asakawa's father said that he had in fact received a call from the police asking him to come down and pick up some items they were keeping at the station, but instead of going to get them himself, he'd told them to contact his son in Kanda. Kanda wasn't too far from Shintomi, where the Metropolitan Expressway Traffic Patrol Unit had their headquarters, and Asakawa senior hadn't felt like lugging a word processor and a VCR home at his age—he was over seventy. So he'd arranged with the police for his son to pick up the items.

Ando's next move, then, was to contact Junichiro Asakawa, who lived with his wife in a Kanda condominium. When he finally managed to get in touch with him that evening, Ando came straight out and told him the situation, or most of it at least. He was afraid that if he aroused Junichiro's suspicions by slapping together a lie or a clumsy cover-up, he might never get his hands on the disk. On the other hand, he couldn't simply repeat the story Yoshino had told him. Ando didn't believe most of it himself, and Junichiro would surely think he was crazy. So he abridged things as he saw fit, ending by emphasizing that there was a possibility that Asakawa had left behind a document that might shed some light on what was happening. Speaking on behalf of the Medical Examiner's Office, he said he'd really like to get his hands on that document and wondered if he might be allowed to make a copy of it, please and thank you.

"I'm not sure there was anything like that in what I was given." Junichiro didn't sound entirely convinced. The way he spoke suggested that he hadn't yet taken a good look at the items.

"Is there a word processor?"

"Yes. But I think it's broken."

"Was there a floppy disk inside it?"

"To be honest, I haven't checked. I haven't even taken it out of the cardboard box they handed it to me in."

"Was there a video deck along with it?"

"Yes, but I threw it away. Was that the wrong thing to do?"

Ando's breath caught in his throat. "You threw it away?"

"I can see why he'd be carrying around the word processor, because of his job, but why did he have a VCR with him?"

"Excuse me, but did you say you threw it away?"

"Yes. It was a total wreck. I'd arranged garbage pick-up for a TV the other day, so I had them take the VCR away at the same time. It was beyond repair. Anyway, I doubt Kazuyuki'll mind."

Ando had almost caught his two quarries, and now, at the last minute, one had eluded him. There'd been a good chance that the videotape that held the key to all this had been inside the VCR, and with luck he'd hoped to get his hands on both it and the floppy disk. He was kicking himself for not having contacted Junichiro sooner.

"Besides the VCR, there wouldn't happen to have been a videotape, would there?" Ando said a little prayer as he asked.

"I don't know. All I saw was the word processor, the VCR, and two black leather gym bags that probably belonged to Shizu and little Yoko. I haven't opened them."

Ando made sure Junichiro understood that he wanted to see them as soon as possible. "Would you mind if I paid you a visit?"

"That's fine," Junichiro agreed, surprisingly quickly.

"How about tomorrow?" Sunday.

"Let's see. I'm playing golf with one of my writers, but I should be back by seven."

"Well, then, seven it is." Ando made a note of the time, and underlined it several times.

At just after seven o'clock on Sunday evening, Ando called at Junichiro's condo in the Sarugaku section of Kanda. The neighborhood didn't feel very residential. Junichiro's building was surrounded by office blocks. The area was eerily quiet on Sunday evenings.

Ando rang the bell and heard a man's voice from behind the door ask, "Who is it?"

"This is Ando. I called yesterday."

The door opened immediately, and Ando was ushered inside. Junichiro was lounging around in a sweatsuit and his hair was wet; he must have just gotten home from golf and taken a shower. Somehow, from his voice on the phone, Ando had imagined him as a tall, nervous man, but in person Junichiro was heavyset and wore a genial expression. As Junichiro led the way into the apartment, Ando reflected that, of the three brothers, the eldest was an editor, the second a Japanese teacher, and the third a reporter for a major news organization. They'd all chosen fields that had them dealing with language, with writing, on a daily basis. Most likely, the eldest had been influential in this regard. Ando himself had been inspired to enter medicine by his older brother, who became a high school biology teacher.

Junichiro went to the closet in the hall and took out a cardboard box. The gym bags and the word processor had been stuffed into it.

"So. You'd like to take a look?" Junichiro sat down cross-legged on the floor and pushed the box in Ando's direction.

"Thanks, I would."

Ando first took out the word processor, jotting down the make and model. The machine's shell seemed to have been rather severely damaged in the crash; the top wouldn't open, and pressing the power button elicited no response. Standing it vertically on his knee, Ando noticed an eject button there on the side. It belonged to a slot, and peering into it he saw a blue floppy disk. He almost shouted for joy as he pressed the eject button. The machine produced a click that sounded to Ando like *bingo!* He took out the desk and held it on his palm for a moment, examining it back and front. The label hadn't been affixed, so there was no title to be seen. But Ando knew immediately that this was what he'd been searching for. It had *sounded* right popping out of the slot.

He wanted to read the disk as soon as he could, and he said to Junichiro, "I'd like to check out what's on here."

"I'm afraid this machine isn't compatible with mine." Junichiro wouldn't be able to use his word processor to open the files on the disk.

"In that case, would you mind if I borrowed the disk for two or three days?"

"It's alright with me, but..."

"I'll return it to you as soon as I'm done with it."

"What's on that disk, anyway?" Ando's excitement had evidently communicated itself. Junichiro suddenly seemed curious.

Ando shook his head. "I don't know, exactly."

"Well, I'd like it back as soon as possible." Now it appeared that Junichiro wanted to read it, too. Maybe his editorial instinct had been stirred.

Ando dropped the disk into his jacket pocket, and knew a sense of relief, but at the same time he was seized with a new desire. Those gym bags... He knew it was futile to hope, but he couldn't rule out the possibility that the videotape was in one of them.

"Would it be too much to ask if I could see what's in there?" He tried to choose his words carefully, somewhat embarrassed at the idea of going through a woman's belongings.

"I don't think there's anything in there," Junichiro laughed, but he handed over the bags. When he looked inside, Ando's faint hope of finding the tape was finally dashed. Mostly the bags contained clothes and disposable diapers. Not what he was looking for. Just as he'd feared, the tape had been inside the VCR when it was trashed.

Still, he'd gotten his hands on the floppy disk, and he had to count that a success. He could hardly stand still as he took his leave. He'd check around at work to see if anybody had a machine that could read the disk. He couldn't wait to see what was on it.

7

Ando poked his head into the Pathology Department office to see if Miyashita was in, but before he had a chance to say anything, Miyashita called out to him.

"Hey, just the man I wanted to see. Tell me what you think of this." Miyashita was holding a printout of something, and he beckoned to Ando with his other hand. Beside him stood Nemoto, an assistant in the biochem lab. Nemoto and Miyashita were built so alike that anybody who happened to see them together couldn't help but laugh. From their height and weight—five-three and easily over a hundred seventy pounds—to the length of their legs, their girth, their faces, even their taste in clothes and their high voices, they were like two peas in a pod.

"Hey, I didn't know you had a twin." Ando uttered the same joke he always did as he approached them.

"Please, Dr. Ando, don't lump me together with this guy," said Nemoto, grimacing. But it couldn't have been too awful to be told he took after his colleague, two years his senior. After all, Miyashita was liked both for his personality and his learning, and had been pegged as a future candidate for full professor.

"Everybody keeps telling us we look alike, Nemoto. I'm telling you, it's getting to be a pain in the butt. Why don't you go on a diet?" Miyashita elbowed the younger man's paunch.

"Well, if I go on a diet, you have to go on one, too."

"Then we'll be right back where we started!"

Then Miyashita offered Ando the printout he was holding, as if to put an end to the stale routine.

Ando spread out the printout he'd been given. He understood its contents at a glance. It showed the results of running a snippet of DNA through a sequencer.

All life on earth consists of one or more cells containing DNA (or, in some cases, RNA). The nuclei of these cells contain molecular compounds known as nucleic acids. There are two types of nucleic acids: DNA (deoxyribonucleic acid) and RNA (ribonucleic acid). These play different roles. DNA is the compound in which genetic information is stored in the chromosomes: it takes the form of two long threads twisted about one another in a spiral, a shape known as the double helix. The sum total of a life form's genetic information is inscribed within that double structure. This genetic information is like a set of blueprints for the construction of specialized proteins; each gene is a blueprint. In other words, genes and DNA are *not* the same thing. A gene is a unit of information.

So what exactly is written on these blueprints? The letters that make up the inscriptions are four chemical compounds known as bases: adenine (A), guanine (G), cytosine (C), and thymine (T) or in the case of RNA, uracil (U). These four bases work in sets of three called codons, which are translated into amino acids. For example: the codon AAC makes asparagine, the codon GCA makes alanine, etc.

Proteins are conglomerations of hundreds of these amino acid molecules, of which there are twenty types. This means that the blueprint for one protein must contain an array of bases equal in number to the number of amino acid molecules times three.

The blueprint called the gene can be thought of, then, as basically a long line of letters, looking something like this: TCTCTAT-ACCAGTTGGAAAATTAT... Translated, this signifies a series of amino acids that runs: TCT (serine, or Ser), CTA (leusine, or Leu), TAC (tyrosine, Tyr), CAG (glutamine, Gln), TTG (leusine, Leu), GAA (glutamic acid, Glu), AAT (asparagine, Asn), TAT (tyrosine, Tyr), etc. etc.

Ando glanced again at the base codes covering the printout, the four letters A, T, G, and C lined up seemingly at random across the page. Segments of three rows had been highlighted so as to stand out from the rest.

"What's this?"

Miyashita winked at Nemoto, as if to say, *you tell him*.

"This is an analysis of a segment of DNA taken from the virus found in Ryuji Takayama's blood."

"Okay...so what's this?"

"We found a rather strange sequence of bases, something we've only seen in Takayama's virus."

"And that's what's highlighted here?"

"That is correct."

Ando took a closer look at the first highlighted series of letters.

ATGGAAGAAGAATATCGTTATATTCCTCCTCCTCAACAA
CAA

He looked at the next highlighted portion, and compared it with the
first. He realized it was exactly the same sequence. In a group of not
even a thousand bases, the exact same sequence occurred twice.


```
                                                                       480
.....................................................................GTTTAAAGCA
      490        500        510        520        530
TTTGAGGGGGATTCAATGAATATTTATGACGATTCCGCAGTATTGGACGC
      540        550        560        570        580
TATCATGGAAGAAGAATATCGTTATATTCCTCCTCCTCAACAACAATTTG
      590        600        610        620        630
CAAAAGCCTCTCGCTATTTTGGTTTTTATCGTCGTCTGGTAAACGAGGGT
      640        650        660        670        680
TTATGAT AGTTTGCTCTTACTATGCCTCGTAATTCCTTTTGGCGTTATGT
      690        700        710        720        730
ATCTGCATTAGTTGAATGTGGTATTCCTAAATCTCAACTGATGAATCTTT
      740        750        760        770        780
CTACCTGTAATAATGTTGTTCCGTTAGTTCGTTTTATTAACGTAGATTTT
      790        800        810        820        830
TCTTCCCAACGTCCTGACTGGGATTTCGACACAAATGGAAGAAGAATATC
      840        850        860        870        880
GTTATATTCCTCCTCCTCAACAACAACGCTTGGTATAATCGCTGGGGGTC
      890        900
AAAGATGAGTGTTTTTAGTATATT... ... ... ... ... ... ... ... ... ... ... ... .. .
```

Above: between #535 and #576, and again between #815 and #856,
one can observe the repetition of the 42 bases ATGGAAGAA-
GAATATCGTTATATTCCTCCTCCTCAACAACAA.

DNA AMINO ACID TRANSLATION CHART

1st base	2nd base				3rd base
	T	C	A	G	
T	Phe	Ser	Tyr	Cys	T
	Phe	Ser	Tyr	Cys	C
	Leu	Ser	stop	stop	A
	Leu	Ser	stop	Trp	G
C	Leu	Pro	His	Arg	T
	Leu	Pro	His	Arg	C
	Leu	Pro	Gln	Arg	A
	Leu	Pro	Gln	Arg	G
A	Ile	Thr	Asn	Ser	T
	Ile	Thr	Asn	Ser	C
	Ile	Thr	Lys	Arg	A
	Met	Thr	Lys	Arg	G
G	Val	Ala	Asp	Gly	T
	Val	Ala	Asp	Gly	C
	Val	Ala	Glu	Gly	A
	Val	Ala	Glu	Gly	G

Base triplets (codons) are translated into amino acids according to the principles outlined in the chart above. For example, TCT is serine (Ser), AAT is asparagine (Asn), GAA is glutamic acid (Glu). "Stop" signifies the end of a gene; the beginning code is ATG.

Below are the abbreviated and full names of the twenty amino acids:

Phe	phenylalanine	His	histidine
Leu	leucine	Gln	glutamine
Ile	isoleucine	Asn	asparagine
Met	methionine	Lys	lysine
Val	valine	Asp	aspartic acid
Ser	serine	Glu	glutamic acid
Pro	proline	Cys	cysteine
Thr	threonine	Trp	tryptophan
Ala	alanine	Arg	arginine
Tyr	tyrosine	Gly	glycine

Ando shifted his gaze from the printout to Nemoto's face.

"No matter where we slice it, we always find this identical sequence."

"How many of these are there?"

"Bases, you mean?"

"Yeah."

"Forty-two."

"Forty-two. So, fourteen codons, right? That's not very many."

"We think it means something," Nemoto said, shaking his head. "But, Dr. Ando, the strange thing is..."

Miyashita interrupted. "This meaningless repetition was only found in the virus collected from Ryuji Takayama's blood, and not from the other two victims." He threw up his hands in a gesture of perplexity.

In other words... Ando tried to find a suitable analogy. Suppose three people, one being Ryuji, had copies of Shakespeare's *King Lear*. Then suppose that Ryuji's copy, and only his copy, had meaningless strings of letters sandwiched in between the lines. There were forty-two bases, and they worked in sets of three, each set corresponding to one amino acid. If you assigned each of these sets a letter, you'd have a series of fourteen letters. And these fourteen repeating letters were found on every page of the play, inserted at random. If you knew from the beginning that the play was *King Lear*, of course, it would be possible to go back and find the meaningless parts that had been interpolated and highlight them.

"So what do you think?" Miyashita looked to be sincerely interested in Ando's opinion. A true scientist, he was always most excited when confronted with the inexplicable.

"What do I think? I'd have to know more before I could say anything."

The three of them fell silent, glancing at one another's faces. Ando felt awkward, still holding the printout.

Something was tugging at his consciousness. In order to figure out what it was, he needed time to sit down and study the meaningless string of bases. He had an unmistakable premonition that there was something here. The question was, what? And if this meaningless base sequence had indeed been interpolated, when had it happened? Was the virus that had invaded Ryuji's body just different? Or had it mutated in

Ryuji's body, with the fourteen-codon string appearing here and there as a result of that mutation? Was that even possible? And if it was, what did it mean?

An oppressive silence fell over the three men. No amount of speculation at this point could tell them how to interpret these findings.

It was Miyashita who broke the silence. "By the way, did you come here for a reason?"

Ando had been so intrigued by the discovery that his original errand had slipped his mind. "Right, I almost forgot." He opened up his briefcase, took out his planner, and showed Miyashita and Nemoto a slip of paper.

"I was wondering if anyone here had a word processor of this model."

Miyashita and Nemoto looked at the model name written on the paper. It was a fairly common machine.

"Does it have to be exactly the same model?"

"As long as it's the same brand, the model probably isn't important. Basically, it's a question of compatibility for a floppy disk."

"Compatibility?"

"Yes." Ando took a floppy disk from his briefcase.

"I need to make a hard copy and a soft copy of the files on this disk."

"It's not saved in MS-DOS, I take it?"

"I don't think so."

Nemoto clapped his hands, as if he'd just remembered something. "Hey, one of the staff members in my department—Ueda, I think—has this very model."

"Do you suppose he'd let me borrow it?" Ando hesitated. He'd never met this Ueda.

"I don't imagine there'd be a problem. He's fresh out of school." Nemoto spoke with the confidence of a senior staff member who knew that a new resident would do anything he asked.

"Thanks."

"No problem at all. Why don't we go over right now? I think he's there."

This was music to Ando's ears. He couldn't wait to print out whatever was on this disk.

"Great. Let's go." Ando dropped the disk back into his jacket pock-

et. Then, waving to Miyashita, he followed Nemoto out of the pathology department.

8

Ando and Nemoto walked side by side down the med school's dim hallway. Ando wore his lab coat unfastened in front, its tails swept back behind him, with his hands in the pockets of his jacket clutching the disk. Neither Miyashita nor Nemoto had asked about it. Ando wasn't trying to keep it a secret. Had Miyashita asked, he'd intended to give him an honest answer. If they'd known it might hold the key to this whole mystery, no doubt both men would have been at his heels right now.

Of course, Ando hadn't seen what was on the disk yet. There was always the possibility that it held something else entirely. He simply wouldn't know until he managed to bring it up on a monitor. Still, it felt right in his hand: the disk was warm from being in his pocket. It was near body temperature. Its touch seemed to tell him that it held living words.

Nemoto opened the door to the biochemistry lab. Ando took the disk out of his pocket, switched it to his left hand, and held the door open with his right.

"Hey, Ueda." Nemoto beckoned to a skinny young man seated in a corner of the room.

"Yes?"

Ueda swiveled in his chair to face Nemoto, but didn't stand up. Nemoto approached him, smiling, and put his hand on Ueda's shoulder. "Are you using your word processor right now?"

"No, not really."

"Great. Would you mind if Dr. Ando here borrowed it for a while?" Ueda looked up at Ando and then bowed. "Hello."

"Sorry about this. I've got a disk I need to access and it's not compatible with my machine." Ando moved to Nemoto's side, holding up the disk.

"Go right ahead," said Ueda, picking up the word processor from where it sat on the floor at his feet and laying it sideways on the desktop.

"Do you mind if I check it right here just to make sure?"

"Not at all."

He opened the word processor's lid and turned it on. Soon the initial menu appeared on the screen. From among the options displayed, Ando chose DOCUMENTS, then inserted the disk. The next screen gave him two options: NEW DOCUMENT and OPEN DOCUMENT. Ando moved the cursor to the second option and hit return. With a whir, the machine started to read the disk. Finally, the names of the files stored on the disk appeared on the screen.

RING 9	1990/10/21
RING 8	1990/10/20
RING 7	1990/10/19
RING 6	1990/10/17
RING 5	1990/10/15
RING 4	1990/10/12
RING 3	1990/10/07
RING 2	1990/10/04
RING 1	1990/10/02

Ando read the file names aloud in a delirium. "Ring, ring, ring, ring..."

Ring!

What the hell! The same word that I got from solving the code that popped out of Ryuji's belly.

"Are you alright?" Nemoto sounded worried. He was peering at Ando's suddenly dazed expression. Ando could barely manage to nod.

There was no way this could be a coincidence. Asakawa had composed a report detailing this whole strange train of events, saved it in nine parts, and entitled it *Ring*. And then that title had extruded from Ryuji's belly.

How to explain this! There is no way.

Ando was in a state of complete denial. *Ryuji's body was completely empty; he was like a tin man. Am I saying he slipped me a message from his abdominal cavity! That he was trying to tell me of the existence of these files!*

Ando recalled the way Ryuji's face had looked right after the autopsy. His square-jawed face had been smiling. Ando had expected that any minute he'd start laughing at him, stark naked on the table, jowls shaking.

Deep down, Ando could feel Yoshino's outlandish story starting to take on the feel of reality. Maybe it was all true. Maybe there really was a videotape that killed you seven days after you watched it.

9

The word processor buzzed ceaselessly as it printed out page after page. Ando tore each page from the printer as it emerged and read through it quickly.

Each page was single-spaced, but still Ando was able to read faster than the printer could spit them out. Wanting a hard copy, he'd decided to print it all out instead of reading it on the screen. Now he found himself getting frustrated by the two or three minutes it took each page to be printed.

He'd ended up borrowing Ueda's machine and bringing it home with him. A quick check had revealed that the total report was close to a hundred pages, more than he could reasonably print out there in the lab. He had no choice but to stay up late at home.

Now he was at the end of page twenty-one of the manuscript, alternating between reading it and taking bites of the dinner he'd picked up at the convenience store on the way home. What he'd read so far followed faithfully the outline Yoshino had given him the week before. But it differed from what Yoshino had told him after lunch at the café in that it contained specific times and places. As a result it was a good deal more persuasive. The reporterly style—no frills—also made it harder to disbelieve.

While investigating the simultaneous deaths by heart attack of four young people in Tokyo and Kanagawa prefecture on the evening of September 5th, Asakawa had come up with the idea that the culprit was some kind of virus. Scientifically speaking, it was the obvious conclusion. And since autopsies on the four bodies had indeed revealed a virus that closely resembled smallpox, it turned out that Asakawa's hunch had been right. It had been Asakawa's guess that since the four had died at the same moment, they must have picked up the same virus together at the same place. He'd figured that the key to the whole case must lie in figuring out where they were exposed to the virus, that is, in determining the route of transmission.

Asakawa had succeeded in finding out when and where the four had been together: August 29th, exactly a week before their deaths, at South

Hakone Pacific Land, in a rented cabin, Villa Log Cabin No. B-4.

The next page, page twenty-two, started with Kazuyuki Asakawa himself heading toward the cabin in question. He took the bullet train to Atami, then rented a car and took the Atami-Kannami highway to the highland resort. Rain and darkness limited the visibility, and the mountain road was awful. He'd made reservations for cabin B-4 at noon, but it was past eight at night when he finally checked in. So this was where those four kids had spent the night: the thought gave Asakawa a jolt of fear. Exactly a week after they'd stayed in this cabin, they were dead. He knew it was possible that the same spectral hand would touch him, too. But he couldn't overcome his reporterly curiosity and ended up searching B-4 from top to bottom.

From something the kids had written in a notebook on the property, Asakawa determined that they had watched a videotape that night, so he went to the manager's office to search for that tape. He'd found an unlabelled, unboxed tape lying on the bottom shelf. Was this what he was looking for? With the manager's permission, he took the tape back to cabin B-4, and, with no way of knowing what it contained, he inserted it into the VCR in the living room and watched it all the way through.

At first, everything was dark. Asakawa described the opening scene like this:

In the middle of the black screen a pinpoint of light began to flicker. It gradually expanded, jumping around to the left and right, before finally coming to rest on the left-hand side. Then it branched out, becoming a frayed bundle of lights, crawling around like worms...

Ando looked up from the page. Based on what he was reading, he was able to get a reasonably clear image of what had been on the screen. Reading Asakawa's description of the opening, an image popped into his head that he felt he'd seen somewhere before. A firefly flitting around on a dark screen, growing gradually larger...then the point of light splays out like the fibers of a paintbrush. It was a short scene, but one that he could remember seeing, and recently at that.

It didn't take long for the memory to come to him. It was when he'd gone to Mai's apartment to try and track her down. He'd found a videotape still in her VCR, and he'd pressed the play button. The one with

Frank Sinatra, Liza Minnelli, etc., written on the label in a man's hand. The first few seconds of that tape had fit this description perfectly.

But on the tape in Mai's apartment, this scene had only lasted a few seconds, before the screen suddenly became a lot brighter. In what had evidently been an attempt to erase whatever was on the tape, Mai had recorded morning variety shows, samurai melodrama reruns, whatever, until the tape ran out. Ando immediately figured out what this meant. Somehow, probably through Ryuji, Mai had acquired the problem tape and watched it in her apartment. Then, when she'd finished, she'd eradicated it, whatever it was, from the tape. She must have had her reasons. But she hadn't been able to erase the very beginning of the tape, so those first few seconds had remained there, lurking. Did it mean that the tape Asakawa had found in Villa Log Cabin had somehow made its way into Mai's hands?

Ando tried to organize his thoughts. *No, that can't be it. The tape Asakawa found and the tape Mai had were clearly two different things.* According to the report, the one in the cabin was unlabelled. But the one in Mai's VCR had a title written on it in black marker. Which meant it must have been a copy.

The one in the cabin was the original, and the one in Mai's place a copy. So that tape had been copied, erased, disguised, transported—a dizzying series of changes. In Ando's mind, the tape, occupying a point between the animate and the inanimate, began to resemble a virus.

So, was Mai's disappearance a result of her having watched that tape? The possibility worried him. She hadn't been back to her room since then. She hadn't been showing up at school, and she hadn't even called her mother. On the other hand, he hadn't heard anything about a young woman found dead from unexplained causes.

Ando let his mind wander for a while, considering all the things that could have befallen her. Maybe she'd died alone someplace unbeknownst to anybody. The thought pained him—she was only twenty-two. The fact that he could feel the first twinges of a crush on her only made it harder to bear.

The printer finally came to the end of another page, with a noise that snapped Ando out of his reverie. In any case, now was no time to be borrowing trouble. At the moment, he'd be better off finding out what was on that tape first.

10

The next few pages contained a thorough description of the contents of the videotape. As he read, Ando could see a TV screen in his mind, filled with shifting images.

Something red and viscous spurted across the screen. This was followed by a view of a mountain that he could tell at a glance was an active volcano. Lava flowed from its mouth; the earth rumbled. The eruption lit up the night sky. Then this scene was suddenly cut off, replaced by a white background, in front of which the character for "mountain," written in black, faded in and out of view. Then a scene of two dice bouncing around on the bottom of a bowl.

Finally a human figure appeared onscreen. A wrinkled old woman sat on a tatami mat. She was facing the camera and saying something. She spoke in a nearly incomprehensible dialect, but he could tell, more or less from the sound of her words, that she was predicting somebody's future, warning him or her.

Next, a newborn baby, wailing. There was no discernible link between scenes. One followed another with all the abruptness and randomness of someone flipping over cards.

The infant disappeared, replaced by hundreds of faces, filling the screen and multiplying as if by cellular division, all against the background of a multitude of voices intoning accusations: *Liar! Fraud!* Then an old television set, displaying the character *sada*.

Then a man's face appeared. He was gasping for breath and dripping with sweat. Behind him could be seen a lush thicket of trees. His eyes were red and full of bloodlust; his mouth was contorted with screams and drool. His bare shoulder was deeply gouged, and blood flowed from the wound. Then came again, from nowhere in particular, the cry of a baby. In the center of the screen was a full moon, from which fell fist-sized stones, landing with dull thuds.

Finally, more words appeared on the screen.

Those who have viewed these images are fated to die at this exact hour one week from now. If you do not wish to die, you must follow these instructions exactly...

And then the scene changed entirely. Instead of the prescribed method for avoiding certain death, the screen now showed a common television commercial for mosquito coils. The ad ended and the previous eeriness returned, or rather, the memory of it.

At the end of this series of bizarre visions, Asakawa had managed to understand exactly two things. First, whoever watched this tape was doomed to die in exactly a week. And, second, there was a way to avoid this fate, but it had been deliberately recorded over. The four kids who'd watched the video first had erased it in a fit of malice or mischief. It was all Asakawa could do to slip the tape into his bag and flee cabin B-4.

Ando took a deep breath and lay the manuscript aside.
Holy shit.

In his report Asakawa had given a painstakingly elaborate account of the strange twenty minutes of images on the tape. He'd made every effort to recreate, using only words, what the video conveyed directly through sound and visuals, and he'd largely succeeded. The scenes still swirled around in Ando's mind, as vividly as if he'd seen and heard them himself. He sighed again, suddenly exhausted. Or maybe it wasn't fatigue. Perhaps it was that he now felt Asakawa's fear as his own, and wanted somehow to push it away.

But even a moment's pause only whetted his desire to know more. Taking a sip of tea, he picked up the next page of the report, and started reading ahead, even faster than before.

The first thing Asakawa did upon returning to Tokyo was to call Ryuji Takayama and tell him what had happened. Asakawa had neither the time nor the courage to solve this thing alone. He needed a reliable partner, and so naturally his thoughts turned to Ryuji, whom he'd known since high school. He also approached Yoshino, but Yoshino refused to watch the video. Regardless of whether or not he actually believed in it, if there was even a slim chance that calamity would befall him as a result of watching the video, he wanted to avoid doing so.

But not Ryuji. As soon as he heard about this video that'd kill in a week's time anyone who watched it, the first words out of his mouth were, *First let's have a look at this video.*

So Ryuji watched the video in Asakawa's apartment, fascinated. And when it was over he asked Asakawa to make him a copy.

The word "copy" made Ando sit up and take notice. Now he thought he could figure out the route the tape had traveled. The original tape from Villa Log Cabin had most likely stayed in Asakawa's possession. It had been in the VCR in Asakawa's car at the time of the wreck, had passed to Asakawa's brother Junichiro, and been thrown away. There was one more tape, the one in Mai's apartment, the one with only the very beginning remaining. This was probably the copy Asakawa had made for Ryuji that first night. It had a title on the label, written in thick letters in a man's hand. It was probably Asakawa's handwriting. When Ryuji had asked Asakawa to make him a copy, instead of using a brand-new tape, Asakawa had recycled an old tape on which he'd originally recorded a music program. This had passed through Ryuji's hands into Mai's. That much made sense. But when had Mai received it? Mai had never mentioned having the tape to Ando. Which meant, Ando supposed, that she'd come across it by chance, several days after Ryuji's death, and watched it not knowing it was dangerous.

In any case, the tape had been replicated in Asakawa's apartment. Ando felt he needed to keep that in mind.

So Ryuji took the copy of the tape back to his apartment and started working on figuring out the erased message (he and Asakawa called this "the charm"). Both men wondered what this weird recording was doing in Villa Log Cabin B-4. At first they thought that it had been shot with a video camera and then left there, but that turned out not to be the case. Three days before the unfortunate youths, a family had stayed in B-4: they'd put a tape in the VCR and set it to RECORD. They'd then forgotten about it and left it there when they went home. So the images on the tape had not been shot elsewhere and the tape brought to the cabin: rather, some sort of unknown transmission had been captured on the tape when the machine was recording. The next people on the scene had been the four young victims. With time on their hands, they'd decided to watch a video; when they went to turn on the VCR, out popped a tape. They'd watched it. The threat at the end must have amused them. *Like we're really going to die in a week if we don't do what it says!* So they decided to play a trick by erasing the solution; that should scare the next guests. Of course, the kids never really believed in the tape's curse. If they had, they never could have pulled such a stunt. In any case, the tape was found the next day by the manager, who put it on the shelf in the office, where it stayed unnoticed by anyone until Asakawa's arrival.

So: how had those images gotten into the deck while it was recording? It occurred to Asakawa that some maniac might have hijacked the airwaves, so he tried to pinpoint the source of such a broadcast. Meanwhile, when Asakawa was out of the house his wife and daughter found the video still in the VCR and watched it. Now Asakawa was urged on by the desire to save not only his own life, but also those of his family.

Then Ryuji made a startling discovery. Watching the tape over and over at home, he had a flash of inspiration. He made a chart and found that the tape could be broken down into twelve scenes, which fell into two groups: abstract scenes that seemed to consist of what might be called mental imagery, and real scenes that seemed to have been seen through an actual pair of eyes. For example, the volcanic eruption and the man's face were clearly things that had really been seen, while the firefly-like light in the darkness at the beginning of the tape looked like something conjured up by the mind—like something out of a dream. So Ryuji called the two groups "real" and "abstract," for comparison's sake. Upon further investigation, he noticed that in the "real" scenes, there were instants in which the screen was covered by what looked like a black veil, just for a split second. In the "real" scenes, these instants occurred at the rate of about fifteen per minute, while in the "abstract" scenes, they didn't appear at all. What did this mean? Ryuji concluded that the black veil was in reality a blink. It appeared in the scenes that were seen with actual eyes, and not in the sequences that were only seen in the mind's eye. Not only that, the frequency of the blackouts matched the average eye-blinking frequency of a female. It seemed safe, then, to consider them eyeblinks. Which led naturally to the conclusion that the images on the videotape had not been captured by exposure in a video camera, but rather taken from the vision and imagination of an individual and placed on the tape by thought-projection.

Ando had real trouble believing this part. The idea that a person could mentally imprint images onto a videotape was simply preposterous. He might be willing, just barely, to allow the possibility of mentally imprinting photographic film, but moving images? That was an entirely different set-up, first of all. In order to press on, Ando had to lay this point aside for the moment, even as he admired Ryuji's perspicacity.

Assuming that someone had recorded the tape paranormally, the next question was: who? Asakawa and Ryuji concentrated on that point, heading to the Tetsuzo Miura Memorial Hall in Kamakura. A researcher into parapsychological phenomena, Miura had devoted his life to tracking down paranormals from all over Japan. The files containing his findings were now housed in his memorial. The two men got permission to examine those files, over a thousand in number, thinking that a psychic with powers strong enough to project moving images onto a videotape couldn't have escaped Professor Miura's notice. And, after several hours of searching, they'd found a likely candidate.

Her name was Sadako Yamamura. She'd been born in the town of Sashikiji, on Izu Oshima Island.

According to an entry in her file, at the age of ten she was already able to project the characters *yama* (mountain) and *sada*, elements from her name, onto a piece of film. These very characters had appeared on the video. Certain that this Sadako Yamamura was who they were looking for, Ryuji and Asakawa boarded a boat for Izu Oshima the next morning. They hoped that learning more about her upbringing and personality would illuminate some of the secrets of the videotape. Sadako was threatening whoever looked at her images with death in order to get the viewer to do something. The tape itself embodied her wish for that action to be undertaken. Which made it crucial that they find out what Sadako desired. At this point, Ryuji already had an inkling that Sadako Yamamura was no longer alive. It was his belief that on the brink of death she'd unleashed her final, unfulfilled desire in the form of a psychic projection, meaning to relay her wish to someone else. Her deepseated hatred had ended up on the videotape.

Between the assistance of the Oshima stringer for the *Daily News* and the help of Yoshino in Tokyo, with whom they stayed in frequent contact, Asakawa and Ryuji managed to piece together a profile of

Sadako Yamamura.

She was born in 1947, the daughter of Shizuko Yamamura, a one-time paranormal who had made a big but temporary splash in the national media, and Heihachiro Ikuma, an Assistant Professor of Psychiatry at Taido University who had gotten into research on para-psychology with Shizuko as his subject. At first, the trio of Ikuma, Shizuko, and Sadako had been received by the public with simple curiosity, and in fact had become media darlings after a fashion. But once a certain prestigious academic society had pronounced Shizuko's powers fake, the masses turned on them, and they became subject to violent attacks in the media. Heihachiro was hounded out of the uni-versity, and eventually came down with tuberculosis, while Shizuko suffered nervous attacks and finally threw herself into Mt. Mihara, the volcano on Izu Oshima.

Sadako was taken in by some relatives on the island, where she lived until she graduated from high school. Once in fourth grade she gained some notoriety within the school by predicting an eruption of Mt. Mihara, but aside from that she didn't display any of the powers she'd inherited from her mother. On leaving high school she moved to Tokyo, where she joined a theater troupe in hopes of making it as an actress. It was Yoshino who picked up her trail from there.

Asakawa called Yoshino from the island and asked him to find the troupe's rehearsal space in Yotsuya, Tokyo. He did, and once there, he found out more about Sadako's true nature from a man named Arima, a leader of the troupe. It had been twenty-five years since Sadako had been a member of his company, but he recalled her very well. She seemed to have some sort of supernatural power; she could project images at will onto the screen of an unplugged television. If this was true, then Sadako's powers far outstripped her mother's. While at the rehearsal space, Yoshino succeeded in obtaining a photo of Sadako. They still had her resume on file, and it contained two black-and-white photos from when she joined. One was from the waist up, while the other was a full-length shot. Both revealed Sadako to have perfectly balanced features that went beyond even the word "beautiful."

Yoshino was unable to determine what became of Sadako after she left the theater troupe, so he faxed the photos and the other information he'd gathered to Asakawa at the *Daily News*'s Izu Oshima bureau.

124

When he read the fax and found out that Sadako's trail had gone cold, Asakawa was devastated. If they couldn't find her, how could they hope to figure out the charm?

Once again it was Ryuji who had a flash of inspiration. He realized that it might not be necessary to follow Sadako's every move. Instead, maybe they should turn their attention to the scene—Villa Log Cabin No. B-4—and try to figure out why the images had shown up there. She had to have some sort of connection with the place.

They realized that all of the buildings at South Hakone Pacific Land were new. It wasn't impossible that something else had once stood there. Asakawa contacted Yoshino in Tokyo and asked him to try a new line of investigation: find out what had occupied that ground before the resort.

Yoshino faxed him the next morning. It turned out that there had once been a tuberculosis sanatorium on the site. He even managed to send them a plan of the facility's layout. He also attached a file with the name, address, and resume of one Jotaro Nagao, age 57, a GP and pediatrician with a practice in Atami. For a period of five years, from 1962 to 1967, he had worked at the South Hakone Sanatorium. The suggestion seemed to be that any further information about the sanatorium would be best gotten from Nagao.

So, armed only with what they'd learned from Yoshino, Asakawa and Ryuji took a high-speed ferry for Atami. It was one week to the day since Asakawa had watched the video. If they didn't figure out the "charm" by ten that evening, Asakawa would die. Ryuji's deadline was ten o'clock the next night. And Asakawa's wife and daughter's time would be up at eleven on the morning after.

The two men climbed back into their rented car and headed off to find Dr. Nagao's office. Their hopes to gain even a tidbit of information from him were granted, in spades. When they finally came face to face with the doctor, both Asakawa and Ryuji recognized him. Near the end of the tape there was a part in which a man was seen from the waist up, panting and sweating, blood streaming from a gouge in his shoulder. Although he'd aged and lost some hair, Nagao was unmistakably that man. Sadako had seen his face up close. Not only that, in her "eyes" he was something wicked.

With typical brashness, Ryuji pressured Nagao until he confessed everything. He told them all about that hot summer afternoon twenty-five years ago...

Nagao had contracted smallpox from a patient while on a call to the sanatorium's isolation ward in the mountains, and that afternoon, the early symptoms of the illness were starting to show. But in spite of his headache and fever, he didn't recognize at first that he had smallpox, and went on treating tuberculosis patients as usual. He thought it was simply a cold. Then he met Sadako Yamamura in the courtyard. She often came to the sanatorium to visit her father, who was a patient there. Having just left the theater troupe, Sadako had nowhere else to go, and she was often up to see her father.

One glance at Sadako and Nagao was overwhelmed by her beauty. He approached her and they began to talk, and then, as if guided by something beyond himself, he took her to an abandoned house deep in the woods. There, in front of an old well, he raped her. It was then that Sadako, in her desperate attempts to resist him, bit his shoulder. Between the bleeding and his feverish delirium, it took him some time to notice Sadako's uniqueness. She had testicular feminization syndrome, an extremely rare condition in which one had both male and female genitalia. A person with this syndrome usually has breasts and a vagina but lacks a uterus and fallopian tubes. Externally, the person would appear quite female, but chromosomally would be XY—a male—and unable to bear children.

Nagao strangled Sadako and threw her body in the well. He then threw rocks into the well after her.

After hearing out Nagao's confession, Asakawa showed him the plan of the resort and asked the doctor to show him on the map the location of the well. Nagao was able to indicate the general area—namely, where Villa Log Cabin was located now. Asakawa and Ryuji immediately sped off to Pacific Land.

Once there, they began to search for the well in the vicinity of the cabins. They found it beneath cabin B-4. The cabin stood on a gentle slope, and when they investigated the space beneath the porch they saw the rim of an old well, covered with a concrete lid. If Sadako's hatred had radiated straight up out of the well, it would have run smack into the TV and VCR in the cabin above. The videotape was in the perfect position to pick up her psychic projections.

Vanishing

Asakawa and Ryuji broke a few boards, crawled under the cabin, pried the lid off the well, and set about the task of finding Sadako's remains. That's what both Asakawa and Ryuji now interpreted the missing "charm" to be: Sadako wanted whoever watched the videotape to release her from that cramped, dark space. The two men took turns descending into the well and scooping water out of the bottom of it with buckets. And when they finally, thankfully, fished from the mud a skull that they took to be Sadako's, it was already after ten o'clock. Asakawa's deadline had come and gone, and he wasn't dead. They were satisfied that they'd figured out the secret of the videotape.

After that, Asakawa took Sadako's remains back to Izu Oshima, while Ryuji returned to his apartment in Tokyo to work on an article. The case had been put to rest. The bones of Sadako Yamamura, possessor of fearsome psychic powers, had been rescued from the depths of the earth. She had been appeased. Neither Asakawa nor Ryuji had any doubt about that.

11

Having read that far, Ando now stood up, still holding the report, and opened the window. Imagining climbing down a rope into a well had given him the feeling that he was suffocating. It was a doubly restricted space; under the cabin it would be dark even in the daytime, and then there was the well, not even a yard across. It gave him a flash of claustrophobia; he had to breathe outside air. Directly beneath his window he could see the dark woods of Meiji Shrine swaying in the breeze. The pages in his hand fluttered too, stirred by the same current of air. The last page of the manuscript was in the printer now. One more page and Asakawa's account would be finished. Ando heard the sound of the printer finishing its task. He glanced back at the word processor only to find a mostly blank piece of paper staring back at him.

He picked up the final page. It said:

Sunday, October 21
The nature of a virus is to reproduce itself.
The charm: make a copy of the video.

And that was all. But it had to be of the utmost importance.

October 21st was the day of Asakawa's accident. The previous morning, Ando had dissected Ryuji's body and met Mai at the medical examiner's office. Although the manuscript ended abruptly, Ando could more or less fill in the rest himself.

On October 19th, Sadako Yamamura's remains had been delivered into the custody of her relatives back home. But that hadn't been the end of things after all. Even as Asakawa sat in a hotel on Oshima composing his detailed report, Ryuji was dying in his apartment in East Nakano. Upon returning to Tokyo and learning of Ryuji's death, Asakawa had rushed to Ryuji's apartment. There he'd encountered Mai Takano and peppered her with what seemed to her strangely inappropriate questions.

Ryuji really didn't tell you anything at the end? Nothing, say, about a videotape?

It was easy to see why Asakawa had been in a panic. He'd been convinced that he'd escaped death by figuring out the riddle of the video-tape, and now he'd found out he was wrong. The curse still lived. And Asakawa was left without a clue. Why was Ryuji dead and Asakawa alive? Not only that, Asakawa's wife and child had a deadline of their own coming, at eleven the next morning. So Asakawa had to figure out the charm all over again, alone this time and with only a few hours to do it in. Logically, he realized that whatever it was the videotape had wanted him to do, he must have done it at some point in the past week without realizing it. Something that he could be sure Ryuji hadn't done. What could it be? Perhaps he spent the whole night wondering. And then finally, on the morning of the twenty-first, he'd had a spark of intu-ition, maybe, and hit upon what he was sure was the solution. He'd made a quick note of it on his word processor.

> *Sunday, October 21*
> *The nature of a virus is to reproduce itself.*
> *The charm: make a copy of the video.*

What Asakawa meant here had to be none other than the smallpox virus. Just before her death, Sadako Yamamura had had physical rela-tions with the last smallpox victim in Japan, Jotaro Nagao. It was natu-ral to assume that the virus had invaded her body. Driven to the brink of extinction, the smallpox virus had borrowed Sadako's extraordinary power to accomplish the purpose of its existence, which was to repro-duce itself. But once it took the form of a videotape, the virus couldn't reproduce on its own. It had to work through human beings, forcing them to make copies of it. If one were to fill in the missing part at the end of the tape, it would run like this:

Those who have viewed these images are fated to die at this exact hour one week from now. If you do not wish to die, you must follow these instructions exactly. Make a copy of this videotape and show it to someone else.

In that light, things made sense. The day after he'd watched the videotape, Asakawa showed it to Ryuji, and he also made a copy for him. Without realizing it, he'd helped the virus propagate. But Ryuji never made a copy.

Sure he had the answer, Asakawa had loaded a VCR into the rented car and driven off somewhere. Undoubtedly he'd planned to make two copies of the video and show them to two other people—one for his wife, and one for his baby girl. The people he showed it to would then have to find new prey, someone else to give a copy of the video to. But that wasn't the immediate problem. The important thing was to save the lives of his wife and child.

But just at the height of his relief at having saved the lives of his loved ones, Asakawa had reached into the back seat and touched his wife and daughter and found them cold. He lost control of the car.

Ando felt he could understand Asakawa's catatonic state now. Not only was he devastated at the loss of his family, but he was no doubt also tormented by a question: what was the true nature of the charm? Every time he thought he had it figured out, the answer slipped through his fingers, transforming itself, claiming another life. Rage and sorrow, and an endless repetition of the question: Why? Why was he still alive?

Ando put the manuscript pages in a pile on the table. Then he asked himself:

Do you really believe this cock-and-bull story?

He shook his head.

I just don't know.

He didn't know what else to say. He'd seen the unnatural sarcoma on Ryuji's coronary artery with his own eyes. Seven people were dead of the same cause. In their blood had been found a virus that closely resembled smallpox. And where had Mai disappeared to? What about that odd ambience in her apartment, which she had seemingly vacated? That hair-raising intimation he'd had that something was there? The traces left on the videotape still in her VCR? Was the tape still propagating? Would it continue to claim new victims? The more he thought, the more questions Ando had.

He turned off the word processor and reached for the whiskey on the sideboard. He knew he wouldn't be able to sleep tonight without the help of alcohol.

12

Ando first dropped by the biochem lab and returned the word processor to Ueda, and then headed to the pathology department. Under his arm he carried the report he'd printed out the night before. He intended to let Miyashita read it.

Miyashita sat with his head down low to the table, scratching away with a ballpoint pen. Ando dropped the report on the tabletop next to him, and Miyashita looked up in surprise.

"Listen, would you do me a favor and read this?"

Miyashita just stared back at Ando in amazement.

"What's going on?"

"I want to know what you think of that."

Miyashita picked up the document. "It's pretty long."

"It is, but there are things in there that will interest you. It won't take long to read."

"You're not about to tell me you've been writing a novel in your spare time, are you?"

"Kazuyuki Asakawa wrote up a report about the deaths."

"You mean, *our* Asakawa?"

"Right."

Miyashita looked interested now as he flipped through some of the pages. "Hmm."

"So, there it is. Let me know what you think when you're done."

Ando started to leave, but Miyashita called him back. "Hold on a minute."

"What?"

Miyashita rested his cheek on his hand and tapped the table with the tip of his pen. "You're pretty good at codes, aren't you?"

"I wouldn't say I'm particularly good at them. In med school, some friends of mine played around with them, but that's about it."

"Hmm," said Miyashita, still tapping on the table.

"Why?"

Miyashita took his elbow off the printout he'd been looking at and slid it over to Ando. "This is why." He started tapping his pen on the center of the page. It was the printout he'd seen the day before, the results of sequencing the virus found in Ryuji's blood.

"You showed me this yesterday."

"I know, but I just can't get over it."

Ando picked up the piece of paper and held it up in front of his face. Into several points in an otherwise unordered sequence of bases, a string of bases in the same order had been inserted.

ATGGAAGAAGAATATCGTTATATTCCTCCTCCTCAACAA
CAA

No question, it was strange for the same string of forty-two bases to appear several times at appropriate intervals.

"And Ryuji's virus is the only one like this?"

"Right. His is the only one with these extra forty-two bases," Miyashita said, his gaze not wavering from Ando's. "Doesn't that strike you as weird?"

"Of course it does."

The *tap-tap* of the ballpoint pen ceased.

"The thought crossed my mind that it might be a sort of code."

Ando gulped. He couldn't remember having told Miyashita anything about what had happened after Ryuji's autopsy. Not about the corner of newspaper, and certainly not about the fact that he'd come up with the word "ring" off of it. And yet now Miyashita was talking about codes.

"Assuming it is a code, who's sending it?"

"Ryuji."

Ando screwed his eyes shut. The idea was one he'd been desperately trying to avoid entertaining, and now Miyashita was shoving it in his face.

"Ryuji's dead. I performed the autopsy myself."

Miyashita didn't seem fazed in the least. "Well, whatever. Just see if you can decipher this, okay?"

Was it really possible that the sequence of bases could be somehow turned into a word? Just as the digits 178136 had quickly yielded RING, maybe these forty-two letters could be made to form words. Maybe they did carry some important message. Had Ryuji himself, from beyond the grave, inscribed this over and over in his own remains?

Ando's hand, clutching the printout, trembled as he felt himself

132

being driven into the same blind alley as Asakawa. But there was no way he could refuse Miyashita's outright request. The idea that it might be a code had occurred to Ando, too, the first time he'd seen the sequence, but he'd buried the thought in the depths of his brain. He was afraid that if he didn't, the scientific framework on which he'd hung his life would be bent further out of shape. Things were threatening to go beyond his ability to absorb them.

"You can keep that. Take your time and see what you can do with it."

Miyashita was supposed to be a scientist. Ando couldn't understand how he could bandy about these unscientific ideas so readily.

"I have faith in you. You'll figure it out," said Miyashita, giving Ando a pat on the butt.

PART THREE

Decoding

1

Ando and Miyashita followed the waitress to a table by the window. The restaurant was on the top floor of the university hospital and boasted a fantastic view of the Outer Gardens of Meiji Shrine. In addition, university employees got a discount. Both men had taken off their lab coats before coming, but still the waitress could tell at a glance that they weren't members of the general public visiting a patient. She handed them the special employees' lunch menu. Merely glancing at it, both Ando and Miyashita ordered the special of the day and coffee.

As soon as the waitress left, Miyashita said, with a portentous air, "I read it." From the moment Miyashita had asked him to lunch, Ando had known he'd start out with that phrase. Miyashita had read Asakawa's *Ring* report and was now ready to comment on it.

"So what did you think?" Ando leaned forward.

"I won't lie. I was amazed."

"But do you believe it?"

"Hell, it's not a question of belief. It all adds up. The names of the victims and the times of death he gives check out. We've seen the incident reports and the autopsy records ourselves, you and I."

He was right, of course. They had copies of the coroner's reports and associated documents for the four victims who'd been at Villa Log Cabin. The times of death given therein accurately reflected what Asakawa had written. There were no inconsistencies to be found. But what took Ando aback was how a pathologist as sharp as Miyashita showed no apparent resistance to the idea of curses and supernatural powers playing a role in all this.

"So you just accept it?"

"Well, it's not as if I don't have reservations. But, you know, when you really think about it, modern science hasn't managed to come up with answers to any of the most basic questions. How did life first appear on earth? How does evolution work? Is it a series of random events, or does it have a set teleological direction? There are all kinds of theories, but we haven't been able to prove one of them. The structure of the atom is not a miniature of the solar system, it's something much more difficult to grasp, full of what you might call latent power. And when we try to observe the subatomic world, we find that the mind of the observer comes into play in subtle ways. The mind, my friend! The very same mind which, ever since Descartes, proponents of the mechanistic view of the universe considered subordinate to the body-machine. And now we find that the mind influences observed results. So I give up. Nothing surprises me. I'm prepared to accept anything that happens in this world. I actually kind of envy people who can still believe in the omnipotence of modern science."

Ando himself had at least a few doubts about the so-called omnipotence of modern science, but evidently they weren't as grave as Miyashita's. How could one feel comfortable in the scientific community if one harbored that kind of skepticism?

"That's pretty extreme."

"I've never told you this, but I'm actually a philosophical idealist."

"An idealist, huh?"

"Like the Buddha said, form is empty and emptiness is form."

Ando wasn't quite sure what Miyashita was trying to say. He was sure that between philosophical idealism and *reality is empty* there was a lot being left unsaid, but now wasn't the time to pursue the finer points of Miyashita's worldview.

"Anyway, was there anything that particularly bothered you about the report?" Ando wanted to see if he and Miyashita harbored the same doubts about it.

"Oh, any number of things bothered me." The coffee arrived, and Miyashita stirred his full of cream and sugar. His ruddy face caught the sun full-on through the window. "First, why is Asakawa and only Asakawa still alive after having seen that videotape?"

Miyashita took a sip of coffee.

"It's because he figured out the charm, no?"

"The charm?"

"You know, the part that had been erased at the end of the tape."

"The bit that wanted to force the viewer to do something."

"So if Asakawa did it without realizing it..."

"Did what?"

"It was right there at the end of the report, wasn't it? 'The nature of a virus is to reproduce itself. The charm: make a copy of the video.'"

Then Ando explained to Miyashita a few things he didn't know.

There had been a video deck in Asakawa's car at the time of the accident, and Ando had found a taped-over copy of the videotape in Mai's apartment.

A light seemed to go on in Miyashita's head. "A-ha, so that's what he meant. Asakawa thought the charm was to make a copy of the video and to show it to someone who hadn't seen it yet."

"I have no doubt that's what he thought."

"So, where was he heading with the VCR on the morning of the accident?"

"Someplace where he could find two people who would watch the tape, of course. He must have been desperate to save his wife and young daughter."

"But he'd have had a hard time showing such a dangerous tape to a complete stranger."

"I imagine he went to his wife's parents. It couldn't have been his own parents, since his father's still alive and well. I spoke to him on the phone just the other day."

"So her parents exposed themselves to a temporary risk in order to save their daughter and granddaughter."

"Looks like we need to find out where they live and check with the local police."

If the video, complete with extortionate addendum, had been reproduced and circulated, then there might well be more victims in the area around Shizu Asakawa's parents' house. But if there were, the media hadn't picked up on them yet. The video's progress was still below the surface, out of the public eye.

Miyashita, too, seemed to have arrived at the thought that the videotape had the ability to spread like a virus. He spoke mockingly. "Looks like you'll be cutting up a lot of bodies."

This jolted Ando into a realization. Judging from the situation, it was more than likely that Mai had watched the tape. It was now almost two weeks since she'd disappeared. Perhaps he'd end up dissecting her himself. He imagined her beautiful form on the operating table, and it horrified him.

"But Asakawa's still alive." He said it like a prayer.

"The biggest problem we have is this: if Asakawa did manage to make two copies of the videotape, why did his wife and daughter die?"

"Put another way, why is Asakawa himself still alive?"

"I don't know. The smallpox virus is tangled up in this, right? In light of that, it makes perfect sense for this 'charm' to be copying the video to help it propagate."

"It makes sense up through Ryuji's death. But the deaths of Asakawa's wife and daughter throw the question wide open all over again."

"So, being copied wasn't what the tape wanted?"

"I don't know."

He didn't know how to interpret the situation. Either the charm had aimed at something else, or something untoward had happened in the copying process. Or maybe the tape killed people who watched it regardless of whether or not they enacted the charm. But that would make it even harder to explain why Asakawa survived.

Lunch arrived, and the two men fell into silence for a while, absorbed in eating.

Finally, Miyashita rested his fork and said, "I find myself in a dilemma."

"What do you mean?"

"Well, if there is such a videotape, I'd want to watch it. But it might kill me. I'd say that's a dilemma. A week's not much time."

"Not much time?"

"To figure it out. It's really gotten me intrigued. Scientifically speaking, what we have here is a video, a medium that attacks the human brain through its sense of sight and sound, which can somehow implant a smallpox-like virus inside the body."

"Maybe it wasn't that it implanted it. Maybe the images on the video somehow influenced the victim's cellular DNA so that it metamorphosed into the mystery virus."

"You might have something there. I'm thinking of the AIDS virus. We don't know its origins for sure yet, but it's thought that something caused human and simian viruses that had existed all along to evolve, and that's what gave birth to the AIDS virus as we know it. In any case, AIDS is not a virus that has been around for hundreds of years. Analysis of its base sequences clearly shows that it's something that branched into two strains only about a hundred and fifty years ago. Through some chance event."

"And you want to find out what that chance event is in this case."

"Me, I think it involves the mind." Miyashita leaned forward until his nose almost touched Ando's.

It was, of course, common knowledge that the mind, as abstract and immaterial as it was, could influence the body in various ways. Ando was well aware of this. One only had to think of how stress could eat holes in the stomach lining. Now Ando and Miyashita were thinking along the same lines. First, the video created in the viewer a particular psychological state that somehow influenced the viewer's own DNA to metamorphose until the mystery virus which resembled smallpox was born. Then, this smallpox-like virus caused a cancer inside the coronary artery that surrounds the heart, resulting in a tumor. In a week's time the tumor reached its peak size, cutting off the flow of blood and stopping the heart. But the virus itself was like a cancer virus—its function was to worm its way into the DNA and cause cellular mutation in the coronary artery's tunica media—and wasn't very contagious. At least, that was what their analysis so far had led them to think.

"Come on, don't you want to see it?" challenged Miyashita.

"Well..."

"I just want to get my hands on that tape."

"No, I think it's best to let sleeping dogs lie. You'd end up like Ryuji."

"Speaking of Ryuji, did you manage to break the code?"

"Not yet. Even if it is a code, forty-two bases is too small a number to work with. It could only contain a few words at most."

This was an excuse. Ando had in fact tried several times to decipher the code, but every attempt had ended in failure.

"I guess I know how you'll be spending your holiday."

That was when Ando first realized that the next day was a national holiday, Labor Thanksgiving Day. And since he didn't have to work the following day, Saturday, it meant he had a three-day weekend coming up. Ever since losing his son and his wife, he hadn't paid much attention to holidays. It was nothing but misery to be home alone, and three-day weekends that he had no plans for made him particularly depressed.

"Yeah, well, I'll give it a shot."

But spending the holiday trying to read a coded message from a dead man sounded pretty dismal. But on the other hand, if he succeeded, then maybe it'd give him some sense of accomplishment. At least it would provide a distraction.

So he promised Miyashita that he'd have it figured out by the end of the weekend. "On Monday, I'll tell you what Ryuji's trying to say."

Miyashita reached across the table and clapped a hand on Ando's left shoulder. "It's up to you now."

2

After lunch, Ando went back to his office and put in a call to the Forensic Medicine Department of Joji University Hospital, in Utsunomiya, Tochigi prefecture. A little research had turned up the information that Asakawa's wife's parents lived in Ashikaga, Tochigi. Any unexplained deaths in that region would fall under the jurisdiction of the doctors at Joji.

An assistant professor came to the phone, and Ando asked him if there had been any patients who'd died late last month from heart attacks caused by blockage of the coronary artery. The man responded with a curt question of his own.

"Sorry, but what are you getting at?"

Ando explained to him that they had seen seven deaths from the same cause in the greater Tokyo area, and there were indications that there could be many more victims. He avoided any mention of paranormal phenomena.

This didn't seem to have assuaged the man's doubts. "So you're contacting medical schools across the region?"

"No, not exactly."

"So why are you calling us?"

"Because your area is at risk."

"Are you saying we're going to find bodies in Utsunomiya?"

"No, in Ashikaga."

"Ashikaga?" The mention of the name startled the man. He fell silent, and Ando could almost sense his grip on the receiver tightening.

"This is a shock. I can't imagine how you know about it. As a matter of fact, on October 28th, the bodies of an elderly couple were discovered there. We did autopsies on them the next day."

"Can you tell me their names?"

"Their last name was Oda, I think, and the wife's name was Setsuko. I forget the husband's name."

Ando had already checked on Shizu Asakawa's parents' names: Toru and Setsuko Oda. It had to be them. Now they had proof. On the morning of October 21st, Asakawa had loaded a VCR into his rented car and driven to his in-laws' house in Ashikaga, where he'd had two copies made of the tape and shown to the old couple. No doubt he'd assured them that if they made more copies and showed them to other people within a week, their lives wouldn't be in any danger. They probably hadn't needed much convincing, regardless of whether or not they fully believed in their son-in-law's outlandish story. If there was any chance that their daughter and granddaughter's lives were on the line, they must have been more than willing to acquiesce. And so Asakawa had had copies made, believing that by doing so he'd saved his wife and child. But on the way home he lost them both at once, and then a week later, the old couple died, too.

"I'll bet you were pretty surprised by what you found in the autopsy." Ando could well imagine the staff's shock at finding the same symptoms in both bodies.

"You can say that again. I mean, given the simultaneous time of death, plus the fact that they left a note, we naturally assumed it was a double suicide. But then we cut them open, and found, instead of poison, strange tumors in their coronary arteries. Surprised isn't the word."

"Hold on a minute," Ando broke in.

"What?"

"You say they left a note?"

"Yes. It wasn't much of one, but a note was found next to their pillows. It looked like they'd written it right before they died."

Ando was disconcerted by this development. What did this mean? Why did they leave a note?

"Can you tell me what the note said?"

"Hang on." The assistant professor put down the receiver, but was back a few seconds later. "It's going to take me a while to locate it. Shall I fax it to you later?"

"I'd appreciate that."

Ando told the man his fax number and then hung up.

He couldn't leave his desk after that. The fax machine was on the middle shelf of a computer cabinet two desks away. He swiveled in his chair forty-five degrees to face the fax machine, and then waited for the transmission to arrive.

He couldn't relax; he couldn't even lean back in his chair. Instead, while he waited, he went over the course of events up to now in his head. Reviewing the past was all he could do. He was too distracted wondering when the fax machine would come to life to start a new train of thought.

Finally, the machine started to buzz and a fax began to roll out. He waited until it was finished, then got up and tore it off. He returned to his seat, spread the fax open on his desktop, and read:

> *To: Dr. Ando, Fukuzawa University Medical School*
> *Here's the note Mr. and Mrs. Oda left. Please let me*
> *know of any new developments.*
>
> > *Dr. Yokota*
> > *Medical School*
> > *Joji University*

Under the professor's scrawled note were a few lines of text accompanied by the Odas' names. The handwriting wasn't Yokota's; he must have made a photocopy of the original.

> *October 28, morning*
> *We took it upon ourselves to dispose of the videotapes.*
> *There's nothing more to worry about. We're tired. Yoshimi and Kazuko,*
> *please take care of everything.*
> > *Toru Oda   Setsuko Oda*

The message was short, but even so it was enough to make it clear that they knew they were facing death. Yoshimi and Kazuko were probably their other two daughters. But who had the previous sentence been addressed to?

What did they mean, they'd disposed of the videotapes?

Did it mean they'd gotten rid of them? It certainly couldn't be taken to mean that they'd copied them.

Ando decided to try and recreate the Odas' state of mind from the beginning.

On Sunday, October 21st, their son-in-law showed up on their doorstep and told them that Shizu and Yoko's lives were threatened by a curse embedded in a videotape. The Odas agreed to copy the tape. But then, that same day, Shizu and Yoko died at the time foretold. Even if the Odas had been skeptical about Asakawa's story at first, now they

144

surely had to believe in the video's power. Then, after the funeral, they had learned the results of the autopsies: inexplicable heart attacks. At this point the Odas must have decided to give up hope of saving themselves. Their daughter and granddaughter had lost their lives in spite of the fact that they'd followed the videotape's demands. The Odas must have thought that they couldn't escape death no matter what they did. Exhausted from all the effort that had gone into the funerals, and perhaps weary of life in general, they decided to refrain from copying the videotape and meekly awaited the approach of death. But if their note was to be believed, while waiting, they had "disposed" of the videotapes that were the source of all this misery.

There was no way for Ando to know how they had disposed of the tapes. They might have erased them completely and then thrown them away, or they might have buried them in the yard. In any case, as Ando now attempted to diagram the video's path on a piece of scratch paper, he decided to grant for the moment that those two copies had been obliterated.

First there had been the one in Villa Log Cabin No. B-4, the source of all the evil, created when a VCR left to record had captured the images on tape. Asakawa had taken that back to his apartment and made a copy for Ryuji. At this point there were two copies, two strains as it were. However, it seemed that Ryuji's copy had found its way into Mai's hands, and had then been erased, all except for the first ten seconds. Asakawa's copy, meanwhile, had passed to his brother Junichiro, who had discarded it along with the damaged VCR. Asakawa's original had begotten two further strains in the form of copies given to the Odas, but these too had been disposed of. In short, the videotapes born of Sadako Yamamura's wrath had now vanished from the face of the earth.

Ando went over the tree he'd constructed again and again, to make sure he had it right. But the tape did indeed seem to have gone extinct. A mere two months after it had come to life at the end of August, having claimed only nine victims, the scourge had died out. *But...* Ando thought. If the videotape killed everybody who watched it regardless of whether or not they copied it, it was obvious that it was going to go extinct sooner or later. Only by virtue of its threat would it be able to reproduce itself, to adapt to its environment and survive. Once the threat was exposed as a lie, the tape would inevitably be driven into a corner.

If it was extinct, that would mean they'd seen the last of these mysterious deaths. If nobody else could be exposed to those images, then there was no fear of anybody dying from inexplicable heart attacks. But a fundamental point now stole back into Ando's mind.

Why is Asakawa still alive?

This was followed by another question.

Where is Mai Takano?

Logically, the videotape seemed to have died out. But Ando's intuition denied it. This wasn't going to be over that easily. Something didn't sit right.

3

Ando picked up a locker key at the front desk of the library, and then took off his jacket on his way to the lockers. It was almost winter. Anybody who saw him, wearing nothing but a shirt, would shiver in sympathy. But Ando perspired easily, and even in his shirtsleeves, he felt hot in the climate-controlled library. He took a pen and a notebook out of his briefcase, then wrapped his jacket around it and stuffed it in a locker.

The notebook was where he'd put the page containing the DNA analysis of the virus found in Ryuji's blood. Ando was determined to have a go at cracking the code today, which was why he was here in the library first thing in the morning, but the moment he looked at the meaningless array of letters on the printout, his eyes glazed over. There was no way he'd be able to figure this out. But when he thought about it, he recalled that he was doing this partly to kill time. He couldn't think of anything better to get him through the empty three-day week-end.

So he tucked the notebook under his arm and headed up to the third-floor reading room, where he took a seat by the window.

As a student playing at cipher-cracking with Ryuji, he'd had quite a collection of books on cryptography at home. But what with getting married and then getting divorced, he'd moved three times since then, not to mention the fact that he'd lost interest in the subject; all those books had disappeared somewhere along the line. There were certain types of codes that he couldn't hope to decipher without the help of character substitution charts and letter-frequency graphs of the kind found in specialist works, and he doubted he'd be able to get anywhere on this one without their help. And since it just seemed foolish to buy them all over again, he'd ended up at the library.

At one point he'd had a good grasp of the basics of constructing and unscrambling codes, but it had been ten years, so he first took a quick glance through a primer on the subject. He decided that his first step should be to decide just what class of code was contained in the small-pox-like virus's base sequence.

Codes can be generally divided into three types: substitution ciphers, in which the letters of the message are replaced by other letters, symbols, or numbers; transposition ciphers, in which the order of the words of the message is changed; and insertion ciphers, in which extraneous words are inserted between the words of the message. The numbers that popped out of Ryuji's belly after the autopsy, which Ando was able to link to the English word "ring," was a good example of a simple substitution cipher.

It didn't take him long to guess that the virus's code had to be of the substitution variety. What he had to work with was a group of four letters, ATGC, corresponding to the four bases, so it was most likely that the code consisted of assigning a particular character to a predetermined grouping of letters. That was most code-like.

Code-like. When the thought occurred to him, it made him sit up and think. The essential purpose of a code is to convey information from one party to another without any third party being able to figure it out. As students, codes had been nothing but a game to them, brain-teasers. But in, say, times of war, when a code's susceptibility to deciphering could sway the tide of a conflict, a "code-like" code would mean one which was, in effect, too dangerous to use. In other words, one way to keep the enemy from breaking your codes was to make sure they didn't look like codes at first glance. If you caught an enemy spy and found he was carrying a notebook filled with suspicious-looking strings of numbers, it would be a safe bet that it was top-secret information, encrypted. Even allowing for the possibility of decoys, when a code is identified as such, the chances of it being broken rise significantly.

Ando tried to think logically. If the purpose of a code is to keep information from the hands of a third party, then a code should only seem "code-like" to the person for whom the information is intended. Staring at the forty-two letters interpolated into the base sequence of the virus, Ando found them extremely code-like. That had been his impression from the very first time he'd looked at the chart.

Now why would that be?

He tried to analyze the source of that impression. Why did it seem code-like to him? It wasn't as if there had never been puzzling repetitions found in the course of DNA sequencing. But in spite of that, this particular repetition seemed meaningful. It popped up everywhere they looked in the sequence, no matter where they sliced it. It was as if it was trying to call attention to itself, saying, *I'm a code, dummy.* The sequence of letters seemed particularly code-like to Ando in light of his experience with the numbers that had popped out of Ryuji's belly. In other words, maybe there had been two purposes to the word "ring" squeezing its way out just then: not only was it meant to alert Ando to the existence of the *Ring* report, but it was also a form of warning. It was as if Ryuji were telling him, *I may use codes again as the situation warrants, so keep your eyes peeled and don't miss them.* And maybe he'd used the simplest kind of substitution cipher as a hint, too.

Given that the mysterious string of bases had only been found in the virus drawn from Ryuji, it was safe to assume that he was the one sending the code. It was an undeniable fact, of course, that Ryuji had died and his body been reduced to ashes, but a sample of his tissue still remained in the lab. A countless number of instances of his DNA, the blueprint for the individual entity that was Ryuji, still remained in the cells in that tissue sample. What if that DNA had inherited Ryuji's will, and was trying to express something in words?

It was a nonsensical theory completely unworthy of an anatomist like Ando. But if he did succeed in making the string of letters yield words by means of substitution, then that would trump all other readings of the situation. Theoretically, it was possible to take DNA from Ryuji's blood sample and use it to make an individual exactly like Ryuji—a clone. This assemblage of DNA sharing the same will had exerted an influence over the virus that had entered its bloodstream, inserting a word or words. Ando could suddenly sense Ryuji's cunning and sheer genius behind this. Why had he inserted the message only into the virus, an invader, and not into his red blood cells? Because, with his medical background, Ryuji knew that there was no chance that DNA from the other cells would be sequenced. He'd known that he could only count on the virus responsible for the cluster of deaths being run through a sequencer, and so he'd concentrated his efforts on the virus's DNA. So that the words he sent would be received.

All of which finally led Ando to one conclusion. Since this code looked to him like a code, it was no longer functioning, in essence, as a code should. Rather, it was just that Ryuji's DNA had no other way to communicate with the outside. The DNA double helix was composed of four bases represented by the letters ATGC. Ando couldn't think of any other way for it to make its will known but by combining those four letters in various ways. It had chosen this way because there was no other available to it. It was the only means Ryuji had at his disposal.

Suddenly all the despair Ando had felt a few moments ago was gone, replaced by a buoying confidence.

Maybe I'll be able to decipher this after all.

He felt like shouting. If Ryuji's will, lingering in his DNA, was trying to speak to Ando, then it stood to reason that the words it used would be ones easy for Ando to decode. Why should they be more difficult than they needed to be? Ando went back and checked his line of reasoning to see if there were any holes in his deductions. If he started off on the wrong foot, he could wander around forever without finding the answer.

He no longer saw what he was doing as merely a way of killing time. Now that he felt that he would actually be able to decipher the message, he couldn't wait to find out what it said.

The rest of the morning, until lunchtime, Ando spent working on two approaches.

The sequence he had to work with was:

ATGGAAGAAGAATATCGTTATATTCCTCCTCCTCAACAA
CAA

The first question was how to divide the letters up. He tried dividing them up in twos and in threes.

First, by twos:

AT	GG	AA	GA	AG	AA
TA	TC	GT	TA	TA	TT
CC	TC	CT	CC	TC	AA
CA	AC	AA			

Taking a pair of letters as one unit, the four letters available yielded a possible sixteen different combinations. He wondered if each combination might represent one letter.

But this immediately led him to another problem: what language was this message written in?

It probably wasn't the Japanese syllabary. There were nearly fifty characters in that, far more than the sixteen allowed by the pair method. The English and French alphabets both had twenty-six letters, while Italian only used twenty. But he also knew he couldn't overlook the possibility that the message was in romanized Japanese. Identifying the language of a code is sometimes half the battle.

But this was a problem that had already been solved for Ando. The fact that he'd been able to replace the numerals 178136 with the word "ring" could probably be taken as a hint from Ryuji that the present code would also yield something in English. Ando was sure of this point. And so the question of language was as good as settled.

The forty-two base letters could be split into twenty-one pairs. But several pairs were identical: there were four AA's, three TA's, three TC's, and two CC's. There were only thirteen unique pairings. Ando jotted these numbers down on a piece of paper and then paged through a book on code-solving until he found a chart showing the frequency of appearance in English of different letters of the alphabet.

He knew that although the English alphabet contains twenty-six letters, not all of them occur in equal numbers in everyday use. E, T, and A, for example, are common, while Q and Z might appear only once or twice per page. Most handbooks on code-breaking will include various kinds of letter frequency charts in the back, among other statistical references. Using such tables and statistics made it easier to determine the language a coded message was in.

In this case, what the figures told him was that in an English phrase of twenty-one letters, the average number of different letters used was twelve. Ando clicked his heels. What he had was thirteen different letters, not far off the average at all. This told him that, statistically speaking, there was nothing wrong with him dividing the sequence into twenty-one pairs and assuming that each pair stood for a letter.

Putting that possibility on hold for a moment, Ando next tried dividing up the sequence into sets of three:

ATG GAA GAA GAA TAT CGT TAT ATT CCT CCT CCT CAA CAA CAA

This produced fourteen trios, or seven unique varieties: GAA, TAT, CGT, ATT, CCT, and CAA. The charts told him that an English phrase of fourteen letters contained an average of nine different letters. Not far off from the seven he had.

Ando immediately noticed that there was a lot of overlap produced by this system. GAA, CCT, and CAA each occurred three times, and TAT appeared twice. But what really bothered Ando was the fact that GAA, CCT, and CAA each appeared three times in a row. If he assigned each triplet a single letter of the alphabet, there were three separate cases in this short passage of the same letter being repeated three times. He knew enough English to know that double letters were not at all uncommon. But he couldn't think of any English words with triple letters. The only possibility he could think of was situations in which one word ended with a double letter and the next word began with the same letter, e.g., "too old" or "will link."

He picked up an English book he happened to spy nearby and started examining a page at random to see just how often the same letter occurred three times in succession. He'd gone through four or five pages before he found a single instance. The chances of it happening three times in one fourteen-letter sequence were basically nil, he concluded. By contrast, dividing up the forty-two letters into pairs produced just one double letter. As a result, he decided that statistically it made more sense to go with the first option and divide the bases into pairs of letters.

He'd narrowed down the possibilities. From here he could proceed through trial and error.

AT	GG	AA	GA	AG	AA
TA	TC	GT	TA	TA	TT
CC	TC	CT	CC	TC	AA
CA	AC	AA			

The AA pair appeared four times, which meant it must correspond to a letter used with great frequency. Consulting another chart, Ando confirmed that the most frequently used letter in English is, of course, E. So he hypothesized that AA stood for the letter E. The second most common pairs in his sequence were TA and TC, occurring three times each. He also noticed that AA was followed by TA once, while TC was followed by AA once. This might be important, since there were also statistics for various combinations of letters. He started trying out various possibilities for TA and TC, constantly referring to his charts.

As far as letters which often follow the letter E and which are also common in and of themselves, the letter A seemed like the best candidate, which meant that TA could stand for A. By the same logic, he thought that TC might correspond to the letter T. Further, by the way it combined with other letters, he guessed that CC might be N. Thus far the statistics seemed to be serving him well. At least, he hadn't run into any problems.

This is what he had:

$$\_ \_ E \_ \_ E A T \_ A A \_ N T \_ N T E \_ \_ E$$

What had once seemed a random jumble of letters now seemed to be taking on the aura of English. Next he tried filling in the blanks based on what he knew of consonant-vowel combinations, always consulting the charts.

SHERDEATYAALNTINTECME

The first three letters seemed to form the word "she," but the rest of it didn't form words no matter how he divided it up. He tried switching the positions of the E's, A's, T's, and N's, and changed other letters around on hunches. When it became too time-consuming to write down the possibilities on paper, he tore sheets out of his notebook, first to make twenty-six cards, one for each letter. It was beginning to feel like a game.

THEYWERBORRLNBINBECME

When he hit on this combination, the first thing that popped into Ando's mind was the phrase "they were born." He knew the spelling was a bit off, but maybe it wasn't too much of a stretch. And the meaning struck a chord with him somehow. But he had a feeling there was a better match out there somewhere, so he kept at the game.

After about ten minutes of playing around, Ando thought he could guess what the result would be, and he stopped. If he had a computer with him, things would be much easier, he thought. The third, sixth, eighteenth, and twenty-first letters were the same. The seventh, tenth, and eleventh were the same. The eighth, fourteenth, and seventeenth were the same. The thirteenth and the sixteenth were the same. The phrase was twenty-one letters long. If he fed those conditions into a computer it would probably come up with the answer, provided he made the proper adjustments for frequency of letter usage. But the computer would undoubtedly come up with several possible solutions. There had to be an infinite number of meaningful phrases in English that satisfied those conditions. How would he be able to tell which one was Ryuji's message to him? Only if there was something about the right answer that would tell him at first glance that it was from Ryuji, like a signature at the end of a letter. But if there wasn't, he'd be lost.

Ando realized he was at a dead end. He hung his head, feeling stupid that it had taken him this long to notice. Back in his student days, when his code-breaking intuition had been more finely honed, he would have caught on to this impasse in a minute or two. He'd have to change the way he thought about this. He needed a new hypothesis.

Ando was so absorbed he hadn't noticed the passage of time. He looked at his watch now to find it was nearly one in the afternoon. He realized he was hungry. He stood up, thinking to go have lunch in the cafeteria on the fourth floor. A change of surroundings would do him good. Trial-and-error and inspiration: he was going to need both if he was going to come up with a solution. And he often got his inspirations while he ate.

The answer to this is going to have to be obvious.

He whispered it almost like an incantation as he headed for the fourth floor.

4

As he ate the set lunch, Ando gazed out the window at the trees down below, and at the kids playing on the swings and the seesaws in the park. It was past one now. The cafeteria had been packed when he arrived, but now there were empty seats here and there. The printout with the base sequence sat on the table next to his aluminum tray, but he wasn't looking at it.

One wall of the cafeteria had floor-to-ceiling windows, so there was nothing to obstruct his view of the children playing. It was like watching a silent movie. Whenever he saw a boy of about five, Ando's gaze was riveted to him. Without even realizing it, he'd stare at the child, and it would take him several minutes to snap out of it.

He'd come to this library with his son once. It was a Sunday afternoon two years before, when they were living in the South Aoyama condo. Ando had suddenly realized he needed to look up some data for a presentation he was scheduled to give at a research conference, so he decided to come to the library. He took Takanori along for the walk. But when they got there, a sign at the entrance said *NO ONE UNDER 18 ADMITTED*. He couldn't very well make the boy wait outside while he did his research, so he gave up and they played in the park instead. He could remember standing behind the swings, pushing Takanori; he could remember the rhythm of the swing. That same swing was in motion now, under the golden gingko leaves. He couldn't hear a sound, couldn't even see the expressions on the faces of the children as they alternately stretched out their legs and tucked them in. But in his mind's ear he could hear his son's voice.

But he was getting off track. He brought his gaze back to the page and picked up his pen.

It was time to get back to the basics of code-breaking. There was no other way to crack this kind of code but to come up with several hypotheses, and then pursue each one of them in turn. When it became clear that one theory wasn't working out, the best thing to do was abandon it with alacrity and move on to the next one. For a message of only twenty-one letters, he wouldn't be able to rely solely on frequency charts and letter-combination rules. In fact, if the code was complicated enough to require a specific conversion key, it ran the risk of being too hard, in which case it wouldn't be able to convey what it wanted to. No, he needed to simply work through a bunch of theories by trial and error. If an idea wasn't working, he needed to abandon it, that was all.

There was one hypothesis that Ando thought he had abandoned too soon, though. It occurred to him that the code might be an anagram.

He returned to the reading room and once again split the forty-two letters into groups of three.

ATG GAA GAA GAA TAT CGT TAT ATT CCT CCT CCT CAA CAA CAA

He'd abandoned this approach because it resulted in triple repetitions of the same letter, a very unusual thing in English. But what if the letters themselves needed to be rearranged? He thought of an example he'd read once, where the phrase "Bob opened the door" had been encoded as OOOOEEEBBDDTPNHR. As it was, the sequence contained far too many letter repetitions to make sense as English, but when rearranged according to a certain set of rules, it yielded a perfectly normal sentence.

This might work, he thought.

But just as he was about to get to work, he stopped. He could see where this was going, too. If he not only had to decide what letters each triplet stood for, but also had to figure out how to rearrange the letters, the task suddenly became a mammoth one. And it wasn't just a question of time. Without a key of some sort, he'd end up with the same sort of problem he had run into with earlier: a plethora of possible solutions with no way to choose among them. He thought of the numbers that had led him to "ring" and wondered if they might somehow be that key, pointing him toward the right order in which to arrange the letters now. But first he'd have to figure out what letters the triplets stood for.

Another dead end.

You need a fresh angle on this, Ando told himself. He was trying to proceed by trial and error, but he felt like he was just trying the same thing over and over. Maybe he was too fixated on the idea of making each set of two or three bases correspond to one English letter.

The solution has to be something unambiguous, something that I can figure out without going through a long, complicated process.

He felt his concentration faltering, his eyes wandering away from the page. He suddenly realized he was staring at the hair of a young woman seated at the other end of the same table. With her head down like that, she looked like Mai Takano, especially her forehead.

Where is she now?

He worried about her safety, especially when he considered that she used to be Ryuji's lover.

Could Ryuji be trying to tell me where she is with this code?

He considered the possibility for a moment, but then discarded it with a derisive laugh as being too comic-book. How adolescent, to imagine himself as the famous detective out to save the heroine from mortal danger. Suddenly the whole thing seemed foolish to Ando. This probably wasn't a code at all. There was probably a perfectly scientific explanation for how that sequence of bases got into the virus's DNA. And once Ando admitted that possibility, he could feel his passion for code-breaking vanish. He was just killing time anyway, right? He was working awfully hard at it.

The setting sun was turning the hairs on his upper arm golden. All the intensity he'd had that morning was gone now. He thought about moving to another seat, where the sun didn't hit him, and started to get up. Looking around, though, he saw he was surrounded by kids, college students or high school kids studying for entrance exams, all dozing behind mountains of books. Moving wouldn't help him get his concentration back. The entire reading room was enveloped in drowsiness. Ando sat back down where he was.

Think about it logically, he told himself. *There has to be a formula.*

He sat up straight. He'd been trying to assign letters of the alphabet to trios of bases, but that didn't work out to a formula. If he could get it down to a one-to-one function, or even a several-to-one function, then the answer would become obvious. One-to-one, perhaps several-to-one... There had to be a formula like that to be discovered.

He stood up. Logically speaking, there was no other way. His intuition told him that he'd moved one step closer to a solution, and the realization blew away his torpor, spurring him to action.

He went to the natural sciences section, found a book on DNA, and started flipping madly through the pages. As his excitement mounted, his palms grew sweaty. What he was looking for was a chart that gave what amino acid each trio of bases formed.

Eventually he found one. He took the book back to his table and laid it out flat, opened to the chart, next to the coded message.

When a trio of bases, a codon, forms a protein, the codon is translated into an amino acid. The principles by which the translation takes place were contained in the chart Ando had found. There are twenty varieties of amino acid. There are four bases, meaning there are sixty-four separate combinations of three that can be formed. With sixty-four combinations standing for only twenty amino acids, it meant there was quite a bit of overlap. It was several-to-one mapping. Each trio of bases signified one amino acid or another (or a stop).

Consulting the chart, Ando wrote the abbreviated names of the amino acids below the forty-two bases of the code.

ATG	GAA	GAA	GAA
(Met)	(Glu)	(Glu)	(Glu)
TAT	CGT	TAT	ATT
(Tyr)	(Arg)	(Tyr)	(Ile)
CCT	CCT	CCT	CAA
(Pro)	(Pro)	(Pro)	(Gln)
CAA	CAA		
(Gln)	(Gln)		

Next he took the first letter of the name of each acid and lined them up:

MGGGTATIPPPGGG

But this meant nothing. And he was still faced with triple letter combinations. It seemed he'd have to figure out what to do with them no matter what. There had to be another interpretation. For example, maybe a third straight repetition of the same letter meant that the first two should be interpreted as a space between words.

He tried that:

MG TATIP G

That wasn't English either.

But all the same, Ando felt he was getting somewhere. He could tell he was closing in on the solution. He didn't know why, but he felt that any minute now he'd come up with a word that made sense.

Met, Pro, and Gln were the ones that were repeated three times. He tried writing them out a different way:

Met
Glu (x3)
Tyr
Arg
Tyr
Ile
Pro (x3)
Gln (x3)

He stared at this list for about a minute, and then he saw an English word he knew.

It occurred to him that the codons repeated three times might signify not "three" but "third." As in, the third letter of the abbreviation for the amino acid.

In other words:

Met
Glu
Tyr
Arg
Tyr
Ile
Pro
Gln

Which meant the solution was: *Mutation.*

Forgetting where he was, Ando let out a groan. The only answer he'd been able to come up with, as a result of logic, method, and trial and error, was this. It was a simple, clear answer, and it had to be right.

But still he had to hang his head. He knew the meaning of the English word "mutation"—that is, he knew what it meant in an evolutionary biological sense. But he had absolutely no idea how he was supposed to take it in this context.

Just what the hell are you trying to say, Ryuji? He didn't speak the question aloud. But even in his own head, Ando could hear his voice tremble with excitement at having decoded the message.

5

He went to the hall, found a pay phone, and dialed Miyashita's number. He doubted his friend would be in, given it was a Saturday evening in the middle of a three-day weekend, but lo and behold, Miyashita was at home with his family. Ando was able to tell him that he thought he'd deciphered the code.

Ando figured Miyashita was probably in his living/dining room; in fact, he could practically see Miyashita's wife and children getting ready for dinner. Miyashita himself was cupping a hand around the mouthpiece to keep out the background noise but was unable to keep his halcyon home life from filtering through.

"Good show! That's excellent. What did it say?"

Miyashita had a loud voice to begin with, and with his hand cupped around the mouthpiece it rang even louder in Ando's ears.

"Well, it wasn't a sentence. It was just a single word."

"Okay, so it was only one word. What was it?"

"Mutation."

"Mutation?" Miyashita repeated the word several times, as if trying it on for size.

"Do you have any idea what it might mean?" Ando asked.

"I don't know. How about you? Any ideas?"

"Not an inkling."

"Listen. Why don't you come over?"

Miyashita lived in a tasteful condo in North Terao, in Tsurumi Ward in Yokohama. Ando would have to take the train to Shinagawa and transfer to the Keihin Express line, but he'd be able to get there in less than an hour.

"Alright, I guess."

"Call me when you get to the station. I know a good bar near the station where we can knock one back and talk it over."

Miyashita's kindergarten-age daughter seemed to have guessed he was planning to go out. She clung to his waist and whined, "Stay home, Daddy!" Out of respect for Ando, Miyashita clapped his hand over the receiver and scolded her. Ando could hear him wandering around the house with the phone, trying to get away from her. Ando felt guilty, even though it hadn't been his idea to go out in the first place. At the same time, he felt an ineffable sense of loss and envy.

"We can do it another time if you want."

But Miyashita wouldn't hear of it. "No way. I want to hear all the details. Anyway, give me a call from the station, and I'll be right there."

He hung up, not waiting for Ando's reply. With a sigh of despair, Ando left the library and headed for the subway station, the harmonious sounds of his friend's household still echoing in his ears.

Ando hadn't taken the Keihin Express line since visiting Mai's apartment eight days before. From somewhere near Kita Shinagawa Station the train ran on elevated tracks. He found himself looking down on houses and the neon signs. At six on a late-November evening it was already nearly pitch-dark. Turning his gaze toward the harbor he saw the Yashio high-rise apartments straddling the canal, their lit and unlit windows forming a checkerboard pattern. A surprising number of the windows were dark for a weekend evening. Ando found himself trying to find words in the patterns of light and dark; he'd had codes too much on the brain lately. On one among the forest of buildings he thought he saw the phonetic syllable *ko*—child?—but of course it meant nothing.

Mutation, mutation.

He kept muttering the word under his breath as he stared into the distance. He hoped that maybe the more he intoned it the clearer Ryuji's intent would become.

In the distance he heard a foghorn. The train slid into a station and stayed there; an announcement said they were waiting for an express to pass. Ando was on the last carriage. He stuck his head out the door to see the name of the station. Sure enough, this was where Mai lived. From the train he could see the street outside the station, lined with shops, and he started looking for Mai's apartment, relying on his eight-day-old memories. He remembered that when he'd stood in her room and looked out the window, he'd seen the Keihin Express station at right about eye level. He could see people waiting on the platform, which meant that he should be able to see her apartment from here.

But he couldn't see very well from inside the train, so he got off. He walked down to the end of the platform and stuck his head out over the fence. The shopping street stretched east at a right angle to the train tracks. Less than a few hundred feet away, he saw a seven-story apartment building he recognized.

Abruptly, he heard the sound of the express approaching from the direction of Shinagawa. Once it had passed, the local Ando was riding would shut its doors and continue on toward Kawasaki. Ando hurriedly looked for her window. He knew she lived in #303, and that was the third window from the right. By now the express had passed, and the bell was ringing to announce the departure of the local. Ando looked at his watch. It was just past six. Miyashita would be eating dinner with his family right now. Ando was reluctant to arrive too early and disturb their precious family time. He figured he was about thirty minutes earlier than he wanted to be, so he decided to take the next train down. He let the local leave without him.

The third floor windows were more or less level with the platform where he was standing. He looked carefully at each of them in turn, but there was no light in any of them.

So she's not there after all.

It had been a faint hope, easily dashed. Then, just as he was about to look away, his gaze was arrested by a band of pale blue light emanating from the third window from the right. He squinted, wondering if he was imagining it, but there it was, fluttering like a bluish-white flag. It glowed so faintly, flickering in and out of view, that he would have missed it if he hadn't been looking so carefully. He leaned even farther forward, but it was too far away. He couldn't quite make it out.

He wanted to go back to her apartment. It should only take twenty minutes or so, which would put him right on schedule for the next train. Without hesitating another minute, he went through the ticket gate and out into the street below.

It was only when he was standing directly below her window, looking up at it, that he was able to figure out the strange light. Her window was open, and her white lace curtain had been blown outside the window, where it was dancing in the breeze, and the neon sign of a car-rental agency across the street was reflecting off the pure white of the lace. Sometimes the primary colors shining on the white cloth showed up like fluorescent paint, which explained the pale blue tinge that was just barely visible from the station. Still, there was a lot about the scene that didn't sit right with Ando. The window had been open and the curtain half closed when he visited eight days ago, but he could distinctly remember closing the window and pulling the curtain to the side before he left. He knew he hadn't left that window open. But there was something that bothered him even more. There was no wind to speak of on this early-winter evening. And yet the curtain had been blown beyond the railing until it was nearly horizontal. Where was that current of air coming from? He couldn't hear any wind. The leaves of the trees lining the street weren't moving. And yet, just above those motionless branches, the curtain danced. The scene was eerily off-kilter. But none of the passersby so much as glanced upward; nobody seemed to notice the odd phenomenon.

The only explanation Ando could think of was a mechanical one. Perhaps a powerful fan was blowing in the room, creating an artificial current flowing outward. But why? His curiosity was aroused.

He went around to the lobby. The only way he'd be able to find out would be to confront that room again.

The superintendent seemed to have the day off. The curtain was drawn on at the counter of his office. The whole building felt quiet, with no signs anybody was about.

He took the elevator to the third floor and then walked toward #303. The closer he got, the smaller and slower his steps became. His instincts were telling him to turn back, but he just had to know. The door to the outside hallway was open, and beyond it he could see a spiral staircase for emergency use. *If something happens, maybe I shouldn't use the elevator. Maybe I should just run down the stairs...* Without knowing what exactly he was afraid of, Ando found himself planning an escape route.

He came to the door marked 303. Below the doorbell was a red sticker on which was written TAKANO. Everything was just as before. Ando went to ring the bell, but then thought better of it. Checking to see that the hall was deserted, he put his ear to the door. He couldn't detect a sound, certainly not the motor of an electric fan. He wondered if the lace curtain was still waving outside the window at this very moment. From what he heard beyond the door, he had a hard time believing it was.

"Mai."

Instead of ringing the bell, he called her name, gently, and knocked. No answer.

Mai watched the video, he reminded himself. And she, or someone, had taped over it, only two days before Ando's visit. The fifth day of her disappearance. Who had done it, and why?

Suddenly, Ando could feel again on his skin the strange atmosphere of the room, like the inside of a body. The water at the bottom of the tub, the dripping, the feeling of something brushing against his Achilles tendon.

Ando backed away from the door. In any case, all four copies of that demon video had been wiped from the face of the earth. The crisis was over. No doubt Mai's body would be found soon. No amount of screwing around here was going to bring him any closer to turning things around, Ando told himself as he started back toward the elevator. He was eager to get out of this place again, even at the expense of leaving without an explanation. He wasn't sure why, but he seemed to feel like this every time he came here.

He pushed the elevator call button. While he waited, he kept repeating to himself, *mutation, mutation*. He wanted to keep his mind on something else, anything. The elevator was taking forever.

From the hallway to his right he heard a resounding snap as a deadbolt clicked. Ando's body stiffened. Instead of spinning completely around to look, he turned his head just far enough to see out of the corner of his eye. He saw the door to #303 open slowly outward. He could see the red sticker: there was no doubt which door it was. Unconsciously, Ando pressed the elevator button again and again. The elevator was spending an agonizingly long time on the ground floor.

Seeing a figure emerge from the doorway, Ando braced himself. It was a woman in a summery green one-piece dress. She took a key from her handbag and locked the door, her face visible to Ando in profile. Ando studied the face. She was wearing sunglasses, but even so, it was clear to him that it wasn't Mai. It was someone else. There was no reason for him to be afraid, but his body was running far ahead of his mind at this point.

The elevator doors opened and Ando slipped inside. He went to push CLOSE but accidentally pushed OPEN instead. Finally, a few beats late, the doors started to close. Then, at the last second, a white hand insinuated itself into the crack between the doors, which reacted by springing wide open again. The woman was standing there. Her sunglasses hid any expression her eyes might have had, but Ando could see that she was around twenty-five, with perfectly regular features. With one hand against the edge of the doors, she stepped smoothly onto the elevator and pressed the close button, and then the one for the first floor. Ando inched nervously backwards until his back and elbows were pressed against the elevator wall and he was standing on tiptoe. From that position, he stared at this strange woman, this woman who had come out of apartment #303, and directed a single question at her from behind:

Who are you?

An odd smell, different from the scent of perfume, tickled his nose, and he made a face and held his breath. What could it be? It smelled like it contained iron, like blood. The woman's hair reached down to the middle of her back, and her hand on the wall was so white it was almost transparent. A closer look revealed that the nail on her index finger was split. Her sleeveless dress was much too light for the season. She had to be freezing. On her legs she wore no stockings, and on her feet just a pair of pumps. He could see purplish bruises on her legs. This shocked him, but he didn't know why. As hard as he tried, he couldn't stifle the trembling that welled up from deep within him.

Shut up in that tiny box of an elevator alone with that woman, time seemed to drag for Ando. Finally they arrived at the first floor, and Ando held his breath until the door opened. The woman walked straight across the lobby and disappeared into the street outside.

She looked to be about five feet tall, with a well-balanced figure. Her tight dress ended a few inches above the knees and showed off her derriere nicely, and she had a lithe walk. With no stockings to cover them, the backs of her legs showed up especially white, making the bruises on her calves stand out even more. The night was so cold that every other person on the street was wearing a coat, and yet off she went wearing nothing but a sleeveless summer dress.

Ando got off the elevator and then just stood there for a while, staring into the darkness after her.

Ando waited for Miyashita in front of the bank like he was told. It was a weekend evening, and the bank was closed. With its metal shutters down, the area in front of it looked curiously orderly. The darkness here was cozy, but as he waited for Miyashita to emerge from it, he couldn't rid his mind of the image of that woman from apartment #303.

He tried, but she was burned onto his retinas. The whole time he'd half-sleepwalked back to the station from Mai's building, and then the whole way here to Tsurumi Station, he'd been seeing her in his mind.

Who was *she?*

The most sensible explanation that occurred to him was that Mai's sister had gotten concerned about her sibling and come to check on her apartment. Ando himself had called Mai's mother and told her in simple terms what he'd found. If Mai did have a sister, and if she too lived in Tokyo, there wasn't anything in the least strange about running into her at Mai's apartment.

But there was something in the indescribable aura that the woman had exuded that negated such an easy answer. Riding in the same elevator with her had shaken Ando to the depths of his soul. She didn't seem to be of this world, and yet, she didn't look like a ghost, either. She'd definitely been there with him in the flesh. But Ando thought he would have had an easier time accepting her if she had been a ghost.

He saw a bead of light emerge from behind a mixed-occupancy office building and head straight for him.

"Hey, Ando!"

Ando squinted toward the light, and realized it was Miyashita, hurtling toward him on a small ladies' bike, complete with shopping basket. He must have borrowed his wife's bicycle.

With a squeal of brakes, he came to a stop in front of Ando. At first, Miyashita was too out of breath to speak. He just stood there, straddling the bike, elbows on the handlebars, head bobbing up and down as he gasped for air. Ando never thought he'd see Miyashita on a bike. The slightest exertion usually left him panting.

"That was quick." Ando thought he'd be waiting for at least ten minutes. Miyashita was never early for anything.

Having parked the bike on the sidewalk in front of the station, Miyashita put a hand on Ando's back and guided him into an alley where every building seemed to have a red lantern hanging from its eaves. His breathing had finally calmed a bit, and as they walked, he spoke to Ando.

"I think I know what 'mutation' might mean."

That explained why Miyashita had come on a bike. He was dying to tell Ando his ideas.

"What does it mean?"

"Let's have a beer first."

As they ducked under a shop curtain, Ando noticed that it said *Beef Tongue*. Miyashita didn't trouble to ask what Ando wanted; instead, the moment they were inside he called for two draft beers and an order of salted tongue. Miyashita seemed to know the proprietor. They exchanged glances of recognition as Miyashita and Ando headed for two counter seats in the back. Those were the quietest seats in the house.

First, Miyashita asked Ando what he had done to figure out the code embedded in Ryuji's virus. Ando took the printout from his briefcase and began to explain the steps he'd gone through. Miyashita nodded repeatedly. Before Ando was half finished, Miyashita seemed to be convinced of the soundness of his method.

"It looks like 'mutation' has to be the answer, alright. The proof of your approach is that it yields exactly one solution." Miyashita patted Ando on the shoulder. "By the way, I'm sure you've noticed what all this is analogous to?"

"What do you mean?"

Miyashita took a crumpled sheet of paper from his pocket and unfolded it. It had something drawn on it. Whatever it was, it had been done roughly, merely to illustrate a spur-of-the-moment idea.

"Have a look at this," Miyashita said, handing him the paper. Ando took it and flattened it out on the bar in front of him.

He understood immediately. It was an illustration of how the DNA double helix inside a cell replicates itself. The strands of the double helix are complementary: when the structure of one is determined, the other one is automatically determined, too. When a cell divides, the two strands separate, each one faithfully creating next-generation copies of the original. This process of copying a gene and passing it down from parent to child can be thought of as the basics of heredity.

This was, of course, elementary to Ando. "What about it?" he asked.

"Think for a minute about the mechanism behind the evolution of species."

There was a lot that still wasn't known about evolution. For example, the basic concepts of Kinji Imanishi's theory differed from those of Neo-Darwinism, but it was impossible to determine, definitively, who was right. All in all, it was "let a hundred flowers bloom" in the world of evolutionary theory; everybody, qualified or not, weighed in with strongly held opinions. But even without decisive evidence to settle the question, Ando knew that recent developments in molecular biology had come close to showing that sudden genetic mutations were a driving force in evolution.

So he answered by saying, with some confidence, "It probably begins with genetic mutation." He felt he could guess where the conversation was going.

"Right. Mutation is the trigger that moves evolution forward. So, how do mutations happen?" Miyashita took a long swig of his beer, and then pulled a ballpoint pen from his breast pocket. Before Ando had a chance to reply to his question, Miyashita was writing again on the illustration. *The reason mutations occur.* Ando tried to peer past his hand at the sketch.

"An error arises in the genetic code—some chance damage or displacement to the genes—and that error is copied and passed down. Thus, a mutation. Are you with me? This is the current thinking on the mechanism of mutation."

Miyashita pointed at his diagram with his pen to emphasize his points, but this wasn't anything that had to be explained to Ando. Genetic damage can be caused on purpose in a laboratory using X-rays or ultraviolet radiation. But, usually, mutations occur at random. The DNA sequence, which theoretically should be faithfully copied and transmitted to future generations, sometimes mutates due to a copying error, so to speak, and as enough of these mutations accumulate through replication, gradually a new species arises. A given mutation can be looked at as one small step toward evolution.

"Remember that analogy I mentioned, my friend?" Miyashita mur-

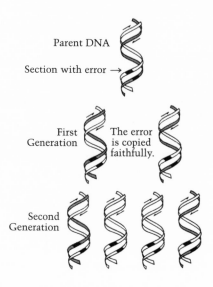

Parent DNA

Section with error →

First Generation

The error is copied faithfully.

Second Generation

mured. Finally it dawned on Ando what Miyashita was getting at. X was like Y. Now that Ando considered it, there was indeed a resemblance.

"You're talking about duplicating videos, aren't you?" Ando finally said.

"Don't you think it's basically the same thing?" Miyashita shoved two slices of tongue into his mouth and washed them down with beer.

Ando turned the paper over and spread it out on the counter, and then borrowed Miyashita's pen and began to make a diagram of his own. He needed to take stock of the points of similarity. Even if it was something he thought he already knew inside out, he knew it often helped him to map a thing out on paper.

On the 26th of August, a videotape came into the world in Villa Log Cabin. On the twenty-ninth, four young people lodging in that same cabin erased part of the end of the tape—the part that said, *Whoever watches this video must make a copy of it and show it to someone else within a week.* The kids taped commercials over this section of the video. To the videotape, it was as if an unforeseen, random event had damaged its genetic sequence, the chain of images. An error was introduced. The tape, now containing the error, was then copied by Asakawa. Naturally, the error was copied as well. Thus far, the process was exactly like the one DNA uses to replicate itself. Not only that, but the erased section of the tape, the message, was meant to play a critical role in the tape's ability to reproduce. In genetic terms, it was a regulator gene. Shock to a regulator gene can make it easier for mutation to occur. Had a trauma to the end of the tape caused the video to mutate?

Ando let the pen come to rest. "Hold on a second. We're not talking about a living thing here."

Miyashita didn't miss a beat. It was as if he'd prepared his response ahead of time.

"If someone asked you to define life, what's your answer?"

Life, in Ando's view, basically boiled down to two things: the ability of an entity to reproduce itself, and its possession of a physical form. Taking a single cell as an example, it had DNA to oversee its self-reproduction, while it had protein to give it external shape. But a videotape? To be sure, it had a physical form—its plastic shell, usually black and rectangular. But it couldn't be said to have the ability to reproduce itself.

"A video doesn't have the ability to reproduce on its own."

"So?" Miyashita sounded impatient now.

"So you're saying it's just like a virus..."

Ando felt like groaning. Viruses are a strange form of life: they lack the power to reproduce on their own. On that score, they actually fall somewhere between the animate and the inanimate. What a virus can do is burrow into the cells of another living creature and use them to help it reproduce. Just as the videotape in question had held its watchers in thrall by means of its threat to destroy them unless they copied it. The tape had used people in its reproductive process.

"But..." Ando felt compelled to object at this point. He wasn't even sure what he wanted to deny. He just felt that if he didn't, something catastrophic would happen.

"But all copies of the video have been neutralized."

There shouldn't be any more danger, in other words. Even if the videotape had been alive in the limited way a virus is, it was extinct now. All four specimens that had been introduced into the world had now been removed from it.

"You're right. The videotape is extinct. But that's the old strain."

171

The beads of sweat on Miyashita's face grew larger with every swallow of beer he took.

"What do you mean, old?" asked Ando.

"The video mutated. Through copying, it evolved until a new strain emerged. It's still lurking out there somewhere. And it's taken a completely different form. That's what I think, anyway."

Ando could only stare open-mouthed. His mug was empty, but he wanted something stronger than beer now. He tried to order some *shochu* gin on the rocks, but his voice faltered and he couldn't make himself heard to the bartender. Miyashita took over, holding up two fingers and calling out, "Shochu!" Two glasses of the liquor were set on the bar before them, and Ando immediately reached out and drank about a third of his in one gulp. Miyashita watched him out of the corner of his eyes, and then said:

"If the videotape did mutate and evolve into a new form during the process of multiple copying, then it wouldn't matter at all to the new species if the old one died out. Think about it. Ryuji went to all the trouble of manipulating a DNA sequence so he could talk to us from the world of the dead. I can't think of any other explanation for why he'd send us the word 'mutation.' Can you?"

Of course Ando couldn't. How could he? He brought the liquor to his lips time and again, but intoxication seemed still a long way off. His head was distressingly clear.

It might be true. Ando found himself gradually leaning toward Miyashita's viewpoint. Ryuji probably meant the word "mutation" as a warning. Ando could almost see Ryuji's face as he sneered, *You think you're safe. You think it's extinct. But you won't get off that easy. It's mutated, and a new version is rearing its head.*

Ando was reminded of the AIDS virus. It was thought that several hundred years ago some preexisting virus mutated and became what is now known as the AIDS virus. The previous virus didn't infect humans, and may well have been harmless. But through mutation, it took on the power to wreak havoc with the human immune system. What if the same thing happened with this videotape? Ando could only pray that the opposite happened, that a harmful thing was now innocuous. But the facts suggested otherwise. Far from becoming harmless, the mutated videotape had turned into something that killed anybody who watched it regardless of whether or not they made a copy of it. If that was any indication, the thing was getting even nastier. And with Ando unable to form any conclusions yet about Mai's disappearance, that left Asakawa as the only anomaly.

"Why is Asakawa still alive?" Ando asked Miyashita the same thing he'd asked him the day before.

"That's the question, isn't it? He's the only clue as to what that videotape has turned into."

"Well, actually...there is one other person."

Ando gave Miyashita a brief rundown on Mai: how the video had made its way through Ryuji to her, how there was evidence that she'd watched it, and how she'd been missing for nearly three weeks now.

"Which means there are two people who saw the tape and are still alive."

"Asakawa's still alive, although just barely. I'm not sure about Mai."

"I hope she's alive."

"Why?"

"Well, why not? We're better off with two clues than with one."

He had a point. If Mai was still alive, they might be able to figure out what she and Asakawa had in common. It might give them an answer. But for his part, Ando just hoped she was safe.

PART FOUR   *Evolving*

1

Monday afternoon, November 26th.

Ando had finished an autopsy on a boy who'd drowned in a river, and now he was filling out a report while listening to the boy's father explain the circumstances.

Ando was trying to ascertain the boy's date of birth and his movements on the day of the accident, but the man's answers were vague and confused, making Ando's job difficult. Sometimes the father would gaze out the window when the conversation flagged, and sometimes Ando caught him stifling a yawn. He looked sapped of strength, drowsy. Ando wanted to finish up as quickly as he could and release the man.

Then the M.E.'s office rang with a sudden commotion. They'd just been notified by the police that another body was coming in, that of an unidentified female. At the moment, they were simultaneously preparing to treat the body and to dissect it. Dr. Nakayama, an older colleague of Ando's, would be in charge of the autopsy. The police had said she'd been discovered in an exhaust shaft on the roof of an office building. This meant the team would have to do two autopsies back to back, so assistants and policemen were running in and out now getting ready.

"The body has arrived, Doctor."

The autopsy assistant's voice rang out. Ando jumped involuntarily and looked toward the sound. Ikeda, the assistant, was standing by the half-open door, facing Nakayama. For some reason, though, Ando felt as though he were the one being summoned.

"Alright," said Nakayama, getting slowly to his feet. "Get it ready, would you?" Nakayama had joined the M.E.'s office two years before Ando; he belonged to the Forensic Medicine Department of Joji University Medical School.

The assistant disappeared, and in his place a policeman came in and approached Nakayama. After a couple of words of greeting, the cop pulled up a chair and sat down next to Nakayama.

Ando looked back down at his own work. But he could overhear the policeman's conversation with Nakayama behind him, and it interested him. He could only catch fragments, words here and there. The officer seemed to be explaining the circumstances in which the body had been found.

Ando stopped writing and listened. The words "unidentified" and "young female" cropped up again and again.

Nakayama asked, "But why was she on the roof?"

"We don't know why she went up there. Maybe she was thinking of jumping."

"Was there a note of any kind?"

"We haven't found one yet."

"I imagine, from inside an exhaust shaft nobody would have heard her cries for help."

"It's not a residential area."

"Where is it?"

"East Oi, in Shinagawa Ward. It's an old fourteen-story building along the Shore Road."

Ando looked up in shock. He recalled the view from the Keihin Express tracks. Beyond the residential district, one could see the Shore Road where it passed through a district lined with warehouses and office buildings. It was just a stone's throw from Mai's apartment. An unidentified young female on the roof of a building on the Shore Road...

"I think that'll do. If I have any more questions I'll give you a call." Ando thanked the boy's father and wrapped up what he was doing. He was too interested in the conversation behind him to be able to put together a report right now. There were still some things he knew he needed to find out, but he decided he'd take care of them later.

Ando slipped his papers into a folder and got to his feet. Nakayama and the policeman stood up at the same time. Ando went over and clapped a hand on Nakayama's shoulder. Bowing slightly to the officer, whom he recognized, Ando said, "The female you're doing next—she hasn't been identified?"

The three of them left the office and headed down the hall toward the autopsy room.

It was the policeman who answered Ando. "That's right. She didn't have anything on her to help us peg her."

"How old is she?"

"She's young, twenty or thereabouts. She'd be quite a looker, if she weren't dead."

Twenty or thereabouts. Mai was twenty-two, but she could easily pass for a woman in her teens. Ando could feel himself starting to choke.

"Any distinguishing features?"

He'd know immediately if he saw the body. But he needed to prepare himself first. Of course he'd much rather hear something that proved it wasn't her. Then he could leave without having to check.

"What's the matter, Dr. Ando?" Nakayama grinned. "Are you more interested now that you know she's a knockout?"

"No, it's not that," said Ando, refusing to play along. "There's just something that bothers me about it." Seeing his expression, Nakayama quickly wiped the leer off his face.

"Now that you mention it, there was something strange about her. Dr. Nakayama should hear this, too."

"What's that?"

"She wasn't wearing any underwear."

"Really? Top or bottom?"

"She was wearing a bra, but no panties."

"Were her clothes in disarray when she was found?"

Ando and Nakayama were both thinking the same thing: maybe she'd been raped on the rooftop, and then thrown down the exhaust shaft.

"No disturbance of her clothes, and at least on visual inspection, no evidence of rape."

"What was she wearing?"

"A thick jumper, knee socks, blouse, sweatshirt. A normal outfit. You might even say conservative."

But she hadn't been wearing panties. November, and she was wearing a skirt and no panties. Was that normal for her?

"Excuse me, but I'm not sure exactly what you mean when you say she was found in an exhaust shaft on a roof," Ando said. He was having trouble imagining the scene.

"We're talking a shaft about ten feet deep and about three feet wide, next to the machine rooms on the roof. It's usually covered with wire mesh, but it'd been partially removed."

"Enough for her to fall through."

"Probably."

"Is it the kind of place you just trip and fall into?"

"No. It's not easy even to get close to. First of all, the door from the elevator hall to the roof is locked."

"So how did she get there?"

"There's a ladder up to the roof from the top of the fire escape. It's built into the outside wall. We think she went up that. It's the only way she could have gotten up there."

Ando didn't see what she could have been doing up there.

"About the underwear. Do you think she could have taken it off herself, intentionally, inside the exhaust shaft?" The shaft was three yards deep. If she'd fallen, she would have hurt herself. Maybe she'd taken off her panties to use as a bandage. Or maybe she thought she could somehow use them to help her escape.

"We looked for them. In the shaft, and all over the roof. And then, just to be sure, we checked around the perimeter of the building, too."

"Why the perimeter?" Nakayama interjected.

"We thought maybe she'd wrapped them around a piece of metal or something and tossed them. Inside the shaft, there was no chance anybody'd be able to hear her cries for help. The only way to let the outside world know where she was would have been to throw something down that might catch people's attention. But that turned out to be impossible, too."

"And why's that?"

"From the bottom of that shaft, there was no way she could've thrown anything past the fence on the roof."

Assuming it had something to do with the angle, Ando didn't press the point further.

"So, it's most natural to assume that she wasn't wearing any panties when she left."

"At the moment, that's the only explanation we can think of."

They stopped in front of the autopsy room.

"Would you like to join me, Dr. Ando?" asked Nakayama.

"Maybe just for a little while." It was an honest enough answer. If it wasn't Mai, he'd sigh with relief and leave. And if it was her...he'd probably leave anyway, entrusting the autopsy to Nakayama. In any event, the thing to do now was check to see if it was her.

Beyond the door, he could hear water gushing from the faucet, as usual. As he listened for other sounds, Ando was suddenly overcome with the urge to flee. His stomach churned, and his extremities quivered. He prayed it wasn't her. It was all he could do.

Before Ando was really prepared, Nakayama opened the door and led the way into the autopsy room. The officer was next to enter. Ando did- n't go in, but only peered through the open doorway at the naked, pale corpse on the operating table.

2

He'd had a sneaking suspicion that the day would come, but seeing the young woman's body up close sent a deathly chill through his body nonetheless. Ando finally approached the table in Nakayama and the officer's wake. He looked at the face from every angle, still unwilling to recognize it. There was mud, dried and hardened, in the hair on the back of her head. Her ankle was twisted unnaturally; the skin over it showed the only discoloration on her body. He figured the ankle was broken, or at least badly sprained. No signs that she'd been strangled. In fact, there were no external wounds at all. The body was well past the rigor mortis stage. Over ninety hours had elapsed since death.

Ando knew the healthy glow her flesh had displayed in life. How many times had he fantasized about holding her and feeling that skin against his? Now he'd never have the opportunity. Now she was a wasted, waxen corpse. The woman he'd been about to fall in love with now lay cruelly exposed on the table, changed into this. Ando couldn't bear the reality, and anger welled up in him.

"Goddamnit," he sighed. Nakayama and the officer turned simultaneously to look at him.

The policeman couldn't hide his astonishment. "Do you know her?" Ando gave a barely perceptible nod.

"I'm sorry," Nakayama mumbled, not being able to tell exactly how close Ando had been to the woman.

The policeman spoke next, slowly and deliberately. "Would you know who we should contact?" Behind the polite tone, Ando could hear a hint of expectation. If he knew who she was, it would save the officer from the drudgery of having to identify her.

Wordlessly, Ando took out his planner and paged through it. He was sure he'd written her parents' phone number in it. He found the number, wrote it on another piece of paper, and handed it over. The officer read it back to Ando.

"You're sure about this, then?" The man's tone was almost obsequious.

"I'm sure. It's Mai Takano, alright."

The policeman rushed out of the room to call Mai's parents and notify them of her death. Ando imagined the scene at their house: the phone ringing, her mother picking up the receiver, an ostentatious voice on the other end identifying itself as Officer So-and-so from the police department, then, *Your daughter is dead...* Ando shuddered. He felt sorry for her mother, about to experience that moment. She wouldn't collapse, she wouldn't break down crying. The world around her would simply recede.

He couldn't stand to be in the autopsy room a moment longer. When the scalpel entered Mai's body, the air would be filled with an odor much worse than what greeted them now. And when the organ wall was cut so that the contents of her stomach and intestines could be examined, the stench would be positively horrific. Ando knew how surprisingly long olfactory memories could last, and he didn't want this one. He knew very well that it was the fate of all living beings, no matter how pure and beautiful, to finally leave an unbearable stench. But just this once, he felt like giving in to sentimentality. He wanted to keep his memories of Mai from being sullied by that smell.

He whispered in Nakayama's ear, "I'm going to leave now."

Nakayama gave him a suspicious look. "You don't want to participate, after all?"

"I still have some work I need to finish up in the lab. But I want to hear the details later."

"Understood."

Ando put his hand on Nakayama's shoulder and whispered to him again. "Pay attention to the coronary artery. Make sure you get a tissue sample from it."

Nakayama was puzzled that Ando had a hypothesis regarding the cause of death. "Did she have angina?"

Ando didn't answer. Instead, he squeezed Nakayama's shoulder and, with a look that warned against asking why, said, "Just do it, alright?"

Nakayama nodded twice.

3

Back at the office, Ando pulled out the chair from the desk next to Nakayama's and sat down in it backwards, hugging the backrest. He waited like that for Nakayama to finish his paperwork.

"You seem rather concerned," Nakayama said, looking up from the report he was writing.

"Sort of."

"Want to see the autopsy report?" Nakayama indicated a sheaf of documents in front of Ando.

"No. All I need is a summary."

Nakayama turned to face Ando.

"Let me get right to the point, then. The cause of death was not a heart attack due to blockage of the coronary artery."

So the hypothesis Ando had shared with Nakayama before the autopsy had been wrong. Ando fell silent for a time, wondering how to interpret this. *So Mai didn't watch the video after all? Perhaps, the tumor didn't get big enough to block the flow of blood.*

He decided he needed to check further. "So there was no sarcoma in the coronary artery?"

"None that I could see."

"Are you absolutely sure?"

"Well. I'll have to wait for the tissue sample to come back before I can say for sure."

For the moment, the telltale tumor seemed to be missing from Mai's artery.

"In that case, what killed her?"

"Probably the cold. She was in an extremely weakened state."

"How about injuries?"

"Her left ankle was broken, and she had lacerations on both elbows. Most likely from when she fell. There were particles of concrete ground into the wounds."

So she'd fallen in feet first, broken her ankle, and was unable to get out of there. The shaft was a yard wide and over three deep, too deep for her to escape on her own. She would have been stuck there, with only rainwater to quench her thirst. Even so, she would have survived for several days.

"I wonder how long she was alive in there." It wasn't really a question. He was merely thinking aloud as he imagined her fear and despair at being left all alone at the bottom of a hole on a rooftop.

"I'd estimate about ten days." Her stomach and intestines were empty, and her subcutaneous fat was largely depleted.

"Ten days." Ando took out his planner. Assuming she survived for ten days in the exhaust shaft, and assuming five more for her body to be discovered, she would have vanished on or about the 10th of November. Ando's date with her had been scheduled for the ninth; the fact that she hadn't answered the phone all day that day pushed the date of her disappearance back at least that far. Indeed, her mailbox had contained newspapers going back to the eighth. Which meant that something had happened to her on the eighth or ninth to make her leave her apartment.

Ando marked those two dates on his calendar.

Something had happened to her between the eighth and tenth of November.

He tried to imagine himself in her place. When she was found, she had on a skirt and a sweatshirt. Her attire suggested she'd just stepped out for a moment, maybe for a breath of fresh air. But, strangely, she hadn't been wearing any panties.

He thought again about the things he'd felt when he visited her apartment. They were still vivid in his mind. That had been the 15th of November. If the results of the autopsy were to be believed, at that point she was already trapped on the roof, waiting to be rescued. In other words, she'd been gone from her apartment for several days. Yet, Ando was sure he'd sensed something in the apartment. It should have been empty, but he had definitely felt something that breathed.

"Oh, and..." said Nakayama, holding up an index finger as if he'd just remembered something important.

"What?"

"You were pretty close to her, weren't you, Dr. Ando?"

"I wouldn't say close. I'd only met her twice."

"Oh. When had you last seen her?"

"The end of last month, I guess."

"That would be about three weeks before her death." Nakayama looked as if he were holding back something important. Ando fixed his older colleague with a stare that said, *Come on, say it.*

"She was pregnant, wasn't she?" Nakayama finally blurted out. For a moment, Ando wasn't sure who he was talking about.

"Who was?" he said.

"Mai, of course." Nakayama was keeping a close eye on Ando's confused reaction. "Didn't you know?"

Ando didn't answer.

"You don't mean to tell me you overlooked the obvious signs of a woman nearing term."

"Nearing term?"

Ando could only parrot Nakayama's words. He looked at the ceiling and tried to recall the exact lines of Mai's figure. He'd seen her once in mourning clothes and once in a bright dress. Both outfits had been tight around her waist and hips, showing off her slim contours. Her wasp waist had been one of her most attractive features. But it wasn't just that. Ando had sensed something virginal about her. And now Nakayama was trying to tell him she'd been pregnant? Nearing term, in fact?

Not that he'd ever observed her that closely. In fact, the more he thought about her the blurrier his image of her became. His memory was hazy. But no, it couldn't be. There was no way she'd been nine months pregnant. For one thing, he'd seen her corpse with his own eyes. Her belly had been so flat it almost touched her spine.

"She couldn't have been nearing term."

"Some women are like that, though. They don't get very big even in the last trimester."

"It's not a question of degrees, though. I saw her dead body myself."

"You misunderstand," Nakayama said, waving his hands. Then he carefully arrayed the evidence before Ando.

"The uterus was greatly enlarged and she had wounds where the placenta had been torn away. The vagina was full of a brownish secretion. And inside the vagina I found tiny pieces of flesh that I believe are from an umbilical cord."

You're out of your mind, thought Ando. But he couldn't imagine an experienced forensic surgeon like Nakayama making such an elementary mistake. Those three pieces of evidence presented by Mai's body could only lead to one conclusion: she'd given birth shortly before falling into the shaft.

Assuming the delivery was fact, could it explain her movements? Perhaps, on or about the seventh, she had gone into labor, and had accordingly headed for an obstetrician. She'd given birth, spent five or six days in the hospital, and then checked out on the twelfth or thirteenth. Maybe the baby had been stillborn. In her grief, the mother had wandered about until she found herself on the roof of the building, where she'd fallen into the exhaust shaft. She'd survived for ten days. And then this morning, her body had been discovered.

It worked out, time-wise. The birth offered a plausible explanation for her disappearance. And naturally she would have kept it all secret from her mother.

But Ando didn't buy it. Leaving aside the fact that, even allowing for individual variation, she just hadn't looked pregnant, he couldn't forget the impression their first encounter had made on him.

He'd first laid eyes on Mai right in the same office. Just before he was to dissect Ryuji, she'd been escorted in by a detective who wanted her to tell Ando all she knew about the circumstances of Ryuji's death. She had tried to sit down, then lost balance and steadied herself with a hand on a nearby desk. Ando had known at a glance that she was anemic. He had picked up the faint scent of blood on her and deduced that her anemia was due to her menstruating. His conclusion had been bolstered by her embarrassed expression as she apologized: "Sorry, it's just that..." Their eyes had met, and they'd had a moment of nonverbal communication.

Please don't worry. It's just the monthly thing.
Gotcha.

Mai had informed him only with her eyes, afraid to create a fuss given the location. The memory of how she'd made her meaning clear without words was still strangely vivid for Ando. He'd performed Ryuji's autopsy on the twentieth of the previous month. That meant Mai, who supposedly gave birth, had been menstruating less than a month before giving birth. It was impossible, of course.

Maybe I misunderstood the whole thing. All along I thought there'd been a silent exchange, but maybe I was fooling myself. Maybe I got it all wrong. But the more he thought about it, the less he was able to believe it. He was confident he'd taken her meaning.

However, the facts revealed by the autopsy flatly contradicted his view of the matter.

Ando stood up and said, pointing to the autopsy report, "Would you mind if I made a copy of this?" He wanted to take it home and read it carefully.

Nakayama held the stack of papers out to him. "Go right ahead."

"Oh, and one more thing," Ando added. "You took a blood sample, I assume?"

"Of course."

"Can I have a little of it?"

"A little, sure."

Ando realized that he had to confirm immediately whether or not Mai had been carrying the smallpox-like virus. If he found it in her blood, it would be proof that she'd watched the video. He needed to determine if the tragedy that had befallen her had its source in the video or was the result of something entirely unrelated. At the moment, all he could do was to amass data, little by little. If he could illuminate the video's role in this, perhaps he'd come one step closer to solving that "mutation" riddle.

4

Soon after he'd encountered Mai's corpse, Ando was notified of the death of Kazuyuki Asakawa. As Asakawa's condition had deteriorated, he'd been transferred from Shinagawa Saisei Hospital to Shuwa University Hospital, but he'd died almost immediately. Ando had been notified about the change in Asakawa's condition, but he hadn't imagined the patient would go so quickly. According to the attending physician, the death came about as the result of an infection, and the patient had passed away peacefully, as if from old age. Asakawa had never regained consciousness after losing it in the accident.

Ando went to the Shuwa hospital and told the doctors in charge of the case to look out for something during the autopsy: a sarcoma blocking the coronary artery, a smallpox-like virus in the tumor. Ando figured these points were crucial in terms of forecasting the future. He made sure the attending physician understood the importance of the situation and then left.

As he walked back to the station, he felt renewed disappointment that Asakawa had never awoken. He'd possessed essential information, and he'd died having imparted it to no one. If only Ando knew what Asakawa knew, he'd have a much better idea what to expect. The future was maddeningly opaque now. Ando didn't know what to prepare for.

The biggest thing worrying Ando right now was whether Asakawa's death had been bad luck or a necessary outcome. The same question applied to Mai, for that matter. Both of them had wasted away and died after accidents—a traffic accident in Asakawa's case, a fall in Mai's. Their deaths seemed to have something in common. But Ando had no way of knowing if it had anything to do with their having watched the video.

As he walked, he suddenly realized that the building where Mai's body had been found was not far from the hospital he'd just left. He'd been wondering why she had chosen to climb to the roof of a shabby old office building; now was his chance to have a look and maybe find out. He needed to go soon, before any of the evidence disappeared.

He decided to go back to Nakahara Street and catch a cab. He'd be there in ten minutes.

After stopping once on the way to buy some flowers, Ando had the taxi let him off in front of a warehouse belonging to a shipping company. All he'd been told at the M.E.'s office was the name of the company and the instruction that the building was to be found to the south of the warehouse; he didn't know the name of the building itself.

Standing on the sidewalk, he stared south at a building. There was no mistaking it. It had fourteen stories, and an exposed staircase spiraled up the narrow space between its outer wall and the warehouse.

Ando moved toward the front door and then stopped. He walked around to the outside staircase. He thought he'd try to figure out how Mai had gone up. She could have taken the elevator to the fourteenth floor, gone out to the fire escape landing from there, and climbed the ladder to the roof, or she could have taken the fire escape stairs all the way up from the street to the ladder. At night, the front door was probably locked and protected by a metal shutter, so she'd have had to go in through the service entrance, which was surely guarded. And if it was too late, even the service entrance might have been locked, the guard gone. If she'd gone up at night, she must have used the fire escape.

But there was a gate at the edge of the second-floor landing, and it looked impassable. Ando climbed up to it to take a look. It was an iron gate, with a knob. He tried to turn it; it wouldn't budge. It had to be locked from the other side to prevent entry. The gate, however, was only six feet high or so, and a light and agile person could scale it without much problem. Mai had been on the track team in junior high; she'd have been able to get over it with little trouble.

Next to him on the landing was a door leading into the building. He tried turning the knob, but, unsurprisingly, this door too was locked. He wondered what time of day Mai had come here. If it had been daytime, she probably would have taken the elevator to the fourteenth floor. If it was night then she must have climbed over the gate and taken the stairs.

Ando returned to the front door of the building, entered, and went to the elevators. There were two of them, and both were waiting at the ground floor. Each floor of the building seemed to be occupied by a different business or businesses, whose names were all written, floor by floor, on a board by the elevators. But nearly half of them had been crossed out. They must have moved without the landlord being able to find new tenants to take their places. The building was quiet and felt rather abandoned.

On the fourteenth floor he stepped off the elevator into a dark hall-way, where he started looking for stairs to the roof. After walking the length of the hall once, he hadn't found anything. Mai would have had to go outside. Indeed, there was a door at the end of the hall, and Ando opened it and stepped outside. The wind off the ocean was so strong that he had to turn up the collar of his coat. It was only here, on the top floor, that he realized how close Tokyo Bay was. There was the Keihin Canal, beyond it Oi Pier, and then finally the Tokyo Harbor Tunnel, which was quickly swallowed up by the sea. From his vantage point, the two black holes of the tunnel entrance looked unnatural. He thought they looked like the nostrils of a drowned man floating face-up in the water.

From here, he also realized why the fourteenth floor had seemed so cramped despite the size of the building. The architects had made the square footage of this story about half that of the other floors, using the rest of the space for the outdoor balcony that encircled the building on all four sides. Stepping out, Ando saw that the landing for the fire escape was actually a corner of this balcony. But Mai's body had been found yet another level up.

Right next to the door there was a ladder built right into the wall, leading up. It looked to be about ten feet to the top.

Trying to imagine what Mai could have been feeling, Ando put the flowers in his mouth, grasped a rung on the ladder, and started climbing.

What made her want to come up here anyway? wondered Ando, as he pulled himself up rung by rung. It wasn't because she wanted to jump. That was clear enough from the way the building had been designed. A jump from the roof would only have landed her a dozen feet below on the balcony. To fall to the ground, she'd have had to leap from the fire escape landing on the fourteenth floor instead.

It wasn't the kind of roof you went up to for the view, either. The water-resistant paint was peeling and cracking, and it gave way unpleas-antly under his feet as he walked across it. There was no railing around the perimeter, and he wasn't going near the edge even if there was a bal-cony not far below.

There were concrete protrusions lined up at regular intervals, and they were shaped like the tetrapods used as breakwaters on beaches. Ando had no idea what they were for, but they were just the right height for him to sit on. Instead of going to the edge of the roof, he climbed up on top of one and had a look around. It was just before five o'clock, and it was the time of year when the sun set earliest. Lights had come on already in the surrounding buildings and the shops down below. Across the canal he could see a red Keihin Express train going by on the elevated tracks. It was actually an express train; it sped past the station platform that seemed to hover in the air. He knew that platform. He'd been on it a couple of times to visit Mai's apartment. Swathed in a diffuse white light, it was relatively empty for the time of day.

Using the station as a reference point, he tried to locate Mai's apartment. He found it only about four hundred yards away as the crow flies; it was right in front of his nose, so to speak. His gaze followed a path along the shopping street, turning right on the Shore Road. Another hundred yards brought him back to the building where he now stood.

Why this roof? There were any number of other tall buildings in the neighborhood. In fact, she could have gone up to the roof of the very building she lived in. He looked around until he found it again. Perhaps because the rooms were all low-ceilinged studio apartments, the seven-storied building was less than half the height of the one atop which Ando now stood. Still, Mai's had a flat space on the roof where one could walk around. At the same time, it was right on the shopping street, so it was surrounded by tall buildings. In particular, there was a nine-story commercial building on its west side from which the roof was easily observed. That was what distinguished the building Ando was on now. Located on a stretch of the Shore Road full of warehouses, there weren't many tall buildings in its immediate environs. No fear that someone might be looking down on you from above.

Ando descended from the concrete protrusion and went to stand between two equipment houses that jutted upward. One was for elevator machinery, while the other seemed to house a ventilation system. There was a large water tank on top of the southern machine house.

Between them was a deep groove that functioned as an exhaust shaft. Walking carefully, testing each step, Ando progressed until he stood right by it. It was cordoned off with a steel mesh, but this had holes in it. The maintenance crew must have decided to ignore the holes on the assumption that nobody but them ever came up here. Ando couldn't bring himself to step any closer. Just one foot on the lip of that dark rectangular crevice and already he felt he'd be sucked in. But he leaned forward and, with trepidation, tossed the bouquet he was holding through one of the holes in the meshing. He pressed his palms together and prayed for her eternal repose. If a technician hadn't come up here to inspect the elevator the day before, Mai would have lain undiscovered for even longer.

Night came quickly. The rooftop was veiled in darkness now, and the ocean breeze swirled in the narrow space Ando occupied, surrounded by concrete on three sides. He shivered. He ought to have come earlier in the day, when the sun would have been directly overhead. Yet, he knew he wouldn't have the courage, even in broad daylight, to peer into the shaft, this hole which had had a dead body in it until just the day before. And it wasn't just the thought of the corpse that was covering him in goosebumps. The idea of awaiting death down in that hemmed-in place filled him with terror. How many days had Mai spent down there, having twisted her ankle in the fall and unable to stand, staring at the small slice of sky just three yards above her, gradually losing hope, until she died? It must have felt like being sealed alive in a coffin floating in the air. Ando felt short of breath. The situation was too unnatural to call it an accident.

From inside one of the machine houses he heard a groan that sounded like cable being reeled in by a winch. One of the elevators was apparently on the move. Ando began taking small steps backward to get out from between the machine houses. Their walls were rough and blackened in places, with the paint chipping off, testifying to how seldom people came here.

He got away as fast as he could, rushing to the ladder and climbing down to the balcony of the fourteenth floor. The bottom rung was three feet above the surface, so he had to jump. Ando missed his footing on the landing. The back of his leg went momentarily numb; he crouched over and found himself at eye level with the bottom rung of the rusty ladder.

He went back inside and headed for the elevators. One of them was slowly making its way upward. He pushed the button for that elevator and waited in front of it.

As he waited, he tried to figure out why Mai had gone up to the roof of this building. He considered the possibility that she was being pursued. The warehouse district would be mostly deserted at night, and perhaps, walking along, she realized she was being stalked. She saw those stairs outside, with the iron gate. Judging that she could climb it but not the stranger, she might indeed have gone for them. Perhaps the person managed to scale the gate after all, and Mai had no place to go but up. Her first mistake, as it were, put her in a cul-de-sac. The ladder leading to the roof would have been her last lifeline. The bottom rung was a yard off the floor. Hoping that her assailant would give up at last, Mai had climbed to the roof. Well? Had the stranger been able to follow her up? Ando tried to imagine what sort of person would have a hard time with a ladder, set perpendicular to the ground, and the image that came to his mind was of some four-footed beast.

The elevator doors opened as the thought occurred to him. The elevator was not empty. Ando had been staring at his toes; he raised his eyes to meet those of a young woman. She stared at him as if she'd been lying in wait for him. There could be no mistake, he'd encountered this woman before, under similar circumstances. She was the one who had come out of Mai's room and shared an elevator with him. The cracked nails, and that odor, the likes of which he'd never smelled before—he couldn't forget her if he tried.

Now he stood directly in front of her, facing her, and he couldn't move a muscle. He was confused. His mind couldn't process what he was seeing and his body escaped his command.

Why. Is. She. Here? Ando flailed about for a reason, which he was doomed not to find. The absence of any conceivable reason was what truly frightened him. As long as an explanation could be come up with, terror could be dispelled.

As they stared at each other, the elevator doors started to close between them. The woman reached out a hand and held them open. The motion was smooth, dexterous. She wore a blue polka-dot skirt, beneath which he could see her legs, bare, unstockinged despite the early winter weather. It was with her right hand that she had stopped the doors; in her other was a small bouquet of flowers.

Flowers! Ando's sight rested on the bouquet.

"I've seen you before, haven't I?" She had spoken first, and her voice drew him in. It was deeper than her willowy proportions had led him to expect.

Ando's mouth hung open until he finally managed to dredge some words out of the parched depths of his throat. "Are you Mai's sister?"

That was what he wanted her to be. If that was who she was, it made sense: her emerging from Mai's room, her coming to this building with a bouquet. Everything would stand to be explained.

The woman made a slight, indecipherable movement with her head. It wasn't quite a nod, nor quite a shake. It could have been affirmation or denial, but Ando decided she'd intended a yes.

She's Mai's older sister, come to leave flowers on the roof of the building where her sister died. It was most natural, quite fitting. People only ever believe what they can understand.

The moment he got that straight, all of his previous cowering struck him as funny. What had he been so afraid of? He couldn't make sense of his own psychology. The first time he'd met her, this woman had given him a strong otherworldly impression. But now that the riddle was solved, that impression faded away like a lie, while her beauty alone came to dominate his view of her. Her long, slender nose, the gentle, round line of her cheeks, her ever-so-slightly slanted eyes with their heavy eyelids. They didn't stare directly at him; rather, they seemed intentionally unfocussed. Within them lurked a seductive glow.

Those eyes. When he'd encountered her the other day at Mai's apartment, she'd been wearing sunglasses. This was the first time he'd been able to see her eyes. Their gaze, full upon him, exerted a strong gravitational pull. He found it hard to breathe, and his chest pounded.

"Excuse me, but..." From the tone of her voice and her expression it was clear that she wanted to know his relationship with Mai.

"My name is Ando. Fukuzawa University Medical School." He knew this didn't exactly answer her question.

The woman stepped out of the elevator and, still holding the door open, motioned him in with her eyes. He had to obey. Her elegant movements left him powerless to refuse. As though enchanted, Ando entered the elevator in her place. They stared at each other again from their reversed positions.

"I'll call on you soon with a request."

She said this just before the door closed. Ando heard her clearly and there was no mistaking her words. The doors as they closed were like a camera shutter, removing her from his field of vision but leaving her image imprinted on Ando's brain.

As the elevator descended slowly, Ando found himself overcome with uncontrollable lust. Mai had been the object of the first sexual fantasies he'd had since his family had ceased to be, but this was far more intense. He'd only been with the woman for a few seconds, and yet he could remember every detail of her body, from the curve of her ankles, bare above her pumps, to the corners of her eyes. And his image of her remained sharp, even as the moments passed. Flustered by the sudden flood of sexual desire, Ando rushed out of the building, hailed a taxi, and hurried home.

In the cab, he thought about the last words she'd said.

I'll call on you soon with a request.

What was her request? Where did she mean to "call on" him? Was that supposed to be some sort of social pleasantry?

He'd rushed out of the building and into a taxi as if pursued by her gaze. He regretted not asking her for her name and number at least. Why hadn't he? He ought to have waited for her to come down from the roof. But he hadn't. Or rather, he couldn't. It was as though his every movement had been controlled by that woman. He had acted against his will.

5

A week had passed since Mai's autopsy. It was December, and the weather had suddenly turned wintry. Ando had never liked winter—he much preferred late spring to early summer—but ever since the death of his son he'd stopped paying much attention to the changing seasons. The morning's drastic chill had forced him, nonetheless, to recognize the advent of winter. On the way to the university he'd stopped in his tracks several times to go back and get a sweater, but in the end he'd simply continued on his way. He didn't feel like going all the way back, and the walking was warming him up.

His apartment in Sangubashi was close enough to the university that he could walk to work if he felt like it. And though he usually went by train, the transfer he had to make despite the short distance never went smoothly. As a result, and because he knew he needed the exercise, Ando sometimes ended up half-walking, half-jogging to and from work. The day had started out as one of those days, but halfway to campus he changed his mind and caught the JR train at Yoyogi Station. He wanted to get to the university sooner than later.

With just two stations to go, he didn't have the time to organize his thoughts in the rocking cradle of the train carriage. This morning he was supposed to look at samples of Mai's cells and Ryuji's through the electron microscope. Miyashita was going to be there, as well as Nemoto, an electron microscopy expert. The thought of what lay ahead made Ando want to hurry.

Up until then, the smallpox-like virus hadn't been found in anybody who hadn't watched the video. There had been no reports of the virus being spread by physical contact. In Mai's room he'd found a copy of the video, already erased. These two facts meant that if Mai's blood cells revealed the presence of the virus, it would be safe to conclude that she had actually watched the tape. The calamity that had befallen her would have been the video's doing.

He was so deep in thought that he almost missed his station, but he managed to jump off the train just before the doors closed. He allowed himself to be swept along with the rest of the crowd toward the ticket gates. The university hospital stood in all its grandeur right outside the station.

Ando poked his head into the lab, and Miyashita turned his ruddy face toward him.

"Finally he shows up!"

Miyashita and Nemoto had spent the previous week making preparations for today's session with the electron microscope. A virus wasn't something one could just pop into a microscope and take a gander at when the mood struck. There were a lot of things that had to be done first, applying a centrifuge, cell sectioning, and so on. The procedure was beyond the pale of a non-specialist like Ando. Given all the preparation it took, Miyashita could hardly wait for the moment. He'd been up since early morning getting ready.

"Lower the lights," Nemoto said.

"Yessum!" replied Miyashita, who quickly turned them off. Although they'd completed the base sequencing some time ago, this was their first chance to see the virus directly, with their own eyes. The virus that had been found in the blood of Ryuji and Mai.

Nemoto went into the darkroom alone and fixed the ultrathin section on the holder. Ando and Miyashita sat in front of the console, staring at the screen in utter silence. Though it was still blank, both men's eyes were active as they chased mental images of what they would soon be seeing.

Nemoto came back and turned off the last overhead light. All set. Holding their breath, the three men watched the screen. Gradually, as the ultrathin section of cellular matter was illuminated by an electron beam, a microscopic world began to open up before them.

"Which one are we looking at?" Miyashita asked Nemoto.

"This is Takayama's."

The green pattern on the screen before them was a universe unto itself. A twist of a dial sent their field of view racing across the surface of the cells. Somewhere in there lurked the virus.

"Try increasing the magnification," Miyashita instructed. Nemoto responded immediately, taking the machine up to x9000. Another pass over the surface gave them a clear view of the dying cells. The cytoplasm gleamed brightly, while the organelles had collapsed into black clumps.

"Home in on the cytoplasm on the top right and increase the magnification." As he spoke, Miyashita's face caught the reflection of the dying cells' mottled appearance and had the dull glow of a bronze bust. Nemoto increased the magnification to x16000.

"More."

x21000.

"There. Stop." Miyashita's voice rose, and he shot a glance at Ando, who leaned forward so that his face was right near the screen.

There they were...swarms of them!

The strands writhed around in the dying cells like so many snakes, biting and clinging to the surface of the chromatin.

A chill ran down Ando's spine. This was a new virus, the likes of which had never been seen before. He'd never seen the smallpox virus through an electron microscope, yet he did know it from medical textbooks. The differences between that and this were obvious at a glance.

"Oh my God."

Miyashita sat there sighing, his mouth hanging open.

Ando understood the workings of the virus: how it was carried along inside the blood vessels to the coronary artery, where it affixed itself to the inner wall of the anterior descending branch and caused mutations in the cells of that area until they formed a tumor. What he couldn't understand was how this virus he was looking at now could have been created via the victim's consciousness. This virus didn't invade the body from outside. Rather, it was born within the body as a result of watching a videotape; it was a function of the mind. That went beyond mysterious and Ando was dumbfounded. It represented a leap from nothingness to being, from concept to matter. In all earth's history such a thing happened only once, when life first came to be.

Does it mean, then, that life emerged due to the workings of some consciousness?

Ando's thoughts were veering off track. Miyashita brought him back with his next comment.

"'Ring,' anyone?"

Ando returned his gaze to the electron microscope screen. It didn't take long to figure out Miyashita's remark; he was angling for something with which to compare the shape of the virus. Some specimens were twisted and some were u-shaped, but most of them looked like a slight-

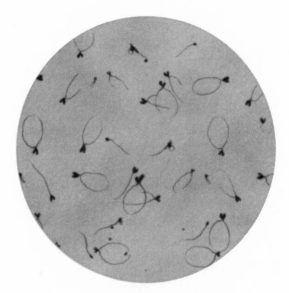

The ring virus (21000x)

ly distorted ring, the kind one wears on a finger. "Ring" hit the nail on the head. There was even a protrusion at one point that resembled nothing so much as a stone on a setting. The screen looked like a view of a floor across which tangled-up rings and snakes and rubber bands had been strewn indiscriminately.

It fell to Ando and Miyashita, who discovered it, to name this strange new virus, and Miyashita's comment was by way of a suggestion. The ring virus.

"How about it?"

Miyashita wanted Ando's opinion. The name was perfect, but Ando felt uneasy for precisely that reason. It was too perfect and made him wonder if a God-like being were making itself felt. How did all this begin? Ando had no trouble remembering: it was with the numbers on the newspaper that had been sticking out of Ryuji's sutures. *178, 136.* They'd given him the English word "ring." Then he'd found that astonishing report, and it was entitled *Ring*. And now, this, which he beheld—a virus shaped like a ring. It was as if some will, changing form with each rebirth as it strove to grow into something ever larger, had chosen this shape as its symbol.

The microscopic universe contained kinds of beauty that came from cyclic repetition, but what Ando saw now was an ugliness that mirrored such beauty. And it wasn't just the abstract knowledge that this virus brought evil to humanity that made it appear ugly to Ando. What he felt was closer to an instinctive hatred of serpentine creatures. Any human being shown the image, with absolutely no prior knowledge, would probably react with revulsion.

As if to prove this, Nemoto, who had little idea of the origin of the virus, was visibly shaken. His hands on the controls trembled. Only the machine remained unaffected, emotionlessly spitting out negatives. Once he'd taken seven photographs, Nemoto gathered them up and went to the darkroom. While he waited for them to develop, he set the ultrathin section from Mai's blood cells in the holder. Then he resumed his place in front of the console and flipped the switch without ado.

"Next we'll be looking at Takano's."

They gradually increased the magnification, just as they'd done with Ryuji's sample. They had no trouble finding what they were looking for. Without question, it was the same virus. They were writhing just like the other ones.

"Identical," Ando and Miyashita stated at the same time. Neither of them could see anything to prevent them from reaching that conclusion. But Nemoto, the electron microscopy expert, was more sensitive to minor inconsistencies.

"That's strange."

Miyashita watched him tilt his head and stroke his chin, then asked, "What is?"

"I'd rather not say anything until I get a chance to compare the photographs."

Ever cautious in all things, Nemoto hesitated to draw a conclusion based solely on his impressions of Ryuji's virus. Science was about proof, not impressions, was his motto. That aside, Nemoto could swear he saw a quantitative difference. It wasn't a variation in the overall number of specimens of the virus present in each sample. What struck him was that, in Mai's sample, there were more broken rings. In Ryuji's sample, too, of course, some of the virus specimens had come undone, making

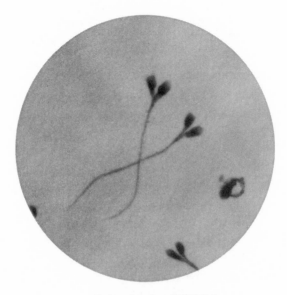

Broken ring virus (100000x)

u-shapes, or snake coils, but most of them were whole and looked like rings. In Mai's case, more of the rings were broken, and stretched out like threads.

In order to confirm his suspicions, Nemoto homed in on a likely-looking specimen and adjusted the focus until the specimen filled the screen. If the normal virus looked like a ring, then this specimen looked like a ring which had broken just on one side of the stone. The "stone" and its "setting" now looked like a head with a flagellum wiggling behind it.

The result was a shape that Ando, Miyashita, and Nemoto were quite familiar with. All three men were reminded of the same thing at the same time, but none dared say it.

6

Nemoto's first impression was borne out when he compared the photos he'd taken of the ring virus. In any given area of Mai's sample, there were more virus specimens that looked like broken rings or threads than in a comparable area of Ryuji's sample. Statistically speaking, roughly one in ten of Ryuji's viruses were broken, while in Mai's case, the distribution was around fifty percent. Such a manifest difference was unlikely to occur without a reason. Ando requested that samples from all the videotape's victims be put under the electron microscope.

It wasn't until the Friday after the New Year's holiday that all the results were in.

Glancing out the window in the lab, he could see that some of the previous night's snowfall still lingered among the dead trees of the Outer Gardens of Meiji Shrine. When he grew tired of analyzing the photos, Ando went to the windowsill to feast his eyes on the scene outside the window. Miyashita never rested though, carefully comparing the photos spread out on the desktop.

Including Asakawa and Mai, eleven people had died after coming into contact with the video. The same virus had been found in each victim's blood, and there was no more doubt the virus had been the cause of death. But regarding broken rings, the victims fell into two groups. In Mai's case and Asakawa's, broken rings made up fully half of what was found in their blood, while in everybody else's samples, only one specimen in ten was broken. It was not a particularly surprising result. It seemed that the fate of the infected person hinged on the degree of presence of the broken-ring virus.

The statistics indicated that once the broken-ring specimens exceeded a certain percentage, the host was spared death by cardiac arrest, though it wasn't clear yet exactly what that percentage was.

Mai and Asakawa had watched the video. The ring virus had appeared in their bodies. Up to that point, they were no different from the nine other victims. But something had caused some of the viruses to come apart into a thread shape, and the broken particles had surpassed a certain level. And that was why, even though they had watched the

Evolving

video, neither Mai nor Asakawa had died of a heart attack. The question was, what had caused the viruses in their bloodstreams to come apart? What set them apart from the other nine?

"Some form of immunity?" Ando wondered aloud.

"That's a possibility," Miyashita said, cocking his head.

"Or maybe..." Ando trailed off.

"Maybe what?"

"Is it something about the virus itself?"

"I lean more in that direction personally," said Miyashita, propping his feet on the chair in front of him and sticking out his great belly. "Thanks to the mischief of the four kids who watched it first, the video was doomed to extinction in the not-too-distant future. To find a way out, the virus had to mutate. All of this is just as Ryuji told us in his message. Now, then: how exactly did it mutate, and what did it evolve into? The answer to that, I believe, lies in the ring virus that Mai Takano and Kazuyuki Asakawa carried. In its irregular shape, to be precise."

"A virus borrows its host's cells in order to reproduce itself, by definition."

"Right."

"And sometimes that reproduction takes place at an explosive rate."

This, too, was common knowledge. One only had to think of the Black Death that ran rampant in the Middle Ages, or the Spanish influenza of modern times, to find examples of a virus proliferating wildly.

"So?" Miyashita urged Ando to continue.

"So think about it. The video tells people, 'Make a copy within a week or you die.' Even if the viewer did so, that's just one tape turning into two. That's a pretty slow growth rate. Assuming the subsequent viewers repeat the process, that's still only four tapes after a month."

"You've got a point, I guess."

"That's nothing to be scared of."

"It's not very virus-like, you mean. Right?"

"If it doesn't increase at a geometric rate, then it's hardly spreading at all."

Miyashita fixed Ando with a glare. "What exactly is it you're trying to get at?"

"It's just that..."

Ando wasn't sure himself what he wanted to say. Was he trying to put a worse spin on things? Certainly there were cases when a single virus spread virtually overnight to thousands, tens of thousands of victims. That was the raison d'être of a virus, to replicate itself simultaneously in large numbers. Having copies made of a videotape, one at a time, was simply too inefficient. The results said as much; only three months after its birth, the tape was now extinct. Unless it had been reborn through mutation...

"It's just that I have a bad feeling about this."

Ando looked again at the photos of the ring virus. Vast numbers of them, piled up on one another. When several specimens overlapped, they looked like unspooled, tangled-up videotape. The psychic Sadako Yamamura, on the brink of death, had converted information into images, leaving some sort of energy at the bottom of that well. The video had been born as a result of the detonation of that energy. It wasn't matter that was spreading, but information, as recorded on videotape and DNA.

He couldn't shake the suspicion that some terrible mutation was taking place somewhere he wasn't aware of. Ando had visited Mai's apartment, and he'd also been to the rooftop exhaust shaft into which she'd fallen. He'd sensed the strangeness of her room and had felt the weirdness of that roof underfoot. Maybe that was why he sensed danger bearing down on him more than Miyashita seemed to. He could almost hear the writhing, of something, accelerate under the earth.

"Do you sense some catastrophe?" Miyashita still sounded pretty relaxed.

"It's just that it's all so grotesque."

Ever since Ryuji's autopsy, Ando had been plunged into the world of the bizarre. Concrete felt soft and clingy under his footsteps, the scent of life pervaded an uninhabited room. One inexplicable phenomenon after another. And then there was the thing Mai had given birth to; the very thought made him shudder. Mai had been dead for a month and a half, and they still had no clue concerning whatever it was she had delivered. Ando doubted that what she'd had was just a cute little baby.

"Don't be so gloomy. Even if it did manage to mutate, there's no guarantee that it succeeded in adapting to the environment."

"So you think the mutated virus might be extinct, too?"

"We can't rule out the possibility."

"Ever the optimist."

"Recall the Spanish influenza virus, the one that swept the world in 1918. They found the same virus in America in 1977, but nobody died then. The first time around it slaughtered between twenty to forty *million* people worldwide, and sixty years later, it was basically harmless."

"I guess a virus can weaken through mutation."

It was true that since the discovery of Mai's body, no more suspicious deaths had come to light. He'd kept a close watch on the papers and worked his contacts in the police department, but so far the net had come up empty. It was possible that Miyashita was right and that the newly reborn, mutated virus had failed to adapt to its environment in the short period it had to do so, and had lost its ability to spread. Maybe it was extinct.

"Any idea what we should do next?" asked Miyashita, kicking the floor and twirling in his chair.

"Well, there's one thing I've let slip."

"What's that?"

"When and where did Mai get her hands on the videotape?"

"Does it matter?"

"It bothers me. I want to nail down the date."

Ando felt he should have checked on this. He'd been too busy analyzing the virus and forgotten. Now, it looked to be the only thing left to do. He was virtually certain that the tape Mai had watched was Ryuji's copy, but he didn't know how or when it had passed into her possession.

7

Finding out proved surprisingly easy.

Assuming that Ryuji's effects, including the tape, had been shipped to his parents' house within two or three days after his demise, Mai could only have obtained it there. So Ando called Ryuji's family.

When Ryuji's mother heard that Ando was an old college friend of her son's, she suddenly became very friendly. Ando asked whether or not a woman named Mai Takano had called on her.

"Yes," the woman replied. She was even able to ascertain the date by looking at a receipt in her household-finance ledger. She'd bought a shortcake to offer Mai. November 1, 1990. Ando jotted down the date.

"By the way, why exactly did Mai visit you?"

Ryuji's mother explained that Mai had been helping Ryuji with a work he'd been serializing by making clean copies of each installment, and that a page had been found missing.

"So she visited your house to look for the missing page, is that it?"

Ando jotted down the name and publisher of the magazine that had been running the series.

And then he hung up. He didn't want to be asked how Mai was doing these days. If he told Ryuji's mother that Mai was dead, he'd be sure to face a barrage of questions, and he simply didn't have the kind of answers that would satisfy her.

Ando sat there with his hand on the receiver long after he'd broken the connection.

On November 1st, Mai visited Ryuji's family home. While searching for the missing manuscript page, she found the videotape. She took it home with her. She probably watched it that very day.

He started to put together a hypothesis based on a November 1st starting point. It took a week for the virus to have its full effect. So something should have happened to her on November 8th. Ando's date with her had been for the ninth. He'd called her several times that day, with no answer. It made sense. She'd either been in her room and unable to pick up the phone or already in the exhaust shaft.

He started to calculate backwards. The autopsy had been able to tell them how long she'd been alive in the shaft, and how long she'd been dead before she was discovered. She had died, according to the evidence, on or about the 20th of November, and she had fallen into the shaft about ten days before. It was perfectly in line with these projections to posit that the virus had worked its changes on her on the eighth or ninth, leading to her fall into the shaft. Thus it was probably accurate to assume that she'd watched the video on November 1st.

The next thing Ando did was to head to the periodicals section of the library to look for the magazine that contained Ryuji's articles. He found it. And in the issue dated November 20th, he found the last installment of Ryuji's work, a piece entitled *The Structure of Knowledge*. This told Ando something.

Mai managed to transcribe Ryuji's article and get it to his editor.

This meant that in the time between her watching the video and her death, there was at least one person she'd definitely had contact with.

He put in a call to the editorial office of the monthly that had run the article and made an appointment with the editor in charge of Ryuji's work. Ando decided he needed to visit the publisher himself; something made him want to actually meet the guy, rather than just talk to him over the phone.

He took a JR train to Suidobashi. From there he walked for about five minutes, looking for the address, before he spotted the eleven-story building that housed the offices of Shotoku, Ryuji's publisher. At the reception desk he asked for Kimura, an editor with the monthly *Currents*. Ando looked idly around the lobby as he waited. Kimura sent word that he'd meet him in the reception area right away. Ando was relieved that the editor had readily agreed to receive a total stranger. On the phone he'd sounded like a man in his twenties, but on the ball. Ando found himself imagining a handsome young man in wire-rims.

Instead, he saw a tubby man in check pants and suspenders, whose bald head glistened with sweat in spite of the season. In every way he failed to match Ando's image of an editor at a major publishing house, especially one who worked for a magazine that chronicled the latest developments in contemporary thought.

"Sorry to keep you waiting." The man grinned broadly and offered Ando his business card. Satoshi Kimura, Executive Editor. He looked much older than he sounded. He was probably pushing forty.

Ando produced his own card and said, "Thanks for seeing me. Can I buy you a cup of coffee somewhere?" He meant to leave the building.

"There aren't any decent cafés around here. But we have a lounge, if you don't mind."

"That's fine."

Ando decided to follow Kimura's lead, and together they boarded an elevator.

The lounge was on the top floor of the building, overlooking the garden in the courtyard. It was quite well-appointed; as Ando sank into a sofa, he looked around and spotted faces that he recognized from newspapers and magazines. It seemed the lounge was a popular place for editors to meet with their writers. Several people were there with manuscripts in hand.

"We certainly lost a good man."

At these words, Ando's wandering thoughts snapped back into focus, and he looked at Kimura's oily face directly across the table.

"It so happens that Ryuji Takayama and I were classmates in med school," Ando said, watching for a reaction. He'd lost count of how many people he'd drawn out with this line so far.

"Is that a fact? So you knew Professor Takayama."

Kimura glanced at the business card in his hand and nodded, seemingly reassured of something. The card bore the name of the university Ando worked for. The man had probably recalled that Ryuji had attended that same university's medical department.

"What's more, I performed his autopsy."

Kimura's eyes grew wide. He stuck out his chin and emitted a queer little cry.

"Well, now, that's..."

Kimura lapsed into silence, staring at Ando's hands, which held a coffee cup. He seemed interested in the fingers that had sliced Ryuji open.

"But I didn't come here today to talk about him," Ando said, putting down the coffee cup and bringing his hands together on the table.

"Why have you come?"

"I'd like to ask you a little about one of his students. Mai Takano."

At the mention of her name, Kimura's expression softened, and he leaned forward. "What about her?"

He doesn't know, Ando intuited. But he had to find out sooner or later.

"Are you aware that Mai is dead?"

Kimura let out an even more curious groan and almost jumped out of his chair. It was almost comical how dramatically his features conveyed his emotions; he was the real Man of a Thousand Faces. He ought to audition for a sit com, Ando thought.

"You must be kidding!" Kimura cried. "Mai can't be dead?"

"She fell into an exhaust shaft on a roof last November and died there."

"I guess that explains why I haven't been able to get in touch with her."

Ando felt a certain closeness to the man, who'd been in the same boat. He had no idea if this Kimura was married or not, but he was willing to bet that the guy had had at least a slight crush on Mai.

"Do you remember the last time you saw her?" Ando asked quickly, loathe to give the man any time to wallow in sentiment.

"We were just beginning to proof the New Year's issue, so it must have been the beginning of November."

"Would you happen to know the exact date?"

Kimura took out a datebook for the previous year and started leafing through it.

"November the second."

November 2nd. The day after Mai had visited Ryuji's parents' house and taken the videotape home with her. Mai had probably already watched the tape by then.

"Do you mind if I ask where you met?"

"She called me to say that she'd finished copying the article. I immediately went to pick it up."

"Went where? To her apartment?"

"No, we met at a café in front of her station. Like we always did." Kimura seemed to want to stress that he'd never set foot inside her apartment, knowing she lived alone.

"When you saw her, did she seem different in any way?"

Kimura looked puzzled. He couldn't tell what Ando meant by the question. "What do you mean?"

"Well, unfortunately, there's still some doubt surrounding the cause of her death."

"Doubt, you say?"

Kimura folded his arms and thought for a while. The thought that what he said might influence Mai's autopsy results made him suddenly cautious.

"Any little bit could help. Did you notice anything?"

Ando smiled, trying to put the man at ease.

"Well, she did seem a bit unlike herself that day."

"Can you be more specific?"

"She looked pale. And she held a handkerchief over her mouth, like she was fighting back nausea."

The nausea caught Ando's attention. He remembered the brown clump of what had seemed to be vomit that he'd found on Mai's bathroom floor.

"Did you ask her about her apparent nausea?"

"No. I mean, right away she told me she wasn't feeling well because she'd pulled an all-nighter writing out Professor Takayama's manuscript."

"I see. So she said it was from lack of sleep."

"Yes."

"Did she tell you anything else?"

"I was in a hurry, you see. I thanked her for the manuscript, we had a brief discussion about the book to come, and then I said goodbye."

"Book. You mean Ryuji's."

"Right. From the very beginning we ran the series of articles on the premise that we'd publish them in book form eventually."

"When's this book coming out?"

"It's scheduled to appear in bookstores next month."

"Well, I hope it sells well."

"It's difficult material, and we're not getting our hopes up. I must say, though, that it's a really good book. Just superb."

After that, the conversation got sidetracked into reminiscences of Ryuji, and Ando found it hard to get back on topic. By the time he'd managed to drag Mai back into the discussion so they could talk about her relationship to Ryuji, the hour Kimura had promised Ando was up. Ando hadn't really learned anything of value yet, but he decided he'd best not overstay the editor's welcome. He doubtless needed to see this man again, and he wanted to leave a good impression. So he thanked Kimura and took his leave.

As Ando stood up, he happened to notice three people entering the lounge. There were two men and a woman, and Ando had seen each of them before. The woman was a nonfiction writer who'd vaulted to bestseller status when one of her books had been turned into a movie. Ando had seen her face on TV and in the weekly news magazines several times. One of the men was the director who'd adapted her work to the screen. But the one who really caught Ando by surprise was the fortyish man who came in with the director. The name was on the tip of his tongue. He wracked his brains. The man had to be a writer or something. As they passed, Kimura spoke to the man.

"Hey, Asakawa. Glad to hear it's going forward."

Asakawa.

It was Junichiro Asakawa, Kazuyuki's older brother. Ando had visited him at his apartment in Kanda in November to pick up the *Ring* floppy disk. At the time, Ando had been so happy to get his hands on the disk that he hadn't said more than a perfunctory goodbye. But when he'd sent the disk back later, he'd included a very polite thank-you note.

He also remembered that the business card Junichiro had given him had borne the name of this publishing house. Whether by mere chance or thanks to the connection, Ryuji's book was being published by his best friend's brother's company.

Noticing Ando, Junichiro seemed to flinch slightly in shock.

"Well, nice to see you again..." Ando bowed, thinking to thank the man again for his assistance as well as utter a proper New Year's greeting. But Junichiro averted his eyes and spoke almost before Ando could get a word out.

"Excuse me."

With that he sidestepped Ando and ushered the writer and the director to an empty table. Ando could tell when he was being given the brush-off. He glanced again at Junichiro, now seated at the table, but the man was deep in conversation with the director now and didn't look his way. He was blatantly ignoring Ando.

He searched his memory for an explanation of Junichiro's rude behavior. Ando thought he'd observed the man well enough in their previous contacts. He couldn't remember having done anything to merit this treatment. He didn't get it. Shaking his head at the man's unnatural attitude, Ando followed Kimura out of the lounge.

8

That evening when he got back to his apartment, Ando filled the tub for the first time in ages. While his boy had been alive, they'd taken a bath together every night. Since he'd been on his own, drawing a bath seemed too much trouble, and he'd gotten in the habit of showering instead.

After his bath, Ando took his copies of the photos from the electron microscope and hung them on the wall. He stepped back and had a good look at them.

One wall of his apartment was taken up with bookcases, but the wall over his bed was bare and white, like a screen. He'd hung the photos there like X-rays on a light box, in ascending order of magnification: x17000, x21000, x100000. The photos were of the virus isolated from Mai's blood. Without taking his eyes off them, Ando stood back a few steps. In one area the ring viruses were piled up on top of each other and looked like a spiral staircase. He concentrated, trying to notice something, anything he might have missed before.

He turned off the overhead light and shone a lamp directly on the photos. Under illumination, it looked as though huge specimens of the virus were crawling around on the white wall. He turned the lamp on a x42000 photo showing broken rings that were stretched out like threads. These showed up in great numbers in Asakawa's and Mai's blood, but hardly at all in Ryuji and others. In Mai's case, there were no signs of any narrowing in the internal membrane of the coronary artery. In Asakawa's case, however, the beginning of a lump had been observed. In other words, even Mai and Asakawa showed slightly different symptoms.

Why was her artery undamaged? Ando turned his attention to this problem. The thread-shaped virus he was looking at now had not attacked Mai's coronary artery, the main target in everybody else. Why was she an exception?

Something tugged at his memory. He opened his planner to where he'd jotted down Mai's movements for late October and November and held it under the light. He'd first met her on October 20th at the M.E.'s office, just before Ryuji's autopsy. Mai hadn't looked well that day. Ando had formed a guess as to why: she was menstruating. It was just an intuition, but he was confident.

He returned his gaze to the photos on the wall. He looked at a x100000 shot of the virus in thread form. He tried to remember his first impression upon seeing it at the university.

Hadn't it reminded him of something, with its oval-shaped head and wiggling flagellum? Swarms of them had been swimming around in Mai's veins, but they hadn't attacked her coronary artery.

What did *they attack?*

His head felt hot. A tiny hole slowly opened, letting in light. It was one of those moments when something previously hidden suddenly begins to heave into view. Ando looked at his planner again, at the date on which he supposed Mai had watched the videotape. The evening of November 1st. The twelfth or thirteenth day after her period.

He took one step closer to the wall, and then another. Toward the ring viruses lashing their flagella.

That's it. They look exactly like sperm swimming toward the cervix.

"Sperm?" he said aloud.

She'd have been ovulating that day.

A woman usually ovulates roughly two weeks after her period, and the egg only stays in the oviduct a maximum of twenty-four hours. If Mai had had an egg in her oviduct the night she watched the video...

The ring virus must have abruptly found another outlet and switched its target from her coronary artery to her egg. Gasping for breath, Ando sat down on the edge of the bed. He no longer needed to look at his planner or the photos. It was just possible that Mai had been ovulating when she watched the videotape. It had been her luck—misfortune, rather—to watch it on the one day of the month. And that was why she was the exception. Of all the females who had watched the tape, she'd been the only one ovulating.

And...

When he tried to deduce what must have happened, Ando's spine froze. But he couldn't hinder himself from arriving at the obvious conclusion.

Countless particles of the ring virus would have invaded Mai's egg and been incorporated into its DNA.

They fertilized her egg.

Although it had evolved, the ring virus's basic nature had not changed. In exactly a week, the fertilized egg would have reached its full growth and been expelled from Mai's body. That had to be why the autopsy found evidence that Mai had just given birth.

But what did she give birth to?

Ando was trembling violently now. He was remembering a certain touch on his foot.

Whatever it was...it touched me.

When he'd visited Mai's apartment, her supposedly empty room, he was sure he'd felt the breath of a living being. Hunched over at an unnatural angle to examine her toilet, he'd felt something soft caress his Achilles tendon where his sock had slipped down. He was sure that whatever had touched him was what Mai had given birth to. Something small enough to escape his notice when he looked around. Maybe it was early enough in its growth stage then to hide in her wardrobe. Whatever it was, he could still feel its touch as it swept across his skin.

Ando's shivering didn't stop. Feeling the need for another soak in the tub, he took off his clothes. He hadn't pulled the plug, so the tub was still full of water. He ran the hot water until the bath temperature was higher than it had been for his first soak. After lowering himself into the tub, he poked his foot above the waterline and twisted it so he could see his Achilles tendon. He rubbed it. It felt perfectly normal, but that didn't comfort him any.

He brought his foot back into the water and just sat there hugging his knees. After a while, a question came to him. He now knew why Mai hadn't gotten a heart attack, but what about Asakawa?

"He was male," Ando murmured.

But maybe he'd given birth to something after all.

Perhaps the water was too hot. Ando suddenly felt thirsty.

PART FIVE   *Foreshadowing*

1

January 15th, Coming of Age Day, was a holiday, which made it a three-day weekend. On the first day of the long weekend, Ando got a call from Miyashita asking if he wanted to go for a drive. The invitation was like a port in a storm for Ando, who'd been wondering how he was going to get through three workless days all alone. He wasn't sure if he liked the way Miyashita asked him—like he was hiding something—but Ando had no reason not to go along. He said yes, then asked, "Where are we going?"

"There's something I want to show you," was all Miyashita would say. Ando figured his colleague had his reasons, and so refrained from pressing the matter. He'd get the answer out of Miyashita when he saw him.

Miyashita picked Ando up at home. As soon as he climbed in the car, Ando asked again where they were going.

"I can't tell you. Now stop asking questions."

And so even as they departed, their destination was unknown to Ando.

The car left the No. 3 Tokyo-Yokohama Freeway for the Yokohama New Road. They seemed to be heading for Fujisawa. They couldn't go too far and still expect to keep it a day trip. Maybe as far as Odawara or Hakone, possibly the Izu peninsula, but no farther than Atami or Ito. After several guesses at the destination of the mystery tour, Ando decided to just sit back and enjoy the ride.

Just before they were to merge with traffic, they came to a halt. The entrance to the Yokohama New Road was always jammed, and was especially so today, at the start of the long weekend. In an effort to keep Miyashita from getting too bored at the wheel, Ando decided to tell him the hypothesis he'd come up with a few days ago as to why Mai alone had displayed no abnormalities in her coronary artery. It was Ando's theory that Mai had been ovulating the day she watched the video, and that the ring virus had shifted the focus of its attack to her egg. Then, just before falling into the rooftop exhaust shaft, Mai had given birth to some unknown life form. Something that had only gestated for a week. If she'd just given birth, that explained why Mai hadn't been wearing any panties.

Miyashita heard him out and then was silent for a time. His striking round eyes seemed to be staring straight ahead, but then he changed lanes with an agility that belied his lax expression, poking his way into the passing lane.

"I thought more or less the same thing when we looked at Mai's virus under the electron microscope," said Miyashita, paying no attention to the blaring horns behind him.

"What do you mean?"

"The broken viruses looked familiar. After a while it hit me that they looked like spermatozoa."

"You too?"

"Nemoto said the same thing."

"So all three of us got the same impression."

"Yes. Sometimes you have to pay attention to intuition." Miyashita flashed Ando a grin, turning his attention from the road ahead.

"Watch where you're going!" As the brake lights of the car ahead drew closer, Ando clenched his leg muscles.

"Don't worry, we're not going to end up like Asakawa," Miyashita said, trying to look unconcerned as he stepped on the brake. But his front bumper was almost touching the car in front of them. Wiping away a cold sweat, Ando wondered if there was something wrong with Miyashita's depth perception. Driving like that they were sure to get in an accident sooner or later.

"Speaking of Asakawa, it's still a mystery as to why he didn't die of a heart attack."

"Right. Men don't ovulate."

"But maybe there was something physically different about him, just as with Mai."

"The virus probably found another exit."

"Exit?"

"A better way to spread and flourish."

Once they passed the exit for the Hodogaya bypass, the traffic snarl eased somewhat, and they made better time. No doubt the road signs had inspired Miyashita to use the word "exit" as he had. He continued.

"You know, it's up to us to figure this out." All trace of his customary nonchalance was gone from his voice.

"Believe me, I'm trying."

Miyashita changed the subject. "What did you do over New Year's break?"

"Nothing. Just lay around the apartment."

"Hmph. I took my family down to a fishing village at the southern tip of the Izu peninsula. We stayed at a little B&B that wasn't even listed on the travel brochures. Guess why I picked such a remote place? Well, one of my favorite novels is set in the village, and I'd always wanted to visit it. In the book it said that if you gaze out over the ocean at the horizon from that village, you see a mirage. I believed it."

Ando couldn't figure out where Miyashita was headed. He just nodded and listened.

"I know it's insensitive to say this to you, but family's a really wonderful thing. We could hear the surf from that inn, see, and it woke me up in the middle of the night. And as I gazed at the faces of my wife and daughter, it sank in just how dear they are to me."

Ando knew all too well the dearness of family. He tried to imagine a New Year's holiday with family in a southern Izu fishing village, where one could see mirages... Alone, the loneliness would be overwhelming, but the presence of loved ones would make the experience heartwarming. Ando began to wallow in thoughts of his own broken home, but Miyashita wouldn't give him time.

"My wife's a real looker, isn't she?"

When Ando replied, though, he wasn't recalling Miyashita's wife, but his own. "Absolutely," he nodded, thinking of how guileless and fresh she'd looked when they'd first met.

"Me, I'm short, fat, and ugly. And her! She's beautiful, and she's got a great personality. I'm a lucky man, and I know it."

Miyashita's wife was taller than him, and she looked just like a very popular actress. Next to her, Miyashita definitely seemed some inferior breed. But he was talented, and if he just kept it up, there was no way he wouldn't get tenure at their med school. Ando laughed ruefully. There was nothing inferior about that.

"So I don't want to die. I think I've been too optimistic. See, all along I've been at this case as a disinterested observer. In fact, I've enjoyed wondering where it might all lead."

Ando had been taking things a bit more seriously. Still, his, too, was the standpoint of the disinterested observer. Even if he failed to solve the case, he wasn't afraid of coming to any particular harm as a result. In that, his situation was fundamentally different from Asakawa and Ryuji's.

"Me, too."

"But I realized that maybe I've been underestimating the danger."

"Realized when?"

"After the holiday, when we got back from Izu."

"Did something happen there?"

"There was no mirage."

Ando frowned. Miyashita wasn't making sense.

"Just because of that?"

"Have you ever visited the setting of a novel?"

"Yeah, I guess." Ando figured that most people felt, at least once, the urge to visit the setting of a favorite book.

"How did it go?"

"Like, 'Well, I suppose this is it.'"

"Was it different from what you'd expected?"

"Most of the time you're bound to feel let down."

"The setting as you'd imagined it from reading the novel was different from the way the place looked in reality."

"I don't imagine it could ever really be the same."

"It was the same for me in Izu. That's the thing. I recognized the place from the descriptions in the book. But it didn't feel right and finally wasn't what I'd imagined. I didn't get to see the mirage."

He didn't say so aloud, but Ando thought that Miyashita's grievance was incredibly juvenile. A novelist inevitably sees things through his own filter and describes them accordingly. That filter is unique to that author, and when readers imagine a landscape for themselves based on it, the result can't help but be at odds with reality. There's no way to accurately convey a scene to another person without a camera or a video camera. Language has its limits.

Suddenly bringing his face close to Ando's, Miyashita said, "On the other hand, what if..."

"You can talk and watch the road at the same time, can't you?" Ando pointed straight ahead, and Miyashita slowed down and moved over into the other lane.

"Do you remember when you read *Ring*?"

Ando could recall the exact date. It was the day after he'd borrowed the disk from Asakawa's brother, Junichiro. Ando had snatched each page up out of the printer and read it eagerly.

"I can even tell you the day. November 19th."

"I only read it through once."

The same was true for Ando. He'd read it once through and hadn't looked at it again. "So what?"

"In spite of that, I remember the scenes, vividly. I still think about them sometimes."

Ando found himself agreeing with this, too. The events and places described in *Ring* were extremely vivid; it was as if they'd burrowed into the folds of his brain. If he tried, he could recall each scene with great clarity. It was a highly graphic report. But then again, what of it?

Clueless as to what Miyashita was getting at, Ando didn't respond.

"I suddenly wondered how accurately the report was communicating the scenes it describes."

Miyashita's expression was still strangely peaceful, given the gravity of what he'd just uttered.

Now Ando grasped the nature of Miyashita's concern. What if the settings they had imagined while reading *Ring* differed not in the slightest from reality? Was that even possible?

"What if it was..." Ando's throat was dry as he uttered the words. The heater kept the car at a comfortable temperature, but it also dried out the air.

"Well, I thought we'd better check and see."

"I get it. So that's why you've dragged me along."

Ando finally knew their destination. They were headed for the South Hakone-Atami area, where many of the events narrated in *Ring* had taken place. They were going to see if the appearance of the various locations matched what they'd seen in their minds' eyes. And of course, two people were better than one for this. Ando and Miyashita could both have a look, discuss the sight, and hopefully come to a precise assessment.

"At first, I wasn't going to tell you until we got there. I didn't want you to be prejudiced."

"I'll be alright."

"I forgot to ask. You don't happen to have been to South Hakone Pacific Land before, right?"

"Of course not. I mean, have you?"

"I'd never even heard of the place until I read that thing."

So neither of them had been there. But when he closed his eyes, Ando could see in his mind the cabins that comprised Villa Log Cabin, scattered across a gentle slope. It was in cabin B-4 that this astonishing chain of events had begun. Beneath the porch was a hole that led to an old well that sank five or six yards into the ground. Twenty-five years ago a woman named Sadako Yamamura had been raped and thrown into the well—the dungeon in which Sadako's vengeful will mingled with the smallpox virus's will to propagate.

That was where Miyashita proposed they go.

Keeping Mt. Hakone, shrouded in clouds, on their right, Miyashita drove through Manazuru toward Atami. According to *Ring*, they were to see signs for South Hakone Pacific Land as soon as they left Atami on the Atami-Kannami Highway. That was the route Miyashita and Ando were taking.

It was the first time either of them had been on the highway. Yet Ando had the illusion that he'd come this way before. Kazuyuki Asakawa had taken this route on October 11th. He'd gone on up a mountain road not knowing what awaited him in cabin B-4, though not without a sense of foreboding, either. It was almost noon, and the sky was clear and bright. On October 11th it had been raining off and on, and Asakawa's windshield wipers had been on. Ando remembered reading that in *Ring*. Asakawa had stared uneasily through the windshield as the wipers scraped back and forth. Both the time of day and the weather were different, but Ando felt like he was suffering flashbacks. He saw the sign on the mountainside for Pacific Land. It looked familiar, the unusual script, in black on a white background. Miyashita unhesitatingly turned left and got on the steep mountain road as though he knew the way well.

The road grew narrower and steeper as it wound between farmers' fields. The surface of the road was in such poor condition that it was difficult to believe it led to a resort. Unpruned branches and desiccated weeds brushed against the car on both sides, and the sound was unpleasant. The higher they climbed, the stronger Ando's sense of déjà vu became. He'd never been this way before, and yet he could swear that wasn't so.

"Does all this seem familiar to you?" Ando asked in a low voice.

"I was just about to ask you the same question."

So Miyashita felt the same way. Of course, Ando had felt déjà vu any number of times before, but the sensation had never gone on this long before. And it was only growing stronger as they drove on. Ando could clearly picture the information center that awaited them at the end of the road, an elegant three-story building with a facade of black glass.

They pulled into a circular driveway leading to the parking lot, and a building came into view. It was the information center, just as Ando had imagined it. He could even picture the restaurant beyond the lobby. There was no need for further confirmation. Reading *Ring* had delivered this scenery to Ando and Miyashita with perfect fidelity. What other explanation was there?

2

A good while later, Miyashita drove down from the mountains past Atami and took the Manazuru Road along the coast toward Odawara. Conversation kept lapsing as each man contemplated the things they'd just seen, the people they'd just met. Ando was too busy worrying about what the day's drive had proved to even glance at the sublime winter sea out the window. The resort, and the cabin with the well under the floorboards, overlay the waves like a mirage; Ando could still smell the dirt. He kept thinking of the man whose face he had recognized.

The various facilities that made up Pacific Land were scattered along both sides of the road between the information center and the hotel. The tennis courts, the pool, the gym, the cottages, everything was built on an incline, whether on the mountainside or in the valley. The slope on which the log cabins stood was actually a comparatively gentle one. Standing on the bank of the road and looking down over the valley where the cabins stood interspersed, they could see far below them a seemingly endless series of greenhouses, in the area between Kannami and Nirayama. Their white roofs flashed in the winter afternoon light. Each and every one of them looked familiar to the two men.

They went down to cabin B-4. They tried the doorknob, but the door was locked, so they went around the back, under the balcony. When they crouched down they could see at a glance the gaping hole where wall boards had come off between two pillars. The hole seemed to have been made deliberately, and they knew by whom. Ryuji had removed the boards so he could pass through. On October 18th, he and Asakawa had crawled through that hole to the space under the cabin, and then climbed down a rope into a well to fish out Sadako Yamamura's bones. A hair-raising feat.

Miyashita retrieved the flashlight he kept in his car and shone it into the space beneath the floorboards. Immediately they found a black protrusion, in more or less the center. The top of the well. A concrete lid lay next to it. Exactly as *Ring* said.

Ando had no desire to crawl in there and peer into the well, just as he'd had no desire to look into the exhaust shaft where Mai's corpse had been discovered. He had come close but in the end hadn't found the courage to look in. A young woman called Sadako had been thrown into the well, to end her life staring at a small circle of sky. Mai had breathed her last at the bottom of a rectangular prism made of concrete. One died in an old well at the edge of a mountainside sanatorium, and the other on the roof of a waterfront office building. One died deep in hushed woods, where branches hemming in from all sides nearly obstructed the view of the sky, and the other by a harbor road where the sea smelled strong, with nothing at all between her and the sky. One died in a barrel-shaped coffin sunk deep in the earth, and the other in a box-shaped coffin that floated high. The peculiar contrasts between the places Sadako and Mai had died only served to highlight their essential similarity.

Suddenly Ando's heart was racing. He detested the damp air beneath the floorboards, the feel of the ground beneath his hands and knees. The smell of soil filled his nostrils until, without his realizing, he was holding his breath. He felt like he was going to suffocate.

Whereas Ando was ready to bolt from the hole, Miyashita was trying to force his fat body into the space under the floorboards. Ando feared that he meant to go all the way to the well, and said, sternly: "Hey, that's far enough."

Miyashita hesitated for a moment in his awkward position. "I guess you have a point," he ceded. Obeying Ando, he started to back out of the hole. They had indeed gone far enough. What else was there to prove?

The two men crawled out from under the balcony and gulped lungfuls of the outside air. There was no need to speak. It was abundantly clear that every detail in *Ring* hewed to fact. They'd proved the hypothesis that the mental images created by the report were identical to the way things looked in reality. Everything was just where the text said it would be. By virtue of having read *Ring*, Ando and Miyashita had already "seen" the place. From the smell of the air to the feel of the dirt beneath their feet, they had experienced everything as Asakawa had.

Yet Miyashita didn't seem quite satisfied. "As long as we've come this far, why don't we have a look at Jotaro Nagao?"

Jotaro Nagao. The name had almost slipped Ando's mind, but he could remember the man's face clearly without ever having met him outside the pages of *Ring*. He was bald, and his handsome face was of a healthy hue that belied his fifty-seven years. Overall he made a first impression of smoothness, and that was true also of his speech. For some reason Ando even knew how Nagao sounded when he talked.

Twenty years ago, there had been a tuberculosis sanatorium on the ground where Pacific Land now stood. Although Nagao had a private practice in Atami now, he had once worked at the sanatorium. When Sadako Yamamura had come to visit her father, Nagao had raped her and thrown her into the well. Nagao had also been Japan's last smallpox patient.

In *Ring* it was written, "In a lane in front of Kinomiya Station was a small, one-story house with a shingle by the door that read *Nagao Clinic: Internal Medicine and Pediatrics.*" Upon reaching the place, Ryuji, always true to form, had throttled the doctor until he confessed what he'd done a quarter century ago. Miyashita was proposing they visit the clinic and see Nagao's face for themselves.

But when they got there, the curtain was pulled across the clinic's entrance. The place didn't seem to be closed just for the weekend; rather, the door looked like it hadn't been opened for quite some time. There was dust beneath it, and cobwebs on the eaves. The whole building hinted at extended, perhaps permanent, closure.

Ando and Miyashita gave up on the idea of meeting Nagao, and walked back to the curb where they'd left the car. Just then, they noticed a wheelchair coming down the steep road that descended from Atami National Hospital. A bald old man sat hunched over in the wheelchair, steered by a refined-looking woman of around thirty. From the way the old man's eyes lolled around looking at nothing in particular, it was clear that he had a psychiatric disorder.

When Ando and Miyashita saw his face they cried out as one and exchanged glances. Although he had aged terribly—twenty years, it seemed, in just three months—the man was instantly recognizable to them as Jotaro Nagao. Ando and Miyashita were able to remember what he had looked like and to compare that image with what they were seeing now.

Miyashita approached the man and spoke to him. "Dr. Nagao."

The old man didn't respond, but the young woman attendant, who looked like she might have been his daughter, turned toward the voice. Her eyes met Miyashita's. He bowed slightly, and she bowed back.

"How's his health?" Miyashita promptly inquired with the air of an old acquaintance.

"Fine, thank you," she said, and hurried away with a put-upon expression. But the encounter hadn't been fruitless. Evidently, the interview with Asakawa and Ryuji that had forced the doctor to own up to quarter-century-old crimes had seriously unbalanced him. It was clear that Nagao had almost no consciousness of the outside world.

Father and daughter passed the clinic and entered a narrow road beyond it. Both Ando and Miyashita, as they watched him go, thought the same thing and it didn't exactly concern Nagao. They were ruminating over the way they'd both instantly recognized the old man in the wheelchair as the one-time clinician. *Ring*, it seemed, had "recorded" not only scenery but people's faces with absolute fidelity.

Ando looked at the sign for the Odawara-Atsugi Highway, and then at the face of his friend sitting next to him. Miyashita was showing signs of fatigue, and no wonder. He'd been gripping the steering wheel since morning.

"You can just drop me off at Odawara," said Ando.

Miyashita frowned and turned his head slightly toward Ando, as if to ask why. "Cut it out, buddy. You know I'd gladly drive you back to your apartment."

"It's such a detour. Look, if I get out at Odawara I can take the Odakyu Line straight home."

Ando was concerned about Miyashita. If he drove all the way in to Yoyogi to drop Ando off, and then back to Tsurumi where he lived, it would add miles to the drive. Miyashita was clearly exhausted, both physically and mentally, and Ando wanted him to just go home and rest.

"Well, since you insist, you shall be dropped off at Odawara!" Miyashita said it like he was indulging the odd whim of a friend, but no doubt he didn't mind not having to drive into Tokyo and out. He was always that way, hardly ever coming right out with a "Thank you." He had trouble expressing gratitude in a straightforward manner.

They'd almost finished threading their way through downtown Odawara to the station when Miyashita muttered, "First thing next week, we'll get our blood tested."

Ando didn't need to ask why, since he'd been thinking the same thing. He had the nasty realization that he'd been transformed from an observer into a participant. All copies of the evil video had vanished, and he hadn't watched it. He was supposed to be safe, but now that he knew the *Ring* report had described absolutely everything with preternatural accuracy... He felt like a physician treating an AIDS patient who suddenly found himself infected via a previously unknown route of transmission. Of course, nothing at all had been proven; it was still only a possibility. Yet Ando cowered, for he felt now that his body had indeed been invaded by something. He'd been paralyzed for a good part of the day by the fantasy that something just like the ring virus he'd seen under the electron microscope was spreading through his body beneath the skin, coursing through his veins, violating his cells. No doubt Miyashita was tasting the same fear.

Aside from its author, Asakawa, Ando had been the first person to read *Ring*. The report described the images on the video minutely. It also described Jotaro Nagao so faithfully that Ando had been able to recognize him at a glance. Naturally, he had to wonder if reading *Ring* might not have the same effect as watching the videotape.

But he'd read it on November 19th of the past year. Two months had elapsed since then, and nothing had happened to him, at least as far as he could tell. He hadn't developed a blockage in the coronary artery and died in a week. Had the virus mutated so that the incubation period was longer? Or was he to be merely a carrier of the virus, one who did not display any symptoms himself?

Miyashita was right. They had to get their blood checked first thing next week back at the university. If the ring virus swarmed in them, too, they had to do something quick. Not that Ando had the slightest idea what.

"What do you plan on doing if you're ring-positive?" he asked dejectedly.

"Well, I won't just sit on my hands. I'll think of something to do." Miyashita spoke in clipped phrases. Ando thought he heard in his friend's voice overtones of fear even greater than his own. That was as it should be in that Miyashita had family to think of.

They entered the traffic circle in front of Odawara Station, went once around in the passenger-car lane, and then came to a stop. Ando got out of the car and saw Miyashita off with a wave.

We're in up to our necks now.

For the first time, Ando felt he truly understood what Asakawa had been through. In Ando's mind he and Miyashita started to blur into Asakawa and Ryuji. Ando corresponded to Asakawa, and Miyashita to Ryuji. Of course, from the physical point of view, and even in terms of personality, Ryuji and Miyashita weren't overly similar. It almost struck Ando as funny. But he was brought up short when he remembered that Asakawa and Ryuji were both dead. He'd cut open Ryuji himself.

He went through the ticket gate and into the station and sat down on a bench on the platform. The cold back of the bench against his spine, Ando wondered if that was what lying on the autopsy table felt like. If that was what it felt like to be dead. Sometimes it was worse to be in the dark, imagining terrors. He figured that in some ways, it was much more grueling to suspect you had cancer than to be told straight out that you did. The uncertainty was what made it so hard. Directly faced with a trial it was possible to endure it with some measure of equanimity. Something in man made being left hanging the worst. So was he infected, or wasn't he? For Ando, there was only one way to overcome the misery of the moment, and it was to persuade himself that his life was spent anyway. Regret at having let his son die could help him overcome his own attachment to life...

But as he sat there in the cold on the platform waiting for the Romance Car express, Ando couldn't stem his shivering no matter what.

3

He settled himself in a seat on the Romance Car. Now he had nothing to do but stare out the window at the scenery. Usually, he'd turn his attention to a book right about now, but he'd neglected to bring one. That morning as he'd climbed into Miyashita's car, he hadn't expected to return by train. Staring at the suburban landscape gradually made him drowsy, and he didn't fight it. He shut his eyes.

When he opened them again he didn't know where he was. His pulse quickened with the unease of having been carried off a great distance in his sleep. He thought he could hear his heart beat. He tried to stretch his legs and bumped them into the back of the seat ahead of him; his upper body jerked. He was jostled from beneath by the distinctive vibrations of a train, and he heard the clanging of a railway crossing in the distance.

I'm on a train.

With a sense of relief, Ando recalled that some two hours ago he'd said goodbye to Miyashita in Odawara, where he'd luckily managed to catch an express for Tokyo. That felt like days ago; it seemed like ages since he visited South Hakone Pacific Land with Miyashita. Hakone felt like some far-off land. Only the highland scenery and Jotaro Nagao's face remained vivid when he shut his eyes.

Ando rubbed his eyes with the backs of his hands and then looked out the window again. Nighttime street scenes flowed slowly past. The train was slowing down now as it approached its final destination, Shinjuku Station. Red lights flashed and bells clanged as they crossed streets. He strained his eyes to read the signs as they passed through a station without stopping.

Yoyogi Hachiman. The next station would be Sangubashi, his station. He wished he could just get off there, but the Romance Car express was skipping all stops before the terminal. He'd have to get off there and get on another train coming back this way, to return two stops. What a pain.

At Yoyogi Hachiman the Odakyu Line tracks made a nearly ninety-degree swerve to run parallel to the dark woods of Yoyogi Park. The scenery was quite familiar to him. He couldn't see it from where he sat, but his apartment was just over to the right. As they rushed through the

station he used every day, Ando pressed his face up against the window
to his left and gazed at the platform.

With a start, he turned to press his face harder to the glass. He saw
a woman he recognized standing on the platform. Wearing only a blaz-
er, hardly dressed for a winter night, she stood at the edge of the platform, very close to the train as it rushed by, staring at the Romance Car
with a nonchalant expression. Although the train was slowing down,
figures on the platform flashed in and out of view in an instant. In that
mere instant Ando's eyes and the woman's had met. He wasn't imagining it; he could still feel the impact from that moment when their gazes
locked.

This was the third time he'd encountered her. The first time, she'd
emerged from Mai's apartment and shared the elevator with him. The
second time had been on the top floor of the building where Mai's body
had been discovered. The elevator door had opened and he'd found himself face to face with her. Though he'd only seen her twice, he remembered her face very clearly.

Ten minutes later, at Sangubashi, he got off an outbound train from
Shinjuku. At Sangubashi Station, the inbound and outbound tracks were
situated in the middle between the two platforms. When the outbound
train stopped and he got off, another train was stationed on the inbound
tracks. As a result, Ando's view of the other platform was totally
blocked. He struggled against the current of passengers heading for the
gates to stay where he was on the platform, waiting for the trains to
depart so he could see if the woman was still there on the opposite platform. Though it had been ten minutes and perhaps his desire to see her
again was confounding him, Ando was curiously sure she was still there.

Bells rang and both trains pulled away at the same time, like sliding
doors opening, revealing a clear view of the opposite platform. In the
sudden stillness his eyes met hers again. His hunch had been right. She
stood in exactly the same place as before, fixing him with the same
steady gaze. Ando returned her gaze and nodded. He was signaling an
intention to comply with her instructions.

Ando slowly began to walk toward the gate. Matching his movements, she went down the stairs on her side. They met at the ticket gate.

"We meet again," she said, as if this were coincidence. Ando didn't think so. He felt that she'd somehow known he'd pass through Sangubashi Station on that train. She'd been lying in wait for him. But it was no use resisting her charms now that she stood before him. Together they went through the ticket gate and turned into the little store-lined street beyond.

4

When he awoke the next morning, the woman lying next to him immediately asked him to take her to a movie that had just opened. It was the weekend, but as they went to the first showing, the theater wasn't too crowded.

The woman sat down leaving an open seat between her and Ando. Until they'd entered the theater, she'd been practically hanging from his arm, but now she suddenly wanted to keep her distance. The seats themselves were luxuriously large, so it wasn't a question of feeling cramped. Ando couldn't figure it out. But if he started listing everything she'd done that struck him as strange, it'd take him all day. All he knew was that she was Mai's sister and that her name was Masako.

He stared at the screen, but he couldn't follow the story. It was partly because he was still sleepy, but more than that, Masako's presence was distracting him. He remembered meeting her at Sangubashi Station the night before, but he couldn't quite reconstruct how he'd ended up taking her back to his apartment. He'd invited her to a bar in front of the station, where, over beers, he'd asked her name.

Masako Takano. I'm Mai's older sister.

Just as he'd guessed. She said she was two years older than Mai; she worked at a securities firm which she'd joined after graduating from a women's college. Everything after that point was hazy for Ando. He hadn't drunk that much, but he could only recall fragments. He couldn't recall who had suggested it, but one way or another, they'd ended up in Ando's apartment.

In the next scene he could recall, there was running water. In this fragment the context was clear. Masako was in the shower, and Ando was sitting on the bed waiting for her to come out.

The water stopped, and then Masako emerged from the hallway. She turned out the lights without even asking him; that moment, when everything went dark, left a strong impression. A second later, Masako pressed her naked upper body against him. Her wet hair was wrapped in a towel, which she held together with her left hand, and with her right, she grabbed Ando's head and pressed his face against her flesh. He felt sucked into her fine skin; his nose and mouth were covered, and he was starting to smother. It was all he could do to push her away enough for him to breathe. Then he filled his lungs with her fresh scent and put his arms around her...

The movie was unremarkable, so Ando spent the time dredging up bits and pieces of the previous night's weirdness. He hadn't been flesh to flesh with a woman for a year and a half. He'd ejaculated three times that he could remember. Not that it gave him any particular pride about his virility. He was about to turn thirty-five, and his managing to do it three times, at least, in one night said more about her beauty than his stamina. Only, now that he thought about it, he realized that everything that had happened in bed last night took place in complete darkness. It didn't matter how pretty Masako was, or how provocative she may have looked; Ando hadn't feasted on her with his eyes. Not only had she turned off the lights, but she'd covered the clock on the bedside table with a towel. She'd made the room truly *dark*, unwilling even to tolerate the faint trace of light coming from behind the face of the clock. Every one of her movements had betrayed an intense attachment to darkness.

Ando was pretending to watch the movie screen, but all the while he was secretly watching Masako. The darkness of the theater set off her beauty even more. Darkness became this woman.

She closed her eyes several times while watching the movie. She wasn't dozing off; her lips were moving. She appeared to be saying something, but Ando couldn't make out what. He leaned forward and to the left, resting his elbow on his knee.

Finally, by looking back and forth between her lips and the screen, Ando figured out what she was doing. Masako was repeating the characters' lines under her breath.

On screen, a bad street girl who had been transformed into a killing machine by a government agency was being sent out on her first mission. In this scene she wore a black dress and carried a huge pistol hidden in her handbag. She was entering a classy restaurant. It was a very tense moment in the film, with lots of rapid-fire dialogue.

Utterly indifferent to the movie, Ando watched Masako as she repeated the heroine's lines. Then, for a moment, Masako's voice and the heroine's overlapped. The movie was in French, with Japanese subtitles, but Masako's Japanese was perfectly in sync with the heroine's

French. It was like a well-done choral recitation. Ando was shocked to see that sometimes Masako's mouth opened even before the subtitles appeared. She couldn't pull off such a feat unless she'd seen the movie enough times to memorize the dialogue.

For a while Masako lost herself in the heroine with a look of happiness on her face that Ando found amusing. But she seemed to feel his eyes upon her and abruptly shut her mouth. She didn't open it again, just staring at the screen thereafter.

As they left the theater, Masako squinted, stifled a yawn, and took Ando's arm. The winter sun shone softly, and Ando decided he'd rather touch Masako's skin directly than link arms with her. He separated his arm from hers and then held her hand. For a moment he felt a chill, but then their skin temperatures evened out, and Masako's hand relaxed in Ando's long fingers.

It was Coming of Age Day, and everywhere they looked there were young women dressed up in kimonos. Ando and Masako followed the crowd from Yurakucho toward Ginza. He intended to take her out to lunch, but had no particular place in mind. He planned to choose some likely-looking restaurant as they strolled along.

Masako kept looking around with evident curiosity at the Ginza streetcorners, and now and then she'd let slip a sigh. She didn't offer much in the way of conversation, but Ando didn't feel ill-at-ease with her. In fact, he felt a surge of satisfaction at being able to quietly stroll around Ginza on a sunny holiday.

Masako stopped in front of a hamburger joint on a corner and stared at its sign on the sidewalk. There was something of the innocence of a teenager in her earnest gaze.

"You want to eat here?" Ando asked.

"Uh-huh," she said, nodding vigorously. Ando went inside, glad he was getting off so cheaply.

Masako's appetite was simply astounding. In the blink of an eye she'd consumed two hamburgers and an order of fries, and was eyeing the counter again greedily.

It turned out to be ice cream she wanted now, so he ordered one and gave it to her. This time she ate slowly, as if she dreaded coming to the last bite. She carried each spoonful to her mouth with great care, but even so, she ended up dripping melted ice cream on her lap. Her stockings were flecked with drops of milky white mixed with bits of strawberry. She scooped up a drop with her index finger and licked it, then grew impatient. She clutched her shin with both hands, brought her mouth to her knee, and ran the tip of her tongue over it. Still in her curled-up position, she rolled her eyes and shot Ando a suggestive glance. There was provocation in her eyes, and Ando couldn't look away. She finished licking up the ice cream and lowered her leg again. There was a run in her new stockings. She must have snagged them with a canine tooth.

Ando had bought her those stockings that morning at a convenience store by the station. She didn't seem to own any; after all, she'd been walking around with bare legs in the middle of winter. Ando felt cold just looking at her, so he bought a pair of stockings without even checking with her. When he handed them to her she ran straight into a restroom to put them on, and she was still wearing them.

The run seemed to bother Masako, because she kept rubbing her knee.

Ando felt he'd never get tired of watching her every move. *She came out of nowhere, and now I'm falling for her.*

He wondered if he really was. Maybe he was just becoming desperate, dissolute. If he'd become a carrier of the ring virus as a result of having read that strange report, if his body was being eaten away by the hour, then his nascent pleasure was something he couldn't afford to lose.

Back in college, he'd read a novel set in a little mountain village that featured a female character who was rather like the woman he was confronted with now. The fictional woman is possessed of above-average looks, but because she doesn't speak and act like others, the villagers have branded her as crazy. She ends up providing comfort to men who have no fixed companions. The image of a woman without a home wandering the woods in a disheveled state, accepting the local men one and all without discrimination, embodied a certain high Eros, aided by the exotic setting. The mountain village gave the story a perfect harmony of character and setting, and at the time Ando had felt that if the author had placed such a woman in the city, the novel wouldn't have acquired the right atmosphere.

Well, he was in Ginza now, smack in the middle of Tokyo, not some alpine hamlet. But Masako had the same aura as the heroine of that book, and her modern beauty didn't seem at all out of place on a stool in a fast-food joint.

Ando suddenly remembered how the novel ended. Alone in the mountains, the woman gives birth to a child, having no idea who the father is. The story closes with that baby's first cries piercing the forest and echoing across the mountainside.

I can't let that happen.

Ando admonished himself. He had to take precautions to protect Masako's body. He recalled that the night before he'd been so overjoyed at the prospect of coupling that he'd forgotten himself and neglected to use birth control.

Masako was running her fingers in a circle over her kneecap, gradually making the hole bigger. The skin of her leg showed white where it peeked through the rent, so white as to make it a shame to cover it up with stockings.

The hole got bigger. Ando stopped her by laying his hand on top of hers.

He asked her, "What were you saying back there in the theater?" He meant to ask why she was repeating the characters' lines.

Masako's reply was: "Take me to a bookstore."

She liked to deflect his questions that way. She asked Ando to do things far more often than she answered his queries. But of course, Ando was incapable of saying no to her.

He took her to the biggest bookstore in Ginza. Masako flitted from shelf to shelf, in the end spending over an hour in the bookstore reading on her feet. Ando, who didn't share that habit, ended up wandering around aimlessly until he discovered, next to the registers, a stack of pamphlets from Shotoku, the publisher. Since he'd visited their offices only the other day, and the pamphlets were free, he picked one up.

The pamphlet included a short essay but consisted mainly of ads for future Shotoku releases.

I wonder if Ryuji's in here? Ando flipped through the pamphlet expectantly. The other day, Ryuji's editor Kimura had told Ando that Ryuji's collection of philosophical essays was just about to be published.

Ando was hoping to see a friend's name in print.

But before he could find it, he was dragged out of the bookstore by Masako. "How about another movie?"

Her plea was a mild one, but the way she gripped his arm and pulled him along suggested she wouldn't take no for an answer. Maybe, while reading in the bookstore, she'd found out about another movie and decided she had to see it. Ando slipped the pamphlet into his coat pocket and asked, "What do you want to see?"

She didn't answer, but simply squeezed his hand and tugged him forward.

He hung back a bit, saying, "Pushy, aren't you?" Then he noticed that she was still clutching an event-guide magazine and came to a full stop. Masako hadn't spent a single yen since the night before. She hadn't made a move to pay for anything, always leaving it to Ando to pick up the tab. He didn't imagine for a moment that she'd purchased the magazine with her own money. Indeed, it wasn't in a bag, and she held it bare rolled up in her hand.

She lifted it.

Ando looked back toward the bookstore. Nobody was coming after them. She'd managed to elude the sharp eyes of the clerks. It was only a three-hundred yen magazine; even if she'd been caught, it wouldn't have been a big deal. As he let Masako pull him along, Ando was beginning to feel bolder than ever before.

5

When he put the key in the lock he could hear the phone in his apartment ringing. Figuring he wouldn't make it in time anyway, Ando decided not to hurry. He turned the knob. When friends called, they usually only let the phone ring five or six times, because they knew how small his apartment was. Hence he could usually guess the caller by how long it took him or her to give up. As he'd expected, by the time he got the door open the ringing had stopped, a sure sign of someone who knew him and how he lived. There weren't too many people who had visited him. It was probably Miyashita, Ando figured, looking at his watch. It was just past eight o'clock in the evening.

He opened the door wider and beckoned Masako inside, then turned on the lights and the heat. Clothing was scattered about exactly as they'd left it that morning. Masako had left her belongings there, seemingly having decided to spend another night with Ando.

Ando's shoulders and back were stiff from watching movies in the morning and afternoon. He wanted a soak in the tub.

Starting to take off his coat, he found the publisher's pamphlet in his pocket. He took it out and placed it on the bedside table, thinking to examine it at leisure after a bath. He'd decided to buy Ryuji's book, and he needed to look up the title and publication date.

He stripped down to his shirt and rolled up his cuffs. He gave the tub a quick rinse and then adjusted the water temperature and started to fill it. It wasn't a large tub, so it wasn't long before it was ready. The bathroom was full of steam, and turning on the fan didn't do much good. He thought he'd have Masako bathe first, so he stuck his head into the other room. She was sitting on the edge of the bed taking off her stockings.

"Would you like to take a bath?"

She stood up. At the same time, the phone rang.

As Ando walked to the telephone, Masako took his place in the bathroom, disappearing behind the accordion-style shower curtain.

It was Miyashita, as he'd expected. As soon as Ando had the receiver to his ear, his friend yelled, "Where the hell have you been all day?"

"At the movies."

Miyashita obviously hadn't expected that answer. "At the movies?" he blurted.

"Two of them, in fact."

"Must be nice not to have a care in the world," Miyashita sneered in heartfelt disgust. Then he continued with his harangue. "I don't know how many times I tried to call you."

"I do go out, you know."

"Well, whatever. Do you know where I am now?"

Where was Miyashita calling from? It didn't sound like he was at home. Ando could hear cars. He must have been in a roadside phone booth somewhere.

"Please don't tell me you're in the neighborhood and you want to come up?"

Now was a bad time. Masako was in the bath. Ando was prepared to refuse if that was Miyashita's plan.

"Don't be an idiot. Think theater, man, the stage."

"What are you talking about?"

Now it was Ando's turn to be annoyed. What right did Miyashita have to criticize him for watching movies when he was going to plays? But that wasn't what Miyashita was up to.

"I'm at the offices of Theater Group Soaring."

The name rang a bell. Where had he seen it before? He remembered—in *Ring*. It was the name of the troupe Sadako Yamamura had belonged to prior to her death.

"What the hell are you doing there?"

"Yesterday I realized that the descriptions in *Ring* were so precise and objective that it was like they'd been observed through the viewfinder of a video camera."

"Me, too."

Why were they going through all that again? Ando spotted the Shotoku pamphlet on the table and pulled it over next him so he could take notes on it. It was a habit of his to take notes while he was on the phone; it calmed him down. His customary phone-conversation posture was receiver wedged between his ear and left shoulder, ballpoint pen in right hand.

"Well, I realized today that there was one more thing to check on. I mean, if we wanted to look at faces, we didn't need to go all the way to

Atami, did we?"

Ando was getting impatient. He couldn't see where Miyashita was going. "Just tell me already."

Miyashita finally came out with it. "I'm talking about Sadako Yamamura."

"Come on, she died in 1966." *But wait...* Ando suddenly realized why Miyashita had visited the theater group. "The photograph."

He remembered reading in *Ring* that Asakawa's colleague Yoshino had visited the troupe's rehearsal space and seen Sadako's portfolio. This was something she'd submitted when she'd joined the troupe, and included two photos, a full-length one and one from the chest up. Yoshino had made copies of them.

"Finally got it, huh? All along, it was easy as pie to feast our eyes on Sadako."

Ando summoned up his mental image of Sadako. Thanks to *Ring*, he had quite a strong impression stored away in his brain. Tall and slender, with only a modest bustline but perfectly balanced in her proportions. Her facial features were somewhat androgynous, but she had perfect eyes and a perfect nose, with nothing about them he would change if he could. He imagined her as an unapproachable beauty.

Ando whipped up some courage and asked, "And how about it? Have you gotten them to show you the photos?"

Miyashita had probably seen them, and the face in the photos and the one in his mind had probably been identical. That was the reply Ando expected.

But what he heard from the other end of the line was a sigh.

"It's different."

"You mean..."

"The face is different."

Ando didn't know what to say.

"I don't know how to put it. The Sadako Yamamura in the photos is not the one I pictured. She's beautiful, no question, but... How can I put it?"

"What do you mean?"

"What do I *mean*? Hell, I'm just confused. But I did remember something. I had a friend who was good at drawing people's portraits, and I asked him once what type of face was the hardest to draw for him. And he told me there wasn't any particular type of face he couldn't draw. He said all faces had peculiarities that made them easy to capture in convincing portraits. But if he had to pick one, he said, the hardest type to draw, for him, was his own face. Especially when the self-portraitist is a very self-conscious sort, it's next to impossible to make the picture match the reality. It always comes out looking like someone else."

"So?" What did that have to do with the question at hand?

"Nothing, I guess. I was just reminded of him, that's all. But take the videotape. It wasn't shot with a camera, right? Those images came from Sadako's eyes and mind. And in spite of that..."

"What?"

"It captured places and people accurately."

"We didn't actually see the video, you know."

"But we read *Ring*."

Ando was getting annoyed. Miyashita seemed to be dancing around the subject. He was like a child who wanted to go somewhere but was afraid to take the first step.

"Look, Miyashita, why don't you just tell me what's on your mind?"

Ando could hear Miyashita take a deep breath.

"Did Kazuyuki Asakawa really write *Ring*?"

Who else could have? Ando started to say, but heard a beep signaling that Miyashita's phone card was about to run out.

"Crap, my card's almost used up. Can your fax machine handle photos?" Miyashita spoke fast.

"That's what the guy said when he sold it to me."

"Great, I'll fax them to you. I want you to check right away to see if she's different from what you imagined, or if I'm just—"

And with that they were cut off.

Ando sat there for a minute with the receiver still on his shoulder, in a daze. The noise of the shower stopped, and the apartment was wrapped in stillness. Feeling a chill breeze, he looked over to see that the window was open a crack, admitting the wintry night air. In the distance, a car horn sounded. The dry, harsh noise testified to how desiccated the outside air was. In contrast, the air inside his apartment was almost wringing with moisture as steam seeped out from the bathroom. Masako was taking a long time.

Ando thought over what Miyashita had said. He could understand his friend's state of mind. Probably he'd spent the whole day on pins and needles, and rather than just sit around and wonder whether the ring virus had entered his body because he'd read *Ring*, he'd decided to act. When he'd remembered that the acting troupe had kept photos of Sadako, he'd gone over to check. Surprisingly, the photos hadn't matched his mental image. Unable to judge whether this was simply due to some blockage on his part, he'd copied the photos, so he could get Ando's opinion. And now he was going to fax them over.

Ando glanced at the fax machine. No movement yet.

He looked away from it. His eyes came to rest on the publisher's pamphlet. He picked it up and started to flip through it while he waited. Upcoming publications were listed in the back. Under the heading "New in February" fifteen or so titles were listed, each one followed by the name of the author and a dozen or so words describing the contents. About halfway down Ando saw Ryuji's name. The title was still *The Structure of Knowledge*, and the summary said it represented "the cutting edge of contemporary thought." On the list it was sandwiched between a romance novel and a collection of behind-the-scenes essays about the television industry, making it seem even more eggheaded. But this was his friend's last work being published posthumously. Ando would give it a read no matter how difficult it was. He circled the entry.

He felt something click in his mind. He couldn't figure out what. Still holding the pen, he thought hard. It seemed to him that he'd seen a familiar word on that page of the pamphlet. He looked again. The bottom half of the page was taken up with a list, in smaller type, of books coming out in March. He looked at the third title from the end.

And then his eyes grew wide with shock. At first he wondered if it was just a coincidence, but then he saw the name of the author.

New in March:

...

...

RING by Junichiro Asakawa. Bloodcurdling cult horror.

Ando let the pamphlet slip out of his hand. *He was going to publish that?*

Now he understood why Junichiro had been so standoff-ish that day when Ando had run into him in the Shotoku lounge. He'd decided to tweak his brother's reportage and publish it as a novel. And since Ando was the one person who knew Junichiro was using his brother's work without consent, it was no wonder he'd been so cold that day, fleeing after hardly the most perfunctory of greetings. Had they talked for long, the subject of the report would have come up, and his editors might have found out. Junichiro obviously wanted to claim the book as being entirely his own.

"It mustn't go to press!" Ando cried out loud. At the very least, he had to get Junichiro to delay publication until it could be established that *Ring* was physically harmless. It was his duty as a medical professional. Tomorrow, he and Miyashita would have their blood tested. It would take several days for the results to come back. If they were positive, if he and Miyashita turned out to be carriers of the ring virus, then publication of that book could have catastrophic consequences. The original videotape could only spread at the rate of one copy at a time. Publication involved numbers of an entirely different scale, ten thousand copies at least. In a worst-case scenario, hundreds of thousands, even millions, of copies would be disseminated throughout the country.

Ando's teeth chattered as he imagined a huge tsunami. A vast, dark wall of ocean bearing down silently, driving before it a wind that he thought he could feel on him even now. He went to the window and shut it tightly. Standing by the window, he looked back toward the hall. Masako stood there, wrapped in a towel; he saw her face in profile. She was rummaging through her bag, probably for underwear.

The phone rang. Ando picked up the receiver, and when he confirmed that it was an incoming fax, he pushed the start button on the fax machine. Miyashita was sending him the photos.

A few seconds later, the fax machine whirred to life and began printing. Ando stood motionless over the black machine, staring at the sheet slowly emerging from it. He felt someone sneak up behind him and turned to look. It was Masako, wearing only panties. She'd draped the towel over her shoulders and was standing directly behind him. Her face was flushed, and her eyes had a new gleam, so lustrous as to make him want to hold her and kiss her eyelids then and there. She wore a strangely resolute expression.

The fax machine beeped to say it was done printing. Ando tore off the fax, sat down on the bed, and had a look. The transmission consisted of two photos, side by side. The printout wasn't quite photo quality, but it was clear enough for him to make out Sadako Yamamura's face and body.

He screamed. The woman in the photos was indeed different from what he'd imagined. But that wasn't why he'd screamed. The photos on the fax were of the woman standing in front of him now.

She took the fax out of his hands and looked at the photos. Ando stared up at her weakly, like a boy getting a scolding from his mother. Finally he managed to wring words from his throat.

"You're...Sadako Yamamura." Not Masako, not Mai's sister—those were lies.

Her expression relaxed. Perhaps she found Ando's consternation funny, for she seemed to be smiling.

Ando's mind went blank. It was the first time he ever fainted in his almost thirty-five years.

6

Ando was unconscious for less than a minute, but that was enough. With no way to process the facts thrust into his face, he'd had no other option but to stop thinking altogether. Perhaps his consciousness would have been able to deal with it if he'd had a little more time, or more composure to begin with. If he'd even remotely entertained the possibility beforehand, maybe he wouldn't have had to faint.

But as it was, it came all too suddenly. To find out that a woman who had died twenty-five years ago was standing right in front of him, and remembering making love to her several times the night before... In that instant he'd gone to the brink of insanity, and his brain circuitry had been forced to shut down momentarily. Most people would faint if they got up to go to the bathroom in the middle of the night and turned around to find a dead person standing there. That's how people escape from horrors presented to them; once you faint, you no longer have to endure the unendurable. Only with that cushion of unconsciousness are we able to prepare ourselves to accept reality.

When consciousness returned to him, Ando thought he could smell burning flesh somewhere. He should have been lying face down on the bed, but somehow he was on his back looking up instead. Had he rolled over himself, or had someone turned him over? Only his upper body was actually on the bed; his legs, though neatly arranged, were hanging out onto the floor. Without otherwise moving a muscle, Ando sniffed the air and listened for sounds. He opened his eyes a slit. He had no intention of reawakening all his senses at once. He meant to ease himself into acceptance. Otherwise he'd probably suffer the same reaction all over again.

He could hear water spurting from a faucet. The sound probably came from the bathroom, but it sounded like the distant burbling of a brook. The noise of the water hid the night sounds of the city. Normally he should have been able to hear the cars rushing by on the Metropolitan Expressway. He eased his eyes open. In the middle of the ceiling two twenty-watt fluorescent bulbs glowed, casting a bright light over the whole room.

Moving only his eyes, Ando looked around the room. Then, gingerly, he sat up. He couldn't see anybody around. Just as he was starting to wonder if his imagination was playing tricks on him, the water stopped. He held his breath without meaning to.

The woman emerged from behind a corner in the hallway. Just as before, she wore nothing but panties and held a wrung-out towel.

Ando tried to scream, but no sound came out. He brushed away the hand offering him a wet towel and got unsteadily to his feet. Then he backed up until he was flat against the wall. He tried to scream her name, but he still couldn't find his voice.

Sadako Yamamura!

He tried to recall everything he knew about her. Twenty-five years ago she'd been murdered, thrown into an old well. She had created that awful videotape by means of thought projection. She possessed paranormal powers. She had testicular feminization syndrome; she was a hermaphrodite. Ando turned his stare on her lower body. There was no visible bulge under the white panties that covered her crotch. Of course, her testicles were not supposed to be readily visible. But Ando had touched her down there last night, caressed her over and over. Nothing had struck him as odd; she was in every way perfectly female as far as he could tell. But he hadn't been able to see. Everything they'd done the night before had been done in darkness. Ando suddenly wondered what her obsession with darkness was meant to prevent him from seeing.

The otherworldliness he'd felt on first meeting her hadn't been off the mark after all. That time in the elevator in Mai's building, he'd been desperate to distance himself from her—just like now. The way she'd just appeared like that from Mai's apartment, he'd had no idea where she'd come from and still didn't.

He had so many questions, but he could hardly breathe much less ask her anything.

He felt that if he wasn't careful he'd collapse onto the floor, and if he did, he'd be in Sadako's clutches. The only way to maintain any dignity at all was to stay where he could look down on her from above.

He didn't take his eyes off her.

Her naked skin gleamed whitely under the fluorescent lights, as if to impress him with the reality of her flesh, as if to assert to him that she was no ghost. This body of hers overwhelmed him, this body whose arms and legs had been so entangled with his last night. What did he need to do to escape from her spell? There was only one answer: flee. Get away from this place. It was all he could think of. What he saw before him was a monster. A woman come back after being dead for twenty-five years.

With his back against the wall, Ando began to move sideways toward the vestibule. Sadako made no move to block him, following him only with her eyes. Ando looked toward the door. Had he locked it when they came in? He didn't remember doing that. The door should swing open when he turned the knob. Warily, Ando moved in that direction. He was in no shape to think about taking a coat.

When he'd put several good feet between himself and the woman, he bolted for the door and stumbled outside. In slacks and a sweater he was dressed much too lightly for the cold, but he spared not a thought for that as he ran down the stairs. It was only after he'd run through the lobby and out onto the sidewalk that he was able to turn around to look behind him. There was no sign of pursuit. He looked up at his windows, still brightly lit. He wanted to go someplace crowded. He ran toward the station.

7

The wind chilled him to the bone. He had no particular destination in mind, but he found himself naturally gravitating toward bright places. He turned his back on the shadowy groves of Yoyogi Park. The skyscrapers of Shinjuku loomed ahead like so many black hulks. Between him and them lay the modest bustle of Sangubashi Station, surrounded by narrow shop-lined streets leading into residential areas. He guessed that even on a holiday there might be one or two places open. Ando's steps took him in that direction. Anywhere there might be people was good enough for him.

It was only when he came to the ticket vending machines at the station that he realized he'd left his wallet behind. He couldn't go back and get it now. He searched his other pockets. He found the little case he kept his driver's license in. He remembered shoving it in his pocket the other day when he'd gone on that excursion with Miyashita, thinking he might have to take the wheel at some point. He'd forgotten to take it out of his pocket when he got home. Luckily he'd tucked some money behind the license for emergencies.

A five-thousand-yen bill. That was all the money he had now. At the thought he felt more lonely than cold. Where was he supposed to sleep tonight? Five thousand yen wouldn't even buy him a night in a capsule hotel.

His only hope was Miyashita. He bought a train ticket, and then stepped into a phone booth. He dialed his friend's number, doubting he'd have gotten home yet. And, indeed, he hadn't. No wonder, he'd only just called Ando from Yotsuya, across town from where he lived. He was probably still on his way home to Tsurumi. Ando decided to head in that direction himself.

It was past nine o'clock when Ando sank into a seat on the train. When he closed his eyes Sadako's face appeared before him as if by conditioned reflex. He'd never had his feelings about a woman change so drastically over such a short period of time. The cold air of mystery he'd sensed on their first meeting had dissipated somewhat on their second, to be replaced by a growing desire for her. When they met a third time, that desire was realized, and the faint beginnings of infatuation had

250

stirred his heart. And then, the fall. She'd lured him up to a high place, had her way with him, and then pushed him off the edge into the abyss. It was unendurable to think that he'd copulated with a woman who should have been dead for twenty-five years. The word "necrophilia" came to mind. Where had this woman come from? Was the part about her being dead a mistake? Or had she really come back from beyond the grave?

It being a holiday, the train was comparatively empty. Only a few passengers had to stand. Across the aisle from Ando, a laborer-type was sprawled across the bench, occupying enough space for three people. His eyes were shut tight, but he wasn't asleep. Proof of this came every time somebody walking the length of the car passed by him and he opened his eyes a crack to fathom his surroundings. His eyes, however, were so heavy and dull that they almost looked dead. Ando averted his eyes from the man. But the laborer wasn't the only one. Every one of the passengers was as pale as a corpse.

Ando hugged himself to keep from trembling. If he didn't hug himself, he was afraid he'd start screaming, right there in the public space of a train carriage.

He accepted a glass of brandy from Miyashita. First he sent a trickle of it down his throat, savoring the sensation, then he drained the glass. He was starting to feel human again, but was still shivering slightly.

"How do you feel now?" Miyashita asked.

"More or less alive."

"You must've been freezing."

Miyashita didn't know yet why Ando had come without a coat.

"It's not the cold."

Miyashita had shown Ando into the room he used as a study. Ando was sitting on the spare bed in the corner. It was where he was going to sleep tonight, but for the moment, he was just rattling its metal bars. Only after downing his second glass of brandy was he able to stop shaking.

"What happened?" Miyashita's voice was gentle.

Ando told him everything that had happened since the previous night. When he finished, he fell backwards onto the bed and let out a whine like a mosquito's.

"I give up! Explain it to me! I'm lost," he moaned.

"Good Lord," muttered Miyashita, utterly thrown for a loop. It was one of those moments when people can't help laughing, albeit bitterly, and that's what Miyashita did, weakly. When his laughter had subsided, he poured brandy into some hot coffee and started sipping it. He seemed to be deep in thought, trying to find a reply that was logical, that made at least some sense.

"The basic question is, where did Sadako come from?" The rhetorical tone suggested that Miyashita had already come up with an answer.

"Tell me. Where did she come from?"

Miyashita turned the question back on Ando. "Don't you know?"

Still supine, Ando shook his head. "No, I do not."

"You really don't know?"

"Tell me! Where did she come from?"

"Mai Takano gave birth to her."

Ando forgot to breathe for a few moments while he tried to think of an alternate explanation. But he could hardly think at all. He'd lost the power of cogitation. All he could do was repeat what he'd heard.

"Mai Takano gave birth to her?"

"The evil video was born from Sadako's mind. Mai watched it on a day when she was ovulating. The ring virus was born in her body and then fertilized her egg. 'Fertilized' isn't the right word, though. It's probably more accurate to say that the nucleus of Mai's egg was replaced with Sadako Yamamura's genes."

"I hope you're going to tell me you can explain the mechanism by which all this happened."

"Think back to when we ran the ring virus through the genetic sequencer. We discovered that it contained smallpox genes and human genes mixed together in a fixed ratio."

Ando sat up and reached for his glass. But the glass was empty.

"So the human genes were..."

"Sadako's. Split into hundreds of thousands of parts."

"Hundreds of thousands of ring virus specimens, each carrying a tiny segment of Sadako's DNA?"

"Despite its being a DNA virus, the ring virus has reverse transcription enzymes. So it ought to be able to insert those fragments into the nucleus of a cell."

A single virus specimen would be incapable of carrying the entirety of a person's genetic information. It simply wasn't big enough. But things would be otherwise if a person's DNA could be split into hundreds of thousands of segments, and each segment parceled out to a different piece of virus. In the photos taken by the electron microscope, they'd seen what looked like countless numbers of ring viruses, mobs of them. It turned out that each one of them had been carrying a part of Sadako Yamamura's genetic code, and together they'd ganged up on Mai's egg.

Ando started to stand up, but thought better of it and sat down again. He always got fidgety when he tried to counterargue.

"But Sadako died twenty-five years ago. Her genetic information shouldn't be able to manifest itself anymore."

"Let's think about that. Now, why do you think Sadako projected those images on a tape?"

What had she been obsessed with at the bottom of that well, on the brink of death? The idea of packing all her hatred for the masses into images that would bring terror to anyone who saw them? Practically speaking, what would she get out of that? There had to be some deeper purpose. But Ando couldn't comprehend what Miyashita was trying to say.

Miyashita tried to guide him toward the answer. "She was only nineteen."

"So?"

"So she didn't want to die."

"She was too young to die."

"Isn't it conceivable that she transformed her genetic information into a code and left it behind in the form of energy?"

Ando's only answer was a sigh.

She translated her genetic information into images and then projected those images? True, Ryuji had succeeded in communicating with them by encoding the word "mutation" into his own DNA base sequence. But the human genome was huge, much too big to be translated into a single videotape.

Ando finally countered with, "Impossible. The human genome is too large."

Miyashita spread his arms to point at the corners of the room. "Take this room, for example. Let's say we were to express the totality of this room in words."

The study was about eight mats large. A desk stood next to the bed. There was a computer on the desk, and next to that a pile of dictionaries. Most problematic were the bookshelves that took up one wall. They were crammed with what had to be a few thousand books ranging from works of literature to specialist works on medicine. It could easily take a day just to list all the titles and authors.

"That's a lot of information."

"But what if..." Miyashita mimed holding a camera. Click. "...you took a picture. You've got it all in an instant. With just one photo you can store most of the information that makes up the sight of this room. And think, continuous images would increase the capacity that much more. It wouldn't be impossible to encode Sadako's complete genetic information that way."

Ando saw what his friend was trying to say, but he still wasn't ready to go along. "Let me think about it for a while," he said, shaking his head. He needed to go back and retrace for himself a path through what Miyashita was saying.

"Go ahead and think. I'm going to go take a leak." Miyashita disappeared down the hall, leaving the study door open.

Of course, what Miyashita had spelled out was merely a hypothesis. But regardless of whether or not the mechanism Miyashita had laid out was actually how it had happened, the fact remained that Mai Takano had given birth to Sadako Yamamura a week after insemination. That seemed to be beyond question at this point. A week from insemination to birth was an awfully short time. Something must have served to hasten the process of cellular division. A cell's nucleus contains chemical compounds called nucleic acids, and cellular division only occurs when the levels of these nucleic acids exceed a certain level. Accordingly, the only way to drastically accelerate the frequency of cellular division is to provide excess quantities of nucleic acids. Perhaps the ring virus had managed this somehow, making it possible to force an incredible rate of growth in the fetus.

The first time he'd visited Mai's apartment he'd felt the presence of something hidden, even though there was nobody there. His feeling had been right. The newborn Sadako had been hiding somewhere in that room. No doubt she'd been very small still. She could have easily found a place to secret herself, in the wardrobe, maybe, or in the cabinet under the sink. Ando hadn't gone so far as to search those places. And because she was still so young, when she'd seen Ando in such a compromised position in the bathroom, she'd laughed. The thing that had touched his Achilles tendon had most likely been little Sadako's hand.

Sadako took over that room in the absence of its rightful inhabitant and grew there, away from the eyes of other people. A week was enough time for her to reach adulthood. And when Ando visited the apartment a second time, she emerged from within it as a full-grown woman.

Ando went over the sequence in his head over and over until he managed to wrap his mind around the hypothesis of Sadako's birth and growth. The theory accorded with what he himself had experienced.

But what about the following days? Having reached adulthood in a week, her lifespan would have been just a few more weeks unless she somehow didn't keep on aging at the same rate. Sadako had come back to life at the beginning of last November, ten weeks ago. And yet her skin retained the youthfulness of a girl of nineteen. Perhaps maturation for her meant simply reaching the age she'd been at when she died?

Miyashita came back, shaking his wet hands, and immediately spoke. "One other thing we shouldn't forget is the vital role of the smallpox virus in all this."

"Yeah, well, Sadako and the smallpox virus seem to be in league alright."

Just before her death, Sadako had contracted the virus from Jotaro Nagao. It seemed that she'd somehow blended with it there at the bottom of the well, over a long period of time, until the mixture had achieved full ripeness. Two beings hounded to untimely extinction had exacerbated each other's potency in their mutual desire to come back to life someday.

"Now, is it true that Junichiro Asakawa is going to publish *Ring*?"

"Yup. Shotoku already has it listed in a brochure of upcoming releases."

"Okay. Sadako and the smallpox virus. Those two threads were twisted into one in the form of that killer videotape. Now they're coming apart, evolving back into two separate strands. One is Sadako herself, and the other is *Ring*."

Ando didn't object. A virus was something that inhabited the gray area between life and non-life anyway, something that amounted to little more than information, whose very nature it was to effect dramatic changes in itself in response to its environment. That it should switch from the form of a video to the form of a book didn't come as much of a shock.

"So that's why Kazuyuki Asakawa survived so long."

Finally, that riddle was solved. In other words, there had been two exits. One was Sadako, and the other was the *Ring* report. And that was why both Mai and Kazuyuki had been spared death by arterial blockage. As long as they had the ability to give birth, so to speak, their lives weren't to be claimed so easily. It made sense. Just as the ring virus that had invaded Mai's body had headed for her womb, in Kazuyuki's body the virus had headed for the brain. It wasn't really Kazuyuki Asakawa who wrote *Ring*; he had been forced to write it. Sadako's DNA entered his brain and made him do it. And that was how he was able to describe things with such video camera-like accuracy. Only his depiction of Sadako, the main subject, was lacking in verisimilitude, according to the logic that dictated that the person looking through the viewfinder won't appear on film.

Ando and Miyashita fell silent, trying to anticipate what was to come.

Just what did Sadako and *Ring* have in mind for humanity? Ando and Miyashita didn't need to wait for the results of their blood tests. They were sure now that they had to find some way to stop *Ring* from being published. Junichiro simply didn't understand how much misery the human race would suffer as a result of the book he was putting his name to. He had to be their first point of counterattack. They'd have to persuade him to reverse his decision to publish the book. But would he listen to them? They weren't sure they could get him to believe their outlandish tale in the first place.

Miyashita slapped his knee and stood up. "Let's go, then."

"Where are we going?"

"It's obvious, isn't it? Your place."

"I told you already. Sadako's there."

"That's why we're going. We're going to confront her."

"Now, just hold on a minute," Ando recoiled. He'd come here to get away from Sadako. It was going to take a lot to get him to go back.

"We don't have time to fart around like this. Don't you understand how deep we're into this?"

Ando did understand. It was obvious that something had to happen to him because he'd read *Ring*. But he didn't care anymore. He wasn't afraid of death, not particularly. He'd been quite afraid of death while his son was alive and his wife had loved him, but not now.

Miyashita hooked a hand under Ando's arm and tried to wrestle him to his feet. "Get a move on. This might be our last chance."

"Chance?"

"Listen, Sadako came to you and entered your apartment of her own free will."

"Well, yes."

"She must have had a reason."

"What reason?"

"How the hell should I know? Maybe she wants you to do something for her."

Now Ando remembered. She'd said something along those lines the second time he met her.

I'll call on you soon with a request.

As Miyashita dragged him out of the study, Ando was thinking that he had no idea what kind of request she might have for him, and that he didn't really care to find out.

8

They parked the car on a street that went by Yoyogi Park. As they climbed out onto the sidewalk, Ando and Miyashita looked up at the apartment building. Ando's windows were dark. It had been well over three hours since he'd burst out of there, chest heaving. It was now nearly one in the morning.

Miyashita lowered his voice and asked, "Hey, are you sure the bitch is in there?" His use of the word "bitch" sounded forced. Ando figured Miyashita was trying to steel himself against the upcoming encounter.

"Maybe she's asleep."

The room seemed quiet, but there was no way to tell from the outside if she was still in there.

"Hey, do the living dead need to sleep?" Miyashita was sarcastically driving at the strangeness of Sadako awakening from a long slumber just to doze off in a place like this.

The two men stood on the empty sidewalk staring up at the fourth-floor windows for a while. Then Miyashita, with a show of fighting spirit, said, "Let's go," and barged on ahead. Ando followed meekly behind. The silence and cold of the night pierced him to the marrow, and he didn't think he could bear standing on the sidewalk much longer. Perhaps, if it had been warmer, he would have been even less willing to go back into his apartment.

Urged on by Miyashita, Ando braced himself and turned the doorknob. It hadn't been locked from the inside. The door opened easily. The place seemed to be empty. The pumps were gone from the concrete floor of the vestibule, as was Sadako's only possession, a small Boston bag. Ando remembered seeing it sitting unceremoniously in the vestibule when he fled.

Ando led the way into the apartment and flipped on the lights. The place was indeed empty.

The thread of his tension severed, Ando collapsed limply onto his bed. Miyashita, though, kept his senses sharp, peering into the bathroom and out at the balcony.

Finally, having searched the place meticulously, he was convinced.

"I think she's gone."

"I wonder where she went," Ando mumbled. But in reality, he couldn't care less where she'd gone. He never wanted to have anything to do with her again.

"Any ideas?" asked Miyashita.

Ando immediately shook his head. "Nope," he said. It was then that he noticed it. On the desk by the window, a notebook had been left open. Ando couldn't remember using a notebook there for some time.

He got to his feet and picked it up. Several pages had been filled with sloppy writing. The first line said, *Dear Mr. Ando*, and at the end it was signed *Sadako Yamamura*. She'd left him a note.

Ando read the opening sentence silently to himself, and then handed the notebook to Miyashita.

"What's this?"

"A message from Sadako."

Miyashita let out a gasp as he took the notebook from Ando. Though he hadn't been asked to, he read it aloud.

Dear Mr. Ando,

As I do not wish to startle you any further, I have decided to leave you a letter. It's rather an old-fashioned thing to do, I know. Please try to remain calm as you read it.

Surely you've figured out by now where I came from. I borrowed the womb of a woman named Mai Takano in order to effect my rebirth into this world. I am perplexed myself as to the exact mechanism by which I was able to come back to life.

My father was an assistant professor of medicine at a university, and he often used to speak to me about heredity when I visited him at the South Hakone Sanatorium where he was a patient. As a result, I know a little about genetics. It may be just a hunch, but I wonder if perhaps, using my psychic powers, I was able to imprint my genetic information onto something. Thinking about it now, I am quite sure that on the verge of death I willed my genetic information to remain intact in some form or other. What I felt was not so much a desire to be reborn as an unbearable revulsion at the thought that Sadako Yamamura and everything she represented would rot away at the bottom of that well, unbeknownst to anyone. What happened to me as a

*result is something that no doubt you, as a specialist, are better quali-
fied to explain than I!*

*My psyche, that which had died in that well, gradually took shape
again within that woman. When I regained self-awareness, what I saw
in the mirror was not my own face. At first, I did not understand what
had happened. My face and my body were not my own; they belonged
to another woman. But the "me" that was thinking that was indeed the
true me. The city, too, looked unfamiliar. The cars lining the streets
were so modern. The apartment (that tiny concrete box), the appliances, the electronics. When I looked at the calendar I found that twenty-five years had passed in the blink of an eye. I realized that somehow
my spirit must have escaped my corpse and then taken up a new body
twenty-five years later. The poor girl whose body I stole was Mai
Takano.*

*My consciousness was not born when Mai gave birth to me. A seed
named Sadako was already putting forth buds in the depths of Mai's
womb. As I grew, it grew, taking up residence within Mai, the master of
that body. By the time I was ready to be born I ruled Mai completely
from my place in her womb.*

*I was able to see things from two perspectives, mother and fetus,
and touch and feel accordingly. With my little hands I was able to
touch the soft folds of my own oviducts, feel them undulating like
waves.*

*As my birth approached, one thing began to bother me. After I was
born, what would become of the Mai-body? Would Mai's soul return,
would that body go back to wholeness as Mai Takano? Somehow I
thought not. I had come to think of that borrowed body as my
chrysalis. Just as the chrysalis cannot live by itself after the butterfly
has grown, the body had to be discarded, having outlived its usefulness.
It might have been a self-serving conclusion, but I felt that Mai had
already died when her body had been usurped.*

*The question then became, where should I be born? If she bore me
in her room, I would be faced with the need to dispose of her decomposing corpse. Judging from how rapidly my fetus had developed, I
thought it would not be long before I reached maturity, and I would
need a place to live. Mai's apartment seemed the most sensible choice.*

This meant that I had no other choice but to be born somewhere out of sight of the neighbors, someplace where I could leave behind the husk and return to the apartment alone. That rooftop was made to order. If I left the husk in the exhaust shaft, it would be some time before it was discovered, and in the meantime I could use Mai's apartment freely.

As our time approached, I made preparations and went up to the roof in the middle of the night. I tied a cord to the metal grate and descended into the shaft. In the process I slipped and wrenched an ankle, but this did not bother the mother-body. I was able to be reborn into this world on schedule. I crawled out of the womb, severed the umbilical cord with my hands and mouth, and cleaned myself off with a wet towel I had readied for the purpose. I was born in the early morning, before sunrise. It was only then when I looked up that I first realized, with a shock, that the exhaust shaft looked quite like the well where I had died.

It was like a rite of passage prepared for me by the gods. I thought of it as a divinely appointed trial; I would not be able to adapt to this world, into which I'd been newly reborn, unless I crawled out of that hole on my own. But it wasn't hard to do. A cord hung down from the rim. I climbed it and was able to emerge from the hole with no difficulty. The eastern sky was growing light and the city was awakening with it. Let me tell you, I drank the air greedily. I felt, quite literally, revived.

A week later I had grown to the age I had been at my death. Mysteriously, I retained all my memories from my previous life. My birth in Sashikiji on Izu Oshima Island, my transient life with my mother as she was subjected to parapsychological experiments, my aged father's time in the sanatorium… I remembered it all. Why is that, I wonder. Perhaps memories are not engraved upon the folds of the brain, but stored in the genes.

Deep within my body, however, there was one way in which I could tell I differed from my previous self. Intuition is all I have to go by regarding the changes in my body, but I know beyond a doubt that I am different from what I was before. I seem to have both a womb and testicles. Previously, I had no womb. Reborn, I have both. I am now a complete hermaphrodite. What is more, the man in me can ejaculate. I learned that as a result of what we did together.

At that point, Miyashita raised his eyes from the notebook and glanced at Ando. Thinking Miyashita meant to tease him about sleeping with Sadako, Ando snapped, "Shut up and keep reading."

But Miyashita was thinking about something else. "'A complete hermaphrodite.' Suppose she—it, maybe?—can have a child without procreative sex? Imagine the consequences."

There are many lower organisms that can reproduce without male-female union. Worms, for example, have male and female parts in one body, and can lay fertilized eggs. Reproduction among single-celled organisms by cellular division also falls under the heading of asexual reproduction. A child born without input from a male and a female would have the same genes as its single parent. In other words, Sadako would give birth to another Sadako. If such a thing were possible.

"If that's true, then..." Ando's gaze wandered uneasily off into space. "Then Sadako isn't human anymore. She's a new species. New species arise due to mutation. This is evolution happening before our eyes!"

Ando tried to pursue the train of logic. The question was how Sadako meant to establish herself as a new species. When a new species arises as a result of mutation, it can find only unmutated individuals to mate with.

For example, suppose a single black sheep is born into a flock of thousands of white sheep. That black sheep must mate with a white sheep. Assuming the result of this mating to be a white or gray sheep, it's easy to see how the trait of blackness must become weaker and weaker until it gradually disappears. Unless there are at least two black sheep, one of each sex, the trait will not be passed on down the generations.

But in Sadako's case, the problem was already solved. If she could reproduce asexually, there was no need for her to choose a breeding partner. If she could reproduce herself, all alone, then all the traits that made her Sadako would be transmitted to the next generation.

However, with one Sadako giving birth to another Sadako, one at a time, the species's rate of increase would be extremely slow, no faster than the videotape's propagation, one copy at a time. And while the species dallied, the human race might corner it and annihilate it. Just as the killer videotape itself had been made extinct. In order to thrive, the new species needed to reproduce itself rapidly and *en masse*. Sadako needed to secure room to survive, perhaps by usurping human habitats, perhaps by flooding in through the cracks. Perhaps she already had a plan...

Ando's thoughts were interrupted when Miyashita resumed reading from the notebook.

This has become rather a long letter, but I assure you that every word of it is true. I have simply told you honestly what happened to me. Why have I? So that you may understand. And now that you do understand, I would like to ask you to do something for me. Why you? Because I believe you, as an expert, have the expert knowledge that will be required.

Ando braced himself reflexively. *Oh God, here it comes.* What if it was something he didn't know how to do? The thought filled him with anxiety.

First things first: I want you not to interfere with the publication of Ring.

Well, that was certainly within the scope of his abilities. All he had to do was do nothing.

I want you not to interfere with anything else I may try to do, either. I want you to cooperate with me.
Please listen to me. It is not my intention to threaten you, but I must tell you that something very bad will happen to you if you interfere. After all, you have already read the manuscript called Ring. *Consider it too late, please, to do anything. If you cross me, you will find a change coming over your body. But I realize that you are courageous and may be willing to resist me even at the risk of death. So I think I must offer you a reward for granting my request. Nothing is free, is it? What would you say if I told you that I could offer you the thing you want most, namely...*

Miyashita stopped reading and handed the notebook to Ando, evidently wanting him to see for himself what came next.

No sooner did Ando read what was written there than he dropped the notebook. In an instant he'd been robbed of the power to think; all strength had been sapped from his body. He'd never dreamed she would offer such a thing. Miyashita must have guessed how he was feeling, and he made no comment.

Ando's eyes were shut. Sadako, he felt, was whispering sweetly to him that he should destroy the human race. That he should take the side of the new species, become its ally, and work on its behalf. Sadako understood that without collaborators among humans, her species could never survive. Junichiro Asakawa, through his efforts to publish *Ring*, was already acting on Sadako's behalf. He probably didn't yet realize it himself, but there was no question Sadako was manipulating him.

But the compensation Ando was being offered in exchange for his soul was more than enticing. How many times had he prayed for that dream to come true? Never thinking that it actually could.

Is such a thing possible? he asked himself. He opened his eyes and looked at the bookshelf. There it was, in an envelope sandwiched between two books. Medically, it wasn't impossible. And with Sadako's help, it might actually happen. *Still...*

He raised his voice in a cry of anguish. If Sadako wasn't stopped now, there was no telling what suffering she'd bring to the human race. As a member of that race, Ando couldn't betray it. In the end the only way to stop Sadako was to destroy her. But if her body was obliterated, his dream would be, too. The only way to make his dream come true was to keep Sadako safe and healthy.

Ando was openly groaning now from the depths of his torment. As he lay on the bed, belly heaving, he saw a figure behind his closed eyelids, a figure that he could not chase away.

"What should I do?" Ando wept. He was incapable of coming to a decision on his own.

"That's your problem," Miyashita said—not cruelly, but with calm self-possession.

"But I don't know what I should do."

"Think about it. If we get in Sadako's way, you and I, we'll be killed on the spot. She'll just find someone else to assist her, that's all."

Miyashita was probably right. Everything was clear when he thought about it coolly. Ando's meeting up with Sadako had not been pure chance. She'd been watching him. None of it was accident, not his brush with her in Mai's apartment, not his rooftop encounter with her, not their meeting at Sangubashi Station. She'd foreseen that Ando would ferret out the truth, and she'd made her moves. Suddenly, Ando felt it was simply impossible to outmaneuver Sadako. All he had to do was make one false move and the ring virus in his body would start to wreak havoc on him.

Miyashita had seen this immediately and drawn the obvious conclusion, but Ando still couldn't quite make up his mind.

"Are you saying I should cooperate with her?"

"What else can you do?"

"What about humanity?!"

"Come on, stop acting like you're a delegate for the whole species. Besides, you've already decided, haven't you? Consider the reward, for God's sake. Are you telling me you mean to pass it up?"

"But it's not fair. What do *you* get out of it?"

"I'll consider it a sort of insurance policy. One day I might be glad I had it, you know. We've no idea what life has in store for us."

Ando realized he was cornered, snared. Decades from now, he would be in the history books, and not as a hero. He'd be remembered as the traitor thanks to whom the human race was driven to the brink of extinction. That was, of course, if there was still a human race to remember him. If the species ended, so did its history.

Why did I ever get involved in the first place?

Remorsefully, Ando thought back to how it had all began for him. How could he forget it? There had been Ryuji's autopsy, and then the code, RING. It was meant to inform Ando of the existence of a report, *Ring*. He'd read that report. If he hadn't read it, he wouldn't be in this mess now. If only he hadn't read it...

Something interrupted Ando's reflections. A thought. There was something else going on here.

"Ryuji," he muttered. Miyashita gave him a worried look. Ando paid no attention, though, as he pursued this new line of reasoning. He was beginning to think he saw a will at work behind all the events he'd accepted as random. Had Ryuji really sent him the words "ring" and "mutation" in code out of pure goodwill? Just to tell Ando to pay attention? Ando began to doubt that. He began to see those hints as course corrections, delivered at moments when Ando seemed about to get off track. Why had Ryuji done such a thing?

There was something else, too. Just why had Mai ended up watching the killer video anyway? If it hadn't been for the coincidence of her watching it on the very day she was ovulating, Sadako would never have been reborn. Where had Mai gotten the tape?

At Ryuji's place.

Why had she gone there?

Ryuji's article was missing a page.

But was it really missing a page?

Only Ryuji knows.

Everything came back to Ryuji.

Ryuji, Ryuji, Ryuji.

He and Mai had been intimate. It wasn't strange if he knew her menstrual cycle. She'd been guided by him on that very day.

Oh Lord...

Ando looked at Miyashita's face, at his eyes narrowed with concern, and whispered, "It's Ryuji."

Miyashita's eyes narrowed even further: he didn't understand.

"Don't you see? It's Ryuji. He's been the one pulling the strings all along. He's behind Sadako."

As Ando repeated the name, he felt his suspicions harden into certainty. Ryuji had been playing all of them. He'd written the script.

Outside the window the sounds of the city at night eddied and swirled. A car passed by on the Metropolitan Expressway with a grating noise as if it were dragging something heavy behind it. Like fingernails on glass it sounded at first, then turned into loud male laughter, an eerie shriek coming from someplace far away. Ando thought it was Ryuji's voice.

He called out to empty space. "Ryuji, are you there?"

Naturally there was no reply. But Ando could sense him. Ryuji was present. The man who had joined forces with Sadako to hunt humanity for sport was in his room, watching how things went, laughing derisively at Ando for noticing too late to do anything about it.

A light came on in Ando's head as he surmised what Ryuji wanted.

Something he was unable to obtain without Ando's cooperation. Ryuji's occult motives were finally clear, but it didn't do Ando any good. It was too late, the course of events was beyond his influence. The only thing left for Ando to do was to join his voice with Ryuji's, with the chuckling in the dark.

Epilogue

On a day so clear it was hard to believe it was still the rainy season, Ando went to the beach. Two years ago to the day, at this very place, his son had died. It wasn't that Ando made a point of coming here on the anniversary. He hadn't come the year before. But today he had a reason to be here.

Unlike two years ago, the waves today were gentle as they approached the shore. White sand stretched away on either side, and here and there anglers stood casting their lines. It was still early summer, and there were no bathers, only two or three families picnicking on plastic sheets.

Ando felt as if he'd been transported back to that fateful day. The waves were different, and there was a seawall stretching out from the shore that hadn't been there before; even the contours of the dunes had changed. To Ando, however, everything was just as it had been. The last two years now seemed to him nothing but one long nightmare.

He sat on an embankment from which he could look down over the beach. Sunlight as bright as midsummer's hit him full in the face. Shading his eyes with his hand, he squinted at a small figure playing at the water's edge. The figure didn't approach the water, but squatted in place, barefoot on dry sand, digging holes and making sand piles. Ando couldn't take his eyes off the figure.

He thought he heard someone calling his name. Wondering if he'd imagined it, he looked around. He saw a stocky man who was walking along the top of the embankment, headed straight for Ando.

The man wore a striped long-sleeve shirt buttoned right up to the top. The shirt looked about to burst; the man's chest and upper arms were amazingly well-muscled. His short neck was wrinkled above his painfully tight-looking collar. The man's blocky, angular face was sweaty, and he was out of breath as he approached, swinging a plastic bag from a convenience store.

Ando recognized him. The last time he'd seen the man, it was at the medical examiner's office, back in October.

The man sat down beside Ando, shoulder to shoulder with him.

"Hey, long time no see."

Ando didn't reply. He didn't even meet the man's eyes, but kept his gaze on the small figure playing near the waves.

"Man, you just disappeared without telling me where you were going. What kind of way is that to treat a friend?" The man took a can of cold oolong tea from the bag, cleared his throat, and drank it dry in a few gulps. When he'd finished, he took out another can and offered it to Ando. "Thirsty?"

Ando accepted the can silently and popped the pull ring.

"How did you know I was here?" Ando asked calmly.

"Miyashita told me that today was the anniversary of your kid's death. The rest was guesswork. You're not that hard to figure out," the man laughed.

Ando had to restrain himself. "What do you want?"

"Look, I had to take a train and a bus to get here. I think I deserve a warmer welcome than this."

"Bullshit," Ando spat.

"Ooh, don't be mean," the man said, a smirk playing over his lips.

"Mean? Where do you get off calling me that? Who do you think is responsible for your being here?"

"Listen, I'm grateful to you, I really am. You worked out just as I expected."

Ando was reminded of just how far this man had manipulated him. In medical school, in their days playing at cryptography, this guy could toss out a code that Ando couldn't possibly break, and then turn around and immediately crack one Ando had wrung his brain to come up with. Ando had felt annoyed and frustrated, but also somehow inspired by the guy's cleverness. Not anymore. Now, he just felt used, and insulted. He found nothing to praise in the man.

Ando looked over at Ryuji Takayama, whom he had helped bring back to the world. Ryuji was facing forward, and Ando looked at his profile, wishing he could see inside Ryuji's head. He wished he knew what this man was thinking. Then he remembered that last October he actually had laid his hands on the man's brain. Not that it helped him understand any of Ryuji's thoughts. And because he hadn't, he'd let Ryuji's codes lead him into a mess. If he hadn't performed Ryuji's autopsy, he would never have become involved.

"Isn't this better for you, too?" Ryuji said in a patronizing tone.

"I don't know about that." That was the truth.

Down by the water's edge, the little figure stood up and waved at

Ando. When he saw Ando make a beckoning motion with his head, the boy came closer, kicking sand as he came.

"Daddy, I'm thirsty!"

Ando offered his son the oolong tea Ryuji had given him. The boy took it and brought it quickly to his lips.

Ando watched his son's pale throat. He could almost see the cool liquid coursing down the little throat. Living, moving flesh and blood.

Compared to the sweat oiling Ryuji's face, the droplets of perspiration rolling down the three-and-a-half-year-old boy's neck were like crystal. Ando could hardly believe they were basically the same fluid.

"Hi there, kid. Want another one? We're two of a kind, you know," Ryuji said, fishing around in his bag.

Two of a kind. The phrase stuck in Ando's craw. It was true, though: the boy and Ryuji had been born of the same womb. Ando found it utterly horrifying.

His son looked at Ryuji and shook his head, then raised his half-finished can of tea and said, "Can I have the rest?"

"Sure, drink up," said Ando, and the boy went back to the water's edge, swilling the can. Ando figured the boy wanted to play with the can after it was empty, maybe fill it with sand. Ando yelled after him, "Takanori!"

The boy stopped and turned around. "What, Daddy?"

"Don't go in the water yet, okay?"

The boy grinned, and turned his back to him again.

Ando didn't have to stress the point. The child was still afraid of the water, as if he remembered drowning. He probably wouldn't go into the water of his own accord. Even though he knew that, Ando couldn't help but be a little overprotective.

"Cute kid."

Ando didn't need Ryuji to tell him. Of course Takanori was cute. He was a jewel, an irreplaceable treasure that he'd lost once. A treasure that he'd betrayed the human race to recover. Ando still wasn't sure if he'd done the right thing.

The reward Sadako had offered him in exchange for his help was to resurrect his son.

Half a year ago, when he and Miyashita had read those words in the letter Sadako had left in his apartment, Ando had found the idea too ludicrous to accept. But that feeling had passed in an instant, and he'd become a firm believer in resurrection. After all, he had Sadako herself as living proof. And he had carefully preserved a sample of his son's DNA in the form of a lock of hair that he kept on the bookshelf. Without some cells from his son, the resurrection would have been impossible. If it weren't for the fact that Ando's hand had brushed against the boy's head in the sea, catching those few strands of hair in his ring, Takanori's genetic information would have been lost forever.

Scientifically speaking, it wasn't difficult. As long as they had a maternal body with the special capabilities—as long as they had Sadako, in other words—modern science could easily take care of the rest.

The first thing to do was for Sadako to inseminate one of her own eggs. With both female and male functions, Sadako was the only one capable of implanting a fertilized egg in her uterine wall with no outside assistance. The next step was to remove this egg and replace its DNA with the DNA of the individual they wanted to bring back to life. True, it took delicate skill to extract the nucleus from one of the cells in Takanori's hair and switch it with the nucleus of Sadako's inseminated egg. But for a specialist, it wasn't all that difficult. Theoretically, it was possible even to resurrect long-extinct dinosaurs, as long as their DNA survived.

The egg with its newly-implanted nucleus was then returned to Sadako's womb. All they had to do now was wait for it to be born. The fetus crawled out of her womb in about a week, and a week after that, it had grown to the age at which the DNA sample had been separated from the rest of the original body. In Takanori's case, it was the moment when the drowning boy's head had touched his father's hand, leaving a lock of hair behind. He even recovered all of his memories up to the point of his death. It appeared that memories were stored in the intron, the "junk" part of the DNA that doesn't contain genetic code.

The Takanori that Ando was seeing now was in all respects identical to the son he'd lost. From his habits to the way he spoke, he was just like he used to be. He had all of his memories of his time with his parents, too, and speaking with him felt perfectly natural.

As soon as she'd presented Ando with his son, Sadako had demanded that he earn his reward. Her request was just what Ando had expected. She wanted him to use the same techniques to resurrect Ryuji. Bringing back Takanori was as much practice as payment. From the beginning, it had been Ryuji's will to be reborn that had allowed him to expel the numerical code from his belly sutures, and then to insert a coded message into the ring virus's DNA. And he'd gotten his wish. He'd gotten a body, and now he was sitting next to Ando in the flesh. It was he who'd been Sadako's partner all along, and a formidable one at that.

This was the first time Ando had seen the resurrected Ryuji. As soon as he'd made sure that Ryuji's DNA had been successfully switched with the inseminated egg's, Ando had taken his son and disappeared. He told no one where they were going, leaving the rest of the operation in the hands of Miyashita and others. He figured that, with Ryuji's conception, his role was over. With Ryuji around, there was no further need for him. Sadako's greatest desire had been to have Ryuji around as a reliable ally.

At exactly what point had she and Ryuji decided to collude? Probably they'd communicated somehow at the DNA level, recognized in each other a valuable co-conspirator, and realized that a partnership would be for their mutual benefit.

But the question didn't really interest Ando. His concern was monopolized now by the problem of how he was going to raise his son. To give himself time to think about it, he'd resigned from the university two months ago, and spent the time since traveling around and seeing the Japanese countryside. He had no particular aim. He just wanted to live at as far a remove from Ryuji and Sadako as possible.

Ryuji reached into a pocket and pulled out an ampoule.

"Here," he said, offering it to Ando.

"What's this?"

"A vaccine made from the ring virus."

"A vaccine..." Ando accepted the tiny glass vial and examined it carefully.

Ando's and Miyashita's blood tests had come back positive. Just as they'd suspected, reading the *Ring* report had made them carriers of the virus. Ever since, they'd both been living in apprehension, wondering when the virus within them would start to act up.

"Take that and it'll take care of the virus. Your worrying days are over."

"Did you come all the way here just to give me this?"

"What, can't a guy go to the beach once in a while?" Ryuji gave an embarrassed laugh. Ando let down his guard a little. No matter where he'd moved, he'd never have been able to relax as long as he carried the ring virus.

"So tell me. What's going to happen to the world now?" Ando asked, putting the vial in his breast pocket and buttoning it shut.

"I don't know." Ryuji's reply was blunt.

"Don't give me that. Together you and Sadako are going to redesign the world and everything that lives in it—aren't you?"

"I can tell you what's going to happen in the immediate future. But after that... Even I don't know."

"Then at least tell me about the immediate future."

"*Ring*'s sold over a million copies."

"A million-seller, huh?" Ando already knew this. He'd seen it in newspapers. The book had already been through several reprints, a fact that was trumpeted in its marketing. But every time Ando saw the word "reprint" it made him think "replication." *Ring* had been able to effect a near-instantaneous mass reproduction of itself. There were now more than a million people carrying the virus.

"They're even making it into a movie."

"A movie? *Ring*?"

"Mm-hmm. They cast the part of Sadako through an open casting call."

"An open casting call?" Ando found himself reduced to repeating after Ryuji.

The resurrected man broke into laughter. "That's right, an open casting call. And who do you think nailed the part of Sadako?"

Ando didn't keep up on show-business news. "Tell me," he said. How was he to know who'd passed the audition?

Ryuji was almost doubled over with laughter. "Don't be such a dullard. You know her quite well."

"Sadako...herself?"

It was only as he said the name that he realized the import of this development. Sadako had always wanted to be an actress. She'd joined a professional theater troupe right out of high school. She was no amateur, she had the training. It wasn't surprising that she'd auditioned, and with her powers, she must have easily captured the casting director's heart. Besides, it was an irresistible role. Sadako would be playing herself. Ando thought he could guess why. She wanted to project her thoughts into the film, so that when the movie showed the killer videotape, it carried her genetic information again. The extinct tape itself was now to be resurrected, and on a grand scale.

And what would be the result? Ando had no idea how big a hit it would be, but it was certain that a fair number of women would go to the theater to see it; those who happened to be ovulating would be visited by the same tragedy that had destroyed Mai. A week later, they would all give birth to Sadako, their own bodies cast aside as used cocoons, abandoned to decay.

And then the movie would hit the video rental shops, and then it'd be broadcast on TV. The images would spread far more quickly than they ever could have through one-copy-at-a-time dubbing. This would be reproduction at an explosive rate. And these new Sadakos would all be able to have children of their own, by themselves. Sadako had managed to work out a method by which she'd have the whole world wrapped instantly around her finger.

"Sadako's going to breed with the media," Ryuji said, finally done laughing and looking up.

"They'll figure it out soon enough, and the movie will be suppressed." Not just the movie, but the book, too. All circulating copies would be rounded up and burned. Ando wanted to believe that humanity would rally.

"Nope. Just think how huge the media industry is, and how many people in it have already been in contact with the virus. Even if *Ring* itself is destroyed, the media is going to be transformed by people who have contracted the ring virus. Just as that videotape mutated into a book, it's going to get into every stream: music, video games, computer networks. New media will cross-breed with Sadako and produce more new media, and every ovulating woman who comes in contact with them will give birth to Sadako."

Ando touched his breast pocket and felt the vial of vaccine. It would be effective only against the ring virus. It would be powerless against mutated media. Without knowing what type of media the virus would

276

mutate into, it was impossible to concoct a vaccine that would be effective against them. Humanity would forever lag behind. Sadako, the new species, would gradually crowd out the human race until finally she'd driven it to the edge of extinction.

"And you're okay with all that?"

Ando himself couldn't peacefully sit back and watch as people died and Sadako took their places. But never mind him. Ryuji was taking an active role in the whole thing, helping it along. Ando simply couldn't understand that.

"You're looking at it from a human standpoint. I'm not. The way I see it, one person dies, one Sadako is born. Add one here, take one there, the total's still the same. Where's the problem?"

"That's totally beyond my comprehension."

Ryuji brought his sweaty face right up close to Ando's. "Now's no time for you to be bitching. You're on our side now."

"To do what?"

"You'll get to intervene in evolution, for one thing. A pretty rare opportunity, if you ask me."

"Evolution? Is that what you call this?"

All the diversity of human DNA would converge with the single DNA pattern that was Sadako. Was that evolution? It seemed rather a point of weakness to Ando. It's precisely because of genetic diversity that some plague victims die while others survive. Even if another ice age comes, thought Ando, the Inuit would be able to live through it, and this would be thanks to diversity, in this case of populations within the human species. If this diversity vanished, then the slightest mischance could lead to the downfall of the whole species. If, say, the original Sadako Yamamura had some defect in her immune system, the defect would be present in every subsequent Sadako. A simple cold could come as a mighty blow to a species.

Ando could only hope that happened. The only path left for the human race was to scrape by and wait for the Sadako species to die out.

"Do you know why living things evolve?"

Ando shook his head. He doubted there was anyone who could answer that question with perfect confidence.

But Ryuji's voice had that confidence as he continued. "Take the eye. I know I don't have to explain this to an anatomist like yourself, Dr.

Ando, but the human eye is an amazingly complex mechanism. It's next to impossible to imagine that a piece of skin evolved into a cornea, a pupil, an eyeball, an optical nerve connecting it to the brain, all in such a way as to make it actually *see*. It's hard to believe it all happened by chance. It wasn't that we started to look at things because there was now a mechanism by which to see them. There first had to be a *will* to see, buried somewhere inside living things. Without it, the mechanism would never have taken shape. It wasn't chance that led sea creatures to first crawl onto the land, or reptiles to learn how to fly. They had the will to do so. Now, try and say this and most experts will just laugh. They'll call it mystical teleology, an execrable excuse for philosophy.

"Can you imagine what the world is like for a creature that can't see? To the worms crawling around in the earth, the world is only what touches their bodies there in the darkness. For starfish or sea anemones waving around on the ocean floor, the whole world is the texture of the rock they're stuck to and the feel of the water as it flows by. Do you think such a creature can even conceptualize seeing? It beggars the imagination. It's one of those things you can't contemplate, like the edge of the universe. But somehow, at a certain point in its evolution, life on earth acquired the concept of 'seeing.' We crawled up onto the land, we flew into the skies, and in the end we grasped culture. A chimp can comprehend a banana. But it'll never be able to comprehend the concept of culture. It can't comprehend it, but somehow it gets the will to obtain it. Where that impulse comes from, I have no idea."

"Oh, so there's something even *you* don't know?" Ando said with all the sarcasm he could muster.

"Pay attention. If the human race goes extinct and Sadako Yamamura's DNA takes its place, in the end it's because the human race willed it."

"Does any species desire its own extinction?"

"Subconsciously, isn't that what humanity desired? If all DNA were united into one pattern, there would be no more individual difference. Everyone would be the same, with no distinctions in ability, or beauty. There'd be no more attachment to loved ones. And forget about war, there wouldn't even be any more arguments. We're talking a world of absolute peace and equality that transcends even life and death. Death would no longer be something to fear, you see. Now, be honest, isn't that what you humans wanted all along?"

By the end of his speech, Ryuji had brought his mouth even closer and was whispering into Ando's ear. Ando, meanwhile, simply kept staring at Takanori, who for some time now had been crouched in the same position, packing sand into his empty can.

"Not me," he replied. His son was special to him, unique. Ando had no desire to see things exactly as other people did. He could say that with confidence.

"Well, whatever," Ryuji laughed, getting to his feet.

"Are you leaving?"

"It's about time I took off. What are you going to do now?"

"What can I do? I'll find a deserted island someplace out of the media's reach, and raise my son there."

"That sounds like you. Me, I'm going to watch the end of the human race. Once it's gone as far as it can go, who knows, maybe a will beyond human wisdom will come raining its wrath down on us. I'd hate to miss that."

Ryuji started walking away along the embankment.

"Bye, Ryuji. Say hi to Miyashita for me."

Ryuji stopped again at the sound of Ando's voice.

"Maybe I ought to teach you one more thing before I go. Why do you think human culture progressed? People can endure almost anything, but there's one thing they just can't survive. Man is an animal that can't stand boredom. And that's what set the whole thing off. In order to escape boredom, humanity had to progress. I imagine it'll be pretty boring to be controlled by a single strand of DNA. Think about it in those terms, and it seems like you'd want to have as much individual variation as possible. But hey, what can we do? People just don't want that variation. Oh, and one last thing—I think you're going to be pretty bored on that desert island."

With that and a wave of his hand, Ryuji walked off.

Ando had no definite plans as to where they were going to live. The future was still too uncertain for that. Prospects were such that maybe no plan, no matter how ingenious, would work. He'd just have to drift for a while and let happen what may.

Ando took off his shirt and slacks. He was wearing swim trunks underneath. He ran to his son, took the boy's hand, and helped him to his feet.

"Let's go."

He'd explained to his son a hundred times what they needed to do today and why they needed to do it. They were going to swim out into the ocean just as they had two years ago, and then, when the boy was on the verge of drowning, Ando would take firm hold of his hand. Two years ago their hands had missed. Today they were going to hold on tight.

In the letter she'd left him, Sadako had written that when she was reborn in the exhaust shaft on the roof of that building, she realized it was the exact same situation, physically, as the bottom of the well where she'd died. And only when she had crawled out of the hole on her own did she sense, intuitively, that she'd be able to adapt to the new world. Ando thought his son needed to undergo the same sort of trial. The boy needed to be put in the same situation he'd been in two years ago.

Takanori had an abnormal fear of water, so strong that it was going to make daily life difficult for him if he couldn't conquer it. As they walked along over the wet sand, Ando could feel Takanori's hand tighten on his in fear every time seawater lapped at the boy's ankles.

Now the boy turned to him with trembling lips and said, "Daddy, you promised, right?"

"Yes, I did."

Ando had already prepared the reward he'd promised the boy for meeting his father's expectations and overcoming his fear of the water. He was going to let him meet his mother.

"Mommy's going to be so surprised."

His wife didn't know yet that their son had been brought back to life. Ando got excited just thinking about the moment when mother and son would be reunited. He'd have to think of a plausible story. Maybe he could say that the boy hadn't drowned after all but had been rescued by a fishing boat; that he'd had amnesia, that he'd lived with other folks for the last two years. It didn't matter how ridiculous the story was. The minute she touched Takanori, alive in the flesh, it would become the truth.

Whether or not they'd be able to make it as a married couple again was another question. Ando wanted to try. He gave himself a fifty-fifty chance.

A particularly big wave came along and started to raise the boy's body off the sand. The boy gave a little shriek and clung tightly to Ando's waist. Ando held his son tightly to his side and waded out into the sea. He could feel his son's heartbeat. That rhythm was the only sure thing in a world facing destruction. It proved they were alive.

Whether you like Japanese stuff

READ

For those unfamiliar with contemporary Japanese fiction, here is a quick overview of some of the most absorbing writing in Japan today — all available in translation from Vertical!

Gangster noir
Ashes **by Kenzo Kitakata**

"*Ashes* depicts yakuza life with a unique understanding and edge-of-your-seat reality."
–*Midwest Book Review*

New Age mystery
Outlet **by Randy Taguchi**

"Her sexual encounters may have a healing power...and the novel's dark twists and turns should keep readers hooked until the surprising climax."
–*Publishers Weekly*

For upcoming titles, visit

or just like good books,

DIFFERENT
READ

VERTICAL.

Comedy of manners
Twinkle Twinkle **by Kaori Ekuni**
"This book is simple. This book is a pearl. This book is like water, clear and loose and natural and fluid." *–BUST magazine*

Ghost story
Strangers **by Taichi Yamada**
"An eerie ghost story written with hypnotic clarity. He is among the best Japanese writers I have read." –Bret Easton Ellis, author of *American Psycho*

Fantasy epic
The Guin Saga **by Kaoru Kurimoto**
"Readers should be cautioned that once you start this journey, it will be nearly impossible to leave it unfinished." *–SFRevu*

SIDDHARTHA ACHIEVES SATORI THIS JUNE,
UNDER THE PIPPALA TREE...

FIND OUT WHY THE EIGHT-VOLUME MASTERPIECE
BY THE GOD OF JAPANESE COMICS HAS BEEN
SELECTED ONE OF THE 25 BEST GRAPHIC NOV-
ELS EVER BY TIME MAGAZINE. THE FIRST THREE
INSTALLMENTS ARE ALREADY IN BOOKSTORES
NEAR YOU!

LIFE BEGAN

IN THE SEA

AND YOURS

WILL END
AT SEA

DARK WATER

KOJI SUZU

Coming to bookstores in October 2004...

Suzuki's obsession with the ocean finds new expression in this prize collection of short stories, all of which have to do with bodies of water. Culled from the period the author was writing *Spiral*, these tales confirm him as an astute observer of human relationships as well as a horror power house. One of the stories, cinematized to great acclaim, is now being remade in the United States.

Coming in 2005: *Loop*,
the *Ring* trilogy's stunning conclusion.